BROKEN LANCE

BROKEN LANCE

Michele R. Sorensen

Deseret Book Company
Salt Lake City, Utah

© 1997 Kevin E. Sorensen

All rights reserved. No part of this book may be reproduced in any form or by any means without permission in writing from the publisher, Deseret Book Company, P.O. Box 30178, Salt Lake City, Utah 84130. This work is not an official publication of The Church of Jesus Christ of Latter-day Saints. The views expressed herein are the responsibility of the author and do not necessarily represent the position of the Church or of Deseret Book Company.

Deseret Book is a registered trademark of Deseret Book Company.

Library of Congress Cataloging-in-Publication Data

Sorensen, Michele R., 1962–1995.
Broken lance / by Michele R. Sorensen.
p. cm.
ISBN 1-57345-270-X (hardcover)
1. Mormons—Travel—Mormon Trail—History—19th century—Fiction. 2. Frontier and pioneer life—Wyoming—Fiction. 3. Women pioneers—Wyoming—Fiction. I. Title.
PS3569.06758B76 1997
813'.54—dc21 97-3187
CIP

Printed in the United States of America

10 9 8 7 6 5 4 3 2 1

IN MEMORIAM

WILDERNESS

20 July 1857
North Fork of the Little LaRamiee River

THE SAVAGE

17 September 1857
West Bank of the North Platte River

WINTER

5 December 1857
The Foothills of the Sierra Madre Mountains

PREFACE

Unusual among western novels, *Broken Lance* is a story of pioneer life as seen through the eyes of a young mother. Wallace Stegner, a novelist and historian who was not a Latter-day Saint, wrote of the pioneer Saints: "That I do not accept the faith that possessed them does not mean I doubt their frequent devotion and heroism in its service. Especially their women. Their women were incredible" (*The Gathering of Zion* [New York: McGraw Hill, 1964], 13).

Callie McCracken is like those remarkable early Saints. A practicing member of The Church of Jesus Christ of Latter-day Saints, Callie has a personality and outlook that are true to those of the women of her day, as are her determination and faith. These qualities give her the unique characteristics of nineteenth-century Latter-day Saint women, and she fits comfortably among historical figures of her time.

Her character provides a vibrant backdrop for the message in *Broken Lance* of Christlike tolerance. In the story Callie is forced to learn to accept a foreign place and a foreign culture. Although she does not condone or enjoy all aspects of her situation, she learns to look for the good in it and to work with it.

Despite its gentle theme, *Broken Lance* is a vigorous account of survival. Suddenly destitute and alone on the prairie, Callie McCracken faces the ordeal of finishing her trek to Zion. Her faith matures as she manages to feed and transport herself and her three children across the savage wilderness we now call the Snowy Mountain Range–Medicine Bow National Forest and the Red Desert of western Wyoming.

Geographical accuracy is a strong point in this story. I came to Wyoming in 1991 from the lush, manicured scenery of Seattle, Washington, and I experienced firsthand the shock of living in a place where wind and sky dominate. When I began writing Callie's story, I traveled her route with my own children, visiting each part of her trail at the same time of year as she traveled it. When she reflects on the vastness of the prairie, it is because my own breath was taken away by its magnitude. When she glories in the natural hot springs near Saratoga, it is because I, too, have washed away aches and pains in that spot. When she builds a shelter against a boulder on Jack Creek, it is because that is where I would have tried to protect myself and my children from the elements. And when she realizes how easily she could have been lost on the Red Desert, her feelings are poignant and immediate because I also have felt lost there in the middle of April's muddy runoff.

For all these reasons, the map included on page xii of this volume depicts Callie's route from the Little Laramie up over present-day Libbey Flats, down French Creek to Saratoga, across to Jack Creek, and then on through Green River to Fort Bridger.

Broken Lance is also a historically accurate work of fiction. In 1857, trouble between soldiers and the Cheyenne Indian—most notably the incident commonly referred to as the "tobacco holdup"—shattered the Fort Laramie Treaty of 1851 and led Colonel Charles Sumner to burn that tribe's tepees and winter supplies (see *Cheyenne Memories: Stands in Timber and Liberty* [New Haven, Conn.: Yale University Press, 1967], 160–65; U. S. Government Report of Captain George H. Stewart, 27 Aug. 1856, Senate Ex. Documents, 34th Congress, 3d Session, no. 5, 108–9).

Across this scene of turmoil wound a newly established route west: the Cherokee Trail. Though comparatively few in number, some Mormon pioneers joined others in taking this shortcut. Callie, her children, and Three Elk are all imaginary characters, but the Cherokee Trail and the struggles of the handcart companies that caused the McCrackens and others to venture out upon it are well documented. Likewise, Callie's techniques for subsistence are rooted in the experiences of Douglas M. Brown, Ph.D., who taught university classes and led outdoor survival expeditions for nine years.

In addition to being historically and geographically accurate and moving quickly through many adventures of practical survival in the wilderness, the strength of the story lies in the characters themselves. For example, Three Elk embodies the Cheyenne ideal of a brave of the mid-nineteenth century. Having a sense of humor, being well-spoken yet of few words, he is generous and loyal. His tribe's morality outlined a strict code that rivaled and possibly surpassed the constraints of Callie's Victorian contemporaries.

Despite their great cultural differences, Callie and Three Elk are alike in their insistence on maintaining honor. His stoicism and her iron will are nearly twin attitudes, yet each must grow before they can recognize and appreciate the other's character.

The changes that occur within Callie and Three Elk lend *Broken Lance* a convincing subtlety not often found in western literature. Beneath the story line run themes of faith, beauty, appreciation, tolerance, integrity, and the ironies in life. Depth lends sophistication to the young pioneer mother whose experiences fill these pages.

I hope you find *Broken Lance* pleasant reading as well as an inspirational story.

Michele R. Sorensen

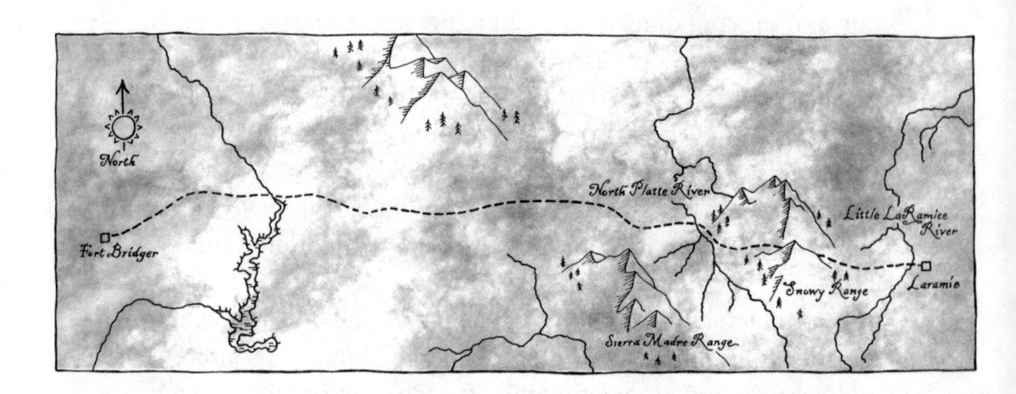
North
North Platte River
Little LaRamiee
River
Fort Bridger
Laramie
Snowy Range
Sierra Madre Range

W I L D E R N E S S

20 July 1857

North Fork of the Little LaRamiee River

ONE

"Feels like a coffin in here."

"Hush, James!" Callie's whisper flew with the intensity of a mother's fear. His mouth could get them killed.

Yet, though she couldn't let on, Callie knew how he felt. It seemed absolute cowardice to hide while everyone else was preparing to fight. She could hear them rushing among the circled wagons, cattle lowing nervously in the center.

Somewhere a woman was crying—probably the young widow, Jane Stickney. Her infant never left her arms, and the whining sound of fear pinched her voice.

Callie could hear the wagon boss, Ike Bullows, chastise a driver to the west. Apparently that wagon hadn't been drawn tightly enough into the ring. Bullows hurled oaths at its owner, demanding he keep cattle away from the gap and not let them break through. Cursing freely, he moved on. For an instant Callie reflected that in a company of Saints this crisis would have the advantage of united prayer; then she began silently trying to compensate on behalf of them all.

To the east Callie could hear round old Widow Lauderberry calling her grown sons to come get extra bullets and powder from her stores.

Then a hand clapped against the side of their wagon bed, and Callie's tight-strung nerves sent a searing jolt through her fingertips and toes. But it was only Ryan Mulloy, greeting her husband, Angus. "Hey, Scottie," he called. "Y' know how to shoot thet thang all right?" Angus's answer was lost in the din. Callie caught only bits and pieces of words as they hurriedly exchanged information about the Indians their scouts had sighted riding out of the north. "A hoard o' twenty er so . . . armed, painted . . . no women er children with 'em, no travois . . ."

She could hear Angus's low voice questioning, and Ryan Mulloy's twangy tenor answering again, "Yep, could be Cheyenne. An' if so, we'd best keep our rifles in hand. Shore as a rattler's got fangs, they been thirstin' fer a drink o' white blood. Why, some of them bucks has been on the warpath ever since the t'baccy holdup near Fort Kearney. I heard Ol' Bull Sumner's gettin' riled . . ."

Dogs ran barking and growling beneath the wagons, unnoticed by their masters. The lowing of the oxen had grown to a feverish roll, like surging water behind a dam.

In spite of the clamor and her own racing heart, Callie thought she could hear Angus checking his gun below the wagon. "Sh-h-h-h-h," she breathed in her little girl's ear. "Sh-h-h-h-h, Susa."

Then all noise abruptly vanished. Only the wind sighed as it brushed tall, dry grass against the bed of their wagon. Callie lay tense. Her arms motionlessly clutched five-year-old Susa against her side, except for one finger that comfortingly stroked the child's silky blonde hair. Young Duncan's eyes stared wide in the darkness beside her shoulder, his breathing quick and uneven. Her older boy, Jamie, cowered in the shallow blackness, hidden from her view except where a sliver of light fell across his hands clenching one of the joists that supported the false floor above them.

The rumble of pounding hooves filled the distance, growing louder. Sudden screams ripped the heavy air: *"Ai-yi-yi!"* The shrill, ratchety whoops of attacking savages mingled with the strange, eerie sound of high whistles.

A gun went off somewhere to the north. Then another. But Angus's weapon was silent beneath the wagon, as she had expected it to be. Angus wouldn't shoot until he could make out the very war paint on their dark cheeks. Callie knew her Highland-born husband of eleven years—so level and cool—wouldn't waste a single shot in nervous anticipation. Whenever Angus fired, he hit what he'd aimed at.

Volleys were being exchanged from both directions before she heard her husband fire. His rifle was secondhand but good—a Sharps carbine that he'd traded work for in St. Joseph. She knew he was shuffling with powder as he reloaded, even though she could no longer make out the sound of his movements above the rattle and slap of gunfire.

The cattle's bellowing had surged to a pitch of frenzy. Not more than twenty feet to the west, she heard a wagon crash over on its side. Callie shuddered and her wagon shook as the thundering river of livestock pressed against their pen and poured through the gap. Their hooves pounded south briefly, turning to run along the north bank of the nearby river. *Even on horseback,* she thought, *it will take the men days to catch them in this wide open plain.*

The screams were mayhem now: war cries, women's terror. Bullets whined and arrows sliced—whit, whit, whit. Men groaned in the agony of pain. Sss-thung! An arrow hit the side of their wagon. "Mamma," someone's baby kept crying, "Mammaaa—"

With one hand, Callie reached over and rubbed Duncan's arm in a gesture for strength. Then, to stop her own terrified quaking, she crushed little Susa even more tightly against her and bent one arm to cover the girl's ears. Jamie said nothing of cowardice now. Their silence bound them in horror as chaos erupted outside.

Soon the fighting was hand-to-hand. Callie heard Angus fire again and then scramble out from beneath their wagon. Scuffling followed . . . a shout . . . a horse whistled and snorted. Unintelligible Indian profanity raked the air. The horse's hooves were nearly on top of them, stomping, rearing.

Then came the sickening thud of a body striking the side of the wagon. It hit the earth without a groan.

Callie held her breath, crushing her ear against the floorboards, straining to know who had fallen. If Angus was all right, he would knock twice against the wagon bed. As always, he had thought through every possibility; he'd created this signal to keep them linked together and give them courage if this moment ever came. *Oh let me hear him knock!* she prayed, silent, desperate. *Let him—*

"Ai-yi-yi!" the whoop began, the warrior's voice wild with triumph. Two feet hit the dirt and shuffled briefly. Then she heard him jump back on his horse. *"Ai-yi-yi-yi . . ."* The savage turned away, his victory shout swallowed up in the melee.

Duncan's eyes were closed, invisible in the darkness. Jamie's hands shook, his knuckles white against the joist. Callie was still praying silently. She shut her eyes tight, but tears continued squeezing out the corners, as she lay with sickening dread in the false bottom Angus had built into their wagon. *Please, let him still be alive. Let him only be unconscious . . . convincingly unconscious.*

Suddenly the wagon lurched. Moccasin-covered feet—not boots—jumped recklessly onto the driver's seat and through the front. Another brute scrambled in the back. Callie listened to the red devils above her, slashing the canvas top, ravaging their possessions and tossing them out. Grunting and heaving, they spoiled irreplaceable provisions, shredded her quilts, shattered her few precious pieces of glass. The ransacking paused for a moment while they spoke in lower tones, their husky voices thick with excitement over some find. Then destruction broke out again.

Callie had clamped her hand over Susa's mouth when she first heard their feet hit, but now she was biting her own lips in an effort not to make a sound. The wagon began rocking wildly, lurching back and forth as the attackers tried to shove her feather tick out between the ribs of the cover. Angus had bought that tick for her in Independence with extra cash he'd earned making wagon beds.

She tried to force her mind back to that moment of kindness, away from the vicious present, as the wagon careened wildly from side to side. Duncan rolled half on top of her, then off again, and the sliver of light that illuminated Jamie's hands leaped wildly through the blackness.

She knew they were looking for her and the children. They were thinking someone would be shivering with fear between the barrels and boxes in the wagon. *Instead, we're shivering below them,* she thought, as a brief, cheap wave of satisfaction washed over her. *We'll cheat the devils of their prize!* Thanks to Angus, those beasts would never discover her little ones unless they made a noise or the wagon completely tipped over, because the trapdoor was on its underbelly.

Angus had thought of that. Uncertain of a new land, of new dangers that hardly resembled the challenges they'd faced in their Yorkshire home, he had lain awake nights, thinking ahead on everything.

"Callie," he'd told her as he fashioned the false floor in the wagon bed, "'tis the children we must be thinkin' of. God'll bring us through to Him whether soon or late. But Susa and Duncan and Jamie, they must have th' blessin's o' Zion, th' cov'nants o' eternity." With this in mind, he'd spent precious pence on a used copy of Piercy's *Route from Liverpool to the Great Salt Lake Valley* and then pored over the sketches during their long sea crossing.

Although a gentle man and a carpenter by trade, Angus's blood flowed from the Scottish highlands and the fighters who roamed there. His father was of the McCracken clan, his mother a Campbell of Glen Morrie. So it was no surprise to Callie that he'd caught on quickly, watching and copying such skills of the frontier as rifle shooting and bullet making. He'd been a tireless observer from the moment they'd reached

Florence, Nebraska. "Our responsibility, Callie lass. Ours t' see that th' wee ones get there."

"You mustn't worry," Callie had told him. "God is at the head of this thing. If Moses could part the Red Sea, He can surely roll back a tide of ignorant natives for Israel's Camp."

Roll back the tide . . . Turmoil was breaking and crashing above her head. Was her husband, honest and good, lying motionless in death below? *Great Jehovah!* she screamed inside her head. *Roll back the tide!*

At last the Indians grew convinced that there were only goods in the wagon. Content with the destruction, one of them leaped down and urged his horse away. But the other jumped to the ground and began chopping with a hatchet at the side of the wagon bed.

Instinctively, Callie tried to draw her feet up, though Jamie was the one nearest the blows. The gun Angus had pushed in with them was beside her. She ran her hand along its cold barrel toward the trigger. Angus had loaded it for her, but how could she shoot, lying on her back, with a child in her arms? Her movement hidden by the noise, Callie rolled half onto her side, pushed Susa away, and pointed the muzzle toward the crashing hatchet.

But the hacking stopped when their water barrel broke loose and fell with a loud crack against the hard ground. Instantly, the brute lit into the other barrel. Next to his chopping, the sound of gushing water was all she could hear. But after it stopped, her ears rang with echoing whoops and screams.

Eventually Callie realized there was only silence outside. The salty taste of blood was in her mouth where she'd been biting her lip, and the rifle had grown warm in her clenched hand. Dry grass scratched again at the side of the wagon.

"Are they gone, Mum?" Duncan whispered.

Susa whimpered softly, the only intelligent part of her

garbled baby sounds was the repeated question, "Where's Papa?" "Be still," Jamie blurted, and his voice cracked.

By this Callie knew her ten-year-old had guessed at the truth, but she was powerless to move or offer comfort. The overwhelming quiet outside their box of blackness filled her with fear against opening the trapdoor. Her terror might even have penned them up until hunger and thirst drove them out—surely they should have waited until night—but Angus was somewhere in the ruin. What if he were lying bleeding on the ground, in pain?

That was the thought that finally forced Callie, with trembling hands, to open the latch on the trapdoor and squint out into the brightness.

T W O

With a gesture forbidding her children to follow, Callie released the latch and silently eased open the trapdoor. The ensuing rush of fresh air revived her senses somewhat, and she forced terror to crouch behind action and expediency. She was met only by the empty sighing of the wind and uninterrupted scraping of tall grass.

Cautiously she let herself down through the trapdoor. In the deathly silence, the sound of her own feet finding the ground made her heart skip erratically. But Callie struggled to keep Jamie from seeing her dread as she reached back and took the rifle he handed her. Cocking it, she was immediately grateful Angus had insisted—against her protestations—that she learn at least the rudiments of shooting.

Callie breathed deeply, bent low, and looked out from beneath her wagon. There was only the dry wind bending the grass, flapping the shredded canvas wagon-tops, stirring across the dead. Callie's eyes slammed shut against the horror, and she forced her mind to close against the wild carnage. Opening her eyes, Callie assured herself there was no other moving form among the broken wagons. The savages were gone.

Then she saw Angus. He lay on the ground, limbs askew in a grotesque angle beside the burst water barrel, his blood mingling with the mud.

Callie choked back a sound that was half sob and half cry as she crawled, gun in hand, toward him. Lifting his shoulders, she saw where his red hair had been torn off, where numerous wounds had bitten through his clothing, where savage knives had mutilated his flesh. She tried to wipe the blood from his face, and pulled frantically at his torn shirt, straining to cover the long horrid gash that plunged into his chest. Grinding her teeth, clenching her eyes, she hugged him to her. Then, in a fit of nausea, she thrust his limp form back to the ground and rose to stumble out into the ring of wagons.

She refused to think during those agonizing moments when she ran from wagon to wagon among the disfigured corpses. Between the heavings of her stomach, she forced herself to turn over each familiar body and confirm that it was indeed dead. All she knew was that in the end she found herself standing back above Angus, beside her own wagon, still clutching the rifle in one hand.

Demons. Devils. Evil fiends from Hell. There were no words big enough to hold the magnitude of her mingled fear and hatred. Yet, in the rush of fierce emotion, Callie felt an engulfing sense of loss as well. The empty wind swept over the dead and brushed past her, running away . . . away.

"Mama?" From inside the wagon, Susa's tiny call was almost swallowed up by the stillness.

"Hush!" The harsh, grating sound of her own voice startled Callie. "Hush, children. Don't come out."

What was she going to do? She couldn't let them see this. She had to hide these mangled, hideous sights from their young eyes.

They didn't protest, and Callie turned, tenderly lifting Angus's shoulders and pulling his long, loose form around past the wagon tongue to the outer side of the ring. Breathing heavily from exertion and heat, she laid him flat, then propped him up against the wheel of their wagon. Yet, no matter what position she tried, the top of his bare and bloody head unsettled her so deeply she could not go on. Where was his hat? She looked around in the trampled grass. Where? Tearing a strip from her petticoat, she bound his head and turned her back.

Among the scattered provisions she found a shovel, and

though her movements were hampered by the shortness and the splinters of its freshly broken handle, she feverishly began scraping out a grave. The ground was hard, dry, and compacted, but she paused only to glance around to be sure she and the children were alone. Her rifle lay cocked beside her right foot at the edge of the growing hole.

Callie's movements were frenzied. Her mind framed only one thought: dig, dig, dig. Tears fell upon the dust, but she turned them away with the shovel, not even registering what they were.

"Mama, I'm thirsty!" Susa called when the hole was half Angus's length.

Duncan immediately volunteered, "I'll get her some water, Mum."

"No!" Callie shrieked.

"We only want to get out and stretch and have a drink," the boy insisted.

"I'm hot in here," his sister wailed.

"No! No! No!" Callie shouted, dropping her shovel and running to be certain the latch was secure. "No!" she cried, hitting her fist on the side of the wagon box. Suddenly the panic in her voice and her own jerking movements became apparent to her. Taking deep breaths, she fought her way back from the edge of hysteria. "You must not," she swallowed, struggling to make her voice more calm, "must *not* come out here until I say. The water barrels are broken, anyway."

"But—"

"No!" she cried, straining for control. "Don't ask again."

Callie had just turned back to her digging when Susa's question caught her, "Where's Papa?"

Callie fell on the ground as if she'd been struck, her empty stomach turning and her vision reeling.

"Where is he, Mama?"

"Gone," she answered at last, looking at his mangled form and wringing her hands. "Gone away."

Pulling herself back onto her feet, she clasped the spade and jammed it against the hard ground.

Twilight had begun to settle in before the hole was near being big enough. Callie had long since realized there was no way she could bury the others. She had to take the children and go. They must get away from this place.

"Mother?" James ventured to call as the light faded and darkness grew.

Unable to answer, Callie kept digging.

"Mother? I can help, if ye like. I can—" His voice cracked again, but he cleared his throat and went on, "I can dig."

"Hold Susa." Callie commanded, surprised again at how brassy and rough her voice sounded. "I can't have you seeing this. It wouldn't do . . . wouldn't do . . ." Her words trailed away with a breathless sound beside the unbroken rhythm of her spade.

As the last purple hints of light gleamed along the western horizon, Callie pulled Angus into the hole and covered him with a three-inch blanket of dry dirt.

Falteringly, in little more than a whisper, she prayed over the grave, returning responsibility for this poor spot to heaven's hands until resurrection morning. Callie was trembling as she rose from her knees, and she realized quite suddenly that the children had been able to hear her every word, for the wind was gone now and the silence was stifling, almost painful in its heaviness. She dropped back to her knees and began another earnest prayer, invoking God to be with them, to protect them and to bless Papa. She must not voice her fears within the hearing of the children.

Three times she began to pray, but her voice gave out. The ache in her throat choked the words so they wouldn't come. Each time Callie felt she could not go on, she looked toward the wagon and forced herself to begin again. But, after the fourth effort, she broke into silent, painful sobs that tore through her entire frame. Still on her knees, she hugged herself tightly, rocking back and forth. Though her mind could not accept the normality of it, twilight dimmed into darkness, and the crickets took up a high, creaky monotone in the grass all around.

Eventually, Callie forced her quivering muscles to calm. She *had* to get her children away from this place soon. Her trembling fingers brushed at the dirt on the front of her dress. Then she wiped at her tears with the backs of her hands. Quietly, determinedly, she willed herself to sing.

Callie's voice had never been soloist quality, but music had often brought peace and joy to her heart. She had enjoyed singing in the kitchen of her Yorkshire home or over her sleeping infants. And now, though her voice was weak at first and soft, even beside the smooth river, a very small part of the pain and terror and loss began sliding away from her across the dark prairie sky.

> Guide us, O thou great Jehovah,
> Guide us to the promised land.

She paused only long enough to draw a shaky breath.

> We are weak, but Thou art able;
> Hold us in Thy pow'rful hand . . .

Defying her voice to give out now, the melody and familiar words of the song carried her prayer along as she sang:

> When the earth begins to tremble,
> Bid our fearful hearts be still;

She looked once more toward the wagon with her hidden children, and her hands fell to the gun that lay across her lap.

> When thy judgments spread destruction,
> Keep us safe on Zion's hill . . .

Slowly, Callie began to feel a growing, almost burning resolve fill some of her inner emptiness. By faith in the God of Israel she determined she would force her way through to Zion.

Singing praises, singing praises,
Songs of glory unto thee-e-e-e
Songs of glo-o-ory unto thee.

A strangely formal feeling settled over the numbing agony. Her nerves were oddly separate from the part of her that had to go on. Her actions became the extension of a mind that ruthlessly determined what it would allow itself to think. If she strayed from focus, she knew all control—all hope—would be lost.

Callie rose, walking straight to the wagon. She put her gun in ahead of her, but, as she was stepping up onto the back, she slipped and fell in something sticky and wet. Her heart tore wildly against her ribs, though her mind recognized the smell. This was where the Indians had dumped the sourdough starter she'd gotten from old Widow Lauderberry when the wagons first pulled out of St. Joseph.

Callie reached for a dangling strip of the shredded wagon cover and tried to wipe her hands and skirt in the darkness. Afraid to make a light, she struggled and shuffled with slippery hands through the moonlit ruins, putting together four packs of provisions. Scraping what she could from the ground and out of broken barrels and sacks, she salvaged rice and cornmeal, and a large portion of coarse wheat flour. From among the scattered cactus and trampled bunches of prairie grass she gathered up dried apple slices she had purchased in St. Joe to keep the children from scurvy. The yeast and vinegar and sugar were gone, scattered to the wind and onto the ground. Her bacon, used mostly for cooking grease, had been thrown somewhere out into the dirt, and she dared not wait for daylight to find it.

Callie searched anxiously for her vial of quinine to fight fevers but could not locate it in the mess. Her tight-lidded bottle of matches was still intact, though, and she gratefully added this, along with her small sewing kit and a dented quart-sized pan, to her pile of supplies. An old knife had been left among her cooking things, and she managed to search out a few usable pieces of India-rubber tarpaulins and a flint-stone from Angus's knife-riddled stores. A long piece of scratchy, rough rope had also been overlooked in the tack barrel.

The Indians had taken Angus's gun, but the rifle he'd given her was continually at her side. He'd also left her cartridges—some in her own pockets and some in Jamie's. Probably two dozen shots, at least.

Gathering what shreds of blankets she could find, Callie made bedding for each of them and bound them in the pieces of India-rubber tarpaulin. Using scraps of canvas from the wagon top, she wrapped up each pack and fashioned strips to bind them to their backs. She hadn't wanted to give Jamie so much, but he would have to haul his full share, for she was carrying most of Susa and Duncan's provisions as well as her own. It wasn't much food compared to their original supplies, but it made a comforting, heavy load on her back and she added to it all the warm clothing she could find. Last she slipped Angus's Book of Mormon into her own pack before crawling under the wagon to the trapdoor.

"Jamie?" She heard him scoot toward the opening. "Come out now, Son."

James quietly helped the other children down through the trapdoor, passing Susa to his mother, and putting his own hand out to steady Duncan's shoulder.

"Don't look around," Callie commanded in a voice that obliterated the possibility of questions. "Keep your eyes on me." Then, with firm, gentle hands, she strapped a pack onto the backs of each of her youngsters.

Grateful for the darkness, she led them away from the ring of battered wagons, out past their father's unmarked grave, down toward the river. They hadn't gone more than fifty yards when Callie stopped suddenly. Huddling the three in a little group, she ran back toward the wagons. After piling up what rocks she could find to guard Angus's grave against wolves, she turned for the last time and looked across the skeletal forms of the broken wagons.

The moon floated like a pale remembrance across the empty sky. Wan light fell from it, settling and pooling along the twin wagon tracks that wound out of the east from which they'd come—tracks that ended abruptly.

Callie went back to her children. In silence and without another backward glance, she led them west through the brush along the north bank of the Little LaRamiee River.

THREE

All of Callie's energy was bent on guiding the children as quickly as possible from the scene of the massacre. Her tight lips defied questions and squelched chatter. James was also filled with determination, as if he wanted to pick up and walk straight to Zion without stopping. Behind her, the resolute sound of his steps made the boy seem much older than ten. He walked steadily into the immense darkness, often reaching back to help seven-year-old Duncan through the trackless sage-brush and around tiny hummocks of prairie grass.

Gratefully, Callie let the two boys follow as best they could in the darkness behind her. She had enough to do, pulling Susa along with one hand and carrying her heavy rifle in the other. Her palms were blistered and raw from digging her husband's grave, but she could not yet feel the fatigue that had set into her muscles and joints.

Tension propelled every step forward, away from the events of the day. Callie's answer to horror was surging determination. Her bastion against collapse was avoidance, almost denial, of the aching fear and emptiness in her heart. Yet, in spite of her strength and defiance, worry began nagging and nipping at her heels.

She felt certain the savages had attacked from the north; that was where the first shots had been fired. Although Callie had no idea where they'd gone, she supposed they had returned where they'd come from. For that reason she had not taken the easy-to-follow trail. She led her little ones in silence, away from the northern route the trail had been following, cutting in a southwesterly direction along the river.

In the hurried silence of fear, the four of them tramped across what Callie supposed to have been four or five miles. The pungent aroma of sage rose from the sparse, bruised leaves beneath their boots at each step. Clouds shrouded the moon. Hardly any light dropped across the ground, but Callie didn't mind stumbling in the darkness if it meant they were better hidden from the heathens' view.

Please don't let us walk into a sleeping camp of the murdering beasts, she prayed silently, fervently echoing the same requests over and over again. *Please spare us from ever seeing another filthy savage.*

At last Duncan tripped over one too many rocks. Callie could hear Jamie trying to urge him to his feet again, but his answer was lost in an unintelligible whine. At the sound, Susa began to cry as well.

"Sh-h-h," Callie commanded, letting go of the girl's hand and turning back to encourage Duncan.

"'Tis a cactus, Mother," Jamie explained, pointing with his toe at a dark patch of small, round, thorny plants. "Th' spines stuck fast when he fell."

Callie knew from recent experience that Duncan's hand was throbbing with a sting from the poison that was worse than the prick. "Hush," she said, kneeling carefully to the side of the dark patch and pulling the seven-year-old into her lap. "Hush, Son. Let me see if I can get them out." She found the large spines easily with her fingers, but darkness made it impossible to see all the tiny thorns in his palm. While Jamie and Susa stood watching, Callie used the tip of her tongue to search for slivers in his tender skin, so her teeth could pull them out.

"There," she said when she could find no more. "All better?"

Duncan nodded his head and laid it against her chest.

"Up we go," she said softly, hoisting him to his feet.

"Please, Mum," Duncan's voice was thin in the darkness. "I'm tired and hungry. Can we stop here? Please?"

At the mere suggestion of a rest, Susa began crying again. The sound distressed Callie in the still night. "Quiet, child. You'll bring a pack of heathens in on us."

Susa's mouth clamped shut in the very midst of a howl, but even after they started walking once more, her dragging feet were slow. Reluctantly, Callie had to admit that her children needed sleep and nourishment.

They had been walking along the rim of ground between the prairie and where the bank fell away toward the river. For most of the night, sage and cactus had been the only obstacles to hinder their steps. But in the last half mile, willows and an occasional elm had begun appearing along the water's edge, singly at first, then in stunted clumps, and finally in a thin, broken curtain.

"Sit here a moment." Callie seated Susa with her back against the rough bark of the nearest tree. She gestured for Jamie to sit there with Duncan, as well.

"No fire, eh?" James asked.

"None," Callie answered as she turned and walked down into the trees. They would need a spot that was somewhat flat but hidden from view. She thought she'd found the perfect place only three feet from the river, a grassy clearing edged all around with willows, until she stepped into it and felt the sharp prick of a mosquito's bite. Then another. She heard the droning cloud even before her straining eyes made out a shadow hanging thick over the water.

She didn't dare leave the children alone and out of sight long enough to hunt up another spot, so she hurried back, swatting mosquitoes from her neck as she went.

"We'll have to bed down here, beneath this tree," she told them softly, keeping her voice too low to carry. After dropping her own pack beside a large, fallen branch, she spread out

Susa's bedding. "You here, Duncan, and you there, Jamie. Put the India-rubber tarp beneath you, like this. And keep the rest of your pack close by."

Carrying the cocked rifle with her all the while, she settled them down and then looked among her things for the rope she'd found in the tack barrel. Its very roughness encouraged her as she ran it along the ground in a loop around her tired children. A woman back in St. Joseph had told her this was the best method to keep snakes away. So, on hot nights when she'd slept outside the wagon, Callie had strung this very rope around herself and Angus, and no slithery creature had ever made an appearance. Claiming a small space against the surrounding wilderness made her feel a little better, as if she were on the offensive, still clutching some control. It was the least tiny comfort she could offer her children now.

Morning isn't all that far off, Callie told herself as she sat down on the fallen branch beside them. Duncan was nearly asleep already, one hand resting beneath his tousled head, the other cactus-prickled one curled up at his chest.

Susa had snuggled into her blankets with the doll she'd made from a spoon. Normally she hummed herself and the wooden playmate to sleep, but tonight the only sound was the slowing of her breath. Before they'd made the crossing, Susa had always been such a rosy and robust child, ever busy and boisterous, that her mother was shocked by how white and frail she looked as she slept. It was a trick of the moonlight, Callie decided, nothing more. Moonlight and her own fears.

She turned her gaze quickly away in James's direction. "Why don't ye sleep, and I'll sit up t' watch?" he asked when she looked at him.

"Hmmm?" Callie jumped. "No, Jamie." Even to herself, her words sounded hard, somewhat condescending. "You sleep. You'll have to carry your own pack again tomorrow, so you'd best catch every wink you can."

Knowing better than to argue, the boy turned over in his

blankets, his face lost from her view in darkness that was both wide and deep. Callie sat resolutely on the log, watching over the dark bundles that were her children at rest. Occasionally Susa and Duncan muttered fitfully, tossing and rolling with troubled dreams. But James lay still and silent. She knew that every so often his eyes were opening and that he was looking toward where she sat, silhouetted against the moonlight. She could feel him watching her, and once she even spoke gently, thinking he was afraid.

"I'm here, Jamie."

"I know," he answered softly, sleepily, and that was all.

But for Callie, rest was a vanished commodity. The more hours that passed between her and the massacre, the more the numbness of her fear and shock wore off. Memories crowded in upon her. The sights and scenes of the battlefield came to her like visions of the very deaths she had willed herself not to see even as she confirmed them: old Dame Lauderberry slumped forward on the floor of her wagon, an emptied box of bullets in her hands . . . Ike Bullows, silent now . . . the strong young Claybourne boys from Kentucky . . . those blond Larson children, a toddler and a set of twins . . . dimpled, bright-eyed Meg Peltzer . . . Ryan Mulloy with his lovely spaniel dead beside him—they'd even killed the dogs! And Jane Stickney, her babe still in her arms. *She's with her husband again,* Callie thought, but this small comfort also emphasized how alone she and the children were.

Worst of all was the memory of Angus as she had found him. At the thought her throat clenched painfully. But she refused to think of him at all. She could not bear it, and she knew it. If she let her mind dwell on him, the pain would be too much.

With a heaving effort Callie thrust this and every other recollection from her mind. Intently she scanned and rescanned the spaces among the willows, the yuccas, and the spreading grass. She strained to catch any unusual sound above the sighing water. But only the crickets sang out in their nightly monotone, while the river eddied softly away toward the east.

Still sitting on the fallen tree with the gun across her lap, she fought to escape remembering. Yet the past crawled around her in the darkness.

Desperately, she turned her thoughts to long ago. If she couldn't ward off memories, she would at least choose them: her Yorkshire childhood and the comfort of her own mother's touch when she had been very small.

She thought of other beautiful things in her life: the smooth sound of her father's violin, the scent of fresh-baked breads in the bakery at the end of the block, the lovely Persian rug Angus had given her when Jamie was born. He'd given her a daring hat with a clutch of bright feathers after the arrival of her second healthy son, and a set of beautiful, small pearls for her ears on the night she birthed his daughter. The rug and hat had been sold to finance this trip to Zion, and Callie had pulled the pearls from her ears and pressed them into her own mother's hand at parting.

Urgently Callie's mind fled back, back in search of a memory that had not been violated by the odyssey that was upon her. Nothing was the same: all the patterns and foundations of her life had been broken. Only what was within her, what she carried on her back, and her three little ones were left to her now.

What in her life had prepared her for this ordeal? Though her youth had not been luxurious, her parents had been frugal with their means and generous with their children. She was not used to hardship. Callie's father had owned a tea and jam shop, providing well enough for her and her older brothers to enjoy some of life's advantages. Old Mrs. Whitcliffe had drilled mathematics tables endlessly into her head and had strictly ensured that the dark-eyed, fine-boned girl could read both words and music. She'd had an excellent education; she'd known civilization.

Sitting among the black trees, Callie considered the fact that she knew nothing of butchering any animal larger than a rooster or rabbit. She knew nothing from making soap to finding her directions in this vicious wilderness. Silently she promised herself that she would use every gift, every experience at her disposal. The higher things of her past would carry her sanity through this desolate journey. Great thoughts would subdue the hideous violence of this frontier, would keep her children separate from it.

"One step." Callie spoke under her breath with intensity that defied the darkness. "One step at a time is how you get to Zion. Even with a wagon boss, you can't get there any faster." She wouldn't think about next week, or even tomorrow. Only one step at a time. Step after step.

Angus would have agreed with that. Angus was such a practical man. He hadn't grown up under the same sheltered conditions she'd known. Born to crofters in Scotland, his family had been driven from their home when he was an infant by the edict of Elizabeth Gordon of Dunrobin Castle, Countess of Sutherland, who unexpectedly had announced that the title of her subtenants would expire on Whitsunday 1813. Never mind how long his people had been there, the clan of Kildonan Parish was left without property or possibility. They huddled together, penniless and starving, until Angus's parents had finally given in and joined the stream of displaced farmers and shepherds that flowed south into Yorkshire's factories, quarries, and mills.

But Angus was different from the rest. He always was. Like his mates, he began working bobbins in a factory before he turned seven. But when the other boys went home, dead tired after running all day to repair broken threads beneath the heavy swinging looms, Angus stopped each night by a carpenter's shop, watching and even helping the workers clean up there. He was a comical lad: skinnier than a broom straw, though his brogue was thicker than potato soup. After a while the manager of the shop began to notice the boy was clever with his hands and a hard worker. Before winter was out, Angus hired on and quickly learned a skill that bought him independence.

Angus had married late, but Callie admired that, too. First he got his parents set in a small home of their own with a rose-covered wicket gate and a kitchen garden beyond. By then, most of his friends had been married, but Angus put together a place of his own before he ever approached Callie's father on the subject. Eyebrows had been raised all over town at the match of a merchant's daughter and this Scottish carpenter, but her father had not found a reason to deny such a practical, kind man. Neither had Callie.

They'd been quite comfortable in the modest home Angus built, not far from either of their parents. With her soft smile hidden beneath the spreading frontier darkness, Callie mused over visions of the rooms where she'd worked and slept, laughed and cried and sung. That little white house was where their children had been born, and it was where she'd first heard the restored gospel.

FOUR

"Callie lass!" Angus called lustily, his voice booming through the front door. "Set two more places if ye will. Here's friends I've brought wi' me."

As he stepped into the kitchen he kissed her softly on the forehead. "Well, aren't ye goin' t' ask who they be?"

Callie looked up from where she was adding milk and water to stretch the gravy. She'd had a hard day: Jamie had stepped on a nail, the neighbor's dog had gotten into her drying laundry, and baby Susa was noisily cutting two-year molars. But when she saw the vigorous grin on Angus's face and his dancing, teasing eyes, all her troubles were worthwhile.

"Why should I?" she answered, mirroring his smile. "If they're friends of yours, they're welcome here."

Quickly, she gave Susa a spoon to teethe on and slid a couple more plates onto the table. As she turned to get the extra sets of flatware, Callie glanced up and saw them standing in the doorway: two men from America.

"Well?" Angus asked, pushing away the pieces of a new chair he was fashioning for her in the firelight. "They've been gone an hour now and there's been nary a word from ye, lass. What air ye thinkin' 'bout those missionaries?"

Callie looked up at him from where she sat mending Jamie's Sunday britches. "What do I think of them?"

"Aye."

"Their English is horrid!"

Laughing, Angus rose and caught her up in his arms, holding her tightly to him.

Even now, sitting on a fallen log in the dark chill of the early morning hours, Callie clearly remembered looking up into her husband's ruddy face, his beard tickling against her cheek. A twinkle that matched his bright eyes shone in his voice. "Ye'll not be takin' after them what ignorantly misuse th' English language, now, will ye?"

"Angus! Angus!" She had laughed, pushing him away from her.

"You mean, what do I think of their message?"

"Their preachin's, lass, I mean their preachin's," he growled cheerfully, not letting her go without an answer.

"Why," she said softly, seriously, "it's true."

Putting playfulness aside, Angus set her gently back in her chair and returned to his seat, but he did not take up the pieces of his project. "Be ye sure what ye're sayin'?"

Callie paused a moment, thought, and then nodded slowly. "Why, yes, Angus. When they spoke, I felt something I've never felt before. I just have a . . . a feeling that what those men said was true." He was staring intently into her face, so she paused and tried to describe what she meant. "How do you know your mother? You can't remember when you first realized who she was . . . that's just something you have always known. Well, what those men said was true, as if I had always known it, but I can't remember from when or where."

"*All* true?"

Callie nodded.

The house was quiet, and only the fire sighed. Angus bent to pick up his plane and a leg piece for the chair he'd been making. But instead of working them against each other, he laid the tool and wood in his lap and leaned forward. "There's a price t' be paid for truth, ye know. Blessings always come with a test shadowin' right behind 'em."

Angus paused and looked earnestly at his young wife, his

wiry red hair and brows blazing in the golden firelight. "This may be the greatest blessin' in our lives, but do ye dare face 't, lass? What will ye say t' Grace Collins when ye meet her on th' street and she knows ye've left her husband's parish?"

"Why," Callie smiled, "the same thing you'll say to Reverend Collins when you meet him."

Angus cocked his eyebrows and nodded, urging her to explain just what that ought to be.

"Good morning, Mrs. Collins," Callie demonstrated in smiling, formal tones. "Perhaps you would do me the honor of allowing me to introduce you to some friends of mine from America?"

Angus chuckled at his wife's teasing. "Aye, ye're a spitfire," he grinned. But then his voice dropped even lower, and his eyes were deeply serious. "But they preach a gatherin' t' Zion, as ye well know. What of yer parents an' yer aunt?"

She paused. Callie hadn't thought of it in quite this way yet. What was he getting at? Was he asking her to go to America?

"Angus," she spoke slowly, thinking as she went. "Imagine that you found the fairest jewel in the world, the most precious thing on the earth. And if—just if the mere possession of this gem could obtain heaven's greatest blessings for you, blessings greater than you had ever before dared to imagine, wouldn't you do everything possible to keep a hold of that jewel? Wouldn't you do absolutely anything to bring it home to our family?"

A pleased expression spread across Angus's face, wrinkling the corners of his eyes. "Shrewd ye are lass—shrewd t' know fine goods th' instant ye see them. An' brave, too." He shook his head with an amused grin that was half teasing, yet halfway terrifyingly serious. "I've always held that ye were th' most determined, headstrong woman on th' face o' this great green earth."

Callie started to protest with customary indignation at his

familiar accusation, but Angus held up his hand to silence her. "Now, t'night, I'm hopin' 'tis true, lassie," he reached out gently and took her small white hand between his callused ones, "because I've read the Book of Mormon meself already, an' I'm yearnin' t' take the wee ones t' Zion."

Callie looked up suddenly from their hands into his eyes. Angus had read an entire book? Zion? America? She opened her mouth to speak but clamped it shut suddenly instead.

"I didn' want t' tell ye lest I be sure. I ken it well—what 'twould mean t' ye t' leave this place, yer home from birth, yer family an' all." Angus's voice was low and hoarse, the brogue thickening even further as he searched for words. "But I be thinkin' the blessings air greater than any cost, an' I'm ready t' work for 'em." He rose and, going to his coat hung by the door, took a small book from the pocket. "When ye've read this," he said, handing the little volume to her with careful emphasis, "an ye're sure it be th' jewel ye were speakin' of, there won't be any price big enough t' hold us back."

What price, God?

These words suddenly seared through Callie's thoughts, leaving a trail of anguished bitterness that jerked her back to the present. *What price?*

Callie looked around in the darkness, calming her breaths, clasping the rifle in her hands, and blinking down fierce emotions. Her eyes fell gently on the sleeping blanketed bundles at her feet, and her mind again sought desperately to escape images of the butchery she'd waded through only hours before.

Some mingled phrases from Paul's Second Epistle to the Thessalonians came forward in her thoughts, and she pressed them softly upon her lips. It was something about the "righteous judgment of God," something about being "counted worthy of the kingdom of God, for which ye also suffer."

Callie sat quietly a moment, straining to recall the rest of the verse. " . . . it is a righteous thing with God to recompense tribulation to them that trouble you," she paused, feeling increasingly satisfied about what she was remembering, even as she knew there was more. "And . . . you who are troubled rest with us, when the Lord Jesus shall be revealed from heaven with his mighty angels, in flaming fire, taking vengeance on them that know not God . . ." Callie paused again, searching her memory for the next bit of the scripture and lingering over this last phrase. "Taking vengeance on them that know not God, . . . and . . . and that obey not the gospel of our Lord Jesus Christ." Eagerly, though softly under her breath, she repeated these words again before finishing, "Who shall be punished with everlasting destruction."

The Lord was with her, she was certain of that. This huge wilderness and its bloody natives were obstacles she would have to overcome—obstacles that would eventually pay for the pain they'd caused a servant of the Most High.

And in her mind she suddenly imagined herself standing beside the bar at Judgment Day. Getting to Zion was going to be hard—she dared not even think about how she would do it—but one day, at the judgment bar, she would stand face to face with the vulgar heathens who had left her children fatherless. Though she hadn't seen any of the fighting, she felt certain she would know the murderers on sight. And she would raise her arm to point a finger in undeniable testimony of their guilt.

On that blessed day she and Angus and the children would be together, reunited in love and happiness that would never again be interrupted. Then, without another thought for the damned souls of the heathen, Callie bent her mind forward on eternity until the quiet light of prairie dawn filtered around her.

Crickets were still humming softly in the grass as Callie rose and stepped out past the trees, looking away toward where the trail wound northward. Her fingers absentmindedly searched the mechanisms of her rifle; then, savoring the security of its weight in one hand, she stretched to shake off nighttime stiffness and chill.

Not far off to her right, a meadowlark whistled his curious tune. How formal he looked for this raw place, Callie thought, all fancied up in his yellow vest and wearing a black cravat. Perhaps the little fellow wasn't native to this wilderness, just trying to pass through like herself. Such things—she and he—did not belong here.

Standing with the fresh air against her face, Callie watched the first pastels of dawn streak the eastern horizon. Away to her left, the white tail ends of prairie goats poked in clusters above the grass. Here and there a goat lifted its slender head to scan the horizon with wide curious eyes. Their spiky black antlers and white cheek patches were clear to her even from this distance. She tried to guess how far off they were, noting how exposed any upright object was on the plain.

As soon as she started the children moving, the wind would scour her little bunch out and find them. *And so might the red savages,* she thought as her eyes strained out across immensity.

The vastness is so bleak, she thought. Around her spread desolation, a void, as if God had run out of materials to beautify His garden and had simply dumped His curious leftovers in this spot. This vicious land possessed nothing of godliness, no room for gentle breezes, smooth water, or soft green foliage—just as there was no room for peace or tolerance, kindness or forgiveness. She hadn't been here long, but that conclusion had been painfully forced upon her.

Although she could not quite make it out, her eyes traced where the Cherokee Trail wound up through the wide grassy expanse at the east, then turned north to follow the mountain range that lay, like a great wall, barring the western horizon. Perhaps she could parallel the trail, walking along the edge of those mountains, the Medicine Bow range. Angus had told her enough of where they were going that she knew somewhere around the tip of the Medicine Bow and out across another open, dry plain, was Fort Bridger. That was what she must find, but she hesitated to leave the Little LaRamiee. She had no canteen for making dry camps and besides, the Indians had attacked out of the north.

Determinedly, Callie turned and walked to the river. Using sand, she scrubbed her hands and face clean in the cold water. After pulling her dark hair straight and running her tiny pocket comb through it, she twisted the brown knot back again and pinned it in place. In the weak light of daybreak, she realized that her dress, a sturdy weave of rusty brown with small yellow flowers, was covered with dirt and blood and dried white paste where she'd fallen in the sourdough. She did not allow herself the luxury of even imagining a bar of soap, warm water, or clean clothes. Without undressing, her gun still at her side, Callie rinsed a flat rock in the river and used its edge to scrape the dried, loose soil from her skirts.

Then she rose and went to stand above her little ones. Jamie was already up, rolling his blankets into his pack. He watched his mother as she looked down on the smaller ones. Susa's beautiful hair shone in the early sun, the same pale gold as her mother's burnished wedding ring. Beside her, Duncan had wormed so far beneath his blankets that not even his nose was showing.

"Get up, sleepyhead!" Callie said, bending to give a teasing tug at one of his dark brown curls. When he was slow to respond, she nudged his behind with her boot and spoke more sternly. "We've miles to go, Duncan."

Susa sat up, yawning, disoriented. Hopefully she would not remember many details from the day and night before.

"Come," Callie said briskly. "Hurry." She didn't dare build a fire just yet, and the only thing that they could eat immediately was the apple slices. This would be quite a treat for the children, and she knew it would swell in their little bellies and make them feel full. "I'll fill each of your pockets with dried apples for breakfast. You can chew them as we walk."

Kneeling her children in a semicircle before her, Callie offered a morning prayer, asking God to hide them from heathens and open the way to Zion. Then, while James helped the younger ones roll up their beds, Callie moistened a strip of cloth in the river and carried it back to wash their faces. As she scrubbed behind their ears and wiped at the corners of their eyes, she vigorously recited for them the same scripture that had given her courage in the night: " . . . taking vengeance on them that know not God, . . . who shall be punished with everlasting destruction!" Saying this, she turned their backs on the warmth of the rising sun and started moving west.

"Mother?" Jamie ventured after they'd been walking half an hour. "Aren't we goin' t' follow th' trail north like we were before?"

"No," Callie answered. "That's the first place the hostiles would look for us."

"Oh," he said, accepting her answer. Callie didn't tell him that along this river was the second, the only other spot where the savages might expect to find them.

F I V E

The sun climbed slowly but with increasing warmth into an ever-deepening blue sky. Grass stretched endlessly off to their left and across the river to their right, shining and rippling in the sunlight. They followed the thin, winding thread of the Little LaRamiee, traveling upriver through the spreading plain.

Callie didn't encourage her children to speak, and for a few miles they walked in silence. For the boys, there was no pausing over the discovery of an old skull nor chasing around through noisy prairie dog towns. Neither did Susa stop to pick the tiny lavender flowers with sticky yellow centers that dared to bloom near the river. Rather, four pairs of feet made a syncopated tapping across the dry earth—a rhythm as continual as the rolling waves of grass.

Callie's mind slid back to the cramped, full-rigged packet ship that had carried her company from Liverpool to New York. After forty-eight wet and rocking days, land finally hove into view. Following a special service of thanks, the flock of British Saints had boarded a rattling, sooty train car. That was how they traveled to Florence, Nebraska, the town that had grown up around what had been the crude shelter of Winter Quarters only ten years before.

Weakened by miserable weeks of crossing the stormy Atlantic in a dank, squalid cabin with daily rations of soup or soft potatoes, fish, and hardtack, Susa and Duncan soon contracted what the newcomers were calling American fever. Even Jamie, though his temperature did not rise, looked pale and sickly. "Gut-shrunk," one of the workers at the depot had called him, "a gut-shrunk, emigrant brat."

Although others among their group—mostly children—were feverish as well, the Saints made no arrangements to rest their ailing members. They would carry their sick and feeble along. Nothing could stop them now, for they were at last on the same continent as Zion.

The McCrackens could have pressed forward with them, but practical Angus decided against it. "'Twas the cart convinced me o' it, Callie lass," he'd explained after he'd looked over a handcart prepared for their company to take. "Green hickory and oak, 'twas made of. An' not entirely bad. Sturdy enou' I trow, for the first thousand miles at least, but I couldn' see it lastin' o'er mountains save God provides a miracle glue."

Vehicles made of green wood had become notorious because of the Willie Company's disastrous, late-season trek only the year before. The news had backtracked across the prairie like wildfire, providing ready fuel for criticism among nonbelievers and kindling fear among the weak. Even for the staunch Saints it was cause for conversation and concern.

With his knowledge of carpentry, Angus felt a special responsibility not to fall prey to the same humanly avoidable tribulations. At least, that was what Callie read between his words, but she ignored Angus's indirect reference to the terror of the Willie Company's suffering. With firm softness she countered, "You speak of the same God who rained down manna."

"Aye," Angus said, and Callie hoped in vain that his face would break into a grin. "But He never has tumbled it into my pockets. Hard work an' careful thought be th' means for all our achievements, lass. Ne'er forget that."

Callie nodded.

Eagerly, Angus had explained his solution, excitement once again thickening his woolly accent. If they dropped behind the other Saints and waited just a couple weeks for the children's cheeks to grow fat and rosy again, Angus could make and sell a few wagon beds. These might even fetch a still higher price if he drove them over to St. Joseph, Missouri.

"The Button," as he called Susa, needed better rest than the back of a crowded handcart could offer. And besides, if he made only three fine wagon beds he would have enough profit to build his family a wagon rather than a handcart. It wouldn't take much longer to purchase a team, if they reapportioned their slim savings.

"'Tis still early in th' year," Angus added.

Callie closed her mind firmly against further echoes of the Willie Company. Their packet had left Liverpool a good three weeks before that group, and, God willing, they wouldn't have to face the same delays. Angus would know what extra time they had to work with.

And on top of that, he had another modification for the plan, an addition that worked like insurance. Angus had heard of a new trail that ran south of the shallow, dirty Platte. The Cherokee Trail, he called it, explaining that not only was it less dusty and overgrazed but it was also less plagued by what physicians called "cholera morbus." The new route was quicker, too. They could make up the time they'd lose waiting for the children's strength to return. Besides, it ran south of the rumored approach of Johnston's army.

"You mean to travel across this wilderness with a pack of Gentiles?" Callie's voice plainly registered her shock.

"'Tis only a matter of time, and there I be m'self."

Angus was right, her words sounded hypocritical, but Callie felt uneasy. If the children hadn't been sick, she never would have agreed to the delay. But then, again, if the children hadn't been sick, Angus never would have thought up such a scheme. He'd always been soft where his "wee ones" were concerned. Too soft.

Callie drew no conclusions beyond reviewing these memories; she wasted no energy wondering what if one thing or another had been different. It was apparent enough: the handcart Saints of her company were probably rolling into the valley by now—or would be within days. Defiantly, she kept walking, her footfalls and three small echoes tracking into the vastness.

They walked into late morning, but now, with bright light and visibility, the going was far more discouraging because it seemed that the mountains hardly grew closer—perhaps not at all. Even distances lied here, throwing off her perceptions.

Overhead, the arching sky deepened into brilliant blue, and puffy white clouds sailed across it like an entire armada of schooners and brigs, squatty barks and speedy clippers. Callie and the children struggled far below among the shadows of their keels, crawling, it seemed, across the dry, dirty ocean floor.

Soon she gave up looking ahead except to keep her bearing on the mountains and scan the horizon for attackers. Her heart could not face the stretch of pitiless desolation that reached away on all sides, its very endlessness hemming her in. She could hardly stand to lift her eyes from the next footstep, lest the view crush her with its immensity and indifference.

Susa and Duncan began to tire, but Callie urged them relentlessly forward, bent on making the green shelter of the mountains by nightfall. It would be safer to build a fire there; she would cook them something with real substance. When the sun was high, she stuffed their pockets with more of the precious dried apples and urged them to drink deeply from the river.

Callie kept the children moving by having them recite. Susa had not yet started school, but she could count to fifty, and Duncan could reach a hundred counting by twos, then fives, and then tens. Jamie had to name the continents and seas, the kings and queens of England, and give the times tables up to fifteen times fifteen. Then they started over, with Susa launching sweetly into Blake's "Little Lamb."

"Little Lamb, who made thee? Dost thou know who made thee?" Her small voice trilled out upon the air like the song of the yellow-vested meadowlarks who had warbled so bravely in the early morning. "Gave thee life and bid thee feed, By the stream and o'er the mead . . ." When her final words chimed, "Little Lamb, God bless thee, Little Lamb, God bless thee," Callie spoke crisply.

"Good. Every word in place and rhythm." She turned to the quiet, brown-haired boy walking behind and to her left. Noticing his cap was getting a hole near the brim, she said, "Now, Duncan, your turn. How far can you get with your Tennyson?"

Duncan looked up at her suddenly, smiling at her subtle wit. "Half a league, half a league, half a league onward." He fell back a pace and elbowed James in the ribs, but the older boy was oblivious to the joke, consumed with walking.

"Begin again, Duncan," Callie admonished, leading her group around to the right to avoid a patch of spiny yucca.

"Half a league, half a league, Half a league onward, All in the valley of Death Rode the six hundred. . . ."

After a few verses Callie paused to pull thistles from Susa's skirt, while Susa pulled them from the imaginary skirt of her spoon doll. Duncan's voice trailed off as he quit walking, " . . . Stormed at with shot and shell, Boldly they rode and well, Into the jaws of Death, Into the mouth of Hell . . ."

Eventually Callie licked her sore fingertips, then straightened, and set their pace again. "Those first three stanzas were correct, Duncan, but start at the beginning again, please."

Duncan rattled on, aware that his affinity for learning and memorization was a continual pleasure to his mother. He reached the end of a flawless rendition and turned to his brother without a breath, "Your turn, Jamie."

The freckle-faced boy groaned. He was so like his father,

not only in his red hair and thick eyebrows but by nature. Recitations were a trial for him, and Callie knew he'd hoped he was finished when he completed the multiplication tables.

"Well, Jamie?" she said, ignoring her insight. "Give us something of Wordsworth, eh?"

"Aye, Mother," he answered obediently but without enthusiasm. "The world is too much with us; late and soon, Getting and spending, we lay waste our powers, Little we see in Nature that is ours." He hesitated. "Little we see in Nature that is ours . . . ," another pause, "It moves us not."

"Start again, James," Callie said. "You forgot: we have given our hearts away . . ."

And so they walked on, with the mother shaping their thoughts and their feet keeping rhythm to the words, their voices caught up and lost on the windy prairie.

And all that long day, the prairie hoppers crackled and whirred around their ankles as they walked. Hoards of star thistles plagued Callie and Susa's long skirts, clinging and poking with every step. Although the spreading, knee-high grass looked velvety at a distance, it was actually scattered thinly in brittle bunches across the dry earth. The soil was broken with cracks like honeycomb, and among the patches of brown grass were pebbles, sharp cacti, and spiny yucca. Beneath the dark, tiny print of her heavy dress, Callie's skin felt stretched and dry as the earth's surface.

"We shall discuss great works; we will think great thoughts," she told her children. "Otherwise we are sheep—or worse, like the heathen who know not God, nor can they stretch their minds to wise, loving, and powerful thoughts like His." Then she began to sing, "God moves in a mysterious way, His wonders to perform. . . ." She matched the music to her steps and vigorously encouraged them to join her. "Ye fearful Saints fresh courage take," step, step, step, "These clouds ye so much dread are big with mercy and shall break," step, step, step, "In blessings on your head."

"Now recite Bell, Duncan. . . . Let us hear Shakespeare, Jamie. . . . Recite Goethe. . . . Give us a psalm. . . . Now Shakespeare again. . . ." And so they went, until their throats were too dry to go on. Then she took another turn, quoting scripture mostly, giving rhythm to their steps.

Even without wagons and oxen to stir it up, the wind brought dusty grit into every breath. Silt filtered through their stockings and inside their clothing, collecting in the creases. Ahead, the Medicine Bow range looked more and more green, more and more inviting. A large, solitary mountain rose sharply above pine-smattered heights at their left, while the river ran toward them through a valley wide with trees.

They reached the mouth of this valley well into evening. Susa, Jamie, and Duncan were fairly perishing for nourishment, so Callie lit a small fire, carefully measured some flour, and baked heavy, unleavened cakes.

Unconcerned with how primitive the meal was, the children wolfed it down and drank from the cool river. Then their tired legs and full bellies were ready for sleep. Her own limbs burned with exhaustion and her mind ached with the effort of mental determination, but Callie would hear nothing of rest. Using strict words and exerting her own sheer willpower, she got them back on their feet, moving one more mile upstream along the Little LaRamiee.

They were walking into the foothills now, but to Callie these mousy-brown hills were mountains. Her Yorkshire years had known nothing to compare with this: no moor was as vast as this plain, no hills towered to such heights.

Yet, she reminded herself, she *had* crossed most of this plain alone and undetected. Following the river, she was beginning to think she could also cross these mountainous hills. Far ahead and to her right, craggy peaks of smooth-creased granite lurched up against the deep sky. The wrinkles were lined with snow, but what she could see of the valley was wide and shallow. Rivers seek paths of least resistance; following this one, she would skirt south of those distant, gray peaks.

Perhaps wagon trains toiled north around the Medicine Bow only because fighting the willows was too hard for the oxen, she reasoned. Angus's efforts at the Big Blue and Cache La Poudre Rivers had given her practical experience with how difficult wagon crossings were.

This valley opened wide, sheltering arms onto the plains. The ascent was gentle so far; trees and water made an increasingly pleasant route. Callie decided to take it—or, at least work her way into it far enough to climb to a high spot and get a good look around her. As she chose a sheltered spot among the trees and bedded her children down, she thought maybe she would even be able to see how far west the range crested.

The elms stretched dark, leafy branches above her and the river slid over the rocks as Callie sang softly to her little ones. Susa asked again for Papa, but her mother abruptly insisted that he was gone away. "Go to sleep!" she commanded, and they dropped off quickly and quietly, though Jamie's rest followed the intermittent pattern of the night before. Even after they were peaceful, Callie continued to sing, repeating over and over a new hymn she had learned from other Saints in Florence, "If You Could Hie to Kolob:"

> . . . The works of God continue,
> And worlds and lives abound.
> Improvement and progression
> Have one eternal round . . .

The melody William Phelps had chosen for the words was too complicated for her to remember, so she matched them up to something from her childhood. Her tune was contemplative and in a minor key, with twists and turns that carried the music onward. The river ran more swiftly here, over a rockier bed. Yet, although her song was almost swallowed up by its noise, comfort flowed in the repetitious, chanting stream of words that poured from her heart:

> There is no end to union;
> There is no end to youth;
> There is no end to priesthood;
> There is no end to truth.

Callie found her small sewing kit and gathered what peace she could from the familiar task of mending the hole she'd noticed in Duncan's cap.

> There is no end to glory;
> There is no end to love;
> There is no end to being;
> There is no death above.

The fire had burned low but was hot and would smoulder for hours. Callie rubbed her sore, puffy fingertips together in the warmth, grateful that, at least for the moment, she wasn't having to pull thistles from her and Susa's skirts. Their skirts . . . these were torn and would need mending soon, too. Callie had sung the long song three times, and even though she did not start up with it again, she cast her eyes about, looking for another job to do. She knew she needed sleep but didn't feel relaxed enough for it.

Then Callie realized what she was doing and firmly refused to spend another night with the ghosts of her memories. She could not let them prey on her strength. Pulling a blanket over her shoulders and still sitting in an upright position with her back against a large rock, she rested the cocked rifle across her knees. Then, willing herself to see nothing but the fire's red coals, Callie stared into the flames until she forced herself to give in to sleep.

SIX

She'd slept for hours, five at least, when her hands jerked her awake, the rifle tightly clamped in them. Had she heard something? Callie's heart throbbed painfully in her throat and her mouth was dry. She rose to her feet and scanned the trees that stood motionless around her in an unusual absence of wind. When she was convinced they were alone, she looked to the children.

Darkness was growing thinner, but daybreak was still a good hour off. How her back ached!—her legs and her back. Her neck was stiff as if something caustic had worked its way into her hinges, corroding the sockets and causing friction. *Nothing more than weariness,* Callie told herself. Then with an efficient snap she folded her blanket before walking to the river. The bank was of smooth round rocks, varied in size and color like children's balls. Carefully she picked her way from one to another, a yard out into the water. In one swift movement, Callie bunched her skirts in the same hand that tightly held her gun and stooped. The water rushing past her free hand was clear, especially sweet after the barrelled water of the wagon train and ship's provisions. And cold! Oh, it was cold.

She made a small mess of porridge in the bent pan she'd salvaged. There was enough for herself and Jamie, who rolled to his feet before the sun had risen and wandered on wobbly legs into a stand of willows. She made another pot for Duncan and Susa, urging them awake with the early filtering light of dawn.

Duncan was quiet, his movements slow and clumsy, as

was usual for him in the morning. But Susa was bright with smiles. She ate her mush quickly and sat very still while Callie braided her honey-gold hair. Chattering softly and constantly, Susa told her doll, Mrs. McGillicutty, about the nice long walk they would take today and how big girls don't complain when there is no salt in the porridge.

Jamie rolled up Duncan's pack for him while he ate and wound up Susa's bedding while her hair was being combed. Within fifteen minutes Callie had said a prayer, recited a scripture, and mustered her troops into walking formation. Girls in front, boys in back, she led out once again.

Ahead, in the lemony morning light, Callie could see that the Little LaRamiee eventually split into two forks, each pouring down out of a different mountain valley. She'd followed the river a long way south, keeping to its shelter, and she knew she didn't want to lapse much farther that direction. Fort Bridger was somewhere more directly west, and that was where she had to go.

The north fork, however, flowed down out of the mountains and swung far to the south before meeting the other fork and running northeast to become the river she was following. This created a bend in the river, and inside it the land scooped away to form a dry bowl. They could probably cover the open space in an hour if the children moved quickly. Even though they would be exposed, crossing this clear expanse would save them as much as a day's travel. A whole day . . . and every day was crucial. Callie stopped walking abruptly.

"Children, I want you to go to the river and take a good long drink."

Susa and Duncan immediately ran down to the water, happy to be taking a break already, but James sensed that something had changed. "What's happening, Mother?"

"We're crossing this big open space here," she answered, pointing out toward her right. "We'll have to hurry quickly—

no recitations or singing—just get the little ones across as fast as we can."

"Are we cutting for those trees over there?"

Callie nodded. "Hurry now, drink your fill." Then she looked her gun over while he ran down to the water's edge.

It was still cocked. She hadn't dared sleep without having it entirely ready to fire. Though she realized the weapon was dangerous to carry like this, she knew no way of bringing the hammer down except to shoot it off. Well, she couldn't do that. So she leaned it against her shoulder with the barrel pointing skyward. James came up behind her, trailing a sibling by each hand, and Callie took Susa's fingers firmly in her own, walking immediately out into the open bowl.

They hadn't gone more than two hundred yards when an immense flock of starlings rose from the grass ahead of them. Wheeling and calling, birds blackened the sky. The sudden beating of their wings set Callie's heart hammering. Jerking her gun into position she fired accidentally, uselessly into the air.

Before the echoes of the report had died away, the children were huddled against their mother, Susa clutching at her skirts. No one moved as the last of the harmless, glossy black birds flapped away.

Callie forced a laugh into the stunned silence. "Ha! Surprised you, didn't I?" When no one answered, she added, "Too small to eat, anyway. It was a crazy idea to shoot one."

James looked at her soberly, too wise for pretending.

Callie wanted desperately to run for the cover of the trees, but they were already committed to crossing this open bend of the river. Jamie, particularly, would be even more frightened if they did not go on. She pulled off her pack and reloaded the gun.

"Well, hurry up, children!" she commanded briskly, hoping they would ascribe her irritation to having missed the shot. "Don't stand crying over your mother's poor marksmanship." She walked forcefully out into the open field, looking every minute from the corners of her eyes for any hostile that might have heard her fire.

But nothing moved. No other birds climbed the air currents, no rodents scampered into their holes. Strangely enough, not a breath of wind stirred about her in the early morning light. The heat began climbing quickly. Wispy tendrils of tall straw and the shorter buffalo grass crunched brittlely beneath her feet. And with each step Callie became more and more dismayed.

The ground was strewn with rocks—not just a few here and there but lying so thickly in the sparse grass that it was often impossible to place her feet between them. Each step twisted at her ankles and made her feet sore through the soles of her boots. Her arm began to ache with pulling, lifting, virtually carrying Susa along. Looking back, she saw that Jamie was no longer helping Duncan. They'd had to spread out and pick their own ways.

"Keep together!" she called in an urgent, hushed voice. "Hurry up."

Then she had to look at the ground again in order to go forward. The rocks forced her to plan each move: stepping over, picking her way around and through. How did grass grow at all here? Yet, somehow, perversely it did, hiding the egg-sized stones of rose and grey. Large white and ochre-colored rocks, some knee-high, humped out of the grass around her. Others made smooth, half-buried mounds, between which the smaller, fist-sized stones littered the ground.

Tall grass caught and tore at her skirt, scratching as she passed. Star thistles nagged them again and Susa began to complain, but Callie flatly refused to stop and pick them out. "Come along," she said, pulling the little girl from one grassy hummock or smooth rock to another.

"Hurry!" Callie called once more, intently scanning the edges of the spreading bowl. "Hurry!" James was slipping and tripping about four yards behind her, and Duncan was even farther back because he was trying to pick his way.

Callie paused only briefly among the few, thin trees that lined a dry riverbed three-fourths of the way across the open bend. And every instant she continued scanning the edges of the clearing while the boys caught up. These trees hardly provided any shade, she thought, noticing that the sun had risen to its midpoint. What she'd thought would take an hour had used up half the day!

Susa pulled at her skirt. "I'm so thirsty my tongue is stickin' in my mouth."

"Hush up, child." Callie heard herself say crossly. "What do you think I can do about it? I haven't anything to give you."

This time Susa did not whimper or whine, but two big tears welled up at the edges of her blue eyes, and she bit her lower lip. "I'm tired, Mother." She spoke softly, unevenly, with hiccoughing intakes of air as she fought to keep from crying. "I'm so thirsty and tired and hungry and . . . and . . . and I want Papa."

As Susa's words fell painfully between them, Callie throbbed with a sudden, intense ache that forced her once again to fight back her own tears. "Hush," she insisted, pulling some stray hair away from her daughter's sunburned face and wiping the tears off her dusty cheeks. "There, now." She had nothing to offer, nothing to say. She could not discuss what had happened nor the carnage she had seen. The only small comfort she'd been able to find was in singing, and—afraid to offer that here—she scooped the child into her arms and held her tightly.

"She hurt?" Jamie asked as he came alongside them.

Callie didn't dare speak, only shook her head.

"C'mon, Dunc!" James called softly. "Quit pussyfootin' around out there! You can go ahead with Susa, Mother. I'll bring 'im right along."

Callie looked down at her freckle-cheeked son. "No," she said firmly. His face had an amazingly hard set to it for a boy of ten. Maturity, determination—even a hint of understanding was clear enough to startle her. But she didn't dare leave him exposed in the field. "No, Jamie."

Heavy sunlight hammered the dry ground and made the edges of the mountains ripple with heat when Callie finally reached the trees lining the north fork of the Little LaRamiee. A hot wind had risen, gusting and swirling about them. It isolated them, preventing them from speaking to one another, choking and blinding them. Yet in spite of how it parched their throats even further—another torture in this gritty oven beneath the sky—Callie was grateful to have it hide their noise.

When they reached the first trees, none of them had any other thought than to get down to the water and drink. Soon Duncan was sitting, curled up with his back against a tree trunk, his cap on the ground beside him.

"Bellyache," he said, when Callie asked if he was all right.

She nodded. "Too much, too cold, too fast." *We're all feeling that way,* she thought, as she gathered twigs and built a fire. Quickly she fried a few hard, dry cakes from flour and water and prayed over them.

"Not hungry." Duncan said when she handed him his. "Hurts."

"Eat anyway." Callie said in a hard voice. "We can't be stopping here. The day's not done."

She turned away quickly before he could object, only to see silent tears streaming across Susa's cheeks. The child was lying curled up in the grass, clutching Mrs. McGillicutty against her chest as she chewed. Callie refused to look at her as well, purposefully speaking into the fire. "Sit up, Susa. Either you'll choke or you'll hurt your digestion that way."

"Oh," Jamie moaned in an exaggerated effort to make the others laugh off their discomfort. "Oh, oh, oh! 'Tis full as a furry tick I am, an' fixin' t' pop!"

Duncan grimaced lopsidedly but didn't answer back. The rest of the meal was forced down in dutiful silence.

When the cakes were gone, Callie literally pulled the younger ones to their feet. A cross tongue was the only motivator she had left, so she used it to herd them further upriver, more safely into the trees. A very large hill loomed ahead on her left, and she determined to climb it for a look around.

She led them a good quarter of a mile up into the draw, thick with white aspen, grass, and pines, before she turned away from the river into the short grass and rocks on the left. "Come," she tugged at Duncan and Susa. "I need to look out from this hill."

"Let me keep them down here," Jamie said. "They can nap in th' tall grass. I'll watch."

"No." Callie said again without even looking back. "No."

Greasewood made the going rough at times, forcing them to pick their way almost as laboriously as in the rocks, but she managed to get them up the hot side of the high hill. There, Callie settled the two youngest ones beneath a short, lone pine. She offered no gentle word or sign of sympathy that might create a chance for them to cry or complain.

"Look," she said, prying a small pink piece of quartz from the dirt. "See what pretty rocks you can find, but don't wander from this spot."

Duncan took her suggestion—he'd always been curious about rocks—while Susa rested her head on her knees, tiredly watching him scrape in the dirt. Jamie trailed his mother up the hill until she paused near an outcropping of creased stone. Gripping her carbine tightly, Callie stood overlooking the bowl they'd crossed and out onto the LaRamiee plain. She was assailed again by the vastness of the prairie before her. Its sheer size was threatening.

Everything looked empty now that she was away from the trail. Endless nothingness roamed as far as the eye could reach, layer upon layer of desolate browns, and then purples in the distance. And all of it was unrelieved by a single person or man-made thing. Callie could see farther than she'd ever gazed before, and still there were no quiet, God-fearing homes to fill up the space, nothing to take up the void, only the hot wind hurrying away.

There was nothing green out there except the tiny line of trees that straggled thin and close to the river. Even the foothills she had worked so hard to reach were sage-covered and barren.

Suddenly she realized that when she left the Cherokee Trail she had left behind every vestige of the world she knew. If she changed her mind and moved away from this river, traveling back out of this valley to parallel the wagon trail, she would be leaving everything that was green and alive. She had no way to carry water, no barrels or canteens.

And then, even as she realized their limitations, her gaze caught against something across the rocky bowl toward the east, out where the sage-covered mountains stretched their arms onto the prairie. Dust billowed up behind five horsemen, riding fast into the north. They crossed the terrain like a cloud's dark shadow.

"Indians!" Jamie breathed.

Callie could almost feel his trembling beside her. She did not answer. Even at that great distance, she was certain the savages were painted and armed for war. Those bronze beasts had brutally claimed the open plain. No wagons would follow. There was no hope of help from the east.

Only one path lay open to her now. She must take her children and travel up this river into the safety of the pine-covered mountains. Once near the top, she could find another stream to use as a trail down the other side. There, Callie vowed, she would find Fort Bridger and compassionate, human help.

S E V E N

Days passed. Callie counted them by making tiny charcoal marks with her fingernail in the back of Angus's Book of Mormon. The wagon train had been attacked in late July, and her calculations suggested that time had slipped through the first week of August while they were still pressing higher and higher into the mountains.

After she'd climbed to look across the LaRamiee plain, Callie rushed her exhausted children up into the valley of the LaRamiee's northern fork. At first she clapped a grateful hand against the trunk of each sheltering tree, urging her little ones forward in silence, terrified by the five forms she'd seen on the eastern horizon.

But as the second day wore into the third, a new realization began demanding her attention. The secluded protection of the mountains was baring its own teeth.

For one thing, they weren't making good time. She was exhausting herself hauling Susa over fallen logs and waist-high rocks, fighting off thorny briers and mosquitoes. Callie silently admitted that they were barely making two or three miles a day. She tried to organize her children into a disciplined unit, but the thickness of the trees and underbrush combined against her.

Soon she resorted to searching out game paths or making something of a trail by leading the children single file. "You'll be last," she'd told Jamie, knowing he would bring up the end best. But Duncan seemed to take perverse delight in letting branches go that swiped his older brother as he came up behind. Sometimes they laughed with boyish silliness while they walked, but their horseplay could vanish in one slim instant, the swinging branches leading to all-out wars.

Although she tried to occupy their minds with recitations and singing, the roaring of the river as it crashed over larger and larger rocks prevented her from hearing their words.

Not only that, but it was all they could do to keep moving forward. The sage-covered mountains that had risen around her gave way to shale-slides and thick timber and even granite cliffs. Callie was forced to cross the river again and again, swinging the younger children along from rock to rock, hoping Jamie had the sense and coordination not to fall in. Sometimes he didn't. Even with her supervision, one child or another slipped into the shallow, icy water daily. Each time she had to stop and build a fire to dry them out.

After the hot, arid wind of the plains, she had initially welcomed the shady pines and aspen. But now, when each day left someone wet and shivering while their clothes hung near the fire, Callie began to worry. The wind blew cool here; winter would surely come early. When would they ever reach the top? How much farther up could these ferocious hillsides rise?

One afternoon the trees broke onto a mountain meadow. Grass lay thick and soft like deep velvet, laced with fingernail-sized flowers of light blue, yellow, and purple. With a yell, Jamie rushed forward past her, entirely forgetting his responsibility at the rear of their line. Duncan was right behind him, running out into the open, catching at the dewy, bearded heads of the tall grass as his legs stretched into a gallop. The grasses whipped about them, sunshine gemming the spray. Callie's heart leapt with happiness she hardly recognized when Susa took after the boys. The little girl's bonnet fell back as she ran ahead, swinging Mrs. McGillicutty high in the air.

Callie no longer worried about crossing open spaces up here. She was thankful for them. Her battle had shifted from fear of Indians to simple survival.

Ahead to her right, she recognized the thorny vines of raspberries. After a steady diet of thin porridge or heavy flour-cakes, Callie's mouth began to water at the mere thought of variation.

Watching Susa, she ached to toss back her own sunbonnet and feel the free wind in her hair as she ran. Easy going again at last! Even though she could see the far side of the meadow, Callie was grateful. She would have been grateful for ten steps that were free of boulders and deadfall.

"Wait!" James yelled out ahead of them. He had stopped running and turned around. "Mother! Stop!"

Suddenly, Callie saw the top of Duncan's tweed cap go down in the tall grass. "Susa!" she screamed, sprinting forward as fear overtook her delight. She caught and grabbed her daughter by the waist, noticing as she ran that the ground was soft and spongy beneath her boots, that murky water oozed up around the soles.

Duncan came to his feet ahead of them; his shoulders and head now above the swaying grass. One side of him was dark with wet mud. He lifted a dripping arm and flung globs of muck high into the air. Susa began to giggle, watching him shake off like a dog, as Callie pulled her toward dryer ground. Jamie came running back toward them, water spraying out beneath his boots as he bounded from one grassy hummock to another. Duncan apparently thought he couldn't get any wetter and plodded along a straight course, slipping and falling twice more as he came.

"Why didn't you stop running when you saw it was so wet?" Callie scolded when Jamie walked up to them and dropped down on the ground.

"Couldn't . . . couldn't stop," he panted. "We was runnin' too fast."

"Were," his mother corrected. "You *were* running too fast."

"Thought maybe the ground would get drier if I kept goin'," Jamie went on, untying his boots to dump water out. "P'rhaps if I ran real fast I could just sort o' fly right o'er th' bogginess, eh?"

Duncan sloshed up to them, trying to stifle a grin so he would look sufficiently put out to escape a scolding. “It's wet out there!” he announced innocently.

Callie glared at him as she pulled up some handfuls of grass and tried to wipe his face. Determined not to lose a day's progress, she wanted to keep walking while the sun was warmest. But the mud was caked onto his cap and plastered through his hair.

“Blow me over!” she blurted at last, “I thought you boys had a few brains between your ears!” Crossly, she stood and, straightening her shoulders, led out across the marsh.

“Just look at ye, Dunc,” Jamie whispered in a teasing, motherly tone. “Ye've no more smarts than a frog has hair!”

Giggling, the children fell into line behind her. But it wasn't long before Callie understood the boys' mistake. The bog was deceptive, and wetness seeped unpredictably up beneath their feet. Droning clouds of black gnats and hungry mosquitoes rose to torment them. She stopped wiping the mud off her children's faces because it seemed to protect them somewhat from bites.

All her attention became bent on getting through the marsh. She had to stop and backtrack, turn right, and then left, searching for a way to get through. The children were slipping and sliding, growing sillier by the minute. Even Callie lost her balance and fell in the muck, still tightly grasping her rifle.

As she rose, she looked up and saw an immense brown creature only thirty yards away. Slowly, it turned its huge head and looked complacently at her, watercress dangling from its slobbery mouth. Eagerly, she brought the gun to her shoulder. Meat! If berries had sounded good, this was beyond belief. She tried to take careful aim, but her slippery hands were shaking with excitement. She squeezed the trigger . . .

Click. Her powder had gotten wet. Quickly Callie dropped her pack and frantically tore into it for the rest of her powder.

“Never mind, Mum,” Jamie said softly, putting his hand on her shoulder. “He's already turned back into th' trees.”

Callie threw the unopened powder tin to the ground, snatched up the pack, and began stuffing things back in. As she reloaded the rifle, Susa said, "Did you see his horns?"

"Antlers," Duncan corrected. "Huge, eh? Magnifeecent!"

"Aye," Jamie answered with admiration, "wider across than Mum is tall, an' what a dangly ol' black beard!"

"The antlers were flat . . ." Duncan mused. "More like a cow than a stag. Oh, for just one mouthful of him!"

"Start walking," Callie commanded briskly, smashing their enthusiasm flat as she rose to her feet. "We can't stand about drooling after what's gone."

The boys kept a respectful silence, aware that this time their mother's frustration with her marksmanship was unfeigned. All the sadder for their former joy, they dragged solemnly along behind her, skirting the bog, backtracking, and pressing forward again.

Eventually, in her usual little girl way, Susa began to hum. When her tune took on words, they were her own version of an old song:

> Oh dear! What can the matter be?
> Dear, dear! What can the matter be?
> Oh dear! What can the matter be?
> Daddy's so long at the fair.

Callie tried to ignore Susa's high voice. Certainly she had enough things to worry her mind. The children were looking thin and pale, and she couldn't deny her own increasing weariness. They needed food, real food. She'd tried once to grab a fish Duncan had spotted in a river hole, but in the water he wasn't where he'd looked to be. The speckled fellow had gotten away as freely as the huge creature in the marsh.

> He promised to buy me a fairing should please me,
> And then for a kiss, oh! he vowed he would tease me,
> He promised he'd bring me a bunch of blue ribbons,
> To tie up my bonnie fair hair.

Callie looked back, noting the airy sound of her daughter's thin song, the dark circles beneath her eyes. Susa caught a deep breath and came around to the chorus again:

And it's Oh dear! What can the matter be? . . .

But the situation was much worse than a failed hunting attempt, Callie thought. Her pack was getting lighter as the flour bag grew emptier. Food supplies had dwindled to nearly half the original quantity. Cooler weather was forcing them to wear all their clothing and still they climbed up, up into these wretched mountains! Where in all heaven's geography did the downside of this thing begin?

Well, she had to control what she could, Callie reasoned. They were nearing a stand of pines whose thick branches spread just above her head and were clear of undergrowth beneath. She tested for firm ground with her foot and then dropped her pack onto the soft carpet of rust-colored needles.

"We'll stop here, now," she announced, noting how surprise lit up the children's faces, for it was still afternoon. "Come on. Help me build a fire to dry us out."

When the orange flames were crackling heartily, Callie stripped the children's clothing and rinsed out the worst of the mud in the stream. Then she propped them up—breeches, shirts, caps, a small gray dress dotted with pink posies—all spread up on twigs beside the fire. "I'll be back soon," she told the children, who lay wrapped up in their bedding beside the glowing heat. She listened to them talk and tease as she walked back to the bog, their voices floating up with the wispy smoke until they were lost in the sighing branches of the pines.

The first thing to do was gather some of the berries that ran rampant across the soggy ground. She would stir these into the flour-and-water concoction her fellow emigrants called "lumpy dick." That would be a fine improvement on their supper porridge.

Second, she resentfully decided, she would give in to the

terrain, making a cut and a seam up the center of Susa's dress so that it would be more like a pair of pantaloons. Bloomers, the Americans called them. Some of the younger, rash women were actually making them as suits for traveling west.

Callie had met two such girls in St. Joe, sitting astride their horses like men, ready to ride out to "Californy." Callie had recoiled at the sight. Everyone knew the rustle of skirts was part of women's grace; it signified who they were. Angus had told her once that he loved the sound they made as she passed. He'd said his earliest memory was the swish of his own mother's skirts as she bustled back and forth near his cradle.

This horrible, hateful place! Callie thought, turning from her berry picking to glare up toward the peaks ahead of her. It had robbed her of a husband's love and security, of civilized living, of food and warmth and cleanliness for her children. And now—now even modest decency was being stolen from an innocent five-year-old girl.

Callie shook herself and went back to picking. "The bloomers will only be temporary," she promised indignantly. She would sew Susa a proper dress at the first opportunity. But for now, the lass could scramble along better in pantaloons, no matter how distasteful they were. Her skirts were becoming seriously torn, anyway. The rips were almost too much to mend. With that decided and her apron pockets and bonnet filled with berries, Callie began walking back toward the children.

The third thing she might do would be to take this evening to shoot some game. She *could* do it. She was capable. And God willing, she would.

As she picked her way back to camp, moving to higher ground, Callie caught glimpses of shiny blue between the trees. There was a lake ahead of them, not far off. Something would come to water there. Whether it was a team of ducks or a deer or that hairy, antlered creature, something would come. And she would be waiting.

E I G H T

" . . . In faith we'll rely on the arm of Jehovah, To guide through these last days of trouble and gloom . . ." Callie sang under her breath as she walked back from her berry gathering near the bog. "When all that was promised the Saints will be given, And none will molest them from morn until ev'n . . ."

Her children's voices were still ringing crisply in the cool shadows of late afternoon. She could hear them some distance off, but now their heart-catching words tore her carefully organized peace apart.

"Shut yer trap!" Jamie growled.

"Don't have to." Duncan spoke defiantly. "You're nobody's master. Susa and I can talk as we like."

"It's true, anyway," Susa piped. "Papa *is* coming for us."

"Now see what you've got her thinkin', Dunc! 'Tis wrong an' 'tis . . . 'tis cruel!"

"Poor Jamie," Susa spoke sweetly as if her older brother had somehow lost faith. "Duncan didn't tell me. I knew it m'self."

"We both heard Mum say in her prayers for God to bless him and keep him safe 'til we're together again," Duncan put in. "He'll be back as sure as sure."

"Ye're a baby." James bit the words out resentfully. Couldn't Duncan see what their mother's prayers really meant?

"Hardly! *I* haven't given up on my own father!"

"Papa will come, Jamie. Don't give up," Susa pled. "He's only gone for help. Dunc told me how, during the fight, he ran to get the caavalrry." She rolled this big word impressively across her tongue as if it were nothing less than a legion of fiery, victorious angels enlisted to assure her personal interests.

Callie could see her children now—they'd put their clothes on, but they were still huddled by the fire. They had sunk so deeply into their argument they didn't even hear her approach. Jamie lunged to his feet and stared at Susa with a shocked expression that his brother and sister apparently mistook for incredulity.

"Just think on it, Jamie," Susa said. "The caavallrrry!"

"There were too many Indians for our wagons to fight," Duncan explained condescendingly. "Of course Father was the one who went for help."

"An' he'll be findin' us soon, he will," Susa chimed. "He's gonna have a big oxcart with fresh-raised bread an' creamy butter. Potato soup with milk, too, . . . and soft, clean blankets. Brother Brigham'll be helpin' find us himself!"

"Th' hole!" Jamie fairly shouted. "Didn' ye hear her diggin' th' hole?"

"Quiet!" Callie scolded, breaking into the circle.

Jamie's fist was in the air. His face was red.

"Stop this!" she said again, urgently.

The older boy turned on his mother. Tears coursed down his cheeks, shining gold in the firelight. He opened his mouth, "But . . . but . . . ," and then clamped it shut hard and ran off into the bushes.

"Want me to go after him?" Duncan asked, apparently astonished by his big brother's collapsed faith.

"No." Callie answered flatly. "No. It's you I need to see, Son. You and Susa come sit beside me." With effort, she pulled a fallen limb near the fire and seated herself on it, dumping the round contents of her bonnet into their little pan.

"O-o-o-oh!" Susa sighed with the kind of bright cheerfulness that doesn't want to talk about serious things. "Berries! Can I have some?"

"Wait," Callie said, wishing she could get the stern sound

away from her voice at least momentarily. Grief had put it there, and she couldn't wrench it out. She knew she couldn't say what she must without that crossness creeping in. It was the only thing between her and tears.

"I haven't talked to you about this because I thought you understood, or I hoped you understood." *I just couldn't bear to,* Callie admitted silently. She took a deep breath and wished there were an easier way. Then, putting an arm around each of them, she snuggled their heads down onto her lap where she wouldn't have to look into their faces. "Your father is dead," she said abruptly. "Killed by Indians. There's nothing we can do about it now." She twisted at their hair with her hands, rubbed nervously on their backs.

"I don't believe it," Duncan's voice was almost inaudible. "It's true," Callie answered, her words escaping in a raspy, determined way. "True, do you hear me? But he's safe with God now, and asking help for us, I'm sure."

"No. You're lying, and I won't go on." Duncan tried to sit up, but she forced his head back into her lap.

"Believe what you will, Duncan McCracken," Callie said, staring into the darkness among the trees and letting the stern sound entirely take control of her voice. "I only tell you this so that you will not carry false hopes on my account . . ." She paused only long enough to draw a breath, "and I've something else to tell you, too. Your father was a brave man who wanted to see you safe in Zion. 'Twas in that effort he sacrificed his very life. If you've got any of that man's courage, Son, you'll walk over these mountains and spite all hell's red fury!"

Callie sat with the little ones' heads in her lap until the fire began to burn low and evening chill crept up around them. She was surprised by their absolute silence which, even after she roused them from her lap and began cooking, hovered oppressively beneath the trees. Susa stared into the curvy red lines of the coals with round, fearful eyes, while Mrs. McGillicutty lay forgotten on the ground a few feet away. Duncan was wordlessly digging tiny holes in the pine-needles. A small pile of shiny rocks lay beside his leg.

She'd expected wailing and tears, or an inability to grasp the facts, but not hopeless silence. *They must have known the truth and just chosen not to believe it,* Callie thought. She shoved more and more wood on the fire, building it high as evening shadows came on.

Jamie sauntered back into camp, pleasantly jovial, arms loaded with firewood. As he came into the light, Callie saw how red and swollen his eyes were, but he kept his voice steady and overwhelmingly cheerful. "M-m-m, smells good!" He rubbed his hands together near the flames. "'Tis hungry I am."

At that moment Callie hated the Scots in him. She hated the way his father's accent came lilting through in his voice, the ruddiness of his hair and features, the hint of something familiar in his movements. She looked again at the swollen eyes, angrily loving him more fiercely than ever before.

"Tired o' th' quiet, too," Jamie said suddenly, turning from beneath her stare. "Give us a story, Mother, please. Tell us o' th' night ye danced with Pegleg Pearson from over Grimsby way, an' how y' made him take th' spike off o' his wooden leg first."

Callie didn't answer Jamie for a moment. She resented his efforts, or rather, the cause of his being forced to grow up so suddenly and thoroughly. *This place,* she fumed inwardly, *this savage wilderness tears families apart, steals decent modesty from my daughter, forces a man prematurely from a ten-year-old boy! Oh, God, what sort of Zion is this?*

"Or maybe, Mother, y' could tell us once more 'bout th' story Grandfather read in his newspaper—th' one where they found th' bones of that great lizard, th' ig . . . ig—"

"Iguanadon?"

"Aye. Remember how those men made a model o' it? 'Twas so big they ate New Year's dinner inside its craw."

And so Callie told about the fossilized bones that had brought the entire world of science to attention. She told other stories, all the funny ones she could think of, including Pegleg Pearson's, embellishing them as much as she could, while carefully leaving out any reference to Angus.

Then, when the night had drawn in thick about them, she heard their prayers, snuggled Duncan and Susa down into their bedding, and spread the rope around them. She took Susa's dress to mend and modify it, giving her daughter one of her own scraps of blanket. Softly, as she clipped and sewed the skirt into pantaloons, Callie sang the comforting nursery songs of British childhood: first "Curly Locks," and "Where Are You Going, Pretty Face?" and then "Oranges and Lemons":

> "Oranges and lemons,"
>   say the bells of St. Clemens.
> "Two sticks and an apple,"
>   say the bells of White Chapel.
> "Bull's-eyes and targets,"
>   say the bells of St. Margaret's . . .

After she'd found them arguing, there had been no way she could follow her initial plan for leaving the little ones to hunt game at twilight. But fresh meat would doubtless strengthen them in both body and spirit. She couldn't afford to worry about Indians hearing the rifle's report, she reasoned as she sang.

> "You owe me five farthings,"
>   say the bells of St. Martin's.
> "When will you pay me?"
>   say the bells of Old Bailey . . .

She would go at dawn to the lake. Surely there would be game there then. She couldn't see for certain if the younger two were asleep yet, but they were very still. Only Jamie tossed and turned.

"When I grow rich,"
  say the bells of Shore Ditch.
"When will that be?"
  say the bells of Stepney.
"I'm sure I don't know,"
  says the great bell of Bow.
"Bong . . . Bong . . . Bong . . ."

Callie sensed that Duncan and Susa were sleeping, but James lay awake in his bedding, watching her. "I'm going out very early in the morning to hunt, Jamie," Callie said as casually as if she'd done it a hundred times before. "I hope to be back before the wee ones even wake. Don't stir them, will you now?"

"No, Mother." His voice was muffled and low. She saw his eyelids droop. Good, she thought, and she sang the last song again for good measure.

" . . . When I grow rich,"
  say the bells of Shore Ditch.
"When will that be?"
  say the bells of Stepney.
"I'm sure I don't know,"
  says the great bell of Bow.
"Bong . . . Bong . . . Bong . . ."

Quiet. When her song was ended, Callie found herself alone with the stillness of high mountain darkness. Quickly, she began to sing again, this time hymns for herself, as her needle poked up and down, in and out. Eventually she would sleep, sitting up as always with the gun across her lap, but until then she would watch—watch and watch and watch until exhaustion overcame her.

Callie woke suddenly, fear twisting in the pit of her stomach like a wicked knife. Something was wrong—the gun was not in her hands! Though her eyes were almost too gritty to open and her throat was raw with fatigue, she threw off disorientation and looked about her.

James was kneeling in the red fireglow, but he wasn't praying. The flames' light licked up his side, his face lost in shadow. Cartridge shells stood neatly in a row, lined like soldiers in front of him. He was rubbing his woolen undershirt back and forth along the shiny rifle barrel.

"Jamie!" Callie breathed, her vehemence accented by the shifting of burning logs and a hiss from the fire. "What do you think you're doing?"

Startled, Jamie jerked, then turned. "Oh, Mother. Y' nearly scairt th' wits out o' me."

"As well I should! That's no toy for you to mess with."

Jamie turned and held it up for her, the stock in one outstretched palm and the barrel crossing the other. The hammer was down, she noticed, though the boy had never shot it off. "Aye, Mother. I suppose you could call it th' strong arm of God that we carry in our own two hands."

Callie ignored his words, gathering up the shells and stuffing them into her apron pocket. She snatched the carbine, laying it in the accustomed spot across her lap. "'Tis too powerful a weapon for a boy. What were you thinking?"

"I was only cleaning it for you, Mother."

"Cleaning it?" Her voice was bitter with disdain. "Cleaning? You could have shot your own hand or leg off!—or killed your brother in his sleep. Pretty condition that'd put me in."

James didn't answer.

"Your father died to get you to Zion. Will you throw away love so dearly spent? Will you carelessly risk such blessings?"

Quietly her son crawled into his blankets and turned his

back to the fire. With an exasperated sigh, Callie closed her eyes to finish the matter. But for a long time she knew that neither of them was sleeping.

The birds weren't yet singing when Callie woke. She felt the rifle with her hands even before her eyes opened. Jamie was asleep at last, and the embers had burned very low. She pushed the log farther into the fire, adding some good-sized fuel to the ashes and blowing softly to keep the tongues of flame from crackling much as they leaped up.

A bright moon was shining in the last of real night. Its light powdered everything, making the bog beyond the trees seem surprisingly white and light, almost as if it were snowy. The air was cold, too, she thought. Like winter. Callie splashed her face and combed her hair by the river, drinking deeply of the icy water. Then she stepped back from the bank and dropped to her knees.

Pines thrust up, tall and black around her. Stars glittered coldly above. "If only Angus were here," she breathed, looking earnestly into the sky as if her gaze could draw him down. Longing rushed in upon her, ever-suppressed memories and surging fondness. Kind, good, practical Angus. The least—the very least—he would do now was give her advice, tell her what to do next, how to hunt. Pulling her shawl tighter around her shoulders, Callie tried to imagine him beside her, tried to feel his strength. But the pines groped upward, the stars glittered impassively, and she was so alone.

What would Angus say? He'd always known what to do. Callie was beginning to get used to the way she often jolted awake in the nighttime, thinking she heard voices—his voice—on the wind. But now everything was so still.

Maybe God would answer the lost feeling in her heart. Maybe He would send her a vision or a guiding voice, maybe even an angel could lead her through the silver moonlight to find some game.

"Dear God," she prayed. "I am alone except for Thee. My children are weak for want of food and pained in their hearts." She squeezed her eyes shut more firmly and clutched the cold steel carbine in her hands. "They are *fatherless* now, Lord!" Her voice wavered, and she clamped her jaw down hard on the words. "Fatherless and starving. Thou must give me the strength of two. Thou *must*."

It would be so much easier if only she could hear a still, small voice telling her what to do—so much easier. The woods ahead seemed dark and cold, impenetrable.

"I'm going out to hunt, now, Lord. I intend to shoot a deer or anything else I see." She waited again. "Please keep my babes sleeping in Thy hands while I am gone."

Callie opened her eyes, but the forest was silent as before, the pines went on reaching blackly upward, the stars were still unmoved. "Hear us in our need, Father. Thou hast power to do all things. Make the animals unafraid of me, so that I may sneak right up on them as they come down to the water to drink." She pondered how Nephi had made a bow and had also hunted to feed his family in a vicious wilderness. Callie closed her plea in Christ's name, pausing a moment to listen, but the forest was still silent.

As she rose to her feet she told herself that God had heard her. Almost holding her breath, she felt her way between the tall pines, noting that she and the children must have climbed very high into the mountains, for there were no white aspen mingled among them anymore. Soon another meadow opened before her, but fearing a bog, she skirted along the trunks at its edge.

Then she saw the lake ahead. A large, fallen pine glowed white in the early morning moonlight, half in and half out of the silvery water. Cool shadows slid out onto the lake's gleaming surface.

Feeling like a shadow herself, Callie crept up and knelt beside the sun-bleached pine. She pulled the heavy barrel of her rifle up and lay it across the gnarled, weathered log, resting the butt against her shoulder, looking through the sights.

Jamie had done a fine job, she thought. She pulled the hammer back carefully, seeing that it moved smoothly. It hadn't ever occurred to her to clean the rifle. She'd fired it off only twice in all this time.

Recalling that Jamie had been able to take the carbine out of its cocked position, she pulled the hammer back farther and felt a click as the tension in the trigger went out. Slowly, slowly, she let the hammer down. Callie breathed deeply, pleased with her discovery. She worked the mechanism several times and then rubbed the barrel with her skirt.

She'd never wanted to touch a gun before, had never needed to touch one. But now she thought that only someone else who had traveled so far into the lonely, brutal wilderness could understand the way she felt about it. Her constant companion at all hours, the rifle was the only tangible safety she had at night, the only physical power she could use to oppose her enemies, the only means by which she knew how to fight off starvation.

Sitting on a smooth, granite rock with her skirts bunched beneath her, Callie looked through the U-shaped sights of her gun and waited for dawn.

NINE

Her mind was strangely empty. Callie typically bent each waking instant toward some useful task, planning how to improve or better accomplish whatever was before her. But now everything was placid, patient, perfectly still. Cold blanketed her shoulders, drooping down along her body, forcing her own inner warmth back as it crept toward her bones.

The water spread without a wrinkle before her, a silent blue echo of her stilled thoughts. The pines rimming the lake stretched their shadows onto the surface like long pointed fingers, pulling it into a void of darkness. Ahead on the right, however, the water had pushed beyond its rocky bank to form a reedy inlet. There she saw the first movements of day.

Morning crested pale against the peaks above her; their image developed on the mirror surface of the lake. Small black birds with red shoulder stripes were soon hopping from reed to reed. Moments later a lone fish jumped less than ten feet from shore, leaving a small round circle that grew and repeated itself across the pool of liquid glass. Then, as the blue predawn light grew ever so slightly, she saw three ducks swimming among the reeds, turning tails up as they bobbed for breakfast along the bottom.

She didn't shoot. The strange calmness that spread over everything was still reaching through her when a young doe walked cautiously from the trees toward the rocky edge of the lake. Silently, Callie pulled the hammer back and fitted her index finger against the trigger. Her hands were frighteningly, exhilaratingly steady.

She could clearly see the white hair beneath the doe's chin, her dainty split hooves as she picked her way to the water's edge. The doe lifted her muzzle to test the air, a thin white veil rising from her nostrils. Her brown eyes were wide as she cautiously bent to drink.

At the same moment Callie saw the tan reflection of the doe's neck meet the water, she tightened her grip to pull back firmly on the trigger. In that split instant Callie thought she heard a voice—his voice—say, "Don' pull back. *Squeeze* it, lassie." She didn't pause to wonder, just squeezed hard.

Her shot rang loud, reverberating in the stillness. The gun bucked, knocking her backward off her stone, but she scrambled to her feet and ran awkwardly across the rocky shore. Birds were flying up; the pink of sunrise flooded around her.

The doe lay where she had stood, her dark-edged muzzle sunk in the water, a bright red stream flowing from her neck, staining the pool. Callie lay down the carbine and pulled at the doe's hind legs until her head was up on the shore. Then the hunter fell on her knees among the bright sun-washed rocks and thanked Heaven.

Callie knew enough to gut her kill immediately—right after reloading her gun. The doe was small enough that she was able to roll it over to remove the hide and to reach the stomach cavity. The job was smelly, even nauseating, because she had to reach in as far as her own shoulders to pull the viscera out. But her spirits soared. She sang as she had not since the massacre, sang with the brightness of increased faith, of hope:

How firm a foundation ye Saints of the Lord . . .

Her voice reached across the still waters, echoing off the deep green of the trees as her broken knife worked against the dark flesh.

Fear not, I am with thee, oh be not dismayed.
For I am thy God and will still give thee aid . . .

Callie's knife was too small for her to quarter the animal and carry it to camp in several trips, so she began to drag the entire carcass along, still singing beneath her breath, exulting in the promise of a satisfying meal. She grew hot and weary, almost dizzy with the effort of pulling her venison back, but did not allow herself to slow.

Food. Rich, dark meat. She tugged and heaved, leaving a bloody red smear across the grass flowers and pine-needles. "Children! Look!" she called as they came tumbling out of the trees. "Here's breakfast to fill you!"

Jamie and Duncan gorged on the strips of juicy flesh as soon as she'd roasted them over the fire. Susa ate ravenously as well, burning her tongue on the first mouthful, but she was too hungry to cry about it. When at last they were satisfied, the children began a pinecone fight that rang through the valley until the branches of the trees danced with their laughter. Callie sat watching them, slicing strips off the hindquarters of the doe, roasting them slowly, and nibbling at them even after she was full.

"'Tis the Sabbath," Callie announced suddenly, when the realization burst upon her. "We'll not be walking to a new camp today" (a chorus of cheers answered these words) "but you'll have to stop that wild play. We shall read and sing and rest, instead."

And it did seem like rest, even though the remaining half of her knife kept sawing at the venison, slicing off thin strips. How could she move this heaven-sent supply? How could she carry it along, further up into the mountains?

Eventually Callie realized she couldn't. There was no way to cure the meat and pack it. She hadn't even a block of salt with which to treat it. So she hung some pieces she'd cut over sticks and cooked them thoroughly above the smoky fire. At least they'd last a few days up here where the weather was so cool. The children would eat well for a time.

Callie slept poorly that night. Her shoulder ached fiercely from the kick of the gun and from pulling the doe back to camp. But worse, she had the sensation of something circling out in the marshy darkness beyond her little pine grove. Though she never saw what it was, she awakened her children very early the next morning, placing her whole heart in the hope of finding the mountaintops and starting down the other side. The wind had a cold, wet scent to it, a heart-catching chill that urged her anxiously on.

Once she'd cut off a generous breakfast, she did not stop to look back at the deer. She felt a dismaying sense of waste at leaving it behind, a concern she did not want to consider. Like the children of Israel and their manna, she could not gather for the days to come. She would have to hunt successfully again.

They left their camp behind them and made good progress along the stream, skirting a bog and walking freely beneath one stretch of tall pines. But then reality set in again, for even with fresh food in their bellies and the freer movements of Susa's pantaloons, they had so very far to go.

That night, when the children were asleep, Callie sat up through all the hours of darkness, staring into the fire. Down the river valley below them, she could hear wolves fighting over the carcass of her doe.

Callie listened to the wolves that first night with choking fear, but soon her own terror—like her longing for Angus—became a familiar part of life. In later nights, in longer hours of darkness, she gripped her rifle and sat awake as their howls curled upward against the starry sky.

She never spoke of the fear and pain that churned within her. Having to stiffen the spirits of Susa and the boys forced her to keep a straight spine. In England her work had been to spread tablecloths and bedcovers; now she soothed a counterpane of faith over the dread in her heart. Each morning brought a cheery face, regular scripture recitations, and hymns. Yet her quiet calm when she'd shot her doe and the soaring thrill of success that had followed were as distant as a dream to her now. How quickly her triumph had frayed and been lost!

Their packs were half empty of their original provisions, the dried venison nearly gone, and Callie had spent six shells in useless hunting. Once, she waded into the icy water and caught three fish with her hands. But the cold exertion so dramatically increased the aching of her joints and fatigue in her muscles that, even hungry, she hesitated to do it again.

And still the mountainside heaved upward, growing more and more rugged, more and more cold. She noticed the uppers of Jamie's boots had begun tearing away from the soles, but there wasn't a needle in her pack big enough to mend them.

Nights were even longer now that the wolves were always around. Several times she thought she saw yellow eyes watching from among the trees. On these nights Callie would not let herself relax at all. She refused to try to remember when she had last slept. Instead she sat staring into the blackness beyond her fire, building the flames high, sometimes reading brokenly from her scriptures, denying herself thoughts of the past but uncertain how to look to the future.

It wasn't many more days before thick forests gave way to grassy slopes. The thinning trees were maimed, and Callie unwillingly read of a hideously harsh climate in their bent limbs and sparse needles. Branches grew only on one side, and many of these pines were no taller than she was. The wind blew even more constantly here than on the prairie—and with a sickening chill.

Soon the grass began to shorten, and massive, lichen-embroidered rocks lurched up from beneath the cold ground. One morning the boys discovered a pocket of snow, and by midafternoon she could see five or six snow patches in every direction.

They must be on top! But her sudden joy was mingled with desperate concern. As Callie left the headwaters of the Little LaRamiee, she was eager, almost frantic to get over the open, desolate flats and head down out of the mountains along another river valley. Two immense granite slabs loomed on her right, the same peaks she had seen from the prairie so long ago, the ones she had been sure she could skirt.

Callie would have liked to walk all night, would have liked not to pause up on the wide backbone of the earth. But she didn't have a choice. The children were too tired to walk longer, and worse—she feared wolves would come again when the light was gone.

Not only was wood more difficult to gather here, but they had to melt snow for water. Finally, after three times the wait she'd been accustomed to in Britain, she managed to boil a handful of rice. Then Callie bunched the two boys and Susa together on one tarpaulin, flinging the other over two stunted pines to form a low, crude windbreak. It barely sheltered their three blanketed forms, but she was grateful for something to cut the wind.

Then Callie settled her own ragged tarp down beside the fire, leaning back on a reddish boulder that stabbed up from the ground. The rock was icy against her back, and from where she sat, the view stretched terrifyingly far. Layer upon layer of blue crawled away into the falling night. The stars came out, tiny impassive pricks in blackness that hung crushingly near. Callie was almost afraid that if she reached out her hand it would scrape against that cold, hard sky. The mountains to which she'd turned for protection were thrusting her up, small and vulnerable, into darkness.

One by one, heavy clouds loomed in from the west, dragging their hanging gray veils of rain toward her, crowding closer and closer until they were snagged between the peaks and the sky. Rumbles and flashes lit their white outlines against the black infinity. Determinedly, Callie pushed away recollections of the gentle growing rains at home. She refused to compare this pulsating anger with the familiar rhythmic patter of soft drops on new spring fields. This sky was huge and menacing, with room for several snarling storms at a time. Violent roaring and yellow streaks of lightning pounded into the immensity around her.

In her exhaustion, Callie had thought her continual anxiety could not deepen, but now her heart stopped short with each thunderous crack. Vibrations tore through her, shaking her frame. She sat awake, trying to watch and protect her children, while the night sky roared above her tiny camp on the bald head of the mountain.

Duncan had always been able to snore through anything, but Susa stirred, mewing frighteneddly in her sleep and clutching Mrs. McGillicutty. Callie scooted closer and patted her daughter's back, absently launching into a steady hymn.

> . . . When the earth begins to tremble,
> Bid our fearful hearts be still.
> When thy judgments spread destruction—

"I'm afraid, Mum." Susa's little voice broke into the singing. "Very, *very* afraid!" she cried, as lightning bit wildly into the night.

Callie sat quiet for a moment, her hand comforting Susa's back as she listened to the rumbling echo away down the mountain. "You mustn't let your fears control you," she responded at length. "Fear and faith cannot be together at the same time. Remember how Alma told his people not to be frightened? He told them they should remember the Lord, for that was who would deliver them. So they hushed their fears and called on God. Faith works mighty miracles on our behalf, too. We need your faith, Chickadee."

Another horrible clap burst above them with enough vengeance to tear open the granite peaks and send them careening down. But to Callie's surprise, Susa was still listening to the very grown-up words she had spoken—seemed waiting for more.

"We need your faith, you see, for God honors the trust of the weak and helpless ones." Callie wasn't sure where the words were coming from, but they sounded good, astonishingly good and true. "You are safe, darling. This is only a storm, and it will pass, as all troubles eventually do."

Susa's heart appeared to be calming, though the thunder kept crashing around them. "You must sleep the best you can and trust God to take care of you. You'll be needing all your energy to walk off this mountaintop tomorrow."

With a quiet sigh, Susa gave up her fears and turned them over to God, just as Callie had said. In spite of the furious storm, her slowing breaths and gently closed eyelids made a picture of peace.

And still the clouds bellowed above, and Callie sat, cradling the gun beneath her tarp, anxiously watching the storm grow in power and fury above her. "Look, Mum," Jamie said, sitting up and sweeping his arm around the horizon. "Three separate thunderheads be scourin' th' sky just as you scoured th' kettles back home."

James looked a lot like his father in the flashing white light. Of course there was no beard and his bulk was so much less . . . but the way he'd swept his arm. There was total absence of fear in his words, just practical respect for the magnitude of the storm.

Was his voice getting lower, too? No, the idea was

ridiculous. He would turn eleven soon, but that was much too young for such changes. She'd heard nothing more than a growing sense of maturity beneath it. He was wearing his father's old red-plaid wool shirt, and she noted with almost perverse satisfaction that it was entirely too big for his hungry young frame.

"We've no time for such talk, Jamie." Harsh condescension stiffened her voice, and Callie once more resented the sound. "God is in command here. These clouds are nothing more than water and wind." Where had her tenderness gone? Her throat ached with the same intensity as the thunder, painful in its tightness. She felt wrung-out, limp. "Sleep now." Callie tried to speak gently, to let love and warmth into her voice, even as another crash drowned out her words.

"But, Mother," Jamie protested. "Let me have a turn watching. You're so tired—" *Crash. Roll. Crash.* "I can shoot th'—" *Crash.*

"Hush. Don't argue with me. You need your sleep to walk tomorrow."

Angus never argued, yet he'd never lost an exchange. As her son lay back down, Callie sensed a familiar silent finality in his movements and felt an inkling of the same respect she'd had for his father. It was as if she didn't really have the upper hand, even though he'd done what she asked.

Though he was lying down, James continued to stare at the storm with quiet, unruffled determination. Callie turned her back to him, leaning sideways against the stone. The flashing clouds began to spit rain, and the fire hissed and popped as the first drops struck the flames.

He's just a child, Lord, she fumed inwardly. *A boy!* Angus was lost to her now. Lost for mortality. *My only reasons to go on are resting right here beside me, Lord. I won't let them be devoured by this cruel place.*

TEN

Rain came as if from buckets. Tiny streams ran between the mounds of stubby turf, uncertain whether to flow east or west. Using a stick, Callie dug trenches around the children's makeshift shelter. Then she threw her own sleeping tarpaulin across theirs to increase its strength against the wind-driven rain. Yet, in spite of her best efforts, Susa began to whine.

"Hush, hush, Chickadee," she repeated softly. "I'm doing all I can."

Even Duncan woke, and Callie could hear the earth squish beneath his tarp as he rolled over. "Can't you make her be still?" he groaned. When his mother didn't answer, he spoke directly to the miserable bundle at his side, "There, there, tiny button, sweet bonnie little lass—shut yer BIG mouth!"

Susa's whine soared into a wail that rang loudly, even through the downpour.

"Ye're a bad egg, Dunc." Jamie said in a low, piercing tone. "If Father was here there'd be a lickin' fer ye."

"Hush, children!" Callie spoke quickly before a quarrel could flare. The fire was drowning. She had to keep it going! Crouching on her knees in the mud, she dug a trench around the sinking flames and blew on the underside of the logs.

"I'm cold, I'm hungry, and I don't have to listen to you," Duncan snarled at his brother.

"Duncan, you shall recite." Callie's demand sounded astonishingly calm in the pounding rain. Her hands were frantically trying to shelter the smoking fire. She had to quiet the noise—

especially Susa's crying—so the wolves wouldn't hear. She had to keep the fire going.

"Huh?"

"Recite. The Twenty-Third Psalm, please, Duncan McCracken."

"The Lord is my shepherd," Duncan began, surprise evident in his voice. "I shall not want."

"Hush, Susa," Callie insisted. "I'd like to hear this." The whining sniffled and subsided.

"He maketh me to lie down in green pastures. He leadeth me beside the still waters . . ."

Callie's hair was falling obnoxiously into her face, and it felt as if a river had made its course down her back. She brushed at the water dripping from her cheeks and blew once more on the last limp flame. Suddenly, with a roar a furious sheet of rain rolled over them, and the last ember went black. She coughed and staggered back from the hissing smoke.

Grabbing her rifle, she stood and scanned the dark flats. Though she saw no yellow eyes in the darkness, she gripped the gun with white knuckles. Its powder was surely wet, but she would use the butt as a club if she must.

Eventually the children slept. Or, at least, after Duncan's recitation they were silent. Though the rain passed long before dawn, everything was wet through in the bitter wind. Callie couldn't even make a breakfast fire, and she felt colder than she ever had before.

Even after the sun came out, Callie had to fight off prickly shivers. She'd been coughing continually during the night, and James looked nervously at her each time she began hacking again. "I breathed in too much smoke when the fire went out," she said, realizing she hadn't much hope of fooling him.

She'd stood alert through all the hours of wet blackness.

Although Callie had never heard nor seen any wolves, she'd been afraid that—even wet—she might fall asleep if she sat down. Without a fire, she didn't dare rest. Beyond exhaustion and worn with fear, she had forgotten to sing or pray.

And then, in the darkest hour before dawn, the children had begun complaining again. Their breath was collecting in clouds about them. Their clothes were rain-soaked and heavy, smelling of cold, wet wool and mud. And their hands and faces were so chilly blue that Callie had gotten them up and walking. As soon as morning's first light was filtering across the flats around them, Callie scanned the western horizon.

Beyond these mountains another chain of rugged peaks lurked purple and snowy in the distance. She thought Angus had called them the Sierra Madres. It was a Spanish or Indian name, she supposed, but she wasted no energy wondering what it meant. One thing was certain: she would skirt them. Once out of the grip of the Medicine Bows, she would look again for the Overland Trail and follow it through the desert at the feet of those snowy peaks before she'd ever cross another mountain chain again.

A wide valley opened ahead of her, curving northwest. This, she decided, was the sure, clear stream that would lead her down from these flats and their summer snowfields, away from the immensity that was crushing her.

Rain-soaked and wind-battered, the boys were too cold to play in the snow. For once the children thought only of walking, and they were able to cover good distance. That night Callie made camp beside the swift stream.

Soon she discovered that this valley's width had been as deceptive as the gentle slopes at the foot of the Little LaRamiee. Steep granite outcroppings narrowed around water that crashed frantically downward. Dense undergrowth alternated with boggy bottoms and rock slides in a miserable, yet almost predictable pattern.

Callie's joints ached fiercely with the effort of moving on.

Her throat itched to cough, and her eyes burned as she tried to stop feverish chills. She had strength for neither joy nor fear. Only the will to keep walking possessed her, the unquestioned decision to go on.

Her morning scripture readings were regular, but her voice dwindled to nothing more than determined rhythm, and her songs were thin. Her prayers were scarcely more than a plea for the strength to do what she must and for the heathens to get justice. The children straggled forward around her without other recitations or singing—Callie was satisfied if she could only keep them moving.

One morning she noticed that she had made seven charcoal calendar marks since they had last taken a day of rest. They were camped in a place where the valley widened into a marshy bottom, the creek caught up in beaver ponds. Sunshine poured brightly down, gathering diamonds off the surface of the water. Beside her, the fire crackled comfortingly. If only she could get warm.

"This is the Sabbath," she told her children as they were finishing breakfast. Her voice grated painfully enough that she did not want to speak or have them hear her. "Jamie, you shall give us a scripture. Can you recall the one I taught you on the ship?"

"Aye, Mother," he answered without his usual reluctance to recite. He scooped the last morsel of mush into his mouth and stood. "Psalm 149: 'Praise ye the Lord. . . . let the children of Zion be joyful in their King. . . . For the Lord taketh pleasure in his people: he will beautify the meek with salvation. . . . Let the high praises of God be in their mouth, and a twoedged sword in their hand; to execute vengeance upon the heathen . . . : this honour have all his saints. Praise ye the Lord.' "

"May we go now, Mother? I heard frogs last night down by the water. I—" Duncan eagerly began.

"After we've had a hymn and you've prayed."

The children stood and sang the Doxology in the freshness of morning. Callie did not bring herself to rise but watched them closely. Their voices were cheerful, though their mosquito-bitten faces needed washing. The boys ought to have haircuts, too, and their clothing looked dismayingly torn and threadbare in the brilliant sunlight. How could it be this bright and not be warm?

"Fine," she said when they were finished. "We'll have more scriptures later," she added, nodding at Duncan. His prayers were usually quick and especially now when he was nearly free. But, for once, Callie did not reprimand him. She thought they looked like a hungry bunch as they ran down toward the river—hungry and thin.

Nearby a bird with a body no bigger than Susa's fist was hopping around on a fallen tree. The tips of its wings and V-trimmed tail looked as if they'd been dipped in black ink. On its head, too, a black V spread above dark stripes that slashed across its eyes. After a moment the tiny bird froze, motionless. Then, with quick force it dived into the grass on the other side of the log.

By the time Callie had wiped at her sore, watery eyes, the bird was back on the log with an even smaller bird sagging from its beak. In a few short, jerky movements, the hunter impaled its prey on a sharp twig and began pecking at the carcass.

To her own dismay, Callie's shock at the barbarous creature was without energy. Viciousness disgusted but no longer surprised her. Even sweet little birds forsook pecking at seeds in this wilderness, actually resorting to cannibalism. She was appalled, but she was too weak to hate any longer—too weak to fume and fury at the violent cruelty on every side or the feelings of insignificance this land forced upon her.

Callie simply closed her eyes and slept. And nothing crossed her mind or disturbed her rest until she jerked awake, still tightly clasping the gun.

Evening was falling all around the children huddled close to the fire, drawing games in the dirt. Susa was halfway onto

Jamie's lap, where he was tickling her so she wouldn't be able to touch her stick to the ground.

"What—" Callie blurted, her mouth awkwardly dry. She tried to grasp the time. "You must be hungry, you—"

The giggling cut off abruptly as the children turned. "Oh, Mother!" Susa was gasping to catch her breath. "We're all right. Jamie cooked for us."

"And he burned the rice to the bottom of the pan," Duncan added.

Callie looked over, but Jamie did not meet her eyes. "Can I bring ye a drink, Mother?" he asked, reaching for something to carry it in.

"I'll fetch one myself," she answered, trying to collect all her body parts and get them standing.

"It was a fine supper," Susa was saying. "Duncan catched the frog he heard last night, and we roasted it over the fire."

Callie's stomach lurched. "Caught, Susa. Not catched."

"He caught it," she corrected. "An' Jamie said to save you some, but we was too hungry. Maybe Dunc can get you another tomorrow."

"Maybe—" Callie answered vaguely as she scuttled toward the creek.

The reddish-brown water was icy cold, and she began to feel refreshed as she splashed her face and neck. She drank deeply and then sat on the bank for a moment, pulling herself together. Once the disorientation of her sleep began to wear off, she actually felt better than she had for days.

A frog, she thought. *A frog?* Quickly she gathered her skirts and rushed back to the campfire. But in spite of her intentions she didn't say anything to Jamie; he was busy straightening her bedding.

Though her knees were wobbly, and Callie had a quivery feeling inside, her fever was gone the next morning. Shortly after dawn, she assembled her troops and began moving downstream once more.

When the sun was halfway into the sky they came upon an area that had been burned. Here the trees were only limbless trunks that pointed eerily upward. There wasn't a fit place to rest for nooning, so they hardly paused in the uncanny charcoal forest.

Then, late in the evening, they came to a wide rock slide that had blocked the flames' greedy path. Whispering pines and green undergrowth beckoned them from the other side. Slowing almost to a crawl, they scrambled over boulders and slid through shifting shale.

That night, as Callie knelt to pray, she was surprised to find that she felt something and was especially surprised to realize that her emotion was gratitude. The blackened ash in the burnt-out area had made their going dirty and unsettling, but walking had been easier. They'd made good time.

And, what was even more amazing, when she sat down beside the fire in the darkness, she found that—at least for the moment—she was not afraid to rest.

Callie woke suddenly, several nights later, and looked about their camp near the bottom of the valley. Something was pressing in the back of her mind, something frail, intangible. Voices? She'd been thinking she heard Angus's voice again. By habit, she assured herself that it was only a trick of the wind, but tonight the pines were unusually calm, no sighing, no swaying. Even the aspen weren't quaking.

No, Callie thought. And she tried to push the feeling away, like cobwebs from her mind. She didn't want to think about Angus. She didn't want to think about anything, anything at all. She'd been resting with a peaceful calm feeling—the same calm that had hung over the lake when she shot the deer.

But now a breeze began blowing, rippling across her

thoughts. What had the voice been saying? What had it been telling her to do?

Far up in the mountains another terrible storm raged on the bald flats. Lightning tore like cannon shot through the sky, and the clouds battled in armadas against each other. Callie shuddered, grateful to be away from there, grateful for the tall pines above her.

Now she was truly awake. She didn't hear the voice anymore, but what had it been saying? She couldn't bring a single word to mind, yet she felt an undeniable and growing conviction. She had to climb up.

The valley was narrow as a bottleneck here and had been tight like that through most of their travel the previous afternoon. It would be hard to climb out of the streambed. Cliffs of granite and shale slides hemmed in the dense undergrowth along the stream.

Callie began gathering things, stuffing them into packs. Her unexplainable urgency was mounting. The lightning was too distant for her to see by and her fire had dwindled low, but she didn't pause to build it up.

"Wake up, Jamie! Duncan—" She shook his shoulder. "Susa! Pop up, Chickadee. Here we go!"

Urgently she rushed them into gathering their bedding, rolling it haphazardly. Far away she could hear a pounding grinding sound beneath the distant thunder. Was it only a ringing in her head? She didn't stop to consider, just got the children moving out of the trees and up into the rocks. Duncan was stumbling clumsily. She couldn't drag both him and Susa.

"Quick, Jamie, give me your pack and bring your brother along."

Without hesitation, Jamie threw his pack at her feet and ran back. "Hurry up, Dunc," she could hear him saying. "Come along!"

The roaring was getting louder now, a horrible crashing sound above them, on up the valley. She scrambled ahead, pulling Susa behind her until, only twenty yards further, a sheer face of granite blocked her flight.

Callie turned to pull Duncan and Jamie up against the granite, looking down into the valley. Through the darkness she could see the tiny pinprick of their fire among the trees below. The rumbling was growing louder, closer. Jamie was saying something, but she couldn't hear him above the clamor.

Then, with a terrific crash, an immense wall of water rounded the bend and tore toward them.

E L E V E N

The roaring, cascading water hit like a fist of stone. Towering pines were hammered flat. Dirt and debris were thrown up into the moonlit night. Callie clasped her children tightly against her. No one spoke as they gazed, awestruck, at the chaos that passed only yards below them.

Eventually the tumult subsided, but the river ran high through the scarred valley. Callie wedged her little ones down into a crevice between the rocks, hoping for a few more hours of sleep. Draping one of the tarps above them, she created a rude shelter between the boulders and the granite cliff.

More clouds were rushing in from the west, but these were softer, hanging lower. They slammed up against the thunderheads, pushed them on over the peaks, and then hung there themselves. Raining steadily, they blanketed the night sky.

Gray morning came through heavy drizzle; the ground was soggy and slick. Callie managed a small fire in the protection of a boulder. Hot gruel might help to warm the children, she thought—even if it was thin. Callie ate hers before waking them and then read from 2 Nephi in the Book of Mormon as they attacked their breakfast.

"'And it shall come to pass that my people which are of the House of Israel, shall be gathered—' Don't slurp please, Duncan," she reproved without looking up. "'And I will shew unto them that fight against my . . . people . . . that I covenanted with Abraham that I would remember his seed forever . . .'"

Soon they were on their way again, with the sun breaking through to spread swaths of warmth across the soaked earth. They couldn't climb out of the valley, and they couldn't go down and find a game trail. The spot where they'd camped the night before was now an impassable mess.

Callie led her children just above the flood line of tangled debris, as a sense of mingled wonder and amazement overtook her thoughts. God was indeed with her. Callie's mind flew back over the times she'd felt His hand reach into their awful plight.

First had been the blazing afternoon when she'd buried Angus and turned her back on the bloody massacre. Her heart could have stopped any instant with sheer anguish, but grief had eased just enough when her song floated as a prayer onto the quiet twilight. Then, again, heaven had been with her when she'd shot the doe. That morning had held the same blue peace, the same penetrating calm she'd felt last night when she'd heard the voice. Seeking that peace again, hoping to hold it with her, she began to sing once more as she led her children along.

> Redeemer of Israel, our only delight,
> On whom for a blessing we call,
> Our shadow by day and our pillar by night,
> Our king, our deliverer, our all.

"Look! Look up there!" Susa tugged at her mother's hand and pointed up the hillside. About twenty feet above them in the cleft of a rock bloomed a flower that looked like a white star edged with trailing purple petals. The swollen stream hadn't reached it, and a lip of granite hung out, protecting it from the rain. Callie noticed, however, that it swayed slightly, and she wondered absentmindedly what breeze could find it there.

"Go ahead, Susa," Callie said. "You can pluck it and then catch up with me." She turned to walk forward, a little more slowly, resuming her song.

We know he is coming to gather his sheep
And lead them to Zion in love,
For why in the valley of death should they weep
Or in the lone wilderness rove?

How long we have wandered—

Susa's sudden scream pierced the air and Callie turned, swinging the rifle up to her shoulder in the same instant. Looking back from her new vantage point she could see a large snake coiled in the flower's crevice. In the heartbeat of silence that followed she also heard its rattle.

Sucking her breath in, Callie caught the rattler in her sights. The gun exploded, bucking so hard she was knocked backward. The snake jerked out from beneath the rock, coiling and twisting in pain. Susa came bounding down the hill, and Jamie was beside her at once, helping her over the rocks to where Duncan had crouched.

Quickly, Callie came to her feet, struggling to reload. Her hands were shaking now as she lifted her rifle and threw another slug into the writhing serpent. Loading again, she would have shot more times, but the coiling contortions slowed.

"I wanna' go look at it, Mum. It's huge!" Duncan's voice rang out eagerly. "It's a monster!"

"No!" Callie answered fiercely, stepping quickly to his side and gripping his shoulder with fingers like a vice. She stood motionless, staring at the dead snake. Inner peace or not, this brutal wilderness was still baring its fangs at her.

"How can there be so many snakes all at once, now, Mother?" Jamie asked as Callie gave him the one small portion of unleavened pancake that was to be his dinner.

"It was too cold up on top for reptiles," Duncan told his

brother, reminding Callie of the good marks he'd gotten back home in his studies.

"Yes, but we never saw any before," Jamie said, still waiting for his mother's response. "And t'day we've seen six."

Callie looked at where she had looped the rope across the ground around them. The soil was so wet she didn't know how they would sleep. Rain had been falling steadily again since sunset, but she'd been afraid to make a shelter against the rocks, since rattlers seemed to lurk in every cranny.

"The ground must be saturated and their holes full of water," Callie said. With effort she kept her voice dispassionate and uncaring. "They're washing right down out of the mountains, just as we are." Then, with a dose of cheer she added, "We'll be out onto the plains again tomorrow. Once we start north, it won't be long before we find the Cherokee Trail again."

Jamie smiled at that. Like a merry dagger, Susa asked, "Will there be wagons?"

"No, dear. No wagons. Sleep, now. I'll wake you early in the morning."

True to her word, the next day they poured out of the widening valley with the rain and the snakes and the swollen river. They were dirtier and hungrier and more tired than she had ever thought possible.

The following morning dawned sunny, though, with a promise of warmth, and Callie slipped away early to hunt. She took a shot at a rockchuck and missed but later hit a marmot. There wasn't much flesh on it to be roasted—especially after the rifle ball mangled it—but Susa brightly assured her mother it was more filling than Duncan's frog. Though hunger still gnawed at the emptiness, and her shoulder was aching again, Callie felt some satisfaction in how her aim had improved. Yet ammunition was running down almost as quickly as their food supplies. She ought to make each shot count for more than one meal. There were other reasons she might need to shoot.

The closer they'd gotten to the open plains, the more her concern about Indians had grown into a desperate thought that peered constantly from the recesses of her mind. She worried about making a fire, but snakes were everywhere and her hope that flames would keep them away led her to risk making small ones. Besides, the weather had cleared, and warm days gave way to starry nights that were terribly cold. She needed fires for cooking and warmth.

The creek spilled down into the wide, sunny valley of the Platte, treeless except along the river bottoms. The ground was swampy beside the river, which was still swollen from mountain streams.

Early the next morning before the children were up, Callie fought through the crunchy, frosted cattails and marsh grass in hopes of discovering a way across the river. She had to get to the other side, sooner or later. Perhaps there would be fewer snakes over there, she reasoned. But the rushing water looked too deep and fast. Snags carried down from the mountains lay partially submerged beneath the swirling current that grasped debris as it sped by. Oh, for a horse to swim them across!

Rather than return empty-handed, she crouched in a stand of bearded, chest-high grass and waited until some ducks flew into the reeds. Callie's third shot was successful, and she carried back a mallard for breakfast. She would have liked to try for prairie goat, if only one would stray into her range. Her rifle wouldn't have mutilated the meat as badly as it did these smaller animals.

"Can we cross here, Mother?" Jamie asked when she walked into camp. He beamed expansively when he saw the bloody mess swinging at her side.

"No," Callie answered. "Eventually we'll hit the wagon trail if we keep moving north, but I wanted to cross early. We've had too intimate an acquaintance with snakes. Stick close by this morning, won't you, children?"

That day, like the preceding two, they struggled across the rolling benches that bordered the east side of the river. It was slow going through the twisted sage and sharp yucca. Often, the pungent sage easily reached as high as Susa's chin. Sometimes the boys ran ahead of her; sometimes they straggled behind. Progress was too slow for Callie to want to mark it. The night before, when she'd made her charcoal mark in Angus's book, she'd realized the calendar had rolled well into September.

Suddenly Duncan screamed, the high deliberate sound of absolute terror. Dropping Susa's hand, Callie raced ahead, not caring how her skirts caught and tore on the grasping sage.

James was already there, throwing rocks at the body of a snake as long as Duncan was tall. The rattler coiled and turned, its fangs caught in the seam of Duncan's boot.

"Get back!" she shouted at Jamie. She raised the rifle, but the snake writhed, wrapping its body around Duncan's boot. "Hold still!" she commanded the terrified boy. "Still!" Turning the gun around she brought the butt down hard against the rattler's thin, scaly head. Its fangs broke loose from the leather. "Shake it off, Duncan! Run away!" Callie yelled, turning the gun around and taking aim.

Her shot caught the snake behind its head. Like Susa's rattler it writhed and twisted for some time after it was dead. But this time she didn't stop to watch.

"Duncan, pull your boot off. Let me see. How deep is it?"

Pale and trembling the boy shook his head.

"Off, Duncan!" Callie shouted frantically. "I've got to see—I've got to lance it." Angus had read in his guidebook that such poison must be sucked out. She had to stop it from traveling up his leg. Callie began digging in her pack for the knife.

"N-n-n-no, Ma. N-n-n-o. I . . . I'm all right."

Angry, Callie sat him down hard and pulled the boot off. Then the stocking. "Where? Where did it get you?" She could see holes where the fangs had gone into the boot, but her son's white skin showed only redness where she'd hit him with the butt of the gun. No blood, no punctures.

"It didn't get me, Mother." Duncan gasped, catching his breath. "It . . . it never broke my skin."

That night, when the children knelt beside their bedding and Callie prayed, she felt the same overwhelming gratitude she'd expressed in the afternoon. They'd given thanks immediately, with Duncan's foot still bare and the dead snake only ten feet away. But now, though her relief was still fresh, the rush of adrenaline was gone.

We cross the river tomorrow, Callie decided. High water or not, this was one brush too many with snakes, one step too close to death.

TWELVE

Morning ushered in a hanging, drizzly rain, but Callie's decision was made. They would cross and escape the infestation of snakes.

"Hold tighter, Jamie," she was saying. "I want your hand to hurt my arm. Then I'll know I'm not losing you."

"Aye, Mother," Jamie answered, his freckled face serious, his grip tensing.

"Remember when you were baptized and you held onto Father's arm like this?"

He nodded.

"Well, 'twill be much the same. I'll hold my arm out for you, but if the water gets too deep, latch onto my shoulder."

Callie tried to smile as if they were on a seaside outing. *If you must, you can swim,* she told herself soundlessly, looking resolutely at the roiling gray water. *There's nothing to learn . . . people just do it.*

The swollen river raced just inches away from her boots and disappeared into the drizzling rain. Snags and debris torn loose from the mountains still rode the swift current, their limbs and roots flashing into sight, bobbing and turning dangerously beneath the water.

Dear God, you led Lehi across the ocean. Callie closed her eyes in fervent silence. *You must do this for me. You must!*

Deliberately, Callie turned again and smiled at Jamie, masking her fear. "I know you're hungry, Son, but don't swallow more than three or four fish while we're crossing.

Otherwise you might get too heavy for me to pull you through!"

The boy grinned, and together they each placed a foot in the swirling water. Then she paused and held him back. Callie turned briefly to look over her shoulder where Susa and Duncan sat, watching. Behind them a waist-high patch of purple-crowned thistles stood firmer against the hanging sheets of rain than the surrounding grass. She looked back down at her own foot and the water washing past it.

"Here we go!" Callie said, stepping forward as gaily as if they were on a picnic. Silently her mind repeated, *Dear God, You must . . . You must . . . You must! . . .*

The pull of the river was cold, instantly numbing her legs. Before each step, she gingerly searched the riverbed for drop-offs with her toe. Pausing after every footfall, she timed her progress to miss being hit by floating branches. And all the way, Callie held her right arm high, gripping the rifle, her left arm clamped in Jamie's grasp. Her heavy skirts swirled around her legs, absorbing water and pulling, almost dragging, her legs out from under her and away downstream. About two-thirds of the way across, Jamie clasped her by the shoulder, and she was glad she'd insisted on leaving his pack behind on the east bank and stuffing Susa's smaller one into her own.

Then the water began to grow shallower, and at last they struggled up onto the western shore. Laughing with relief, Jamie flopped to the ground and began dumping the water out of his boots. Callie dropped her pack and wrung out her cold skirts. Then she turned to wave at Duncan and Susa.

"You did fine, Son," she said, putting a wet hand on his shoulder in tenderness that had become rare. "Fine."

They were standing at the base of a small rise, and Callie began walking up it to warm her legs before she plunged back in to fetch Duncan.

"I'll build a fire t' dry out th' wee ones when they get

here," Jamie called after her. "That water feels as if 'twas run straight off o' ice."

"Yes, you do tha—" Callie's answer was cut short by her first glimpse over the hill. This wasn't the west bank at all, but only an island! Another fork of the river curled northward ahead of her. Callie waited until she could hide her dismay before walking back toward her son. "No, Jamie. Not yet."

The boy paused in gathering firewood.

"Take a look from up there. We've another water frolic ahead of us."

Curious, Jamie dropped the sticks and ran up the hill.

"Let's not be wasting all day," his mother called after him. "We haven't got time to play in every little creek if we're going to be getting on to Zion!" She waded immediately into the water, lifting the rifle higher and higher as the water rose around her. "I'm going back now for Duncan." But the determined impatience in her voice belied a sense of desperation. Angrily she blinked away frustrated, frightened tears. As the sucking eddies rose around her legs, Callie's breath caught in her throat. Drawing all her strength into one immense effort, Callie willed her faith to overcome the muscular pull of the river.

This was the order she'd planned to ferry her children across. During the long night's wait, Callie had reasoned that bringing James first was best when she did not know the lay of the riverbed that faced her. And she would save Susa for last, because the girl was at least twenty pounds lighter than Duncan. Hopefully, Duncan could walk some of the way, but no doubt she'd have to carry Susa every step. *One at a time,* she told herself as she picked her way back across the channel. *First get them all to the island. Then through the second crossing. Don't think of both crossings at once. Just get everyone to the island first.*

Her dark, heavy skirt twisted and clung against her legs. With conscious effort, Callie continued to reach deep inside herself, demanding strength to repeat this back-and-forth ordeal five more times. She could feel the children watching her, but there was no way to make the struggle against the current look easy.

She hated leaving Susa alone on the shore. Callie barred images of snakes and Indians from her mind as quickly as they formed, but their effect was still felt as she lugged the rifle back and forth on every crossing. "Don't move from this spot, Susa," she said, bending low and looking into the child's eyes. "I will come back for you, so don't try to follow me. No matter what happens, stay right here."

Then Callie hoisted Jamie's pack and made sure Duncan had a secure grip on her arm. By the time they were across, he was trembling with the effort, but no sooner did he stand in knee-deep water than she pulled her arms out of the pack and handed it to him. James had come out from the island into the water, and he grabbed hold of the pack, too, using it to pull Duncan toward shore. He paused, apparently wanting to tell her something, but she avoided delay. Turning right around, Callie fought her way back into the rushing current.

Looking again across the water, Callie's heart pinched painfully at the sight of the forlorn little figure, ridiculous in her modified skirt and already dripping from the drizzly rain. "My Susa lies over the ocean," she sang out, across the sweeping expanse of water between them. She had to gather her breath and take a couple steps before she could continue the next line. "My Susa lies over the sea!" It was hardly singing, more of a breathless shout, but it was all she could offer the tiny girl, standing alone in the tall grass. "My Susa lies over the ocean . . ." Callie bent her concentration on catching another breath, on finding the next solid step—"Oh bring back my Susa to me!"

Susa was standing at the edge of the water, not even trying to laugh at her mother's joke, frightened tears streaming down her face. Trembling with cold, Callie strapped Duncan's pack onto her own front, hoisted her daughter on piggyback, and raised the rifle above her head again.

"Brave-up . . . Chickadee!" she said as brightly as she could, her words broken by heavy breathing. "Duncan"—*pant, pant*—"thinks this"—*pant*—"is great fun."

"Duncan's mad," Susa quavered, and her tiny fingers clenched in a strangling grip around her mother's neck. Callie put up her empty hand to loosen the choking hold, and then, raising the rifle higher and higher as she went, stepped into the water again.

Once across, Callie rested briefly on the island, but there was no getting warm in the drizzly rain. Numb with effort, she began supporting Jamie through his second crossing. Six yards from the western bank, Callie stumbled and the water swirled dizzyingly around her. She caught a foothold just as the current slammed the boy up against her. Biting her lip, she raised her gun higher. It took all her strength to hold steady as Jamie wrapped his arms around her waist.

"I can do 't from here," he said, as soon as they were within ten feet of the western shore. "This side isn't as deep as the other was."

Callie could feel herself shaking with fatigue as she took off the pack and handed it to him. Her feet were numb, and she fought to keep her jellylike knees from buckling.

"Build that fire, now," she told him as she turned around. "We'll all be needing it."

"Mother!" he said, grabbing her arm as she turned to go back. "Leave th' rifle wi' me. 'Tis only more weight t' be wearyin' ye further."

Callie turned away from his gaze and stared back toward where Duncan and Susa were waiting. What if Indians came, or someone stumbled over another snake? Without responding, she waded away through the rushing water.

"Why won't ye leave it, Mum?" he called after her. "I can shoot. Father taught me."

Callie didn't know how to answer him, couldn't think of words to explain how responsibility and fear were heaped into one immense burden she could not share.

"Build a good fire, Jamie," she called back over her shoulder. "Then look in my pack and see what you can find to fill us up when this is done." She knew there were a few chunks of the mallard wrapped in a scrap of tarpaulin. Perhaps they would each gnaw a piece of that.

She refused to face how tired she was as she carted Duncan over from the island. When they were nearing the western shore, Jamie waded out into the water and helped his brother through the shallows. He'd apparently had some trouble lighting a fire with wet wood, but he returned at once to the task, Duncan squatting nearby and leaning over to shield Jamie's flint and tinder from the rain. This time Callie went all the way to the shore and hesitated before plunging back in.

Noticing that something was wrong, Jamie left fire-making to offer her a chunk of the cold roast duck. But Callie had no stomach for it. She waved him away and began pacing up and down the bank. She had to force some warmth into her limbs before she could go back after Susa. She considered sitting down and hoping this weakness would pass, but logic told her she'd never get warm in wet clothing and rain. Besides, Susa was standing right on the brink of the water again.

Callie's hands were mottled, water-wrinkled, and pale. She rubbed them vigorously together, bending the stiff joints. Frozen like this, she could let Susa slip from her grasp without even knowing it. So she swung her arms in circles. Perhaps the effort did warm her some, but it also emphasized how weak she was getting. *Mighty God,* she cried inwardly. *You must. You MUST!*

She was having trouble thinking beyond her next step—and even that was becoming a conscious effort—but as she neared the island she could see fresh tears brimming in Susa's blue eyes. At that moment, almost as if it were a familiar surprise, Callie's sluggish thoughts registered the knowledge that Susa still needed to see a brave face.

"Hop on, Chickadee," she said through gritted teeth. "This is your last ride from me!"

She should have been aware of it—should have remembered the spot where she slipped with Jamie—but in her exhaustion Callie stumbled again.

"Hold tight," she commanded Susa, trying to regain balance while the awkward pack scooped water on her front. Flinging back her free hand, Callie grabbed her daughter's boot. With her concentration divided, the stock of the rifle caught full against the current. She swung around, trying to keep her left hand's grip on the slippery barrel.

Susa's courage suddenly vanished into hysteria. Screaming shrilly, she clutched tighter at her mother's neck, choking her. Callie let go of the tiny boot to loosen her daughter's fingers so she could breathe. And in the same effort, Susa's grip was lost. Her wet hands groped wildly as the water tore her away.

"Susa!" Callie shouted, frantic. She grabbed her daughter's baggy pantaloons as the little girl hit the water, but a snarl of debris had also caught the rifle. Callie couldn't bring it around. Susa's pantaloons were tearing. Her screaming had given way to coughing. She was gagging for breath with a desperate, rasping sound. Then the fabric tore entirely, and the current swept her away.

Dropping the gun, Callie lunged after her daughter with both hands outstretched. She lunged again and again. Helpless, panicked, she fought to catch hold of the bobbing form ahead of her. A rock loomed up in the water, and Susa struck hard against it. The coughing stopped. With one last immense lunge, Callie caught hold of Susa's boot. Wrapping her arms around her daughter's middle, she found her tiny body inert, no longer struggling. Heavy with dread, Callie tore her daughter from the clutch of the wild river and fought her way back upstream toward the boys, hunting for a place where she could climb out.

The water felt strangely warm against her legs. A sickening sulphur smell filled her senses, but Callie fought for the edge and pushed Susa onto the sodden grass. James was there, pulling his sister up by her limp arms, Duncan right behind.

Callie could not recall climbing out of the water and onto the rain-soaked bank. The only thing she saw was how blue Susa's lips were and how her eyes rolled back in her head.

THE SAVAGE

17 September 1857

West Bank of the North Platte River

THIRTEEN

Callie woke to see a distorted moon floating lightlessly in and out of misty clouds. Disoriented, she tried to sit up but lay back with a groan. Every part of her ached. She felt as if she had been beaten all over—and cold! She hadn't known cold like this could exist—ice right in the marrow. Did she have any body warmth left at all?

Memory jarred her thoughts like a flash of hard steel. Susa! She recalled the grip of pounding water as if it were still bearing down on her, the horrible sound of Susa's gasping, the limp silence. This memory was followed by a vague one of pulling herself onto the bank, of staggering toward Jamie's fire, of gathering Susa close.

Dazed, Callie had stripped the wet clothing off the motionless little body. After wrapping Susa in the driest scrap of blanket she could find, she'd sat rubbing her daughter's extremities with desperate anxiety, murmuring all the while in a soft stream of mother-babble. Jamie heated some water, but Callie could think of nothing with which to make a poultice. Susa never moved.

Callie had risen and begun drying herself by the fire as best she could. Suddenly the weight of her own cold exhaustion and helplessness had borne down on her with more force than she could resist. Biting hard against her lip, she fought off a fit of weeping. She prayed desperately that some small spark of warmth was left in her own wretched body and pulled her daughter tight against herself. Then she wrapped the piece of blanket around both of them and battled hysteria with sleep.

All these memories swept over her as if in one thought: the anguish of powerlessness, the weary bone-chilling cold, the futile endless worry of what to do next.

Immediately Callie felt with her hands. She couldn't tell for certain that Susa was alive, couldn't be sure she was gone. What had she been doing here, wrapped up together like this? Trying to give some of her own warmth to her daughter, she recalled. But she was so cold herself!

Callie rolled out of the blanket and stood up, thrashing her aching arms through the air in an effort to start her blood moving. She wasn't the least bit hungry, but maybe if she ate something . . .

A small circle of embers glowed orange in the darkness. Her nose wrinkled at the smell of smoke hanging over their camp in the cold night air. Moving closer, she discovered that the boys had cooked a little mush in the kettle. A few spoonfuls were stuck to the sides of the pan, as if they'd felt guilty eating the last of it. The empty cornmeal bag lay on the dirt beside the fire, and Callie remembered the rice had run out three days before. *Only a handful of flour left in my pack, and probably wet now, too,* she thought. *Then it's gone—all of it.*

Turning away from the pan (she had no stomach to eat the last of it either—that would have been like taking food from those boys' mouths), Callie squinted into the darkness. In the glow of the embers, she could see that Jamie had spread his blanket on top of Susa's and was sharing with Duncan. Gently, she tried to make Duncan's scrap stretch a little farther down on Jamie's legs. As she leaned over, Callie noticed that Jamie had strung the lasso around them, just as she had done each night since they'd left St. Joseph.

The sight of the thin hemp rope struck her as pitifully ironic. Emotion welled painfully in her chest, and she turned abruptly from the lean, famished boys to look down on Susa.

Her tiny darling seemed asleep: lingering, barely breathing, yet not gone. The young mother bent, placing her cheek just above Susa's mouth. Yes, the child was breathing faintly, she was sure. Her daughter was pale, almost gray—frighteningly so. Callie shivered violently and then turned and began fumbling in her pack, searching for Mrs. McGillicutty with her fingertips. She'd insisted Susa's precious possession stay secure in a pack, and now she was glad. Gently, she parted Susa's blanket scraps and slid the hard spoon doll between her arms. Again, painful agony pressed down inside her chest.

Callie turned away once more, stepping back to where the boys rested, making one more futile effort to cover them better. *What more have mothers ever been able to do,* she wondered, *than cover their sleeping ones?*

Turning, she looked habitually for the gun, thinking she would check to be sure it was dry and undamaged. But then she remembered the sucking river, the snag it had caught on, the moment she had thrown it away to save Susa. Callie stood blinking, staring at nothing. Her hands hung limp at her sides. This loss was a bigger practical problem than her exhausted mind could fathom or face. She simply stood, looking off into the darkness toward the west, stunned.

Why didn't some horseback rider see her fire in the night? She knew God could do it. He could send an army if He chose. Why didn't He do something? He could arrange anything. What more faith could any human being show than she had? She tried to imagine her vision was able to pierce the darkness. If only she could see the dim glow of Zion out there in the night. She stared until her eyes began to burn and then realized she had to move again or she'd freeze on the spot.

She'd come so far. So far! An immense terrain of rivers and mountains and heaving ocean waves lay behind her. By comparison, Zion was close. The number of miles before her was insignificant against the thousands she had traversed. Yet barren reality stretched impenetrably before her. "Vain dreams of Zion's glories," she heard herself mutter, suddenly wondering if that was all her hopes had ever been. "Sweet dreams curdled in the wilderness and left to rot on the dry plains!"

All the blood, sweat, and anguish of her family cried against the wilderness. Her soul demanded justice. But what could she do?

A vague half-realized answer formed darkly in the back of her mind, an answer she accepted as a possibility for the first time. She was startled at having even allowed it to form into conscious thought, but there it was, plain and clear: Keep going until the end.

Callie had never thought, never accepted that it could end this way. Nauseous weakness washed over her as she turned her back on the vast betrayal that reached through the darkness between her and her dream.

She knew she should build up the fire, but her ankles were leaden with fatigue. Her fingers ached until it seemed impossible to bend them. She swallowed hard but was unable to subdue the inertia that had taken possession of her. She cast her mind about again, trying to ignore this weakness she could not overcome.

The drizzle had lifted, but in the wet air the cold was relentless. As her eyes fell once more on Susa's still form, physical pain tore through her chest. "Oh Lord!" she breathed, dropping to her knees. Her voice trembled, almost wild in the dim firelight. "Lord! Hast Thou brought us here, preserved us to die slowly, one by one?" Silent blackness stretched above, clamping her beneath it like cold, impenetrable iron. "Then hear my last request: Have done with it!"

Her words quavered in the darkness, fell on the still air, and were gone. Callie knelt a moment longer as if waiting, though for what she did not know. Then at last she rose and, using her feet, pushed some of the sticks Jamie had gathered onto the fire.

With her rifle lost in the turbulent river, her hands felt strangely empty. Sitting up seemed useless. All she could do was sleep and let the morning find her as it might. So she lay down again beside Susa.

Sometime in the night Callie thought she heard a violin. Sweet strains of melody swayed around her, warmer than any thought or sensation she'd had in days. Lingering phrases echoed familiarly through her sleep-clogged thoughts. And in her dreamlike condition she assumed her father had come for tea, bringing his beautiful old instrument with him.

She began setting the table, laying out her best china and the lace-edged napkins from Brittany. She lit two new candles at the center of the table and chose silver teaspoons that caught the flames' glow in their rounded bowls. Sugar. Cream. Heart-catching strains from his violin wrapped themselves around it all.

Realization suddenly jerked through Callie, blotting out the comfortable scene. She had nothing to serve! The rice was all gone and the cornmeal, too. She had nothing to mix with her handful of flour, so she couldn't begin to make a proper biscuit.

She would have to borrow from a neighbor. It wouldn't do to have him catch her like this. Perhaps Mary Greaves would lend her some jam or marmalade. Her eyelids were heavy, like cold iron, but Callie forced them open and struggled to rise.

She could *feel* the light around her even before she managed to fully open her eyes. Brilliant light was blinding her, blanketing her. Golden and soft, Callie knew if she could stay within this light the frosty chill would melt away forever. *Surely the fire must have died down by now,* she wondered, blinking. But this was indisputable light. And in the center of it she saw Angus.

Callie knew instantly that the business about tea and biscuits had been a dream. But this was no mistake!

Angus's wiry red hair was back in place, his arms were unbloodied, his hands open toward her. His torn chest, now covered with a clean white shirt, was whole and broad, and she longed to bury her face in it, to be wrapped in his embrace.

But with this awareness came the complete, coherent memory of her plight. All at once she realized the Lord had answered her prayer! She was dying, she reasoned, and her husband had come to guide her home.

"Angus," she breathed. "I am ready. Take me with you!"

She reached out her arms, thinking she could clasp him to her. But Angus was just beyond her grasp, gazing at her fondly, beatifically. In a blaze of recognition, Callie understood that all the light, all the warmth emanated from a sense of peace and love. She could feel his deep concern and sorrow for her pain, but his words shocked her. Though Angus's mouth never opened, it was unmistakably his voice that answered tenderly. "Nay. I canna' take ye yet, m' love." Then he urged softly, "Sing, Callie lass. Sing."

No! Callie thought, a cold flood of resentment washing through her. *I don't want to sing anymore!*

Angus's head tilted, his gaze fixed even more intently on her than before. Suddenly Callie realized he knew what she was thinking, so she explained, "A song can't tame this wilderness. It's too raw. Don't you see? We don't belong here!" And then she pled with all the energy of her soul, her arms reaching toward him again. "I want to rest with you, Angus! I am so tired. I don't know what to do. I don't want to sing anymore. I won't even try."

Angus's smile vanished, and across his face rushed a surge of absolute grief. "Sing, lass," he commanded firmly. "Sing!" Then more gently, almost pleadingly, he added, "All the angels o' heaven be singing wi' ye."

Callie squinted blankly into the brilliant light. Angus's words made no sense to her. But the warmth was a language she understood perfectly, and she wanted her children warmed too. She wanted Jamie to see his father. And as the thought hit her she flung her hand out, reaching for the boy.

"Jamie!" she whispered, turning to look at him as she grabbed his leg and shook it. "Wake up. Your fa—"

She stopped. Though Jamie stirred and curled his knees up toward his chest, she did not try again to waken him. For the moment she looked away, she realized Angus had gone. Night plunged back into darkness; the brilliant warmth fled. Only three small coals glowed dully among the ashes of her fire, three small coals with tiny waves of redness rippling between their white, charred edges.

Sing, Callie thought. She didn't want to lose the warmth entirely or the sense of his companionship. The only real advice he'd given her was to sing. So, kneeling beside the glimmering remains of the fire, she grasped at a song. "Our foes have rejoiced when our sorrows they've seen, but . . ." Something was wrong. She couldn't quite get the melody to run ahead of her. And once she'd faltered, searching for the notes, the words abandoned her, too.

After a while, her thoughts echoed Angus's words. She would have given in to stubborn, indignant feelings, but the peace had been too lovely and she didn't want to lose that. She didn't want to lose the last of the warmth, the sense of Angus's companionship. So she took a deep breath and tried patiently to form her voice around another song. "When the earth begins to reel—" No, that wasn't quite right, either.

Normally, she would have kept singing, forcing her way through, right or wrong, until the tune and words began to merge as they ought. But in the lingering peace, she couldn't bring herself to go on if the song was wrong. And she couldn't think of another.

Taking a deep breath once more, she closed her eyes and waited for the peace to come back to her more fully. There had been violin music—clear tones, rich with soul-wrenching sweetness. Perhaps she could call them back into her mind.

But no forceful walking rhythm came to her. No strident hymn took possession of the moment's tender passion, nor promised victory for God's chosen Israel. Instead, the gentle waves of a melody began lapping at her thoughts. Eyes still closed, voice tremulous, she opened her heart and rode out upon the music with these meek words:

> Lead kindly light, amid the encircling gloom;
> Lead thou me on!
> The night is dark, and I am far from home;
> Lead thou me on!

As Callie sang, her voice cracked and the fervor behind her words worked like a confirmation, sealing them into her heart.

> Keep thou my feet;
> I do not ask to see
> The distant scene—
> One step enough for me.

At the end of the first verse, Callie sat very still, relishing the comfort of the light and warmth that had visited her in the darkness. Although she was the only one kneeling beside the embers, she enjoyed a greater nearness to God than she had ever known. She felt a sense of His presence and caring that surpassed the rational understanding that had brought her across the ocean and half a continent.

Prayerfully, she sang the first verse again; then the second followed as though her own heart had written the words:

> I was not ever thus,
> Nor prayed that thou Shouldst lead me on.
> I loved to choose and see my path; but now,
> Lead thou me on!

Again, at the end of the second verse she paused, and now the stillness had nothing to do with emptiness or loneliness. Cold darkness did not breathe hopeless impossibility. Callie looked at each of her sleeping children, and, for the first time in weeks, the sight did not bring a weight of fear and impending failure. Forsaking desperation, she opened her heart wide on the third verse, not to command or invoke, but with the humble yearning of faith.

> So long thy pow'r hath blest me, sure it still
> Will lead me on
> O'er moor and fen, o'er crag and torrent, till
> The night is gone.

Then, even more softly, but with growing surety she added:

> And with the morn, those angel faces smile,
> Which I have loved long since, and lost awhile.

FOURTEEN

Gray fog hung low all around their camp, and the fire had smoldered to nearly nothing. Cool, moist air filled her lungs as Callie sat up, breathing deeply in the absolute stillness before sunrise. Somewhere in the back of her memory, the clear timbre of a violin rolled on and on, with meaning unspoken, yet intrinsic in the notes: " . . . So long thy pow'r hath blest me, sure it still will lead me on . . ."

Rising quietly, so as not to disturb Susa, she walked a few paces away and dropped on her knees in silent prayer. Then she returned to build up the fire, hoping to radiate enough warmth to drive away the mist. She bunched up a handful of grass, rubbing it against her skirt and putting it near the embers to evaporate some of its moisture. As she was searching for some relatively dry twigs, she recalled a story one of the missionaries had told her.

He had described how Joseph Smith needed help in getting to town to accomplish some task that lay before him. She could not recall exactly what the situation was, but she clearly remembered that he needed a horse. She also remembered that he prayed for one and then went about his work, fully expecting the animal's arrival. She pressed her handful of grass against the coals and watched gray smoke seep through, curling upward. *That must be perfect faith,* she thought as she blew gently, until tiny orange flames sprang up, *to simply get up and go on without doubts.* Best of all, she recalled, the horse had arrived that same morning, ready for use, just as Joseph had asked.

She snapped the bundle of twigs and sticks she'd gathered into tiny pieces and slowly fed them to the fire, building up a golden blaze. Then she rose and went down to the river for a drink. She found a shallow spot where the current eddied away from the main stream. Already, early sunlight seemed to be burning off the morning fog; but mist rose more thickly from the water in this spot, and it carried the strange pungent sulphur smell she'd noticed the day before. A whitish-yellowish mineral deposit was crusted on the rocks where they were partially submerged in the water. She pulled up one sleeve and dipped her hand curiously into the river, only to jerk it out again with surprise! Warm—the water here was warm! Yesterday, in her frantic concern over Susa, she'd thought the sensation of warm water was merely the result of her slipping senses. But now, now she was sure. This water was really warm.

Callie had heard of such things, where the water was heated deep in the ground. She knew that there were places, like the spas and baths in Germany, that claimed their water contained healing minerals.

Gleefully, she pulled up her other sleeve and plunged both hands into the water, scouring them with sand from the bottom of the pool. She tossed back her wrap and splashed water onto her neck, scrubbing and rinsing as she hadn't done in weeks. Callie drank deeply of the smelly stuff, thanking the Lord for her good fortune.

Turning, she started back to camp to get the pot and fetch water for washing Susa. But as she turned into the bushes again, something caught her eye. Something purple and round was hanging heavy on the underside of the bushes upriver. Plums! She pulled one, sending bright drops of dew flying up from the branch as it recoiled. When she bit into it, her mouth puckered at the sweet-sour taste. She held it in her teeth, sucking the juice and eagerly pulling off another. Then another and another—the dewdrops caught the sun, sparkled, and pattered around her as she plucked plums until her apron was full.

Running to the water, she dropped her cache into the quiet pool, penned it in with a circle of rocks, and then ran crashing through the bushes back to camp. "Duncan! Jamie! Wake yourselves!" she called, her voice singing out with joy into the clean light of morning. She grabbed up the kettle and her broken knife and started back toward the river. "I'm fixing a fine breakfast for you," she announced, pausing to look back, "but you must follow me down here and wash first."

Jamie yawned and stood up. "Hear that?" He said, pulling the cover off his brother and folding it. "Ye'd better be up, Master Duncan, and washin' thet handsome face o' yours! Y' never know what splendid person we'll be meetin' in th' wilderness t'day!"

Callie didn't pause to care about his joke. She could hear Duncan whine, "Aw, Jamie, give the blanket back!" as she hurried toward her supply of fruit.

Washing half the plums, she cut them deftly in two and dropped them into the pan on top of the cornmeal residue. Then she scooped water in and hurried back to the fire. Halfway there, she met Jamie coming toward her, still carrying the blanket Duncan wanted.

"Good morning, Son," she smiled. "That steaming pool right there has fine warm water for you." He crinkled up his nose good-naturedly. "Don't mind the smell," she grinned. "Just put your face in it and get clean."

"Come now, Duncan," she said, striding back into camp, where the boy was still curled in a ball, half-asleep and grumbling at his brother. "Stop that noise if you're wanting any of my plum pudding."

At these words, Duncan sat up, cast an astonished smile toward his mother, and ran down the path after Jamie.

Callie steadied the pot on some rocks beside the flames, then turned to examine Susa. "A drink?" the little girl asked, stirring when her mother brushed her hair back from her face. "Please, Mum?"

Callie's heart soared at the words. Susa was weak and pale, and on the side of her head a great bruised knot had swollen up, reddish and crusted with dried blood. But she was speaking again.

"A drink you shall have!" Callie smiled and kissed her daughter's cheek. "And plum pudding, too! All you can eat of it."

Turning away, she searched for something in which to carry a drink to Susa. Even at the same moment as her joy leaped at hearing her daughter speak again, the gravity of their situation pressed down on her. There was no way the child could go on. She would not be able to walk much for days, and autumn was settling in. The morning mist and nighttime cold were sure signs that she couldn't afford to wait in this quiet oasis, to drink the warm water and eat the plums. She needed a horse to carry the child, and she needed to hurry west.

"How's the Button?" James asked, strolling back into camp and dropping an armful of sticks beside the fire.

"Better," Callie answered, smiling thanks at him for the wood. She shook the last of the flour into her pudding pot and held the empty bag out to her son. "Would you be so kind as to fill this with water for her?"

"Aye," Jamie answered as he went, and Callie bent over the pan, stirring vigorously. She hadn't realized she was singing to herself until Duncan dropped to his haunches on the other side of the fire, rubbing his hands together before the blaze.

"Aren't those the words of 'The Pillar in the Cloud,' Mum? I thought 'twas only a poem."

"Yes, Duncan. But poems set to music often become hymns."

"I like it," he said, pushing a stick further into the flames. "Especially that part you were just singing about the angel faces that smile."

Callie went on stirring the pudding, all wrapped up in concentration so as not to betray the deep emotion behind her own meaning for those lines.

"Wasn't it written by some popish fellow?" Duncan continued amiably.

"Yes, but there's no false doctrine I can see in it. 'Twould please me if you'd learn it all."

"Then sing again, will you? I'll listen closer this time."

Callie grinned. Oh, he'd get it quickly, right enough. She'd only have to sing it two or three times before he'd have all the words. "Lead kindly light amid the encircling gloom, Lead thou me on . . ."

Her voice carried the words; her hands stirred the thin pudding, and she allowed thoughts of her precocious boy to run on. He was so bright and quick to learn. When they arrived in Salt Lake City, she'd put him in a top-notch school. Maybe she could find him a benefactor. He could study law, or perhaps medicine. She'd—

"Smells good!" James said, bursting back into camp. "Here's th' water for Susa. It took a bit o' time 'cause I rinsed th' bag so th' water would be clean."

"Thank you, Jamie," Callie said, handing the stick she'd been stirring with over to Duncan and taking the dripping flour sack. "After breakfast, I'd like you to help me move camp over there, under that cottonwood tree. It's not so low in that spot, and the mists won't hang there as heavily at night."

Softly, in a confidential tone, Jamie asked, "Are we staying put today because o' th' Sabbath or because o' Susa? How bad is she?"

The Sabbath! Callie realized that with all that had happened, she'd forgotten the day. "Because it's the Lord's day, Jamie," she answered.

He stared at her perceptively with something close to hurt in his eyes, and she realized that he knew better. Annoyed that she couldn't keep anything from him, she added, "But also because of your sister. Susa took a serious hit to her head."

"I saw th' knot," he answered. "And I'm wondering if I ought t' gather a woodpile for several days. She won' be walkin' soon."

Callie drew a deep breath, at once exasperated and somewhat gratified by the responsible tone behind his words. "Listen, Son. I'm praying for a horse." She hadn't actually done so yet, but in that moment she decided she would. "And I'm looking for one to come. That's how we'll keep moving."

James cocked one eyebrow at her words—looking for a horse to come wandering along in this wilderness?—but he respectfully kept a straight face. "Aye, Mum," he answered seriously, "then I'll be prayin', too." He looked off toward the river. "Suspect I'll catch a mess o' fish later. It won' be takin' me too long to fetch wood enou' for one day."

"Make it two or three," Callie answered. "But remember, 'tis the Sabbath. We've got scripture reading to do." She pulled her handkerchief from her sleeve and moved closer to Susa. Dipping it into the flour sack, she moistened her daughter's forehead. "Can you sit up and drink a bit of this, Chickadee?"

She'd just finished washing Susa when Duncan called out, "Puddin's thick! Can we eat it now? Please, Mum?"

Susa ate only a little, complaining that her belly ached, but the boys virtually inhaled most of what was left. Callie stewed some more plums to finish off the rest of her own hunger, as well as the boys'.

Later, she held a Sunday service, read Ether's great passages on faith from the Book of Mormon, and sang hymns with the boys. In the warmest part of the day, she moved their camp to the higher ground beneath the largest cottonwood tree. The spot was quite near the river, yet screened on all sides by willow and plum bushes so that they couldn't be seen from far off.

She sorely missed the presence of her gun, feeling even more vulnerable than before. Although she sent Duncan and

Jamie several times to search for it along the riverbank, and even dared to wade back out into the river herself, no trace of it could be found.

Five times, Callie went alone into the bushes and prayed specifically for a horse, explaining her need and even walking around to be sure one wasn't somewhere in the undergrowth along the river. She asked anxiously for a gun, too—any gun! Some sort of weapon was necessary to obtain food. And when Susa began to moan and fuss, she prayed a blessing on her daughter.

Susa had slept most of the day away, periodically waking to retch up whatever bits of food or liquid she'd managed to swallow. So Callie sat up with her through all the long, restless night. She held the aching, bruised head in her lap and stroked the ends of the child's flaxen hair while singing her favorite nursery songs. The events of the night before had lifted her lonely desperation and made her heart lighter during the day. New energy and peace had made her worries more bearable, though no less real. There was a definite relief in knowing that she did not have to force this odyssey through alone. Callie had resolved to trust her "kindly light," letting it take responsibility for the outcome.

But that small taste of peace and companionship had left her hungry for more. She couldn't keep from imagining the singing of a violin, the brogue-thick lilt of Angus's dear voice, the awesome golden light. It was just as well that she didn't have to try to find sleep, Callie told herself, looking tenderly down on Susa's tiny features. She'd tucked her broken knife into her apron tie, but it didn't do much to appease the defenseless feeling that accompanied the loss of her rifle, nor the silence of the uncertain darkness around them.

With morning's light, Susa asked again for water. So Callie rose, stretched, and went to fetch some that was fresh. She was still groggy and half-awake as she walked into the mist that had risen off the river again and settled along the bottoms.

Callie was praying as she went among the willows and plum-bracken, reminding the Lord that she desperately needed a horse, not to mention a weapon for protection and obtaining food. Her faith had not diminished, but unlike her prayers of earlier days, there was less demand and more petition. "I cannot stay here, and without a means of carrying Susa I cannot go on . . ."

Suddenly Callie stopped. Clamping her mouth shut hard on a scream, she clutched at the broken blade tucked into her apron strings and stared. A form was coming toward her in the mist—not a deer nor an antelope, but surely four-legged. The creature was light gray, or rather smudgy-white, almost as if it were materializing right out of the fog. It moved aimlessly toward her, making animal noises in the bracken. And the smell . . . yes! Callie had never thought she'd be so overjoyed to catch the familiar, warm scent of horse.

Without a thought for lurking savages or the origins of the beast, Callie hurried forward. Here was her horse! The one she'd asked for, the one the Lord had sent! And it seemed not the least bit afraid as she held her hand out and clicked her tongue against the roof of her mouth in a friendly way. "Come, fellow," she murmured. "Sweet fellow."

Callie moved slowly forward through the fog, one palm outstretched in greeting, the other resting on her knife, all her faculties bent on not startling this heaven-sent gift. It was standing about six feet away, above her on a misty embankment. She looked straight into its eyes as she reached a hand up, ready to knot her fingers in its mane. Only then did Callie realize something was tied to its back. Something brown and ungainly, something slumping off the far side.

Determined to grip that mount and never let go, Callie kept moving forward even as her mind began to recognize the shape of a moccasined foot dangling beyond the withers nearest her. She ignored the flashing thought that it might be a trap. She'd prayed this horse here, and it was hers. Her heart jerked within her throat, and her breathing stopped entirely, but she continued moving forward until her fingertips sank into the coarse hair of the pony's mane.

The dark form on its back did not move. Callie put her other hand up to be smelled and then nuzzled, as she peered across the pony's neck at the slumping savage. He was obviously wounded and apparently unconscious. She could see that he had tied himself on in a lying forward position, with a piece of white man's cloth, probably the ruins of someone's workshirt. One hand hung limply, and the other was tangled in the same mane as her tenacious fingers. His head drooped so that she couldn't see his face, but blood had clearly run from his chest down the horse's withers and foreleg.

He was armed to the teeth, she noticed grimly. There were feathers tied in his hair, and a scalp dangled from his belt. Knotted into the pony's mane were not only Indian scalps but white men's.

Maybe he's dead, she thought hopefully. But at this close proximity she could see his back moving up and down in unmistakable, shallow breaths.

Behind the initial wave of fear, Callie's first impulse was victorious revenge. Something sweetly exuberant rose inside of her at the sight of a red savage devastated and defenseless. Still keeping one fist clenched in the pony's mane, she let go of the knife and picked up a stick with her other hand. He was close enough for her to touch, but she used the stick to poke him. "Hey!" she said. "Hey, you!"

The savage groaned. He lifted his head and his eyes fluttered open, struggling to focus.

"Hey!" she repeated, poking him again. She wanted to see just how dangerous he was and prayed he would be too weak to respond.

The redskin's vision fused for an instant, and he swept his gaze across her and then looked beyond as if ascertaining where he was. He wasn't afraid of her at all, she thought, and the fact was an irritating surprise. Callie dropped the stick and pulled the broken knife from her apron strings. Didn't he know she was going to have his precious horse?

Gritting her teeth to steady herself and not moving an inch closer than necessary, Callie stretched out her hand and cut away the ragged piece of broadcloth that bound him to his mount's back. Then, firmly, she tugged on the thick mane until the pony took a step forward. Even that slight movement was too much, and the wounded savage slid heavily to the ground. He landed with a grunt, rolling onto his back.

Callie intended to leave him there. He would die soon enough in his condition. She clucked again to the pony, pulling him away toward camp.

But then she stopped. The brute was fully armed, and she had lost her gun. She'd seen a lance thrust through the same cloth he'd used to tie himself on. Perhaps he carried a better knife among his things. She turned and looked back. The heathen was lying where he'd fallen in the mud, staring at her, too stupid even to be afraid. Again she felt indignation rise within her. Visions of the massacre leaped distinctly before her eyes. "Serves him right," she said aloud. "Murderer."

Callie could feel her mouth begin working as an intense desire rose within her to spit right into the audacious paint-smeared face. That would be merely trifling justice for the atrocities his kind had inflicted.

But she held herself in check, only glaring, not spitting into his dark, emotionless eyes. The wilderness had not got such a hold on her yet—at least not such a hold as would make her forget she was a lady, a civilized Englishwoman who would never stoop to spitting, even on this savage. Never!

The question was, what *would* she do with him?

F I F T E E N

"Mother!"

Callie jumped. She had no idea how long she'd been standing there, glaring down at the wounded savage.

"Susa's asking for ye, Mother!" James called.

"Do what you can for her, but *don't* leave camp," Callie answered, turning her head partway to call over her shoulder, without ever taking her eyes off the redskin. "I'm going to be a minute."

What would she do with him? The lance was partially beneath his fallen body, and his knife was thrust in a sheath at his waist. She wanted these, needed them. A heavy, hairy hide that had been beneath him on his horse had slid off with him when he fell. She could use that, too, as well as the beaded leather bag that had remained hanging around the horse's neck when its rider had fallen.

The redskin continued to keep his eyes fastened on her. They were hazy and weak with loss of blood, but she could see no fear. That continued to rankle her, upset her thoughts. Callie wanted to leave him there; he would obviously die soon if left alone. She knew it—why didn't he? Why didn't he understand that she had taken his horse with its pack and that she could take his weapons, too? She could take them, and she would, along with that dark, hairy robe whose warmth Susa so desperately needed.

Her mind never once equated taking his things with stealing; she was taking back a few necessities from maggots that had robbed the very lifeblood of her family. She was sure he understood it, too. And, being literate as she was, she knew the law. Had the army been there, it would have been on her side. So was God, obviously, since this was an exact answer to her prayer.

Suddenly it struck Callie why he wasn't afraid. The answer was so plain! He'd recognized her at once for what she was, a representative of civilization. He was expecting mercy from her—counting on it, obviously.

Callie looked, grimacing, at the scalps knotted into the mane of her pony, and then looked quickly back at the savage. Perhaps he knew the teachings of Jesus Christ, she thought suddenly. What if he'd learned that Christ taught men to love their enemies? Naturally, he wasn't capable of such noble virtues, but what if he expected them from her? What if he knew her moral code, even while she was taking his weapons and turning her back to walk away?

That thought brought another wave of the same sweet exhilaration she'd felt when she'd discovered his vulnerability. But with it came an obligation to live what she professed, to represent civilization and Christianity as she knew them. Next to revenge, the tugging of conscience left an aftertaste in her mouth, a pinched, angry feeling inside her. Callie knew what she must do.

But only until she reached help, she insisted. That was more than anyone could expect. She would leave him with the first authorities who would make him stand trial and pay for his atrocities.

"Jamie!" Callie called. "Come here. Duncan, you stay beside Susa. Don't move until I say—understand?"

"Yes, Mother," the younger boy answered back.

She could already hear Jamie plunging through the misty bushes. "Mum?"

"Here, Jamie," Callie said, "we need to tether this horse. Bring me your blanket and the rope."

"Aye!" Jamie answered, exuberant over the discovery of a

horse. "Your prayer, it's—" His words were cut off abruptly when his gaze followed his mother's and he saw the fallen Indian.

"Go on, Jamie. Be quick about it," she commanded curtly.

He hurried back into the bracken and returned almost at once with his torn blanket and the rope. Taking the rope, she cut it in half, tied one half around the pony's neck, and tethered the pony to a tree. Then she took the other half of rope and looped it purposefully in her hand.

"Did ye kill him? Is he alone?"

"I'm certain he's alone. He came in this pitiful condition, having tied himself to stay on his horse." The hard sound of her own voice amazed Callie, as did the insight of Jamie's next question.

"D'ye suppose he was tryin' t' get here, to th' warm water? He's wounded. Maybe he thought this place could heal him."

"Perhaps," Callie said, remembering how he'd looked past her, as if taking his bearings. She hoped he wasn't seeking more of his kind in this vicinity. Callie took the blanket and dropped it on the ground. Handing her stick to Jamie, she announced, "I'll be tieing him up now, and I want you to stand over him. Not too close, mind, but near enough to strike him hard with this."

"I won' let him hurt ye," Jamie said in a grown voice. "But I'm wishin' we had th' gun."

Callie noticed her hands were shaking, and not wanting Jamie to see, she stepped briskly forward. She rolled the savage over on his back with the toe of her boot. He made no move to resist when she grabbed his wrists and tied them together, trussing him up like a pig going to market. Then she snatched the knife from his waist and tucked its blade beneath her own apron string. "There!" Callie concluded, dusting her palms off with finality, as if she'd managed to tie and disarm a vigorous, strong man.

"Are we takin' him t' camp?"

"Yes, but he can't walk. We'll put him on that blanket of yours and drag him back. That way it won't damage this heavy hide."

Jamie's eyes were huge circles in his hungry face, but his mind was quick and he was alert with the stick. "What'll we do wi' him?"

"Turn him over to the authorities, as soon as we find some. He's a brutal murderer."

Callie fought the tiredness that wrapped itself around her in the rays of the warm sun. Susa was napping. The heathen was teetering in and out of consciousness. Her boys had gone down to the river to catch fish for supper. It made her nervous to have them go, of course. She was even worried about having them stray into the bushes to relieve themselves. What if this brute had been attempting some sort of rendezvous with comrades near this place?

Callie glared at his still form, unable to guess his age. His skin was smooth, unbroken by whiskers or hair upon the chest. And in that way he seemed almost boyish to her. Yet, time had worn creases into his forehead above the black, heavy brows. When he was coherent, his dark eyes revealed an unmistakable depth of experience, the result of passing of years, and, she reluctantly admitted, a surety of purpose—or at least a lack of fear—that left her trembling.

He wore a leather breechclout and fringed leg-coverings suspended by a thong. Hiding his wound was a long leather shirt reaching halfway to his knees, and on top of that was a breastplate made of long white beads—bone, she supposed. His moccasins were ankle-high, made all of one piece of leather and decorated with trade beads. On his head was a circular patch of something that stuck straight up, black like his own hair, but she felt certain it was not human. She wondered absently what it was, though her curiosity was not strong enough to make her venture near him. Through that headdress, whatever it was, ran a large feather, sticking out horizontally from his topknot. On the left-hand side was the feathered end, with the flanges trimmed in a strange, angular way. And the quill end protruded from the right-hand side, with a smaller, pure white feather dangling by a fine thong at the tip.

Beneath this headdress, his straight black hair was pulled into two braids, each wrapped in buckskin strips and colored with brilliant vermilion. Around his eyes he'd painted a mask of the same vermilion-red on one side, eerie white on the other. It was an altogether brutal sight, and she turned her face away.

The lance felt firm, solid in her hands. For the hundredth time, Callie offered a silent prayer of thanks. It didn't give her as much courage as the gun, but it was better than a plain stick. The shaft was made of hardwood bound with strips of leather, including a thicker binding for the handgrip that was polished by use. The stone point had been chipped evenly from a piece of flint. She ventured a finger along its edge, then jerked her hand back, a tiny ribbon of blood seeping from the tip of her finger. How, she wondered, could that ignorant person achieve such keen workmanship? Immediately she answered herself that savages, by their nature, were skilled in murder and plunder and whatever it took to accomplish those ends.

Callie noted that the stone tip was secured tightly by bands of leather and sinew and at the base of these dangled a thin lock of black hair and two more cropped feathers with white and black tips like the one in his headdress.

Impulsively, she reached out her hand to pull these off. Then, discovering how securely they were fastened, she pulled his knife from its sheath.

It was a steel knife of standard design: familiar because it had been made by a blacksmith with the white man's understanding of metal. The blade was strong and sharp, honed with obvious care, and clean. Lifting the point, Callie began forcing it beneath the sinews that held the hair and feathers on the lance.

She glanced at the heathen's face a moment to see if her cutting would upset him, but he watched her, impassive. Callie hesitated again, considering. If she were going to use this lance, she would have to get rid of those barbaric talismans dangling from it. On the other hand, she had purposely left the scalps tied in the pony's mane as proof of its former owner's crimes. Perhaps this, too, would turn out to be some sort of court evidence. She glared at the ghastly thing but refused to do anything that might shorten her prisoner's sentence. With an air of terse finality, Callie knotted the hair so it wouldn't brush against her hand.

Then replacing the knife at her waist, Callie looked off toward the plum bushes where her new horse was browsing. She'd left the scalps in his mane, it was true, but she'd had no patience with the war paint and the way his tail was tied up. After cutting the leather thong around his tail—Jamie had been standing over the bound Indian all the time with a big stick—Callie had hurriedly led her new mount down to the river's edge. On his right shoulder and left rump were the gruesomely distorted prints of the savage's hand, streaked as if the fingers had been dragged across the hide and then, without ever lifting it up, the palm had been clapped down hard. It looked violent to her, in the color of blood, and she'd wasted no time scrubbing sand and water over the pony's hide until all the vermilion paint washed downriver.

Then, standing right there in the edge of the water, Callie had raised her eyes heavenward and asked the Lord to bless her with competence and insight to care for this horse. She told the Lord that she was going to call him Cyrus, after the Old Testament king who'd allowed the Jews return to Jerusalem out of Babylon. And then she'd solemnly dedicated Cyrus to the purpose of carrying her children to Zion.

Callie looked at Cyrus now, cropping green leaves and

grass. A year ago, this mangy creature wouldn't have amounted to much in her eyes. She hadn't been trained in horseflesh, but even she noticed the wild eyes and lack of familiar discipline, the untrimmed hooves, and the potbelly of a horse fed only grass. Cyrus's mottled, smudgy color didn't reflect what little she knew of careful breeding, either. His chest was narrow, his rump small, and his legs short. Yet, even as her eyes took in these characteristics, her gaze betrayed greater veneration than she would have had for the finest equine specimen on earth. This horse was her answer to prayer, and that made everything about him beautiful.

Now that he was here, Callie intended to stay only another day or two. Surely Susa would be able to sit upright for a little while by then. In the meantime, she and Cyrus would take the lance and try to obtain more food.

"Mum?" Susa stirred, whimpering as she turned.

"Here, love," Callie said, quickly dipping a scrap of blanket in the kettle of water and wiping Susa's forehead with it. At least she was keeping water down now. "How about a drink?"

Susa's blue eyes fluttered open, and she gazed up into her mother's face. Carefully, Callie helped her into a sitting position, bracing her arm as a backrest for her daughter. Then she pillowed Susa's head in her lap and sang softly to her, gently stroking her temples, combing the pale blonde hair with her fingers.

> The Lord my pasture will prepare,
> And feed me with a shepherd's care.
> His presence will my wants supply,
> And guard me with a watchful eye.
> My noonday walks He will attend,
> And all my silent midnight hours defend.
> When in the sultry glebe I faint,
> Or on the thirsty mountain pant,
> To fertile vales and—

"Look!" Duncan shouted, running into camp with James striding close behind him.

The Indian jerked, coming back to consciousness suddenly, but then he lay still once more, his dark eyes searching the boys. Callie jumped, too, first at Duncan's shout and then because the savage had moved so suddenly. Her grip was knuckle-white on the lance, but she recovered herself.

"Look! You'll never believe it, Mum! I caught this one just as the other was biting his tail!" He held out two good-sized fish for her to see, the first one's tail having been stuffed in the other one's mouth.

"Why, Duncan," she smiled, "what a clever boy you are!" And then she winked at Jamie.

"Aye, clever," he said, his voice dripping sarcasm. "Crafty and witty as th' day is long."

"Don't mind him," Duncan announced, leaning over Susa with the fish. "Have you ever seen anything like it, Susa?"

The corners of Susa's lips curled faintly upward, but she turned her head away.

"Look at this," he coaxed, pulling the fish apart and rhythmically squeezing the larger one's jaw so that it opened and closed its teeth and its eyes bulged.

"She's not up to your fun," Callie advised, pushing him back gently.

"Here's th' third one," Jamie said, "an' I found a few more plums for th' Button. Seems we've nearly eaten them all."

"Thank you, boys," Callie said, hiding her disappointment that the entire afternoon's effort had yielded no more than one scant meal.

"Put the fish here in the kettle, and I'll cook them up soon. Maybe we should look in that first." She gestured toward the large, beaded leather bag, hoping there would be something worth eating among the savage's provisions. But not knowing what she'd find, Callie didn't dare suggest her purpose aloud.

"What's this?" Duncan asked, picking up a piece of gear

she had dropped near the leather bag when she'd unloaded Cyrus.

"His shield," James answered, showing Duncan how a warrior's arm could fit through the bands on the back.

Duncan's hand traced the design of triangles that circled the outside in that same vermilion-red with which the savage had marked himself and his pony. "This is swell," he breathed. "Can I have it, Mum?"

Callie cared nothing for the shield, with its primitive, geometric designs dyed into the leather and stretched over a round frame. She was beginning to say so when Duncan shoved it up close beneath her chin.

"What d'you think these are?" he asked, pointing to three stylized creatures at the center. "Can I have it? Do you suppose he painted them himself, Mum? What are they?"

"Stags, Duncan," Callie said with careful control, pushing the thing out of her face. "Probably some superstitious hunting charm."

"Aye, Dunc," James agreed, bending to look at it. "He's painted 'em. Look at th' size o' their antlers. First-rate, eh?" He reached out and rapped the leather with his knuckles. Duncan answered smartly, and they were off dueling one another, testing the shield in giggly, boyish fashion.

Callie sighed and then watched her captive closely for a moment. His lids were half open, his eyes observing their play with his shield, but she couldn't see any signs of anger in his face. Not that he looked pleased—he simply didn't reveal anything. *Well,* she thought, *it suits him right to have them play with it. He won't be needing it anymore, anyway.*

Sliding Susa's head from her lap, Callie reached over to the beaded leather bag. She'd had the foresight to wash the hide at the same time she'd washed Cyrus. It was a huge thing, with the hair still on one side, and she'd decided it must have been from a buffalo. She hadn't wanted to wrap her daughter in lice—not that she'd seen any, but why take chances? Since it was hardly showing any signs of getting drier, and the sun's intensity had begun to fade with the approach of evening, Callie pulled it from the bushes where it was spread. Stoking up the fire, she used sticks to prop the hide nearby, hoping to speed its drying. She wished it could be ready today; then Susa would have enjoyed a good night's rest, rolled up in the warmest thing possible.

"Keep back from Susa," she reminded the tussling boys. "And *him*."

Then she bent and peered into the beaded leather bag. Hanging at its side was a waterskin made of an animal bladder. Probably buffalo, she reasoned half with disgust and half with interest in its manufacture. With more of these, she could set off away from the river and travel cross-country, making a dry camp when necessary.

Loosening the drawstring as suspiciously as if a rattlesnake might be lurking inside, Callie peered into the bag. Dark strips of dry meat lay in it, as well as sausagelike tubes. They appeared to be entrails stuffed in the German fashion with some sort of mixture. The boys had quit their rambunctious play and come to stand over her, watching. Callie glanced up at the savage and then cut off one of the tips of the sausage and smelled. She knew he was watching her, knew the boys were, too, but no decency of civilization could keep her from making a face. The odor was obnoxious. Fat, berries, and meat had been stuffed in there and kept for some time.

Disappointed, she crammed the sausages back into the bag. She'd hoped to boil some with the fish for dinner, but not now.

"We'll hold those back, boys," she told them, summoning a smile to replace the grimace that had taken over her face. "A last resort, you know." She wasn't entirely sure it was food.

"What about that dried meat, Mum? D'ye suppose a broth o' that'd be nourishin' for Susa?"

Callie's stomach turned over fiercely, asserting the reality of just how famished they all were. She couldn't afford to be choosy. "Jamie," she ordered, "take this knife," handing him the broken one in her apron pocket, "and go sharpen some green willow sticks. Duncan, put the fish over there in the grass and fill our pan with water."

Callie reached into the pack and pulled out a large handful of the dried, twisted strips of meat. "'Twill do us all a bit of good to drink the broth of this," she muttered. Grabbing some sticks, she built up the fire and placed the meat in the water Duncan had brought.

"Now, Son," she told him, "give this to our guest." Callie handed Duncan the waterskin and one of the sausages. She wanted to watch the savage, to see just how much of the concoction he ate and if he had any special method for getting it down.

Duncan looked at her, surprised, as if waiting for her to change her mind.

"How's he going t' eat wi' his hands tied, Mum?" Jamie asked from where he sat, whittling points on three sticks. Callie didn't answer right away, and James twisted the largest end of the stick into the ground. He skewered the fish so the willow rod bent nicely, the slight weight of the meat causing it to lean over the blaze.

"I'll . . . I'll untie him," Callie announced at last. Grabbing up the lance, she crossed the camp determinedly and stood over her prisoner. "He won't ever be able to face the demands of justice if he starves." She glared down at him for a moment, her scowl conveying the fiercest warning she could muster. And she wished with all her heart that he'd wince, even just a little.

S I X T E E N

The savage neither cringed nor made any other move. When she untied his hands, he didn't even seem to care to rub at the red marks her rope had made on his wrists. Callie promised herself she wouldn't tie him up quite so tightly next time. He hadn't struggled at all.

Duncan set the sausage and waterskin on the torn blanket where the redskin had lain all day. Then he hurried away, trying not to show his eagerness to get to the other side of the fire. Callie watched her son out of the corner of her eye, amused by his forced bravado yet glad he was wary. She noticed that James still clutched the broken knife, but the Indian did nothing suspicious. As he reached falteringly for the water, Callie caught her breath. Fresh blood stained the blanket beneath him. He could hardly move!

How had she forgotten this man had fallen from his horse? How had her fear of him blinded her so much? She hadn't given him a drink all day!

"Jamie!" She spoke only the one word but it contained a legion of command. Her son stepped closer, broken knife at the ready. Callie laid the lance on the ground and knelt beside the savage's head. Her breath would not come; her heart pounded, screaming against her chest. *Help me, Father!* she pled.

She slid one hand beneath his braids and lifted his head. He did not look at her now but concentrated on the waterskin, watching as she lifted it to his lips. A sizable portion dribbled down his chin and fell away, but the savage swallowed weakly.

Then again. He breathed, and each breath seemed to catch and hurt inside him.

After another drink, she laid him against the bloody blanket with a soft touch. Stepping back, Callie stood looking down on her prisoner again for several minutes. Then she replaced the sausage in the bag with the others and started making broth. Although she kept the lance nearby while she worked, she did not tie up the Indian right away.

Handing Duncan her tattered handkerchief, she sent him to moisten it in the warm water at the pool. She also told him to change the contents in the savage's waterskin for fresh water from the mineral pool. After she had nourished the Indian with broth, she intended to pull back that breastplate and take a look at his injury.

There was no compromise in tending his wounds, Callie told herself. She would have done the same for any dog she found, hurt and howling in the road.

Callie stirred the broth, glad to see that the savage had fallen asleep again, relieved that his eyes no longer followed her. Although the dried meat was unsalted, it possessed a hearty red flavor they'd all missed. Once she and the boys finished the fish and chewed the broth's water-softened chunks of dried meat that were too big for the invalids, Callie braced Susa's back and spoon-fed her the hot liquid.

True to her intention, Callie nursed her prisoner, dribbling broth into his barely responsive mouth. He made no effort to thank her but continued to watch her movements with emotionless eyes. Even when she lifted his beaded breastplate and glowered at the bloody leather shirt beneath it, he made no attempt to communicate. So she removed it. Then, using her new knife, she slit the lacings that formed the side seam of his long-sleeved tunic-like shirt. Then, seeing the extent of his bleeding, she continued to cut the lacings that ran in and out of small awl-holes until she could pull the entire shirt off. It caught on something at his neck, a small bag on a leather thong. She cut that, too.

Callie gasped involuntarily at the sight of the redskin's wound. His chest had a bullet hole not much bigger around than her little finger. Fresh blood seeped steadily along its periphery. His back, where the bullet had exited, was a bloody tangle of ragged flesh. The blanket on which she'd dragged him to the campsite was soaked with blood from his shoulder. Although she did not think any of his vital organs had been damaged, it appeared the bullet had entered his chest, torn up the flesh between his ribs, and glanced off the shoulder blade as it exited. The bullet's course had not been a fatal one, but without care the savage would certainly die. Proof of his peril oozed steadily from the grizzled injury before her eyes.

By the fading light she did her best to wash the blood away. Would he ever make a sign of thanks or cry out against the pain? He hardly seemed human!

The evening was silent except for the savage's raspy breathing and the sound of the water as Callie cleansed his wounds, rinsing her handkerchief in the kettle and swabbing at him again and again. The boys sat quietly on their bedding, watching her efforts. Susa continued to doze.

Cleaning away the blood was a losing battle because new flowed in as she wiped off the old. There was some coagulation along the edges, but free flow persisted from inside his chest. The nighttime chill was beginning to settle over them, but Callie did not bind the wounds because she hadn't any rags or blanket scraps to part with. She did fold the blood-soaked portion of his blanket away, sliding the torn remains of the broadcloth shirt he'd had beneath him.

Callie stood and straightened her back. After tossing the panful of bloody water into the bushes, she turned. "Jamie, you and Duncan take Cyrus down to the river for a drink. Then I think you boys had better get some rest."

Obediently they wandered into the bushes while Callie settled herself to mending the tears and holes in her skirt for the first time since the river crossing. She was just finishing this task when the boys returned, said their prayers, and crawled into their blanket. She checked to see how well Jamie had tethered the pony, then read to them for a while from the Book of Mormon. At the end of the sixth chapter, Callie sighed, made her daily charcoal mark inside the back cover, and put the book into her pack. The boys had long since fallen asleep.

She sat alone in the firelight, the lance across her lap, staring at the redskin. Relaxed sleep had become almost foreign to her, an impossible luxury, though her mind and body ached with exhaustion.

Sounds of the night closed in behind the darkness. Coyotes yipped and whined further upriver. Susa gave a muffled sigh and rolled to her side. Callie hoped that tonight she would rest well; there had been several signs of improvement in her condition during the day. Cyrus's stamping nearby in the darkness was a peaceful, reassuring thing. But the presence of Cyrus's former owner was more upsetting than the pony was comforting.

Maybe he'll die before morning, Callie thought, eager at the convenience of this possibility. Then she wouldn't have to face the question of what to do with him.

Back home, she'd have been embarrassed to have anyone know the frank callousness of her deliberations. But she admitted to herself that being so much alone in the agonies of this raw place had led her to base practicality and mental candor that would at one time have shocked her. In Yorkshire she'd never have had to deal with a problem like this.

She couldn't kill him, or leave him, which was the same thing. But she must have his horse. Cyrus *was* hers. She'd prayed him there. So the only simple solution was for the savage to die quietly on his own. Callie considered magnanimously praying for the Lord to spare this poor creature from lingering in pain. But something inside her—something born of conscience and that same frank wilderness honesty—told Callie that her motives for such a prayer weren't altogether selfless and were better left alone.

She sat there for a long, long time, staring at him. In spite of his wounded condition, the savage made Callie too nervous to sleep deeply, though she dozed a few times, jerking awake almost before she'd lapsed into rest. She felt as if a snake had crawled into her camp.

He was weak, she knew, and probably harmless. After all, no one could fake that kind of blood loss. But Callie would not rest with a snake near her children. Until he was dead and buried, she mustn't trust him. And even then she would put long miles between herself and the savage just as fast as she could.

Loneliness followed the darkness. Callie had supposed that after the amazing night when Angus had come, coping would be easier. She'd always thought that spiritual manifestations took the pain and trouble out of life. Now she knew that wasn't necessarily true. God had the power to erase misery, but for some purpose He'd chosen to let her struggle. That was a hard thing to know. Callie's intellect reasoned that rather than eliminate trials, God often chose to strengthen her against them. But her heart cried like a child against the suffering. The blackness of night, the lonely wind, the cries of wild animals in the darkness, the horrible bleeding savage—these things composed inescapable reality.

Remembering that gold-lit night, Callie took memory as a promise and held tight. She would use its peace to rouse her courage now. She wanted the brilliant light to come again, wanted to have the warmth she'd known. How could it be summoned? More in an attitude of heart than an effort of words, Callie knelt and prayed.

The idea came to her slowly, forming itself in the back of her thoughts, even as her mind worked at other things. If she tried it, she might save the redskin's life. But she didn't want to think about that, didn't even want to entertain the notion that he might pull through. The Indian stirred on his blanket, pulling his arms around his bleeding chest in an effort to keep warm. Callie shoved two more sticks onto the fire and went back to her prayer, but the thought would not leave her alone. It was another choice—a choice she didn't want to consider, but one that was among her options. She didn't want to do it any more than she'd wanted to bring the heathen into her own camp. But, for the sake of her conscience, it slowly became the next thing she had to do.

Callie forced herself to begin singing softly and to gather the things she would need. She filled the kettle with water, as well as the waterskin. Taking the savage's cut-off leather shirt, she rinsed it in the river until the worst of the blood was gone. Then she stoked the fire into a hot blaze and propped the shirt on sticks nearby. He would need its warmth to see this night through.

She rummaged in the bushes momentarily, cutting a green willow branch slightly thicker than her thumb. He'd need this, too, long before he'd be caring about the warmth of his shirt. What else? Bandages. She would have to make some if she were going to try to save him. Reluctantly, Callie pulled up her skirt and tore two long strips from her petticoat, starting where she'd left off tearing bandages for Angus's head. She wound them up into a little ball that she thrust in her apron pocket.

"Jamie," she spoke softly, touching the boy's shoulder. "Jamie, we've a job to do."

"Eh?" the boy said, rolling out from beneath his blanket and grabbing the broken knife he'd set on the ground near his head.

"We'll be needing that," Callie pointed at the knife. She wasn't going to use the new good one; she couldn't risk damaging it in the fire.

Jamie rubbed the heel of his hand against the corner of one

eye and squinted at her. "What? Oh, this." He held the knife, handle outward, toward her. "Why?"

Callie didn't know how to answer, so she said nothing. Snatching a large stone, she placed it at the edge of the blaze and put the knife on top of it, with the broken tip pointing in.

Still standing and blinking, James faltered, "Why, Mother? What job? Is Cyrus hurt? Is he lost?"

Callie was still not sure how to answer. She dropped suddenly to her knees and began praying in a stream of quickly mumbled words. Without looking up she grabbed Jamie's pant leg and pulled him down beside her. Obediently, he clasped his hands before him and joined her, his mouth forming the words of a bewildered and rather all-inclusive prayer.

Before long she stopped, so he said amen as well. Checking the knife, she found it glowed red in places, yellow in others. "It's got to glow hotter than this," Callie announced, wrapping her fingers in her handkerchief and lifting the knife off the rock. She pushed the blade directly into the coals and stepped back.

"Jamie," she said, watching the yellow-hot metal begin to lighten even further. "It will be ready soon." When he didn't answer, she turned her gaze from the fire and looked directly into his face. "The redskin will die, you know. He's bleeding to death. But I can't face God if we haven't done everything possible to save him."

Jamie nodded, eyes wide.

"We've got to see if we can't sear his wound shut. Cauterize it."

Jamie blinked and swallowed hard.

"We'll need to tie him, now."

"Aye, Mother." His voice cracked, but Jamie moved to where she'd looped the rope.

"Help me," Callie said, picking up the five-inch willow stick and turning. She looked at the Indian then for the first time since she'd started her preparations and jumped. His eyes were following her again: dark, liquid in the firelight. She wished he were unconscious from the start.

Fighting down her own nervousness, Callie crossed his wrists and tied them together across his abdomen. Tension had once again robbed gentleness from her touch, but she gave him a swallow from the waterskin. Using her handkerchief, she and Jamie tied the stick into the savage's mouth so he wouldn't bite off his tongue. Then, wrapping her hand in her apron, Callie retrieved the knife, its blade all yellow-white hot, and stood over the Indian.

Her prisoner made no sound, but the emotionlessness of his face wavered. His eyes widened, the whites showing. His nostrils flared against uneven breathing.

Jamie bent, holding the Indian's arms, looking wide-eyed at his mother.

"Turn your head!" Callie commanded, her voice like stone. "Look away and recite."

"Uh," Jamie faltered.

"Now!"

"Uh . . . one times one is one. One times two is two. One times three is three." He felt her bend down and paused.

"Don't stop. And don't let go of him!"

"One times four is four," Jamie said more loudly, his mouth working as fast as it could go. "Five ones are five. . . ."

Callie knelt and put one hand over the savage's eyes.

"One six is six. One seven is seven. . . ."

Then she pushed the broken tip of the knife into the bullet-hole and against one side. There was a terrible hiss and the Indian's shoulders jerked. Jamie held his arms firmly; he heaved his weight forward against the Indian's arms, but the patient's whole body convulsed. Callie jumped back, pulling the hot knife away rather than burn anything besides the wound.

A sickening smell rose, and she could see sweat beading up all over the Indian's skin in the firelight. He hadn't made a sound! Callie bent again, forcing her resolve to see this through quickly. She touched the blade down again into the dark hole. The savage's muscles wrenched and then shivered spasmodically. His eyes rolled back in his head, and he went limp. She moved the knife, turning it thirty degrees to the left, working clockwise, trying not to think.

Jamie rose to his feet and crashed awkwardly into the bushes at the edge of the firelight. Callie could hear him retching, and her own nausea rose in a wave. She fought it back, drawing a deep breath, only to smell the odor of burnt flesh.

What if the savage was dead? What if the pain had killed him? Suddenly Callie, too, found herself on her knees in the bushes, the bloody knife fallen from her hand into the grass beside her.

When she returned to the firelight, James was kneeling over the Indian. She took the waterskin he held out to her and rinsed her mouth.

"Still breathing," the boy said softly.

Callie nodded, not certain whether she could trust her voice yet. Bending, she put the knife back on the fire to heat again and slumped down onto the ground.

She could hear Jamie drinking from the waterskin right beside her. She knew this must be a nightmare for him, knew she ought to say something to ease it. Her head was light, almost lifting off her shoulders, when she suddenly began to feel giddy, beyond clear-thinking control.

"Multiplication tables!" she blurted in a strange, pinched voice. "One times one is one. Two times two is . . ." she droned, throwing her arm around her son and pulling him close.

Jamie sniffled and turned a tearstained face up at her. Seeing her smile, he made a hiccoughing noise halfway between a laugh and a sob.

"Let's think of something better than arithmetic when we go back to it," she said, wiping away his tears with a shaky hand. "I dare say he won't struggle against you all that hard, now."

She hoped he could feel the pride in her voice, hoped he could see it in her eyes. Hoped that for once this wicked place wouldn't steal the evidences of her love.

Then a wave of exhaustion rolled over her, followed closely by dizziness. Forcing her energy reserves, Callie snatched the knife out of the fire and flung herself furiously back at the chore. The stench assailed her nostrils, and the sight of flesh turning black and hard beneath the knife sickened her, but she paused only to reheat the knife and to empty her belly once more.

Jamie helped her turn the savage onto his stomach. Blood welled from his back, but Callie pressed the white-hot blade into the hole with fierce determination. Though the shredded flesh of his back seemed endless, she was determined to stop every point of seepage. He might die of weakness. He might never regain consciousness. There was always the possibility of infection, but this savage wasn't going to bleed to death now. Not at her hands.

Then she wrapped him tightly, using the bandages she'd torn from her own already-shortened petticoat. When his chest was swaddled, she rolled back on her heels, waiting to see if she had succeeded, watching with pleasure when no blood oozed through.

Then Jamie helped her pull the unsewn shirt back across the savage's torso. Callie untied the gag from her patient's mouth and used her handkerchief to mop the sweat off his forehead. Impulsively, she poured more water across her handkerchief and washed the mask of war paint from around his eyes.

Wringing out her handkerchief and placing it to dry near the fire, she spoke cheerily, "Well, we're finished now. Off to bed with you, Jamie."

Gratefully, he crawled beneath his blanket. Then Callie

curled up on the ground beside Susa, the lance filling the gun's accustomed place at her side. She listened to the nighttime until Jamie's breathing slowed into a deep rhythm. And even after that, she lay for a while, feeling the stillness of the camp around her. Her contentment wasn't so much a feeling of triumph—although there was a sense of accomplishment in having finished the task—as a measure of relief, of completeness, a feeling of peace.

Callie's hollow stomach and reeling head had carried her somewhere beyond fear and pain. She lay quiet, watching the stars spin brightly above her until she slept.

SEVENTEEN

"Wake up, Mother!" Duncan insisted, shaking Callie's shoulder. "The sun's been up for the longest time. You're not sick, are you?"

Callie sat up and forced her eyes open, feeling as if gravel had been piled beneath the lids. The sun was bright and warm. Then she saw Duncan's worried face and resisted the temptation to lie back down. "What's wrong?"

"Everyone's asleep!" Duncan moaned. "I'm always the last one up, but today nobody's moved. I've already scrubbed my face. See?" He pulled down his shirt collar for her to examine the pink flesh of his neck, "And I caught a pair of breakfast fish. Susa asked for a drink, but then she went back to sleep. Jamie won't get up, and *he*—" Duncan inclined his head with significance to the Indian on the far side of the campfire—"he looks like maybe he's dead."

Callie scrambled to her feet and stood over the Indian. His color had paled, and his closed eyes had dark hollows beneath them, but she could see his chest moving in weak repetition.

"Don't worry," she said, pulling Duncan's cap off and tousling his hair. "He's not dead yet, and the rest of us are fine. Now, let's see those fish you caught."

Duncan's fish were small, but Callie praised him and then set to work skewering his catch. "Jamie," she called when the fish looked ready. "Rouse yourself, Son. You need something nourishing inside you."

"Look at Jamie!" Duncan teased his lethargic brother. "He's

as sluggish as an early-morning lizard looking for a sunny rock."

Callie had to admit the boy's eyes were only half-open.

"Yeah," Duncan went on, "he's even a little green!"

At this Callie stifled a chuckle, knowing Jamie must also have the same hollow, queasy feeling she had. But she was about to stop Duncan's joke when she saw Jamie stick out his tongue in short, flicking motions. Suddenly, he thrust out his hand and grabbed his brother's leg. The wrestle was on, the two boys tussling in the dirt at her feet.

Ten-year-old Jamie had done a man's part last night, Callie realized. And he took teasing like a man, too, but the child in him still rolled and kicked. Well, she was glad. She didn't want him growing up any faster than he must. Maybe, though, she'd take him hunting with her.

Callie was sure the dried meat in the Indian's pack had been buffalo. And Duncan had pointed out buffalo leavings in the vicinity of their camp, so she hoped she might find a herd if she took Cyrus and looked.

She realized the plan was daring—to think she and Jamie could bring down one of those immense, shaggy creatures. But it would provide rich, red meat to dry and another warm robe. Then, using a waterskin and the dried meat, she and the children could strike out more directly west, free of the river.

She rested most of the morning, cooked more broth, and cared for her patients. To her delight, Susa showed further gradual improvement, sitting up without help and showing occasional interest in what was going on around her.

Callie hovered near her most of the morning, but when the afternoon sun glowed golden and warm through the autumn-crimsoned tree leaves, she stepped over to where she'd piled the Indian's things. There was the bag of provisions, the shield she'd let her boys play with, the breastplate, the tiny bag she'd cut from the savage's neck, and his bow and arrows. Perhaps if she practiced . . . she told herself that shooting a bow couldn't be much different from shooting a gun. True, she hadn't been much of a marksman, but the quiver held several arrows. Back in the wagon train, she'd seen buffalo once before. Recalling their lumbering run, she anticipated a good chance to get off more than one shot.

Lifting the bow, she studied it a while, figuring out how an arrow fitted against the string. Then, nocking one in place, she took aim at a bush and drew back. Nothing happened. The string hardly moved; the arrow didn't launch.

Taking a deep breath, she braced her feet apart and pulled with all her might. This time the string drew back farther, but she didn't release at the right time, and the arrow swerved clumsily into the ground about three feet away.

Annoyed, Callie snatched it up from the grass and nocked it into place again. Bracing her feet once more, she gritted her teeth and pulled with all her might. This time the arrow flew five yards, but she didn't even see it. The bowstring had twanged back into place and raked her arm as it passed. Before the arrow ever hit the ground, she was on her knees in the grass, holding her forearm and fighting back tears.

Suddenly she felt the sensation of someone watching and jerked her head up. Sure enough, the heathen, his gaze weak and heavy-lidded, was staring at her again. Angrily she snatched up a rock and raised her arm to throw it at him. Then, checking herself, Callie turned, stone in hand, and stormed away into the bushes.

She walked the riverbed awhile, pretending to search for more late-season plums. And when her temper had at last cooled down, she made her way to where Cyrus was tethered. The lance would have to be her weapon; the horse would speed her search.

This time, the savage wasn't going to have the pleasure of watching her experimentation. "I'm going to look for bison," she told the children. Then she grabbed up her rope, told Jamie to keep an eye on Susa, and led Cyrus around some willows out of sight from the camp.

"Now, boy," Callie announced, rubbing his velvety nose when they were alone, "I'm told horses like to be spoken to, so I'll tell you what you must do. You've led for me well enough, but I've never straddled a horse's back before."

Cyrus smelled her, letting her stroke his nose and ears for a moment, and then he curled back his upper lip and whinnied. "Well," Callie grimaced at his yellow, grassy teeth, "I'll take that as a friendly gesture."

She led the pony to a large rock. Then, hitching her skirts high, she climbed the rock and nervously lowered herself onto his back. Cyrus sidestepped slightly, but she managed to land on top of him, although too far toward his rump. Callie dug her heels in to scoot forward, disliking the way his coarse hair poked through her clothing.

Suddenly Cyrus wheeled away from the rock, coming down straight-legged and hard. A wrenching jolt ran up through Callie's spine. On his next step, the earth rushed up to meet her.

Unsteadily she got on her feet, shaking her head to clear her vision and her mind. She grabbed the rope and tied the pony to some bushes on the other side of the rock before she climbed up. "Now," Callie said from on top of the rock, summoning her firmest, most commanding voice. "You belong to me and we are going to ride you to Zion, so stand *still!*"

Cyrus looked at her, his eyes as emotionless as his former owner's. Callie bent to lay her hands at the base of his neck again, when he shook his muscles from shoulder to rump. She drew back, surprised, and then determinedly prepared to remount as soon as the shaking stopped. Putting her hands on his back, she swung her right foot to the far side and lowered herself onto him in front of where she'd landed last time. And once more, there was no problem in that.

She could feel Cyrus breathing, his ribs moving up and

down beneath her thighs, as she clutched the Indian's leather-strap reins in her right hand. Leaning forward along his neck, Callie loosened the rope from around the bush, squeezing tightly with her feet for balance.

Again Cyrus spun abruptly to the right, coming down hard on straight legs. Again Callie skidded painfully in the dirt.

The third time she mounted, Callie was breathing heavily. Every muscle in her frame tensed as she bypassed the reins and knotted her right hand in Cyrus's mane. Her belly tightened as she braced, ready for him to spin right again. She leaned forward once more, untying the rope from his neck and feeling around his girth with her feet for a foothold.

Again Cyrus lunged right, shooting forward. Callie stayed where she was, lying against his neck as he stretched into a run.

"Yippee!" Jamie and Duncan waved their caps and whooped as she raced by their camp. Callie hardly heard them. She clenched her teeth against the hammering rhythm of Cyrus's crashing, pounding hooves. She had no control at all of where he was going; the reins lay somewhere beneath her torso. Afraid to loosen her grip and feel for them, Callie held onto his mane and dug in with her heels to save her life.

Cyrus ran and ran. Tears streamed from Callie's eyes, and the wind blew them across her cheeks. Her muscles screamed with the effort of hanging on, and she wondered about bailing off, but she could not imagine walking away from a fall at that speed. There had to be a way to slow down. Cyrus was puffing as he drew in air, and she knew he would eventually get winded, but could she never hang on that long? Maybe, if she could get herself into an upright position, or at least approximate one well enough to grab the reins and pull back on them . . .

Callie waited until they were on level ground without trees and with a grassy break in the sage. She tried to sit up a little, felt with one frantic hand beneath her, and caught the leather thong. As she pushed herself into a sitting position, her legs swung down. Callie tried to pull backward without pressing her feet into his sides, and Cyrus slowed abruptly, breaking his gait. Within three steps he'd come to a complete stop. Callie, however, kept right on going until she hit the ground.

The grassy sage flat weaved as Callie pushed herself upright onto wobbly legs. Cyrus waited obediently, watching her as she stumbled forward to grab his rein. "Well," she panted, "I rode you . . . just as . . . as I . . . predicted. And I'm going . . . going to ride you . . . again . . ." There was a very long pause as she considered what she'd said, and then she added, "tomorrow."

She leaned against Cyrus, catching her breath while he noisily cropped grass. A feeling of triumph grew steadily inside her. Callie realized she had learned two things: first, pulling back on the rein would stop him, and second, if she held on with her heels, Cyrus would spin away and run.

After a few minutes, she tugged his head up from the grass and began walking back toward the river. But she hadn't walked long on her aching, quivery legs, when Callie began to think she would rather ride, if only she could do so at a sane speed. She was covered with bruises that made walking uncomfortable, and her legs were still quaking. Besides, she admitted to herself, she wanted to see if she could master him into walking. She scanned the sage flat but saw no rock to mount from.

"Cyrus," Callie announced, bringing him to a standstill, "we're going back to camp at a civilized pace—understand?"

Then, placing her foot in the V of a large sagebrush, she half-jumped, half-pulled herself across Cyrus's back. Intent on keeping her heels loose, Callie maneuvered herself into position and waited. Nothing happened. She pressed her boots into his flanks lightly, then again, and her mount began walking forward. Walking!

Sweet elation swept over her. She stroked Cyrus's shoulder

and offered a prayer of thanks. The afternoon was nearly over, and night would be closing in before she could recover all the distance they'd run, but she didn't mind this speed at all.

She had traveled nearly halfway back when she saw some shaggy brown creatures rolling in a mud wallow near the river, not far from a stretch of willows that burned as red as foxtails in the light of the setting sun. Exuberantly, she watched the dark, distant shapes. Buffalo! She'd completely forgotten to look for them. But here they were, and this on-the-hoof food supply seemed in no hurry to leave the area. She didn't try to get closer because she didn't want to give them reason to go.

She couldn't get one without the lance and before dark. But she and Jamie would come this way again. First thing in the morning, they'd have some fresh meat!

Callie and Jamie crouched low, peering over the grassy swell at a handful of buffalo. The bulky animals had wandered during the night, but she'd managed to locate a portion of the herd grazing along a shallow gully.

"I'll be jiggered," Jamie breathed. "How're we going t' bring one o' *them* down?"

Speechless, Callie stared at the dark, massive shapes grazing contentedly before her. She'd never seen live buffalo this close before. She hadn't understood how immense they were at the hump nor prepared herself for their wild scruffiness. She'd been expecting a rather large, undomesticated cow. But at the sight of their massive, lowered heads and polished black horns she felt a threat—a sense of veiled peril beneath their apparent serenity. Gripping the lance more tightly, she wished it felt less like a stick and more like a weapon in her hand.

Callie studied her intended victims carefully. An old cow browsed along the far side of the grassy bowl, periodically lifting her head to sniff the air and look around. The only bull she could identify was a young one, and he seemed to be less the leader of the herd than was the cautious old cow. But, she conceded, he was a dangerous-looking animal. There were three other, more complacent cows, each with a calf nearby, and, after watching the herd for a while, Callie determined that she would target one of the yearling calves. She couldn't imagine thrusting her spear through the rib cage of anything so bulky, but she bit her lip and determined to do it anyway.

"What are ye thinkin' o' doin', Mum?" Jamie repeated his query at last.

"We'll be needing to trick them, because we'd never take one of those by force," Callie said, as curious as Jamie about what she was going to do.

"Aye," Jamie nodded. "Those have been my same thoughts. I'm wonderin' if we canna' trap 'em somehow."

"Precisely," Callie said.

Jamie ventured, "If I spooked 'em, an' herded 'em down th' swale, d'ye think—"

"Yes!" Callie broke in eagerly. "Yes, Jamie. You walk around to the west so they can't see you and then cross over into the dip from the far side of those rocks." She pointed to a jumbled tangle of rocks and brush that formed a tight neck at one end of the grassy bowl.

"I'll come over the top where that old cow's standin'—eh?"

"Exactly. And I'll be hiding down near the rocks. When one of the calves runs by . . ." Callie glanced down at the lance meaningfully.

"Aye." Jamie's voice, though hushed, surged with obvious excitement. His eyes were bright as he added, "But 'twill take me a while to get all around 'em without that old cow a-noticin' me."

"Then you'd best hurry," Callie said, already moving backward from the crest where they'd been watching. She left Cyrus tied in some bushes and made her way slowly toward the outcropping of rocks.

The sun rose past its zenith while she waited for Jamie to

come up on the far side of the herd. She worried that her boy had nothing with which to defend himself, worried that he must get the beasts moving away from himself without any of them turning angrily on him, worried that they'd run some other direction than toward her trap.

And, as the autumn sun shone warm across her bonnet and shoulders, Callie whispered prayers for strength and safety and success. The rain that had washed them down out of the mountains and dogged them nearly every day along the river must have been unseasonable, because now it was warm again—just like summer. She scanned the horizon, absent-mindedly rubbing the shaft of the lance with her skirt just as she'd often polished the barrel of her gun.

Then, with a whoop, Jamie appeared on the horizon, waving his cap and shouting outlandishly. *Don't scare them!* she thought, sucking her breath in apprehensively. *Just ease them.* But the cow raised her head only long enough to look at Jamie. Kicking her hind hooves up in the air, she plunged down the slope and crashed past the rest of the herd. Callie looked down, firming her grip on her lance, and when she raised her eyes, all the bison were racing toward the narrow defile where she crouched.

E I G H T E E N

Callie braced her feet against the rock as the snorting noses and pounding hooves drew nearer. The bisons' movements appeared awkward and stiff while they were feeding, their gait lumbering when first startled, but now she was dismayed by the speed with which they swept down on her. She was tempted to cower behind the rocks, safe from hooves and horns, until they were gone. How could she possibly thrust this little stone-tipped stick through one of their heavy chests? She would be thrown, Callie realized, dashed against the hard ground. But she forced a mental image of dark, rich meat dripping over the fire and sharpened her resolve.

Clenching the lance beneath one arm and in both hands, she selected a yearling calf at the back of the herd. Then, taking a deep breath and gritting her teeth, Callie leaped from behind the rocks. All her weight and strength were hurled with the lance.

Callie aimed for the ribs as the oncoming rush roared past, but intimidation caused her to hesitate one vital instant. And that moment's vacillation, coupled with lack of experience, made her spear-tip strike just before the rear flank but behind the vitals of the calf. Impaled by the animal's momentum, the point plunged through the yearling's heavy hide. The force of the impact dashed Callie violently against the ground. She tried to hold on and was dragged a few feet, but then the shaft was ripped from her hands.

Choking on dust, with the breath knocked out of her, Callie struggled to rise. Her lance was running away, dangling like a pin in a gigantic cushion! She tried to run after it, until a fit of coughing overcame her and she stumbled. She forced herself to stop, to think clearly. The waterskin was back with Cyrus. Jamie was a long way off, sprinting toward her down the grassy slope where the herd had been grazing.

She ran to Cyrus, gulped some water to quiet the dust in her throat, and untied him. Then, climbing a rock, she mounted the pony and rode to Jamie. Before this, she'd insisted he ride while she led—it had seemed impossible to mount again, once the bruises surfaced from the day before—but now her anxiety for the lance pushed urgently.

"Quick! Climb up here!" she demanded, reaching one hand down in an effort to pull him up. Her heels dug in as she struggled to keep from slipping, and Cyrus started, but she jerked back viciously on the rein until Jamie was behind her. Then Cyrus leaped to the right and forward, plunging after the disappearing quarry. He moved easily into the fluid, ground-eating gallop Callie had survived the day before, but she feared falling at this speed. She pulled back on the rein, anxious to catch the buffalo, yet afraid of going too fast. Cyrus settled back into a jarring, impatient trot.

"What are we doin'?" Jamie asked, his arms tight around her waist, his body jerking up and down against her back.

"Retrieving the lance." Her voice was terse. She *had* to get the lance back. If the beast weren't mortally wounded, at least her spear might fall out where she could find it. Quickly she breathed a prayer along those lines.

Coming up over a rise, Callie caught sight of the bison. The main body of the herd was noisily splashing into the river about a half a mile away. But just down the hill below her was one that had fallen behind. It was the wounded one, she decided, though she was unable to make out the lance protruding from its side. Cyrus saw the straggler, too, and Callie fought to hold her excited pony back.

The lone buffalo was working its way along the prairie,

parallel to the river. Becoming aware of her, it picked up speed again in a desperate sprint to escape. Suddenly Cyrus laid his ears back and jabbed ahead, breaking into a run that would overtake the buffalo's uneven strides in no time. Jamie's hold was torn loose by the unanticipated bolt. He toppled off behind her.

"Jamie!" Callie screamed. "Jamie!" The wind tore his name away the moment she cried out, but she didn't dare look back. It was all she could do to hang on as her eager mount sped forward. She couldn't afford to fall; she had to get that lance back. The wind whipped her bonnet off. Tears streaked backward from her eyes.

Callie could just make out crimson splashes among the buffalo's hoofprints. The ground was a blur beneath her, the grass, the rocks, the patches of wet red. But blood implied success, and she leaned forward more closely, clenching Cyrus's mane with white-knuckled, iron fists.

Cyrus was closing in now, and she wanted somehow to stop him, to dismount and run up beside the buffalo where she could grab the lance. She tried to pull on the rein with one hand, but it was jostled from her grasp. Though she hauled back on Cyrus's mane, he continued charging forward, drawing in close on the panting animal's right side. She could see pink froth at the calf's mouth, could see its brown eyes rolling so that the whites were wide around it, could hear its hollow, barrel-chested breathing.

Then she saw the lance. Callie yanked again and again at Cyrus's mane, but he persistently matched the buffalo's strides, hanging close to its right side. The lance protruded forward from the wounded animal's groin on the left. How could she get at it? She managed to reach down and gather the reins again; she pulled hard to the left. Cyrus edged in closer to the buffalo.

Desperately, Callie dragged on the reins, throwing her torso back against the pull. Cyrus's head jerked up and his rhythm broke. He was blowing hard now. His gait was choppy. He nearly halted, sidestepped, and then broke forward again the moment she slacked even slightly. She fumbled to hang on, struggling to keep her balance.

"No!" Callie shouted. "No! Go that way!" She wrenched the reins hard to the left, and Cyrus's gait faltered again, his lope now as bone-jarring and uneven as the trot had been. But he swung left, moving alongside the buffalo on the same side as the lance.

The shaft dangled beside her, just beyond reach. Callie leaned forward and down, trying to grab it. Fear of falling between the two animals shot through her and snatched away her breath, but she reached again, stretching out the fingers of her right hand and clutching Cyrus's mane with her left. Some uneven change in the ground and Cyrus's choppy gait threw her balance off as she leaned. Callie felt herself slipping. Flailing her arms out, she caught the lance on the way down.

She hit the ground hard. Her side exploded with pain; the lance hurled from her grip. For a moment she couldn't see clearly.

She tried to get to her feet, but a cramp seized her left leg. She grabbed it, pulling it up against her chest, rubbing it with shaky hands.

Looking up again, Callie saw the wobbly bison calf stagger, blood spurting from the hole in its side. It leaned precariously to the right, fell heavily, and with one final paroxysm, heaved its final breath.

Callie tried again to walk. Reeling, she paused, drew three deep, deliberate breaths, and limped forward to stand over her kill. Triumph spilled through her. She reached for her knife even before her panting breaths had slowed. She couldn't wait to feed this to Susa, to see the strength fresh meat would infuse into her small body. She couldn't wait to serve it up for the boys, to show it to that arrogant savage.

Callie pulled the knife from her belt with trembling, eager hands and raised it over the buffalo's still form. Where should she begin cutting? It was so big. The hide was thick and vast beneath the point of her knife.

Exhilaration swept over her again at the sight of all this meat, and she rose to her feet in delight. She walked around the carcass twice, looking at it from all angles. Then, impulsively, she stepped up on top of it, threw her arms upward, and shouted, "Hosannah! Hosannah!" into the deep blue bowl of the sky.

"Wha—?" Jamie shouted, coming into view from behind a dip in the prairie. "You hurt?"

Startled, Callie jumped back to the ground. She was suddenly self-conscious, suddenly aware that the cramp in her leg was tensing relentlessly, aware of a dull, growing ache in her shoulder, a pounding at the base of her skull. The front of her head smarted with sharp, stabbing pains.

Jamie ran up beside her, breathing hard. His face was flushed; perspiration streaked down from his forehead and around his eyes. He wiped the back of his sleeve across one cheek. "Are ye hurt?" he repeated.

"Hurt? No." Callie answered, trying to steady her voice. "No. I . . . I'm fine." All at once, she threw her arms around him and hugged him tightly. "We did it, Jamie!" she whispered. Then letting him go, she shouted. "We did it!"

"Aye!" he cheered in answer. "Hurrah for us! Hurrah for a fat supper!"

"A hundred fat suppers!" she laughed.

"A thousand!"

Then the prairie fell quiet around them. Callie felt the wideness of the grasslands stretching in every direction. She heard a late-season grasshopper drone among the dry weeds, saw that Cyrus was chomping a patch of short curly turf halfway to the river, noticed blood on Jamie's cheek.

"Are you cut, Son?"

"Nah," he spoke quickly, but she saw that his shirt was torn. He followed her gaze to his arm. "Sorry about that. At least th' sage didn't snag me as bad as my shirt. But this is worse," he said, lifting one foot into the air. The sole of his left boot flopped loose from its uppers, unstitched almost to the heel. His face was a mix of boyish amusement and worried distress. "Can ye fix 't?"

Callie answered with a smile and reached out a hand, wiping some of the blood off his cheek with her still trembling fingertips. She looked at it, wondering where it had come from. She couldn't see any injury on his face.

"That?" Jamie asked. "It's yours. Ye've a grand scrape just behind an' above your eye, Mum."

Callie stared at her fingers, then gingerly explored her forehead with them. There was a bloody spot, rough with dirt, reaching back into her hairline. The salt of her fingertips made it burn.

"I guess 't got there when ye hugged me," he said, holding out her sunbonnet with one hand. Then, in a hopeful voice he added, "I'll run to th' river and wet my shirt. Ye can use it t' wash up."

"No." Callie took the sunbonnet but did not tie it on. She picked up the lance from where it had fallen and looked it over solicitously, like an old friend. "No, Jamie. Let's offer a prayer of thanks. Then we'll walk down together and get a drink as well as a wash. We've a lot of hard work still ahead of us."

"What did you do after you got the hide off?" Duncan asked, his eyes bright in the firelight.

"Cut some meat, of course," Callie answered, though it hadn't really been that simple. Actually, she'd tried to move the calf, to position it as she would any other animal, but the buffalo was huge. She felt like she was carving up a horse, only worse. In all honesty, it had been an exasperating, nearly impossible task.

"Tell us again how big it was, Jamie," Susa begged for the sixth time.

Jamie stood on tiptoes, with his arm extended to its full height. "This big at th' hump!"

Duncan chortled gleefully, and Susa clapped her hands in delight.

Callie turned her pieces of meat, watching with satisfaction as the flames jigged brightly around them. Their juices oozed along the edges, dripping down to sizzle among the coals. Her mouth watered. "Did he move or waken?" she asked Duncan, nodding her head in the direction of the prisoner.

"No. Not much. He opened his eyes a few times. That was all."

She'd given him a drink when she untied his hands upon returning, but that wasn't much liquid for someone in his condition. Callie didn't trust her aching legs to hold her up very steadily, so she held the pan out to Duncan and asked, "Suppose you could fill this for me?"

"Sure, if Jamie will come along."

Susa giggled, "Duncan's scared of the dark!"

"Am not!"

"Hush," Callie scolded, turning the meat again. "That's not nice to tease, Susa," she added after Duncan had turned and stalked off toward the river.

"But it's true, Mum. He *is* scared."

Callie's fingers toyed with a six-inch rip in her skirt. She let the warmth of the fire ease her joints like a caress against the deep aches she'd incurred during the past two days. Then she realized she'd been negligent in answering her daughter. "That may be true, Susa, but it isn't kind. If you can't say anything nice, don't say anything at—"

A remote animal call rose from the bushes upriver. It soared upward like a coyote howl, but with a deeper, broader sound, and descended back down the scale. Callie couldn't guess what it was, but she saw the savage's eyelids blink open.

The sound came again, hornlike in the distance, and Duncan crashed back into camp, the pan sloshing in one hand, his eyes wide. At the edge of the firelight he caught himself, tried to regain composure, and asked in a quavery voice, "Hear that?"

"Aye," Jamie said. "'Twill eat ye up!"

Susa fell into fits of giggling, covering her mouth with her fingers. Duncan turned red.

But the sound didn't come again, and soon the boys had a makeshift game of checkers drawn in the dirt. The Indian closed his eyes again. Callie put meat in the pan and began boiling it for her patient. At least Susa would be able to chew actual strips now instead of existing on broth.

"Supper is ready," Callie announced, lifting the meat from above the fire. "Duncan, will you say grace?"

The boys scooted closer and Duncan pulled a serious face. But Callie noticed a mischievous quirk playing at the corners of his mouth and twinkling in his eyes. He elbowed Jamie as if to say: *get this.*

"Dear Lord," he began. "Some hae meat that cannot eat, Some would eat that want it, But we hae meat and we can eat, And so the Lord be thankit. Amen."

"Duncan!" Callie remonstrated, stifling her amusement. "I hardly think the Selkirk Grace is anything but a slap in the face of our great blessings this day. Let us hear your prayer again—not Robert Burns's—and with greater sincerity, or I'll tie your tail in a knot!"

She'd meant the words to sound severe, but there wasn't much bite in her threat. She was too glad to have food—too proud of her kill—to be cross with her boys.

Duncan repeated his prayer, in his own words, with earnestness, although the content was virtually the same. And then they fell to eating. The younger boy was full of questions: How hard was it to get the knife through the buffalo's hide? Did they wrap those pieces of meat in the hide in order to drape and balance them across Cyrus's back? Was he skittish? What parts did they cut and bring? Yes, he understood they'd purposefully brought the bladder and the hide, but what were they eating right now? Loin or rump? Callie was content to let Jamie answer while she gnawed the chewy meat, savoring the strength in it.

Afterward, she fed and nursed the savage, washing his face and hands, checking beneath his bandages for infection. There was none, though he was alarmingly weak. His face was still a mask to her. She couldn't guess what he was thinking, even though his eyes were more focused than before. Why couldn't he force a polite smile, or make some other sign of thanks?

She tucked the boys in and then lay quiet herself, relaxing the aches in her tired, battered body. Sometime during the deepest darkness, after the moon had set and on toward morning, the sound they'd heard from the distant river bottoms came again. But this time it was nearby.

Callie sat up, feeling for the lance as the call resonated in the blackness outside her camp. Beginning with a high whistle, it slid down several octaves into a series of heaving, repeated grunts. Whatever it was, the creature was big. The very resonance of its lungs unnerved her. Her nose wrinkled at the fetid, musky smell that wafted across the still air.

She found herself kneeling on top of her blanket, clasping the lance tightly and wondering if buffalo had greater cognitive powers than she'd supposed. Would they attack for revenge?

Piercing, shrill tones echoed through the night, but it was the low, rumbling bellow that caused her to quake inside. Maybe it was a predator that wanted to eat her chunks of freshly slaughtered buffalo. But beasts of prey wouldn't announce their presence before attacking—would they?

Callie considered building up the fire since that usually frightened away wild animals. Yet she hesitated, unsure, and as the moments passed, she began to realize that the beast in the darkness had no immediate intention of striking. Instead, it went on calling and calling.

That was when she heard another sound, hardly louder than a whisper. An echo was rising into the night, from within her own camp: *"Hunh-ha, Hunh-ha, eh-ha, eh-ha, eh-ha . . ."*

NINETEEN

The heathen was chanting! Astonished, Callie reflexively gripped the lance even tighter. Until this moment, he had made no noise, but now he seemed to be in league with the creature. Had he, by some mystical primitive power, called the beast here to avenge his capture, to set him free? Callie didn't know what to think. She didn't know what was out there, didn't know the savage's intentions, and couldn't decide which thoughts were preposterous and which ones were plausible. She wanted to somehow silence him, but she didn't dare.

The chanting went on, weak, almost inaudible. Callie knew with instinctive certainty that the Indian had sunk as low as the threshold of death. He paused periodically, winded with the feeble effort of singing. But then she would hear him again, undeniably euphoric despite the droning ceremonial rhythm of his answer to the bugling call, *"Mo?e, mo?e, mo?e, eh-ha, eh-ha. Mo?e, mo?e, mo?e, eeeh-ha."*

Eventually a series of short barking calls came from across the river. *Probably coyotes,* she thought. The creature moved off toward them, still whistling and bellowing. She heard its feet crashing in the water, heard another less massive call answering from the other side. When it was gone, she noticed gratefully that the Indian had stopped chanting.

At last she slept, though lightly. Her bruises cramped and ached dully, her head throbbed, and she kept squeezing with her fingertips to be sure the lance was still in her grasp.

Callie woke with a start. He was chanting again! Dawn was bursting in brilliant orange across the sky, inflaming the leaves of the river bottom's trees and the grass of the open plains. The savage's song was almost inaudible, soft and deep in his throat, with his head turned away from her toward the rising sun.

Callie got up, curious whether her movements would stop him, hopeful that they would. His song was filled with all the emotion of which she had thought him incapable. He chanted in ceremonial reverence, his voice undulating with feeling as it rose and fell along a strange, nasal scale. The Indian kept on singing, unflinchingly gazing east. When the sun at last cleared the horizon, he ended the chant and closed his eyes. Then silence pressed uncomfortably in on Callie. She methodically went about checking her cache of meat, glorying in every precious chunk, spreading them out on top of the curling hide. But the savage's whispery voice seemed to hang like uncanny vapor in the early-morning air.

"Two can play at that game," Callie muttered under her breath. And she began to sing, almost as if she were trying to reclaim her camp from her prisoner's heathen chant.

> Jesus, lover of my soul,
> Let me to thy bosom fly . . .

She built the fire up for cooking breakfast, pausing between verses to blow on the coals.

> Other refuge have I none;
> Hangs my helpless soul on thee.
> Leave, oh, leave me not alone;
> Still support and comfort me.

The words and familiar rolling, lyrical melody comforted her. So Callie repeated them all again while she combed her hair and braided it into a neat twist at the nape of her neck. Then she sang the final chorus one more time, slightly louder, just for good measure as she walked down to the river to fetch water.

> All my trust on thee is stayed;
> All my help from thee I bring.
> Cover my defenseless head
> With the shadow of thy wing.

The children were still resting peacefully when she returned, scrubbed clean. Warm mineral waters had soothed the worst pangs and throbs from the day before, and she felt refreshed. Her fears of the night had disappeared, leaving her resolved to control the situation. After all, the savage was weak, nearly dead. Callie set some water to boil and decided to let the children rest a little longer. This might be a good time to tend to her prisoner. Then she could have one chore out of the way before her little ones needed attention.

Callie bent over the savage with the waterskin. "Want a drink this morning, Chief?"

The Indian looked at her without answering but drank when she lifted the moisture to his lips. "It is good." He spoke with soft satisfaction, in recognizable English.

Callie jumped at the sound of his voice, letting his head fall from where she'd been cradling it. He winced at the unanticipated pain, but she ignored his discomfort. "You . . . you talk!" Her words were an accusation.

The Indian blinked, as if this statement of fact required no answer.

Callie persisted, "How have you come to speak English?"

After a long pause in which he seemed to be weighing the validity of her question, the savage answered, "I stay long time Fort Laramie. Many bluecoat soldier."

"But why didn't you tell me?"

Ignoring her consternation, he rolled his eyes toward where she'd heaped his things. "Bag," he said. "Give bag."

Dumb with surprise, Callie went to the pile and lifted the

beaded leather bag in which she'd found provisions. *Of course,* she thought, *he's hungry. That's a sign he's getting stronger.*

But the savage lifted the fingers of one hand upward and to the side indicating for her to stop. "Small," he said. "Medicine."

Medicine! Why hadn't he told her he had medicine in that plain little pouch? Callie searched among his things, afraid she might not find it, but it was there, beneath the shield, the drawstring cut where she had taken it off his neck.

"Here."

With unsteady hands, the Indian opened his pouch and removed a few dried feathery leaves and creamy blossoms that gave off an aromatic fragrance. He put these in his mouth and began slowly chewing, softening them to a pulp.

"Why didn't you tell me you could speak English? Why, you never even—" Indignation caused her words to fail.

The savage went on chewing. When he was satisfied with the consistency of his concoction he gestured for Callie to pull back his bandages. Then he pressed the pulpy leaves into the bullet hole. He wiped half of it into her hand. Callie stared stupidly down at the slimy stuff, so he indicated that it was for his back.

Callie rolled him over and spread the ooze across his burned, torn flesh. Then she rewrapped the bandages around him. When the treatment was all finished, she rolled the Indian onto his back, gave him another sip of water, and moved her face directly in front of his.

"Who are you?" She spoke with slow emphasis, wanting to be sure he understood, demanding he answer.

"Man must rest." The savage closed his eyes. For him the conversation was over.

Callie was incensed. How dare he go on for days without any sort of communication? How dare he? Well, she'd see about that. She wouldn't feed him again until he answered a few questions.

"Who are you talking to?" Susa asked from beneath the folds of her buffalo robe. When Callie didn't answer right away, Susa added, "I'm frightfully hungry, Mum. May I have some of the meat you brought yesterday?"

Callie rushed to the fire and began working at once on breakfast. She was thrilled to see her daughter hungry, anxious to get her up and around soon. The boys woke when they smelled the meat cooking, and Callie was soon busy with camp chores.

Later that morning, she began slicing most of the meat into strips to dry. The job was a messy one, and she had gotten deeply engrossed in the monotony of it when she heard Susa giggle. The happy sound made her smile as she bent over her task. But then she heard the giggling again. Callie had sent the boys to fetch willow sticks with which to fashion drying racks, so what could Susa be laughing at? She turned suddenly around. Susa was sitting beside the Indian, stuffing leftover bits of breakfast meat into his mouth almost faster than he could chew.

"No!" Callie commanded, rising quickly to her feet, bloody knife still gripped in her hand, cross that she'd have to wait longer now if she were going to use food as leverage for talk. "No!"

Susa looked up, surprised. The Indian stopped chewing abruptly.

"Don't touch him."

"But he's hungry, too, Mum."

"Come away." Susa rose obediently and came toward her mother. "Listen," Callie said more gently, sitting down on a rock and holding her messy hands away from her dress. "You can't play with him. He's very dangerous."

Susa deliberated a moment, furrowing her brow and puckering her lips in concentration. "He doesn't look dangerous to me—just sick."

"Well," Callie laughed, happy to see her daughter up after

so long. "Leave him to me. Why don't you run along down to the river and see what's taking your brothers so long?"

Susa turned to go and Callie called after her. "Mind you, Chickadee, don't go near the water!"

"Yes, Mum."

She bent back to her task, carving one hunk after another, placing them in a pile at her right.

"Should cut narrow and more long, Lucky Woman."

Callie turned and glared at the Indian, who seemed obnoxiously amused by her inexperience. "Why didn't you tell me you spoke English? Why didn't you talk to me?"

"What you do more important than what you say." The savage answered matter-of-factly, a nasal sound surrounding his pronunciation. After a moment's pause he added with expressive significance, "White man's words are empty."

"Then why are you talking now?"

"Mo?e come in darkness. Make new medicine. It is good."

No, Callie thought, *more likely it was the rich broth that gave you strength.* But she kept her cynicism to herself and he went on.

Holding up three fingers, the savage said, "Three. Three mo?e." He pronounced the word with a glottal stop at the center and pointed at his shield. "This my name. I am Three . . . hmmm . . . Elk. Three Elk of the *Tse-tsehese-staestse.*"

"I don't know that tribe," Callie responded.

"You do not know much," Three Elk said frankly. His eyes glanced appraisingly at the condition of her camp. "Big cold come. Where your lodge?"

Callie absorbed this. She realized it was true as pertaining to things of the wilderness. She didn't know much, but she was learning—and quickly. They'd gotten along so far. She chose not to argue, swallowing her pride in an effort to keep him talking.

Slowly, clearly, she asked, "Where are you from . . . ah . . . Three . . . ah . . . Mr. Elk? Are there others looking for you? Where are your friends?"

Three Elk lifted his left hand, opposite the wounded shoulder, and made a gesture that seemed to say "who knows?" "They go back to my people," he said. "My people you call . . . Cheyenne."

Callie cringed at the word. Cheyenne. Then he *was* a brutal murderer just as she'd suspected. She'd seen Cheyenne handiwork. Revulsion and horror stiffened her back, hardened her eyes, but Three Elk seemed not to notice.

"Your Colonel Sumner makes big fighting with *Tse-tsehese-staestse.*"

"*Colonel* Sumner?" Callie came to her feet. She stood beside Three Elk, looking down on him, her voice urgent. "Where is he? Can we get to him?"

Again, he made the irritating, nonchalant "who knows?" gesture. It obviously didn't matter to him. "My people go now to winter camp. Soon *hesta?se* comes."

"What comes?"

"*Hesta?se* . . . snow. Big cold." He gestured widely with his hands. "Big snowing."

"Listen," Callie spoke intently, kneeling down beside him in a friendly manner. "I must find this Colonel Sumner. Have you seen him? Can you tell me where he is?"

Again the gesture.

"No," Callie insisted. "I *have* to find him." Her lower lip wavered, and she struggled against a sudden, embarrassing rush of tears. This savage would not see her break down. "You have to tell me more than that. I *must* find him."

"I am tired," the wounded man said, closing his eyes again to terminate the conversation. And that was all. Three Elk was obviously finished talking.

Exasperated, Callie stormed back to her work area and furiously shooed away the green-bellied flies that had begun to swarm along the meat. She slashed it viciously into strips. Well, she could be just as stubborn as he was. Fuming as she worked, Callie went over and over their conversation in her mind.

Three Elk was probably hiding something. Perhaps he was afraid she would turn him over to that powerful colonel. Maybe she should threaten the savage, tell him of her intention to see him face justice. No, then he would clam up, and she'd never get him to talk. Well, one way or another, she'd drag it out of him. She would find out where the colonel was, even if she had to give Three Elk his very freedom for the facts.

Three Elk did not speak again as she finished cutting the meat, fashioned awkward-looking racks from willow twigs, and hung the strips near the fire to dry. He never made a sound, as she hovered above her project, shooing away flies and birds and scolding the boys when they stirred up dust. Callie busied herself with mending and preparing their things to move on. She spread out the calf's hide, tieing it to a makeshift square frame just as she would have blocked a piece of knitting or weaving back home. And she used her broken knife to scrape away the crust of dried blood and fragments of flesh that clung to it.

Callie needed the Indian to explain how to treat the bladder so that it could serve as a waterskin, but asking went against her grain. So she avoided it, making plenty of work elsewhere.

Three Elk woke every so often throughout the rest of the afternoon. Callie could always tell when he surfaced; she could feel him staring at her back. And that irritated her, for she could not escape his scrutiny.

In an undisguised way, his gaze followed her around camp. Indignation flared each time she turned to discover the intensity of it. He seemed to contemplate her very soul with his eyes—but worse, he seemed to only half care what he discovered. His face registered no reactions: he appeared entirely unconcerned with making judgments, noticing only facts. His ability to look through her, to stare dispassionately at her with such amazing candor and without judgmental conviction, unsettled her.

Slowly Callie began to realize that he did not see her as his captor, nor as his nurse, nor even so much as a woman, but only as a curiosity. The presumption it implied! The very condescension ate at her composure. That contemptible, illiterate savage thought no more of her than she did of him!

So each time Callie caught him watching, she made a point of striding over and giving him a drink. "Fluids are good for healing," Callie insisted, though she knew his health was not her primary motivation. *Either he'll drown, or he'll learn some manners!* But even then, the heat of her resentment continued to burn.

Callie began to consider what a relief it would be to get rid of the Indian. Although he didn't eat much right now, being weak, her stores would last longer without him. Besides, she couldn't imagine how she was going to move him.

"Are we 'bout ready t' hit th' trail again, Mother?" Jamie asked. Susa and Duncan were already asleep, and Three Elk, too, apparently. Mother and son sat near the fire, he in his blanket and she on a log, trying to figure out how to mend his boot.

"True," she mumbled, wrapping a strip of the uncured buffalo hide around and around the toe. "We've got to be getting west if we hope to reach Zion." Then, after a moment's pause, she added, "Susa's much better."

"Aye."

"—But she can't walk far. You saw how long she napped when you children came back from the river."

"She napped there, too. Just lay on th' banks an' watched me an' Dunc cut th' willows."

Callie knotted the ends of the leather where the laces

began. “There,” she said, tossing Jamie’s boot into his lap. “Hope you can still get your foot in.”

“If Susa rides,” Jamie asked, nodding his head in the direction of the motionless Indian, “what’ll ye do with him?”

That was exactly what Callie wanted to know. What was she going to do with the Indian? His very presence posed a continual, exasperating problem. She knew he couldn’t walk more than fifty yards, but she wasn’t about to let any savage sit behind Susa on her horse.

Callie began building up the fire, keeping it hot and high to speed the drying of her meat. “Well, James McCracken,” she answered, “when you’ve figured that out, why don’t you let me know?”

TWENTY

The next morning when Callie woke, Jamie was hunched like a shadow in the thin predawn light, whittling shavings off a stick onto the coals of last night's fire. The matches were gone, but he still carried a little piece of flint. Rather than use it today, Jamie was reviving the fire by feeding it shavings. With each stroke of his broken blade, a curly piece of tinder fell; its edges coiled, then darkened, then burst into flaring light.

Callie watched him momentarily, noticing how absorbed he was in the task. She had been up and down all night, keeping the flames high to dry the meat faster. Now she realized she must have eventually lapsed into deep sleep and let the fire die completely.

"Good morning, Jamie." Callie rose, leaving the lance beside the spot where she'd been lying. She eyed the strips of meat as she turned each one carefully. With luck, maybe she could get them packed and travel a few miles west before dark. "If we keep the fire up, these ought to be dry enough by afternoon."

"Then we'll be on our way again? Swell!" Jamie grinned, pushing larger sticks onto the returning flames. His stomach growled loudly and Callie looked over at him, startled.

Jamie wrapped his arms around his middle. "Just a pang."

"Hunger pangs?" Callie asked. "With all this meat?"

Jamie looked up at her, chagrined and almost penitent. "Can't help it, Mother. Buff'lo goes right through me. Duncan, too. But we didn't want t' tell ye. Me an' him be partic'larly grateful t' have it."

Callie smiled at him understandingly. Her stomach had also

been troubled by the red meat, especially after so long on thin gruel. But what could she do?

"When we reach Fort Bridger," she told him conspiratorially, "we shall both ask for a big hunk of brown bread."

"Aye!" the boy grinned. "And then eat and eat 'til we're sick!"

"Jamie!" Callie remonstrated with voice and eyes.

Susa giggled from over beneath the buffalo robe.

Jamie jumped up and pulled her from her warm nest. "Aye, 'twas you I heard a' gigglin'!" He tickled her ribs.

"Yes! Yes! Let me go, Jamie!"

"All right, lassie. I'll let ye be if ye promise ye'll eat yer fill o' bread wi' us at Fort Bridger. I'll find butter for you, sweet. Bread and butter all day long."

"I wi— I will! . . . Jamie, . . . only let . . . let me go!"

"Enough of that," Callie scolded. "Fetch me some water, Son, so I can make breakfast."

Jamie wasn't gone long for the water, and after that he restocked the woodpile. Callie noticed his eyes were extra bright this morning, and he often glanced over at the savage. "Why don't you and Susa go down for a last wash at th' river, Mother?" he asked after breakfast. "I'll feed 'im for ye." Jamie tossed his eyes toward the Indian. "Dunc can handle th' fire."

Wondering what he was up to, Callie considered. She'd intended to have one last refreshing scrub in the warm water. James really ought not be handling the care of the savage. He was only a boy, after all. But then again, their prisoner had never shown any violent antagonism. Surely she could be allowed a moment's peace. "Give him this," she told the boy, gesturing to the remaining water-softened, boiled meat. "And plenty of water. I dare say he can hold up his own head enough to drink."

"Aye," Jamie nodded.

"Be careful!"

When Callie and Susa returned from the edge of the river, both boys were about thirty yards from camp, throwing all their weight against a ten-foot sapling. The trunk was springy, and Duncan and Jamie laughed uproariously as they bounced around trying to bring it down.

"What are you doing?" Callie demanded.

"Mum!" Duncan cried. "Jamie talked to the Indian after we fed him. We told him we have to be going on to Zion and we were afraid you'd make him walk. But it will kill him if he walks now, Mum. I just know it!—and Jamie does, too. So we told him the problem, and he had an idea."

"He what?" Callie's voice was impatient. Why was he telling things to the boys and being so tight-lipped with her?

"Yes. He told us how his people move their sick. You know they live in tepees, follow the buffalo. Everyone has to go."

Without looking up, Jamie went on cutting at the sapling with the broken knife. Callie eyed both boys calculatingly. "He spoke to you?"

"Yes, Mum! Yes! His people make a drag of two poles that they strap to their ponies. We can strap one to Cyrus!"

Skeptical, Callie glared over at the savage and then back at her eager boy.

"He says if we must go somewhere, this is the way he can travel. In a few days, though, he says he will sit on the horse himself."

Ha! Callie laughed inwardly. *He thinks! He won't be sitting on my horse ever again.*

"He'd rather we left him here," Duncan went on volunteering information, "But I explained how you plan to turn him over to the authorities."

Lovely, Callie thought. *There's goes the element of surprise behind my other bargaining tool.* But perhaps she could still salvage some value from the threat. At least this pony-drag plan might make it possible for them to get back on the trail.

"What did he do when you told him that?" Callie asked.

"Nothing."

"Was he afraid?"

Duncan shrugged. "Can we make one, Mum? Can we take him with us on a pole drag?"

"Yes," Callie answered, drawing a deep breath. "Jamie, leave off with that. You boys go down to the river and find a pair of thin tree trunks washed up along the bank. That way we won't spend all day wearing down our knives as if they were axes. Susa, come with me, and we'll pack the meat that's already dry."

When the boys returned, Callie directed the construction of the pony drag, according to Duncan's description of what Three Elk had said. The sun was well past its zenith when she finally had the packs ready, her stretched buffalo skin lashed to its frame, and the savage loaded onto the drag. "Up you go," she said, boosting Susa on Cyrus's back. As the boys let loose a cheer and ran ahead, Callie started her group out onto the prairie toward the sinking sun.

The ride was dusty and jarring, and she could see Three Elk was in pain. Callie gave him a sip of water every so often, but she didn't speak to him, nor did he say anything to her.

They pitched a dry camp that night, having traveled about five miles, she supposed. Susa fell asleep halfway through eating her dinner, but she seemed refreshed in the morning so Callie pushed on.

They traveled steadily all day, shouldering hill after hill, the pony drag bouncing in spite of her efforts to avoid the biggest clumps of sage and stubborn grass hummocks. Herds of prairie goats fled like tan clouds skimming away in all directions across the dry-brown plain.

She followed drainage bottoms as much as possible; there the grass was smoother, the sage not as tough. She sent the boys running ahead, constantly working to choose the smoothest ravines that would lead her west. But ridges barred her way, and sooner or later all the drainages curled south into the towering, snow-covered mountain peaks.

Well into morning, as the sun was just reaching the fullness of its warmth, a steady wind came out of the northwest, kicking up dust, making each breath gritty. A growing layer of dirt formed all over Three Elk and the pony drag, but it would have been useless to brush him off.

Everyone was parched by late afternoon when the wide grassy swale they were following hooked directly south into the tip of the mountains. Callie wanted to go westward, but a series of dry, uninterrupted sage-covered ridges humped into the distance, with one tremendous rise barring the way. Ahead to the south, a clear swift flowing stream rushed from steep heights to empty in a series of red willow-fringed beaver ponds high on the valley floor.

"We'll pitch camp up there," Callie called, though her words were mere formality. The boys had already run far ahead, eager to sink their hands in the water. Callie pressed steadily forward until she was above the beaver ponds, where the water ran swift between gold-leaved aspen. Then, with a sigh, she lifted Susa from her perch and let Cyrus drink. As soon as she stopped, the Indian pulled himself up off the drag. Callie watched him lie on his stomach, favoring his right shoulder, splashing water on his face and head and drinking deeply.

She scooped a handful of water, upstream from the horse, and then straightened her back and studied the land around her. Golden aspen lined the streambed, their leaves chattering beneath the fingers of wind that reached down into the hollow. Callie listened to them while Cyrus gulped, her mind drifting effortlessly through thoughts of gratitude for the cool drink.

"No much water, Lucky Woman," Three Elk told her, gesturing at the horse. "He drink too fast."

Surprised, Callie glanced away, pretending to look for the children. The redskin's advice galled her. She didn't want an ignorant savage telling her how to do things—especially since he was probably right. Impatient, she pulled Cyrus's head out of the water and led him away. Unfastening the drag, Callie set the hungry animal loose on a patch of tall grass.

Then, still thirsty herself, she returned to the stream. Three Elk was on the bank where she had left him, lying quietly, watching her again. Seeing him, Callie nearly suppressed her own need for water and walked away—but then, in a burst of determination, she stomped back down to the bank, dipped her hands full, and sank her dusty face into them, just as she would have done if the savage had not been there.

"How much before you make lodge?" Three Elk asked casually, using his hand to indicate that he meant distance.

"We will continue traveling west to Fort Bridger. I'll get help there." Callie dried her face on the underneath side of her apron. "Duncan tells me he has already informed you that Fort Bridger is where you will pay the demands of justice."

If he understood her threat, Three Elk gave no indication. "Too far," he said with matter-of-fact finality.

The assurance with which he rejected her plan was perturbing. Callie glared icily.

"This day hot sun day. Many hot sun days we have seen. Other days coming not so good."

"I can handle rain, Mr. Elk." Callie's voice was impatient.

"No rain. Big snowing."

Callie let her eyes tell the Indian how highly improbable she thought snow was. The weather had been warm and dry—even hot in the afternoons. There hadn't been a single cloud in the enormous blue dome of sky.

"Go too slow," Three Elk said with emphasis. He was hunting through his memory for each individual word, using hand gestures to get the point across. "Too slow to cross dry place before snow is made."

Callie looked down, retying the lace on one of her boots. This savage was not going to intimidate her. He obviously didn't want to face the magistrate at Fort Bridger, and that was all there was to it. He was stalling—nothing more—stalling and trying to frighten her.

"I won't quit now," she declared. "Besides, your pony drag slows us more than anything. You shouldn't complain, you know." Callie realized her voice sounded peevish. He'd been tough, downright stoic, but she had so many things to worry about. They must go on, and the last thing she needed was trouble from him.

She expected Three Elk to be hurt by her assertion, to close his eyes and refuse to speak as before. But the Indian watched Callie searchingly. When she had finished retying the second boot and was bracing her hands to stand, he said, "Lucky Woman make camp here. Not cross dry place for seven, . . . eight moons."

His appellation and assertive advice galled Callie. "I told you, I will not quit after coming this far. I've traveled farther than you can possibly comprehend. I've brought my children over oceans and continents. And I *won't stop now!*" Thoroughly exasperated, Callie stood and straightened her dress. "Besides my name isn't Lucky Woman. It is McCracken . . . *Mrs.* Angus McCracken."

Again, Three Elk seemed neither hurt nor troubled by her outburst. He folded his arms across his chest, cradling his left hand in his armpit against the wound, and stared off toward the west.

Later that night, as Callie sat reading her Book of Mormon by a spark-snapping fire, the Indian spoke again. "*Mo?ehe-no?hame-amesto?ee-seo?o* is slow," he gestured into the darkness toward the dark shape of the pony drag. "Big snow come. Three Elk build lodge, stay here in cold time."

Callie did not look up from the pages of her book but considered the savage's words. Reason told her that his reticence came from being loath to stand trial at Fort Bridger, but his words didn't sound as much like the plea of a frightened criminal as a simple statement of fact. He did not intend to go on.

No! Callie wanted to shout at her aggravating prisoner. *She* was the one in control. She was the one who fed the group and led them west and made the decisions. She killed the buffalo. She carried the lance.

Three Elk was a burden. And Callie couldn't deny what a temptation it was to leave him behind so she could travel faster. Looking up at the heavy ridge that barred travel to the west, she considered. Pulling the pony drag over that sage-covered crest wasn't something she wanted to tackle.

Under normal circumstances, taking the heathen to Fort Bridger would be the right thing to do. His eternal soul would benefit more if he repented of his murderous ways in this life than if he waited for the next.

But she really ought to think first of her children. This fine weather would eventually have to turn cold. Her precious strips of dried buffalo meat would ultimately run out. Perhaps putting all her responsibilities in perspective, she'd better leave the savage behind. He'd already slowed her too much, and she wasn't sure how to get him over that ridge. Besides, she'd done right by him—more than anyone could fairly ask—in saving his life when he was bleeding to death.

She could treat him with charity, leave him as much food as he'd had the day she found him. He could keep the smelly sausages and a few strips of dry meat to replace the ones she and the children had eaten. Not too much, though. The stubborn mule probably wouldn't last long by himself in his weakened condition—not even a week. And she needed all the provisions she could muster for keeping life and limb together among her own.

"Fine, Mr. Elk," Callie looked up from her scriptures with resolute eyes and a crisp tone. "I shall leave you here. I need not be hauling you across the prairie when I have my own family to look after. You may remain in this camp. Then, subsequent to my arrival at Fort Bridger, I shall advise the colonel of your whereabouts. He will undoubtedly send some men to apprehend you."

Three Elk showed neither relief at his freedom nor concern at being left alone. "*E-peva?e.* It is good," he said simply and lay down in his blanket.

Frost formed heavily during the night, making Callie even more anxious to be under way. At least sunshine would reach and warm them up on top of the plain. Light certainly wasn't going to strike this gully until the sun was high in the sky. She wondered if Three Elk had thought of that, though she had no intention of asking him.

She handed out strips of dried meat and then quickly began packing and assessing which things to take and which to leave. Cyrus and the lance were hers, as well as the rope, the hunting knife, the buffalo robes, and the dried meat. She cut the rawhide robe, still in its frame, off the pony drag. Then she broke the frame on opposite sides, so she could fold and tie its bulk onto Cyrus's rump. Next Callie placed a few strips of dry meat in Three Elk's beaded bag, alongside his sausages. No need to be hauling his shield or bow, she decided. She piled them, along with his breastplate, near the campfire.

To Callie's surprise, Three Elk was on his feet, using his good arm to drag a pine bough toward a large boulder further up the ravine. On a fifteen-foot-wide bench above the creek, but well beneath the rim of the spreading desert, Three Elk stopped and dropped his burden. He leaned over for a moment, bracing his hands on his knees and panting hard. Callie walked slowly upstream toward him, curious.

Aspen circled the south-facing bench, their leaves littering the ground with gold, spreading out like a brilliant patchwork quilt. One tree had fallen where its base had split a little over four feet high. The trunk was still partially attached to the fallen treetop; its uppermost end trailed leafless branches against the ground. Callie watched sweat bead along the Indian's forehead as he lifted the leafless end of the fallen aspen and struggled to pivot it. He stumbled, fell, but immediately worked his way to his feet again, grappling with the fallen trunk.

"Wait! I'll help ye!" Jamie called, running past her and helping to lift the log. Together the two of them twisted the end of the aspen until it was running directly north-south, two-thirds the width of the ledge. They strained against it again and again, trying to force it into the notch of a tree just about level with Callie's nose. The savage worked steadily, unflinchingly, but his color was pale and his breath came in ragged gasps. Fresh blood stained the back of his shirt at the shoulder. At the sight, Callie hurried to throw her weight against the fallen trunk until it slid into place.

Then the Indian used that crossbar as a roof-beam and ran other pieces of dead wood between it and the top of the boulder he was building against. Duncan and Susa helped pile pine boughs and brush across the roof and then in lean-to style walls. Slowly the shelter took shape: closed on three sides, with a low door toward the east and a round smoke-hole between the roof and the rock.

While Callie was using the hunting knife to cut pine boughs, and tossing them down to Susa and Duncan, Three Elk stopped his work and stood beneath the tree she was working in. Using his good arm, he reached something up toward her. Surprised, she took it. Looking the furry thing over, Callie realized she was holding the sheath to the knife she had taken off the Indian the day she'd found him.

"Thank you," she said, trying not to sound stunned.

Three Elk nodded once and then turned back to the business at hand.

What, she wondered, *caused him to do that?* His actions

appeared to be the result of pure generosity, but that couldn't possibly have been his motive. She was sure his savage mind didn't comprehend emotions beyond its own self-interest. *Besides, he can't be giving me things when I've already taken whatever I choose. He must want something.*

Was he hoping to buy her good favor? No, she was leaving now, so it was too late for that. Was he thanking her for helping him build a shelter? Callie didn't think so; he'd never made any attempt to thank her before. Maybe he thought she would be frightened out on the desert and return to him here. But that was too absurd and presumptuous even for him, she decided. No, he must be trying to buy her favor and hoping she would not send out the authorities once she reached Fort Bridger. Well, he was going to be disappointed. *She* couldn't be bought.

"Aren't you going to drop any more?" Duncan asked, startling his mother from her thoughts.

"No," she said, fastening the sheath to her apron strings and sliding the knife into it. "It looks like he has enough, and he'll have plenty of time to gather more if they're needed."

Callie dropped to the ground, brushed the pine-needles from her skirts, straightened her bonnet, and walked downstream to fetch Cyrus. Without conversation, she lifted Susa onto the pony's back and picked up the lance as if it were her walking staff. "Come along, boys!" she called. "James! Duncan! Farewell, Mr. Elk," she said in formal tones. "Perhaps we shall meet again, though I doubt it."

Callie wondered what he would say, waited for words of thanks or kindness, but Three Elk only raised his hand, palm out, and nodded with slow dignity.

"Good-bye!" the children called as they topped the rise. "Good-bye! Good-bye!"

Callie looked back to see the savage, standing motionless and straight, watching them. Then he was cut from view as she hurried out of the stream's gully and onto the open plain.

TWENTY-ONE

In spite of the temperate weather, Callie discovered that none of the small prairie flowers she'd seen east of the Platte were blooming anymore. Brown, brittle grass bunches soon gave way to nothing but sage among the dust and pebbles. The day was warm, even hot—or, at least, the sun was pleasant. Wind blew cool and continual, sweeping across from the northwest in powerful gusts.

Climbing toward the huge ridge in the west, they passed a few tan valleys lined with trees of blazing color, similar to the draw where they'd left the Indian. But the desolation that stretched before her was all dried up. Honeycomb cracks crisscrossed the earth's surface beneath thin, twisted trunks of sage.

Her boys ran ahead, kicking a rock back and forth between them, and Susa leaned precariously, dozing to the rhythm of Cyrus's monotonous plodding. Callie fell back and put up a hand to steady her daughter.

Without actually thinking about it, she began to listen to the silence beneath the sound of hooves and footfalls. Suddenly she realized the crackling whir of grasshoppers was gone. When they'd been on the prairie before, there had been a continual buzz and snap as bugs flew away beneath her feet.

Oddly enough, the farther they went, the fewer living things she saw—not only hoppers but larger creatures as well. The skimming herds of prairie goats were growing fewer, even birds were more scarce. Once her eye caught the scurry of a rockchuck as it disappeared into its hole, but that was all. This plain spread around them, full of emptiness greater than she had seen before—greater and wider and all crouched down beneath the unceasing wind.

Callie wondered where the hoppers and all the other creatures had gone, but she didn't dwell on the mystery. The great absolute was the land. It spread beneath the reaching sky: buckling, imperative, consuming. Against its vastness Callie sang. But the wind raced by, snatching her words and running off to the east. So she hummed and drew comfort from the resonance in her head. Music was her method, the one Angus had approved of, the only means she had for feeling less insignificant in the face of vastness. Her song asserted their presence, kept them from being swallowed up by the wild land.

As they walked, cracked soil gave way to a hard pavement of pebbles on hardpan. Although they reached the big ridge that had worried her, Callie could hardly register any change in their position against the mountain peaks to the south. In spite of a half-day's moving forward, it seemed they had traveled no distance at all. Water-cut ravines rose and fell before them like towering waves on a frenzied sea.

That concerned Callie, but she didn't let on to the children. "Glad to be at it again, aren't we?" she asked. And when Duncan complained of getting tired, she cheerily reminded him that every step brought them that much closer to Zion.

Callie was also disturbed by the lack of water they were passing. Drainages had been cut all around her, but nearly every one was dry, growing nothing taller than sage. All she could do was pray vigorously, so that was what she did. She made a dry camp with a merry fire before telling her children lighthearted stories and tucking them into their blankets. And then, as she sat by the fire with her scriptures, Callie congratulated herself on what a tremendous relief it was to move forward without the added burden of the savage.

At dawn, after saying her morning prayers, Callie paused and considered the fact that she had crossed mountains and conquered rivers. The surrounding vastness seemed less intimidating when she concentrated on the idea that once they got around the mountains to the south, she would find Fort Bridger. Mentally she thanked heaven for food and water, for the lance and the pony.

Later, as she started her small brigade forward once again, Callie looked down at her hands. Rough, chapped, trail-worn, they were not the clean, efficiently domestic hands that had left Yorkshire. Yet they were still her hands. She felt the vigor of her legs with each step she took forward. These legs had carried children over stony peaks and across rivers. They'd straddled a horse, and the strength of her arms had killed a buffalo. With God's help, of course, Callie reminded herself. But divine approbation only served to enhance her good spirits. She basked in the elation of knowing her lonely journey would soon end. This was the last leg she would have to face without responsible companionship from other adults. Civilization no longer seemed beyond reach.

The sun was still young in the sky when a cobalt-gray bank of clouds lifted above the northwest horizon. Slowly their hue became even darker as they crawled upward, blotting out the sun. Around her, the open ridges spread in an unprotected expanse of soft, creamy gold. The contrast between the light grass and the dark, angry sky frightened Callie; she would have to find shelter quickly.

Until now, she'd thought the constant wind had been gusty and strong. But suddenly, as the cloudy menace swelled before her eyes, wind struck them in full force. It was all they could do to move forward.

With the onslaught of the gale, the temperature also plunged. What had begun as a pleasant morning turned suddenly to biting cold. There was nowhere to stop and hide from the storm, no protection among the winding, barren ridges from the wind's fury.

"Those clouds frighten me, Mum," Duncan said.

Callie looked up and saw nervousness worry Jamie's face

as well. The only difference between the two boys was that one knew the futility of speaking his fears aloud.

"We shall have to find shelter," Callie announced. Although their situation made her words redundant, the children took courage from her voice. "We'll keep on walking until we do. Jamie, wrap that blanket around Susa and pull her bonnet closer over her face," she commanded, without pausing in the progress forward.

She and the children passed a lone patch of yuccas whose dry pods rattled in the wind, their spines tossing wildly. The round skeletons of thorny bushes careened by, running before the storm. Callie prayed urgently as she walked, dragging the pony who, until now, had always been easy to lead. With each step she struck the base of the lance against the ground and used it to pull herself forward. She would have tried to encourage the children, but communication was growing impossible in the face of such high wind. It whipped the words from her dry mouth and shot stinging bits of sand and small rocks up off the ground.

The gray clouds grew ragged as they rose overhead, driving snowmeal into the empty space between the sky and the prairie. Terrified, Callie stopped Cyrus and dug through her packs. "Duncan," she tried to speak, but the words were driven back into her mouth. "Duncan . . ." she screamed, "here." Offering her hands as a step, she boosted the boy up behind Susa. Then, using the rope, she tied the big buffalo robe around the two children and lashed them onto the horse. Certain that the storm was her greatest danger now, Callie slid the lance through the rope, securing it to Cyrus's side.

Then she began cutting the rawhide robe from its frame. Jamie stood beside her, trying to hold it down until she could get it free. Wind tore at the huge pelt like a sail, breaking apart her makeshift frame even as she cut it loose from Cyrus's side. "Jamie!" she shouted, wrapping the stiff hide around her boy.

"Hold . . . hold onto . . ." she fought to make him hear her, "Dunca— . . . leg . . . so."

The boy nodded, or at least she thought he did. He was on the south side of the horse, and that was all the protection she could offer.

Callie dug again into the pack, pulling out every scrap of fabric or leather she could find and bundling each of them as best she could. While she was trying to tie her precious handkerchief around Susa's pink hands, the wind wrenched it from her cold-clumsied fingers. Even before Callie could jump after the fluttering cloth it was lost in the gathering whiteness of the storm.

Callie was certain her daughter was whimpering, though she could not actually hear the sounds. Summoning patience, she demonstrated for Susa how to thrust her hands into her armpits. She gestured for Duncan to reach around his sister and to grip the buffalo robe with all his might.

Icy snow pellets and flying sand blasted her cheeks as Callie moved to the horse's head. Pulling at his bridle, she heaved forward, urging him to begin walking again. But Cyrus refused to budge.

When she threw her full weight against the leather strip for the fifth time, Cyrus took a tentative step, then another. Callie faced into the wind, narrowing her eyes to slits and fighting to keep them open. Even at that, she could hardly see through the dust and tears that rushed to cloud her vision. She was having trouble distinguishing the ground ahead, but she was sure Cyrus was turning on her, veering south. Yes, by the force of the wind she knew he was, for it was no longer steady at the front, but swinging around her right and coming from behind.

"No!" she shouted at the animal, jerking angrily again on the Indian-style bridle. "No! This way—"

She managed to force him to go full circle, but Cyrus had no sooner gotten turned west again, than he continued the pivot and came up facing east once more.

Despair gripped Callie like an iron fist. She dropped to her knees on the rocky ground, clutching the wretched blanket around her shoulders, her lips forming words of ardent prayer.

Cyrus stumbled a step forward, almost walking over where she knelt in front of his hooves, beneath his neck. Firmly, Callie pulled his head back and continued her supplication. Again the pony tried to move with the wind, this time deliberately swinging his head and forelegs around as if to bypass the woman at his feet. Callie jerked the reins fiercely this time—she had to reach heaven with her prayer, and she couldn't do it while contending with a horse. She gripped the reins tightly, close to Cyrus's nose, and began praying again in earnest.

" . . . Lead kindly light amid the encircling gloom, Lead thou me on . . ." the words hung, quivered across her ears, undeniably there, but only for an instant. Perhaps it had been nothing more than the shrieking wind, she thought. Then it came again: "Lead thou me on . . ."

Bunching her flapping skirts, Callie struggled back up to her feet. She peered into the dimness of the storm. Was Duncan singing?

"Lead thou my feet. I do not ask to see . . ."

The storm roared down upon her, hitting the ground like ocean waves roaring upon a distant strand. Callie fought to hear as desperately as a drowning man grapples for air. Yes, it was Duncan singing—and Jamie, too. Only the children.

" . . . lead me on. I love to choose and see my path but now, lead thou me on . . ."

Cyrus pressed forward more firmly, knocking her over with his shoulder as she tried to resist. The leather strip slipped from her stiff, icy fingers. Callie threw out her hands, groping after it unsuccessfully. Cyrus was moving quickly, sweeping back to the east, his rump toward the storm. Callie fought the wind to get back on her feet, bunching her skirts with one hand and clutching the blanket around her shoulders with the other. The pony had almost left her behind before she flung one hand out again and lunged after him, clenching her fingers into his ice-clotted tail.

Callie could make out Jamie's dark form ahead of her on the right, now. She could see the bundle that was Susa and Duncan and felt better knowing she could touch them if she only reached out her hand. At least this way she could watch to be sure no one was lost in the snow.

Her vision was better, once she wasn't peering into the wind. But she couldn't make out anything more than a few yards away. The distant mountains were entirely lost from sight, and this barren place offered no other landmarks. Following the horse was a foregone conclusion, for she no longer had the force to direct him nor any sense of where she wanted to go. So Callie gripped his long, tangled tail and let his momentum pull her.

The raw cold was more bitter than any she had ever endured. Her breath formed crystalline white on her eyelashes, and her cheeks stung. Behind them, the wind gnashed and bit at their backs. And though the icy temperatures gnawed inward from their extremities, Callie soon realized that the pace Cyrus set was saving their lives by keeping their blood pumping. "Shake your feet and arms every so often, Duncan!" she shouted, finding it slightly easier to communicate now that he was downwind. "Make Susa do it, too!"

They walked through an eternity of white. Snow moved past them in shades, sheets across the wind. Eventually Jamie's steps tired, and Callie pulled him back beside her where he, too, could hang onto the tail as if it were a rescue rope. Hours passed with only the rocking motion of the riders ahead and the roar of snow-laced wind at their backs. When the blizzard finally blew over, the sky began to clear and the ice pellets tapered off. Wind never stopped beating against them, and Cyrus never ceased plodding on through the shallowest of the drifts and places where the storm had swept so hard the barren ground was still dry.

Night let down, and Callie could not see anything except white snow in the gloom about her. But with the wind continually at her back she guessed that Cyrus was still leading them east. Callie reached with numb hands into her pack, pulling out sticks of dried meat for them to chew and kept on walking behind the horse. She wanted to seize control, call a halt, build a fire. But the sage desert offered no useful wood, and she hadn't seen any buffalo chips between the mounds of windswept snow. Callie looked down, watching, hoping that the minute she saw anything combustible, she would still have the use of her hands to set it on fire.

Every so often, she rubbed her cheeks and nose with the back of her rag-wrapped hand. She was startled by how soon her face went numb again after she quit rubbing. "Wiggle yourself," she commanded Jamie. "Susa! Duncan! Shake yourselves all over!"

"May I lie down instead, Mum?" Jamie begged, his voice a rasping plea, his lips so numbed by cold that she could scarcely understand. "Only a wee moment?"

"No, Son," Callie answered gently, her heart aching for him and tears stinging her eyes. From the way her own legs ached, she knew how his must feel. She let go of Cyrus's tail and rubbed Jamie's back roughly. But without a handhold, she couldn't keep up the pace and had to quickly grab on again.

"Please?" he begged after a long while.

"No!" Callie half-shouted the command. "No. If you lie down now, I won't be able to get you up again."

She didn't need to say more. Jamie gave her no other response than to keep plodding uphill and down until suddenly Duncan shrieked. "A light!" Callie saw the bundle within his arms jerk and knew Susa had once again been sleeping. "There it is again! A light!"

"Aye!" Jamie yelled. "Halloo the house!" He let go of the pony's snow-caked tail and ran forward with an uneven gait on frozen, painful feet.

Callie hurried up to the horse's shoulder, her tired eyes working to make out the scene ahead. Cyrus walked straight toward the light, and she discovered they were climbing a narrowing defile.

Ahead, a small fire burned within a crude shelter that looked like nothing more than a hollow in some snow-covered rock. Silhouetted in the glow she could see Jamie's crazy dance of delight, and another form standing still and straight, wrapped in a ragged wool blanket.

Eagerly she fumbled at the knots around Duncan's and Susa's buffalo robe. "Hurry," Susa pled, as Callie struggled to set them free. "Hurry, Mum!"

At last the two children half-tumbled, half-jumped from the pony's back and ran on wobbly legs toward the flames. Callie walked around Cyrus, following where the children had gone.

"Lucky Woman," the silhouetted form spoke the name with a familiar, unhurried voice.

Stepping closer, Callie squinted against the light. And to her surprise she thought she saw a friendly smile play around the corners of Three Elk's eyes.

TWENTY-TWO

Three Elk had been delighted about their return. He made no pretense of hiding his relief that Callie and the children had survived the storm. The Indian showed Callie how to rub snow against the shrill pain of extremities bitten with cold. Then he followed the snow-rub with ice water and chased that with soakings which grew progressively warmer. He worked beside Callie, as she rubbed the children's hands and feet with her own pale, white hands that trembled against the searing pain of being reclaimed.

Even Jamie cried out, though Duncan was worse, and Susa was writhing and weeping freely. Their commotion filled the small shelter. Callie noted Three Elk's gentleness, especially with Susa. But once he had done all he could for their comfort, his patience quickly waned. "You cry like sick crow," he told the boys disgustedly. Putting his good hand in his armpit to simulate a wing, he flapped it and made a series of grating, squawking sounds.

At once the commotion ceased. Susa began wailing again as soon as she'd caught her breath. Jamie broke a grin, but Duncan's face was sullen, and he went on rubbing his toes petulantly.

"Cheyenne boy is warrior young," Three Elk grunted disdainfully. "He not cry like baby."

In spite of his harsh words, the Indian did not seem angry. Callie realized that he thought his people's ways, knowledge, and even their children were superior. His attitude irked her, but she was in too much pain to dwell on something so absurd.

Meanwhile, Three Elk went outside and, because he'd added a front to the shelter with a loose frame of woven boughs, Callie couldn't see what he was doing. After a while she grew curious enough to push aside the door-cover and peek out. In the snow-lit darkness, she could see he was unloading her belongings from Cyrus. And, from the way he was dumping them into the snow, his concern for the horse's needs was obviously foremost in his mind. Shame washed over Callie as she realized that in her eagerness for warmth she'd entirely forgotten their mount. But Cyrus had been trained not to stray from where he'd been left, and the one who had trained him remembered.

As Callie hurriedly crawled from the shelter, she realized that for Three Elk the simple act of unloading Cyrus was a laborious task. He seemed to struggle as fiercely against pain and weakness as she did against the cold wind.

He'd piled her things unceremoniously in the snow and was going over the horse, removing clumps of ice from its fetlocks and hooves. Wishing she'd known to do that, Callie began carrying her goods inside. Fatigue caused her legs to tremble; her resistance to the cold fled entirely, as she struggled to make one little trip after another. Jamie came to the door and took the packs as she handed them to him. Their provisions made only a pitiful, paltry stack, but Callie was so spent that it was all she could do to lift—not drag—the things out of the snow and pass them through the door.

Three Elk stood holding the horse's head. Callie watched his gentle handling and friendly muttering to the animal. She could see that he was shaking and that perspiration beaded his brow in spite of the cold. He leaned heavily on its neck as he whispered into its ear, then turned it loose toward the aspen and willows along the creek. The soft sounds, nasal tone, and glottal stops of his language were obviously comforting to Cyrus, for he turned to nuzzle the Indian's face before disappearing into the darkness.

This open display of affection shot a pang of jealousy through her, but Callie told herself she was immune to such emotions. Three Elk's relationship with Cyrus did not affect the ownership of the animal. And she purposefully ignored what was going on until she realized that Three Elk had no intention of following the horse or tieing it up. "Hey! You can't just let my horse go!" Callie demanded.

Three Elk did not bother to answer her. He walked, bent and wobbly against the gusty wind, back into the warmth beneath the boughs. Callie stood for a moment frowning after him, but not wanting to chase the horse and picket it. Well, if Cyrus strayed, Three Elk could hunt him up. She was too cold to do it now and would insist he do it later.

Three Elk lay quietly on the robes as Callie struggled to contain the screaming of her hands and feet and face while they warmed a second time to the fire. Susa was still thrashing and crying, so Callie divided her time between rubbing and comforting the children and arranging their meager provisions along the draftiest wall of the shelter next to the door.

Soon Three Elk was sitting upright again. Wordlessly, he boiled strips of dried buffalo by dropping fire-heated rocks into a leather bag from among his things. Callie saw him add a few leaves from his neck pouch but did not have the energy to entertain feelings of distrust or suspicion. When he offered the concoction to them, James and Duncan ate ravenously, and as soon as they were finished, Three Elk cooked more.

Unlike the boys, Susa could hardly eat a bite. She tossed and turned, alternately wringing her hands, gripping her feet, and clutching at her stomach. "I can't eat, Mum," she wailed. "Me stomach's in knots with the pain. Oh! Ow-w-w! Ow-w-w! Ow-w-w-w-w-w-wie!"

"See here, now, lassie," Jamie said, scooting her onto his lap. "Aren't ye able even t' swallow th' hot broth first? 'Twill settle yer belly and warm yer insides."

"That howling of yours is louder than a pack of coyotes!"

Duncan growled. "You're old enough to buck up, Susa, like the rest of us." Then, realizing how waspish his voice sounded, he added, "Besides, you wouldn't want to bring wolves down upon us, would you?"

"Oh, Jamie," Susa cried, putting her arms around her big brother's neck. "Are the wolves out there even in this cold?"

"They're often abroad in th' black o' night, but I'm thinkin' this storm's got 'em holed up at home wi' their missus and their wee ones."

Callie noticed the white spots on Jamie's cheeks, at the center of brilliant pink, and she realized how much they, too, must be hurting. But he went on encouraging Susa and getting the warm broth down her one sip at a time.

The children finally stopped crying over their aching hands and feet. Or rather, they stopped their wakeful noise and escaped into whimpering, fitful rest that filled the close quarters beneath the shelter with moans. Even Jamie, who showed self-control while awake, gave way to deep, long groans and tossed beneath his covers. Three Elk was lying quiet on the other side of the fire from Callie, with the children between them.

Callie wanted to sleep. But the flaming, tender flesh of her extremities made it impossible. Besides, the children's discomfort added to her own. And all the time, the rude shelter cramped down around them, trapping her and pressing in even as it rescued them from deadly cold outside.

Where had the storm come from so suddenly? Why? Questions assailed her mind whenever she tried to rest. *How could God have let this happen?* Once again she felt deserted, frustrated even beyond what her own thoughts could define. Callie refused to try to sing in such tight quarters, penned up with a savage as she was. And so, she found herself cornered by her thoughts.

She was haunted by the inexorable power of this wilderness. It had crushed her again. Swept over her and beyond . . .

yet it did not exult in its victory. Its complacency upset her most. Callie did not think of nature as an animate thing. If it had been a person of some sort, she could have attributed qualities to it, could have thought of it in terms of good and evil, like Satan being after her soul. But the wilderness was untamed nature, nothing more. The vicious mountain heights, the swollen rivers, and the sudden storms were not premeditated or calculated attacks against her. The wilderness did not care about her at all. It was just out there following laws which were so vast and powerful that she hadn't means to fight them. Or so it seemed.

But God had control. He made the laws and machinations of nature; they were obedient in His hand. She had trusted that for her sake and for her faith He would bend them. Again the questions multiplied. If God did not intervene, it must be because He wanted her here. *But why?* That was more than her frustrated, exhausted mind could comprehend.

Angrily, Callie rose and began patting Susa's back, hoping to quiet her whining. She started through a mental inventory of her goods. Like a ship becalmed at sea, she had only so many provisions and so much time. Quietly she counted, going over rips and holes in their clothing, estimating which ones she had enough thread left to mend, lamenting lost buttons. She cast her eyes around the dim shelter: its corners, its uneven roof of sticks and boughs, its dirt floor. Snatching up Angus's Book of Mormon from among her things, Callie opened it but found she was too tense to read. The words trailed through her mind without meaning—nothing more than a rattle of familiar sounds.

Crossly, Callie quit in the middle of a sentence and thumbed through the pages to the back cover. Eyes watering in the dim, smoky light, she counted the days she'd marked with charcoal lines. One hundred and twenty-one. One hundred and twenty-one days or—she worked out the sum—tomorrow would make four months since the massacre on the prairie.

That had been a Tuesday and—she separated the tallies by sevens—this day had been a Tuesday as well. Callie licked her lips and began counting again. At fifty-seven, she abruptly slammed the book shut. Why was she double-checking? The days didn't matter! One hundred and twenty-one days or three hundred and nine. How long didn't make any difference. What mattered was that they still weren't in Salt Lake City, still hadn't even reached Fort Bridger.

Instead they were crammed in this hole, squeezed together among rags and dirt like a pack of vermin. She glared across the children at the Indian's still form. He was sick now, still weak from the wound, but what would happen when his strength came back? Would she need to be afraid of him, to watch every minute until the onslaught of winter was over? A white woman in such a small space with a savage . . .

Callie reached for the knife in her apron strings, but found the sheath Three Elk had given her, as well as his knife. She wondered momentarily about his motives, refusing to believe he'd actually expected her to return. He had been trying to buy freedom from the justice of law—nothing more.

And still the closeness bore down on her: the moans of the children, the unsteady flickering of the dim light, the creaking and shifting of their shelter as the wind reached down into the hollow and gusted around the rock.

Suddenly she could stand it no more. Pulling her blanket behind her, Callie crawled to the doorway and thrust aside the cover Three Elk had woven of boughs. Once outside, she replaced it and flung her blanket around her head and shoulders. Miserable tears coursed down her cheeks as Callie gave in to shivering sobs. The wind persisted though it had driven the clouds away and unfolded a night of brilliant immensity. Leafless aspen stood all around her, their twisted branches reaching hopelessly, like gnarled, cold-bitten fingers toward lovely, jewel-bright light.

A shuffling sound was followed by the shaking of the door

as Three Elk slid it aside and crawled out. Callie watched his movements. He revealed no pain, made no grimaces, gave no moans, but his nostrils flared wide as he came slowly to his feet. He was breathing deeply, intentionally, against every exertion. The Indian stood beside her, looking up at the cold expanse of stars that thronged the black sky.

"Have you a family, Mr. Elk?" Callie asked eventually, her tone an accusation.

"Yes. A wife, a son."

"Aren't you worried about them? Who will take care of their needs in this weather?" Anxiety made her words angry, and she unleashed her fury on him freely.

"My brother cares until I come." The Indian's words were calm, imperturbable.

"Your brother?" Callie asked, looking suddenly toward him. Even in the darkness, she could see the ragged gray tiredness that rimmed his face, but there was no mercy in her voice. Scowling back up at the stars she demanded, "But what of him? Doesn't he have responsibilities of his own? Doesn't he have a family? Mouths to feed?"

"Yes."

"Then how can you possibly stay here? Don't you long for your own people? You say your boys are brave men and mine are babies. Yet you calmly submit to this wilderness and let it rule over you." Callie paused only long enough to draw breath. "How is it that you buckle under? I cannot believe you are as manly and courageous as you pretend, when you let a storm make you crouch in this hole like an animal!"

Silence hung on the cold between them, and Callie began to think Three Elk would refuse to answer. She was sure she was right; having the last word proved it.

But the savage surprised her by speaking softly at last, with his ever-present sense of carefulness and reserved control. "Long darkness is big cold."

Callie was shivering violently now, but she did not want to

withdraw her question until he explained himself or admitted defeat. She glared up at the reaching treetops and the glittering, far-off stars. "So what?"

Again the moments drew out before Three Elk spoke. "I am *vohkoohe.*" He poked one hand out of his blanket and made a hand sign for a small animal with long ears. "See? Rabbit. Big cold is *ho?nehe* . . . hmmm, big dog . . . ah, volf."

"*W.*" Callie corrected, her voice severe. "Wolf." She couldn't imagine what he was getting at.

"Wolf," Three Elk repeated in his usual nasal tone. He shifted his feet, wobbled slightly, caught himself, and went on. He seemed to care that she understand this, and she was too angry to acknowledge his physical weakness. "Wolf is big. More big than rabbit. If I am wise, I see more suns when wolf go 'way. If I am foolish—if I not wait smart—I am eaten. I never see my people more."

Callie did not respond. She was too tired and disappointed to accept the prudence of his words. Expedience galled and humiliated her; it hammered at the very foundations of her faith, and at that moment she hated it. She wished she hadn't spoken to him in the first place.

That was when Three Elk pulled his gaze fully down from the sky and peered directly, meaningfully at Callie. His eyes looked deep into hers with the same amazingly dispassionate discernment that had so often unnerved her before. "Two kind of rabbit," he said in a voice that was cool, firm, emphatic. "One foolish. One wise."

He turned abruptly and pulled aside the door of the shelter, gesturing for her to crawl inside. Callie did not argue; there was nothing else to do.

TWENTY-THREE

Callie woke the next morning feeling sheepish about the anger she'd unleashed on Three Elk. He certainly hadn't caused the storm and penned her up in this hovel. Although she resolved to make a frank apology the first chance she got, her determination weakened as the day went on.

She knew the efforts of the night before had taxed Three Elk's limited energy. She realized that a straight diet of dried meat wasn't the best nourishment for speedy healing—nor were the rest of the conditions they were living under. But her contrition began to fray as Three Elk slept on and on past the bounds of normal rest. This savage, she finally decided, was plain lazy. He was going to sleep the entire day away!

Afternoon shadows stretched long and blue across the snow that had piled beneath the rim of the gully when she went down to the creek. This was her seventh trip to fill the waterskin that day. She had cooked meat, fetched water, and applied constant effort toward keeping the children content in such a small space. Considering her own lingering exhaustion, it had been quite a strain; she was glad to be free of that tight place, even if it meant facing the gusty cold.

The sun had shone all day through a sky of distant, chilly blue. Although its light was bright, its rays exerted very little warmth against the wind. The day seemed too cold for melting, but in some places the snow had disappeared, leaving wet soil behind. Duncan asked her if wind could cause enough friction to melt the snow. Callie didn't know how to answer his question, so she simply pointed out that all but the hardest, dirt-crusted snowbanks had blown east.

"To England, Mum?" Susa had asked.

"Not that far, Chickadee," Callie chuckled. "Not that far." But now, walking across the creek-bank of frozen mud, and stooping to roll a stone through the thin ice that had frozen over her dipping hole, Callie faced the isolation she'd been trying all day to avoid. This wasn't just an early, passing storm—it was the onset of winter. Even if warm days were to come, she didn't think she should dare to cross the heaving desert and risk meeting another fury like the one of the day before. That blizzard had blown itself out quickly enough, but Callie was beginning to realize what a miracle it was that she and the children were alive.

Accepting her situation meant confronting the realities she had been so irrational about the night before. She was stuck in this wretched hole for the winter, stuck with a savage who was content to eat and sleep and let her do all the work as if she were his slave.

"Well, you lazy heathen," Callie muttered through clenched teeth as her shivering red hand dipped the waterskin into the icy stream. "You've a grand surprise in store! I'm no squaw. As soon as you're able, you'll find yourself up and acting like a real man." The frigid water made her fingers smart so fiercely that she laid the waterskin beside her on the frozen bank and, wrapping them in a corner of her blanket, began to blow on them.

The first thing she'd have him do was build a necessary and confine other refuse to a midden. She'd heard how deserted Indian camps were a mass of filth and offal and could not be used again for some time. Well, *her* camp would be different. She wasn't going to walk through their own accumulated leavings all winter.

After that, she would make sure the shelter was enlarged to cover the full breadth of the twelve-foot rock against which it had been built. The Indian and the boys could do that, as well as help her find fresh game. Unsupplemented, her buffalo strips would not last more than three weeks among all five of them.

Downstream an owl called into the gathering blue darkness. "Who, who? Who, who? Who-who-awww!"

And I will begin earnest lessons for the children, Callie promised herself as she picked up the waterskin and started back along the path. Susa could begin learning her letters out of Angus's Book of Mormon, and the boys could continue with math tables and memorization. *Regardless of our pathetic condition,* she resolved, *these months will not be lost. Maybe something of civilization will even rub off on Three Elk.*

Callie crawled into the shelter and warmed herself by the fire before going back out to fetch a night's supply of wood. Three Elk was still dozing; the boys were making a game of flicking woodshavings into the fire, and Susa was lost in make-believe with Mrs. McGillicutty.

But when she was back outside again, gathering wood in the last of wan daylight, Callie thought once more of Three Elk. Maybe he would show some intelligence and learn to read. He seemed to be fond of Susa, and if she were learning, perhaps he could better himself, too.

Could it be that God had restrained her progress toward Fort Bridger because the savage needed to learn? What if Three Elk were to grasp reading, to study the Book of Mormon, and to go back to his tribe and save his people? The idea was grandiose but not entirely impossible. The prophet Nephi had foreseen that the gospel would come to the Lamanites through the Gentiles. Why hadn't she considered it before? After all, that volume of scripture was a history of *his* own people.

Callie felt warmer than she had in days, and she picked up sticks with a more eager hand. She could survive the winter if only she knew her placement was God's will; she could endure nearly anything if she believed He had a purpose in it.

Returning to the shelter, she found Susa quarreling with Duncan. "He pushed on my foot again after I told him not to!"

"Not on purpose!" Duncan asserted.

"Dunc knows it hurts, Mum. He isn't being careful."

"We all need to be careful," Callie said, trying to organize the tumbling, awkward stack of fuel she had set beside the door. Meanwhile the squabbling kept on.

"Stop!" Jamie cried. "Hold off, you two! 'Tis enough o' ye pokin' each other. Keep t' yourselves." His voice boomed loud in the shelter, shaking clear through Callie's tired frame.

"You're not my master!" Duncan grumbled.

"Quiet, Duncan," their mother interposed. "And thank you, Jamie. That will be enough. You take care of yourself and I'll handle your brother and sister."

"Sorry, Mum," Jamie answered. "Guess we're all cross wi' bein' cooped up." Then his face suddenly blanched, and he hurried from the shelter.

Hasty rushes outdoors had been the boys' pattern all day. Callie insisted on their staying warm inside for at least one day until their frostbitten parts looked better because logic told her that those places were more susceptible to being frosted again. But her efforts to keep them inside had been only partially effective because their stomachs were aching and queasy. *At least,* she hoped, *we will have a necessary soon.*

She boiled meat in water again, and as soon as it was ready, Three Elk roused conveniently. After blessing the meat, Callie divided up shares.

"No good," Three Elk said as she handed a portion to Jamie.

"What do you mean?"

"No good to belly," Three Elk pointed at the buffalo and then touched his stomach. He made a sour face. "Boy has bad belly." He reached into his beaded leather bag, pulled out the sausages, and gestured for her to hand him the knife. Callie hesitated but then gave it to him. He cut a three-inch sausage in half and presented part to each boy, the knife to her. "Eat."

Callie squinted skeptically; Duncan's nose wrinkled as he

sank his teeth into the first bite. Oblivious, Three Elk showed as much satisfaction as if he'd provided them with a slice of cake. *"Mal de vache,"* he told their mother as if sharing a confidence.

"Mal de vache?" she repeated the words and then brightened. He was speaking French! The badness-of-cow, or cow-sickness, was the way her mind translated the words, but she still didn't understand Three Elk's meaning.

"Too much . . . hard . . . tough . . . meat make belly bad. *Mal de vache.* Need *ameske.*" He pulled out another sausage and, using his fingernail, broke open the casing, took a glob of fat on his fingertips, and spread it between them. "Tomorrow, Lucky Woman dig roots for boy. *Mal de vache* go 'way."

Callie bristled, nearly speechless at his announcement. "Why, Mr. Elk, I hardly . . . I mean, the ground is hard and cold!" Although she was incensed by his giving a command, she was also desperate. She searched his face for the slightest suggestion that he was mocking her. "I have no spade. Don't you think that if I knew where to obtain a potato, an onion, or a carrot, I would have done so by now?"

Three Elk returned her stare, his eyes registering a mild sort of contemptuous surprise. *This woman,* his expression seemed to say, *doesn't know how to dig for roots!* He leaned back against the shelter wall and laughed.

Callie could do nothing but swallow her indignation. Her own stomach had been peculiarly troubled for days, and although she did not want to admit that she was willing to eat one of his sausages, she urgently wanted to know if there really were potatoes nearby.

She tried to make polite talk with the savage over their dinner, asking questions about what his people subsisted on. But the red man was silent as he ate, unwilling to speak until the meal was finished. Later that night, after reading scriptures and putting her children to sleep, Callie found she couldn't rest until she knew the truth. Prodding him from sleep with the butt of the lance, she asked, "Excuse me, ah, Mr. Elk. Do you honestly know where potatoes are, or are you trying to make me feel foolish?"

Three Elk sat up and spread his hands in innocence. "Potato? I know not this word."

"Roots," Callie repeated impatiently. "Onions, maybe? Carrots? Turnips?"

"Roots," Three Elk echoed. "Food is here," he gestured, spreading his good arm expansively. "But must know to look." He considered before he added, "The good day for . . . *e-hovo-htanene,*" he gestured as if he were gathering, "this day is gone 'way. Already women have made the work."

"Obviously, the best time to harvest is gone," Callie tried to keep exasperation from edging her voice, "but can we find anything left after this first hard sweep of cold?"

"*Haahe!* Lucky Woman," the Indian said, chuckling and folding his arms over his chest, "you can find."

Hearing these words, Callie relaxed and let her anxiety fall back as she stared into the fire. Comfortable memories of home pressed upon her, of neat green gardens with tidy hedgerows, herbs drying in bundles along rafters, hot golden yeast rolls steaming from the oven, cows lowing to be milked at dusk, and sheep bunching in the meadows. Suddenly she remembered she had awakened Three Elk and that he was waiting patiently across the fire from her. Although he sat perfectly still, she could see he was alert because his dark eyes gleamed in the firelight.

Graceful civilization had been ingrained in Callie; she floundered to make the situation match her manners, never allowing herself to consider the ludicrousness of it. "May I offer you a drink, Mr. Elk?" she asked, lifting the waterskin and holding it out toward him.

Three Elk waved her away with a gesture of his fingers.

After a moment's silence Callie asked politely, "What is your wife named? And your boy?"

"*Na-htse?eme?* My wife?" Three Elk seemed surprised. "This one is being called *Veskeehe-menotse.*"

Callie made a sloppy attempt at repeating the word, and grinned clumsily. "What does it mean?"

"Sweet Berries," Three Elk answered, curling his second finger against his thumb to illustrate size. "Small, red. Good to belly."

"Ah," Callie breathed. That was nice. "And the boy? Last night you said you have a son. What do you call him?"

"*Onone-voneske.* Little Dog." Three Elk put his front teeth out over his lower lip and put his two hands up in front of his chest. He gave a few short, yipping cries, and Callie laughed outright, covering her mouth with delight. His imitation of a prairie dog was so perfect she could not restrain laughter, but Three Elk did not seem to mind. "Always he is running here . . . here . . . here. Talking, talking, talking." He opened and shut his fingers against his thumbs and yipped a few more times with amused affection.

"And your brother?"

"Masaha-ome," he said, but he appeared to be stumped by the idea of translation. "This one is lodge," he explained at last, gesturing around the shelter they were in. "Crazy Lodge." Then he breathed deeply and said, "*E-peva?e.* It is good. What of your people, Lucky Woman? Where your man?"

Callie felt suddenly cold, as if the wind had pierced their snow-buried shelter. "My husband's name is Angus McCracken," she heard a voice say; it was that other voice of hers, the hard one beyond tears. "On the North Fork of the Little LaRamiee River . . . last July. . . . There was a massacre on the prairie beyond those mountains," she pointed east. "Everyone was killed. Angus, too. Killed by Cheyenne."

The warmth and closeness between them dissolved. The promise of friendship vanished as they remembered they were adversaries, caged together beneath a pine-bough roof.

WINTER

5 December 1857

The Foothills of the Sierra Madre Mountains

TWENTY-FOUR

Callie sat on the cold shore of the beaver pond, rubbing life back into her numb feet and ankles as she looked at the pile of cattail roots and the bundle of clover she had gathered. It wasn't much, for sure. Five hungry people would make short work of her efforts, and she'd be down here again tomorrow, she knew. But she would rather take off her shoes and stockings, hike up her skirts, and wade into the freezing beaver pond than spend all afternoon digging those tough, scrawny roots Three Elk had first suggested.

Not that she'd minded their flavor much, really. The chewy root had an oily, sweetish taste. But even though it didn't thicken out underground like the turnips in her kitchen garden, it couldn't be pulled. Marshalling the children and arming them with sticks, Callie had led them outdoors and set them at the task. At the end of the first day it took little genius to discern that they'd spent more energy digging than they would derive from eating the roots.

So here she was, wading out into a reedy, ice-sheeted beaver pond to dig roots and gather greens. Three Elk had explained, using his hands as much as his improving English, that she would find cattails, clover, and watercress near the pond with a "beaver lodge." Sure enough, Callie discovered that under puckered stretches of snow lay a thin pane of ice, like a sheet of glass. And beneath it might be watercress, where the stream flowed swiftly, or clover, in the boggy areas.

If only the wind would stop whipping her! Callie clapped her nearly numb hands together several times, trying to restore circulation. She pulled on her stockings and boots, laced them tightly, picked up her gleanings, and began walking upstream. Tomorrow perhaps she'd bring some dry tinder and Jamie's flint. Then she would be able to build a cozy fire and warm up before she started the walk back to shelter.

Only one thing worried her about that idea: she didn't want to stay away from the shelter a moment longer than necessary. She wasn't uneasy about Three Elk hurting her children—if that were his plan, he'd had plenty of opportunities long ago. But she wasn't so sure about his relationship with them.

She could tell Jamie liked Three Elk, and Three Elk liked her son. He'd taught him to play some guessing games where he used sleight of hand to trick the youngster. His skill demanded close attention. The savage had bragged endlessly about betting on horse races, reveling in the prowess he seemed to think his successes had gained him.

"Did Cyrus ever win any races for ye?" She'd heard Jamie ask once.

"No. This one is buffalo-runner. Hunter. Fast, yes. But I see when other horse faster. I bet. Win me plenty." And then the rascal had boasted on, recounting the story of some poor creature kept by the Southern Cheyenne and called Burned-All-Over-Horse because he had so many brands. Apparently Three Elk had bet on this one during a treaty celebration several years ago, and had come away with impressive winnings. At least *he* was impressed with the loot. Callie had been disgusted.

Her distaste soon turned to abhorrence, however, when the heathen taught Jamie to gamble with some small sticks he carved. He'd even let the boy win his earring, purely for the purpose, she was certain, of addicting him to the game.

"I won't have it! None of it!" she told Jamie, leading him outside by the ear and speaking her mind. "You must never, never, never again wager with that scoundrel! He'll corrupt you, Jamie! He'll rob us blind. He'll turn you into a gambler and disgrace the father who died to save you!"

"Aye, Mother," Jamie had answered, immediately penitent. "'Twas only a game t' pass time."

"Only a game!" Callie raged. "I'd have thought more of you than to invite such evil habits into our camp and contaminate your little brother and sister. They look to you, Jamie, and I count on you to keep them safe from such wickedness when I'm away."

"I'll never do it again." The boy's voice had a solemn sound, but Callie was too cross to let him off so lightly.

"Not only will you never do that again, lad, but you'll give the heathen back his filthy earring—understand?"

"Aye, Mother. Aye," Jamie said over and over until she'd loosened her hold and sent him to fetch sticks for the fire.

That had been two days ago, and there hadn't been any gaming with the savage since then. But she wouldn't put it past the brute to think up another unscrupulous means of influencing her children.

Callie's feet were past tingling with pain as she neared the shelter. But she approached quietly and paused outside, hugging the bundle of greens against her chest and leaning close to hear what was going on inside.

"Shirt Inside Out tell what happen. He say War Shirt is dead; Plum Man sit with body."

"I'm not sure I understand," Callie heard Jamie say. "A chief named Plum Man, another man called Shirt Inside Out, an' a third man named War Shirt were huntin' prairie goats near Fort Kearney, right?" There was a pause in which Three Elk must have nodded affirmatively because Jamie went on, "An' while War Shirt pursued th' kill, th' other two waited for a stage t' come down th' trail—"

"Wagon road."

"—Wagon road, so they could ask for tobacco."

Callie winced. She hoped Three Elk didn't have any of that stashed away in his beaded bag. Again the pause before Jamie went on.

"Why didn' they just split their plugs with War Shirt when he came back?"

"They would do this thing . . . s-s-split, as you say. War Shirt say 'No.' He get own tobacco."

"But when he approached th' stage they shot him?" Jamie asked.

"Treaty say bluecoat soldiers friends. Cheyenne friends. *Ve?ho?e* lie. War Shirt is dead. Many Cheyenne dead."

"Other Cheyenne, too?" Jamie asked. "Did you kill th' people in th' stage?"

"I am 'way, hunt deer, when Shirt Inside Out come back. He take friends, White Hawk, Spotted Horse, Shot In Head, Tall Reed, others. They hunt stage."

"Did they catch 'em?"

"No. Too late. Horses . . . ah . . . horses played out. Three suns pass. Old Bear—he look from tree—he see many bluecoat soldiers coming."

"They attacked your village?"

"We hide. They shoot tepees, no shoot Cheyenne." Pride at his people's cleverness swelled Three Elk's voice—pride and anger. "Other camp not hide. Ten Cheyenne dead, ten hurt."

Jamie whistled low. "So ye called th' treaty off, I s'pose, and ye hit th' trail, lookin' for blood?"

After a moment's pause Three Elk spoke, "Actions mean more than words. My friend War Shirt die. I have bad face for white man. I take many scalps for broken treaty, count much coup."

Callie couldn't stand silent a moment longer. She kicked open the door cover and crawled inside. Hot words stung her tongue, but when she saw Three Elk's face the stream of words she'd meant to say was clipped short. "No massacre brings the dead back to life," she substituted tersely, biting her lip against the tears that welled close to the surface.

"Lucky Woman speak true," Three Elk answered, leaning back and closing his eyes.

"Oh, no," Callie told him. "You're not going to end this conversation that way. I'll have a word with you, red man. This boy is young and impressionable. You shouldn't be filling his mind with tales of depredation and murder."

"He can think."

"He's only a child! A young boy," she insisted.

"His thoughts . . . these are thoughts of a man."

Callie groaned. *You can't argue with a heathen,* she decided. *Their logic is bad. Their ability to reason must somehow be impaired.* Out loud she said, "He is *my* son. Don't tell him your stories about tobacco and gambling and glorifying the evils that come of it. Why don't you do something useful? Teach him how to get us fresh meat or something like that?"

Immediately Callie regretted the suggestion; she didn't want Jamie in any danger. She'd been trying to protect him from the wilderness. She wanted him to grow up civilized, not hardened by all this viciousness.

Turning away, Callie spread out a hide and put her burden down on it, sorting the roots from among the bits of clover. "Just . . . just try to do something useful, will you? Just keep to things that are useful."

Callie regretted her words, but Three Elk acted on her request. While he hadn't the strength to walk far, he could sit outside their shelter where the wind wasn't as keen and the sun was warm. From there he gave directions to the boys. He sent Jamie and Duncan scouring the hills for large, flat rocks and whittling sticks to make snares. Both boys were eager to learn.

The snaring technique turned out to be simple. A flat, heavy stone was propped up on one end by a stick, and between where the two met, another stick slanted down at an angle. On its tip they pushed something for bait, and when a small creature came to wiggle it free, the rock fell with a crushing blow. The secret to success, Three Elk emphasized, was to find the right game trails on which to set the traps and to sing the song for "taking meat."

"That's silly," Duncan said, hurrying off to set up his first snare.

But Jamie was curious, "What song's that?"

Three Elk began intoning a chant with the resonant, nasal sounds Callie had heard him use before. *"Hunh-ha, hunh-ha, eh-ha, eh-ha, eh-ha . . ."*

The sound was not unlike the song he sang every morning when the sun rose, nor the one he sang when it set. In fact, she wasn't sure she could tell his chants apart, although the savage seemed very serious about it. *"Haa-he!"* he said abruptly. "That my song. You must sing own song."

Jamie nodded, but the Indian was not satisfied. "Sing," he ordered.

Jamie looked sideways over at where his mother was cutting up cattail roots. "Hunh-ha," he began, tenuously, "hunh-ha—"

Before she could object, Three Elk threw up his hand. "No. Your song for taking meat."

The boy sat silent for some time, and Callie waited, giving him room to work through this himself. Then suddenly, Jamie's face brightened and he burst out in his boyish, off-tone voice, "How firm a foundation, ye Saints of the Lord, is laid for your faith in His excellent word!" Tapping the fingers of one hand to his cap in good-bye, Jamie ran upstream into the forest. "What more can He say, than to you He hath said? You who unto Jesus . . ."

Callie could still hear the chorus echoing down the ravine after he was gone from sight. She chuckled. "Sounds like he'll scare off most everything before they even get a chance at his bait."

"He learn," Three Elk answered calmly. "He learn."

Jamie did learn. He and Duncan set traps all over the ravine. And after five days, Jamie brought home a rabbit, while both boys caught several chipmunks near the necessary and the midden.

But the buffalo strips were running out, and Three Elk didn't seem to be getting much stronger. Callie realized that if they were going to have meat, a regular daily meal, it was up to her to provide it.

She took Cyrus out one morning to scout the valley, carrying flint, a small bundle of dry tinder, and the warmest buffalo robe. Heavy gray clouds formed a tattered blanket across the sky, but between their edges the sun was warm. Callie rode Cyrus down the sloping bottom of the valley and picked their way across sage-scattered ridges, laying the lance before her as men rest their rifles across their horses' withers.

She rode all day, singing softly to herself and scanning the horizon, but no buffalo were to be found. And although black-horned prairie goats sped away leaving dust-puff trails across the desert, she couldn't kill the speedy creatures with just a lance. In fact, there was nothing out on the bare ridges she could catch.

This realization desolated her. Turning Cyrus back up the bottom of the valley, Callie listened to the tall dry grass brush against his legs. Hungrily she hunched forward over her aching stomach and began to pray. "I've done all I know of, Father. What more is there?"

Suddenly a grouse shot out of the grass at Cyrus's feet. Its wings were held high, its legs waddled awkwardly forward until it lifted off the ground, flew a few yards, and dropped down to run again. She had seen sage grouse before and knew they were good to eat. Agnes Lauderberry's boys had come in with several one night on the trail. The old woman had complained loudly about plucking fool-hens, as she called the brown and white birds, but not about eating them. At that time, Callie had thought such a mouthful not worth the trouble, but this one looked like a genuine feast.

With a kick, hardly realizing what she was doing, Callie raised her lance. Jabbing Cyrus's flanks with her heels, she leaned forward and gave chase. The bird swerved suddenly, running off to the right, and Cyrus cut after it before Callie realized what was happening. The ground rushed heavily up at her. She met hard dirt with a thud that knocked the air out of her chest. *Falling never hurts any less,* she thought, lying still until her senses calmed down. The she picked herself up and hurried to see that her lance wasn't broken. Cyrus forsook the grouse and came to stand over his rider while she cherished the lance, fearful of damage, running her hand over its shaft and crossing her thumb along its blade.

"This is a wild goose chase, old fella'," she said as she rose, leaning against the pony to catch her breath. "Or a wild grouse chase!" Callie chuckled to herself, but amusement was momentary. She couldn't spear grouse any more feasibly than she could run down the prairie goats.

But what if she waited for game to come to her? Where one fool-hen lurked, there was probably a bevy. What if she lay still—very, very still? If she were on her stomach beneath the buffalo skin, perhaps they wouldn't recognize her as a threat.

Eagerly, Callie rode Cyrus up the valley to where there were some willows and set him loose. Then, walking back near the scene of her fall, she gathered a big handful of seeds from the sagebrush. Callie sprinkled these around on the ground before stretching herself out downwind of her seeds and covering herself with the hide.

How will I kill them? she wondered. So far she'd considered the idea a clever one. But what chance did she have of getting enough force and speed in this position to impale one of the birds? After puzzling for a while, Callie realized that she did not have to stab with the lance. If she held it very still and upright, perhaps the fool-hens would think it nothing more than a thin tree. From there she could bring it down and—*whap!* If nothing else, it would surely stun one of the birds.

Eagerly, Callie braced the butt of the lance against the ground and raised the point up into the air. Getting it well balanced between her hands, she rested her cheek on one arm and began to wait. The sun was warm; the robe protected her from wind so that she soon grew snug and drowsy. She hadn't known she was dozing until something hit hard across her face and back.

TWENTY-FIVE

The lance. She must have relaxed her grip enough that it had fallen. Absurdly grateful no one had been there to see her "fierce" hunting, Callie raised the lance back into an upright position. Then she clucked softly as if she were feeding a coop of chickens. *Come out, all you fool-hens, wherever you are,* she called mentally, considering the way hunter and prey were well-suited to one another. To keep from falling asleep again, Callie began chewing one of the sage seeds, twisting it between tongue and teeth and sucking at it.

Holding still was difficult. And being perfectly motionless was impossible. Her muscles began to pinch with spasms and the little rocks beneath her pressed up like daggers. For a while it seemed she might explode as a stray hair tickled her upper lip and a nagging itch insisted she scratch her ankle. But through persistence Callie found that by flexing all her muscles—just barely exercising them in infinitesimal ways—she could keep her limbs from cramping up.

Eventually a lone field mouse came running by to investigate her seeds. Callie had just realized she was hungry enough to eat even such a tiny rodent, when a small tan bird with black markings flew down and attacked it. After an instant of being violently pecked, the mouse lay dead. The bird dragged his prey off toward a lifeless sage branch, where he impaled the limp creature, ate his fill, and flew away.

Callie's mind reached backward, wondering where she'd seen something like this before. And then she knew. Up in the mountains she'd seen another tiny bird, just like this one, kill an even tinier bird in the bracken. She remembered the indignation its aggression had aroused in her, remembered her resentment toward the bird's out-and-out violence. She'd been appalled, even though she was past letting the viciousness of the wilderness surprise her. But now it was as if she were recalling the feelings of a stranger.

The bird was hungry. That was all. What she'd witnessed today amounted to an honest, open answer to a direct need. How could she hold a simple beast responsible for wrong when it had only been trying to fill its stomach? Hadn't she been about to kill that very mouse when the bird came along?

These impressions raced through Callie, deep below the level of words, beneath the defined thoughts of her conscious mind. She didn't so much *think* them as *feel* them. She didn't realize that most of her plan in killing the grouse had come to her in hunches and feelings. Actually, she didn't think about it much at all because, in spite of the recent rodent murder, some fool-hens were beginning to peek out of hiding and to wander toward her seeds.

Callie's ride back to camp was exhilarating. Although the ragged cloud blanket had settled into a sheet of gray that smelled of snow, Callie was exuberant. No fewer than five fool-hens had wandered near her hiding place during the course of the afternoon. Two hens and a cock had met her lance without even seeing doom fall.

Callie sang out in full voice while her dim shadow ran ahead and darted around Cyrus's hooves like a hunting dog.

> D'ye ken John Peel with his coat so gray?
> D'ye ken John Peel at the break o' day?
> D'ye ken John Pee-e-e-e-el when he's fa-a-ar a-away
> Wi' his hounds and his horn in the mornin'?

One of her husband's old ditties came rolling up within her, matching the pony's gait as he sauntered home. Callie sang in the brogue, with a joyful twist of her tongue, rolling the R's as she had often heard Angus do.

At the sound, Jamie came running down the spine of the ridge, jumping sage clumps with Duncan and Susa close behind. Without attempting to hide her satisfaction, Callie held up the three sage grouse by their feet, calling, "Make a spit, Master McCracken! We've fresh meat t' sup on!" Cheering, the children turned and ran for the shelter.

Three Elk made no attempt to suppress his pleasure at Callie's success. They made a party of it, singing and laughing, and Callie offered a sincere prayer of thanks. Then Three Elk gave gifts to Callie and Susa of some small buttons he had carved from bone. They were round and smooth enough that Callie, still caught off-guard by the gift, marveled at the workmanship. She was less enthusiastic about the Indian's presents to the boys but decided against speaking hard words that might mar the day's satisfaction. Besides, Jamie and Duncan laughed and blew on their shrill bone flutes as if these were toys they had always wanted.

Three Elk pulled one from his things, using it to show the boys that it was possible actually to play real notes. Callie listened, remembering the old celidh songs of the Scots, the ancient twisting melodies that wound sad and mysterious, just beyond the reach of memory.

"Let's show Three Elk our appreciation by entertaining him," she suggested, shaking off the moody feeling the whistles gave her. Duncan looked eager, while Jamie became suddenly absorbed in scrutinizing his new whistle. But when she said, "Susa first," the redheaded boy looked up.

"Aye, lassie," Jamie grinned eagerly. "Show Mother what ye' mastered t'day while she was out fetchin' meat."

"Jamie helped me, Mum," Susa said, opening the Book of Mormon. "And see? I can read the beginning without mistakes! From 'the First Book of Nephi,'" she began, her tiny pink finger following along each word, her voice halting and without inflection. "'His Reign and Ministry. Chapter One. . . . I, Nephi, having been born of goodly parents . . . and having seen many afflictions in . . . my days . . . nevertheless, . . . having had a great knowledge of the goodness and the mysteries of God . . .'"

Callie's heart swelled at the sound of her daughter's little mouth shaping itself around difficult words, pausing, her eyes squinting and then looking to Jamie for encouragement. How she loved that boy! His gentle, good-natured ways brought Angus close again.

"Lovely, darling," Callie clapped when Susa had finished. "Absolutely marvelous! Tomorrow, you shall sit on my lap, and we will read even further!"

Then she insisted the boys recite, taking turns verse by verse, through Coleridge's *Rhyme of the Ancient Mariner.* She was encouraged by how well they did and took particular pleasure in Duncan's natural flair for giving the words meaning.

When he said,

> The ice was here, the ice was there,
> The ice was all around:
> It cracked and growled, and roared and howled

she felt the falling snow outside more keenly. And when he reached the famous stanza,

> Water, water, everywhere,
> And all the boards did shrink;
> Water, water, everywhere,
> Nor any drop to drink

Callie thought how even Hobson, the boys' schoolmaster back home, would have been pleased with her teaching. She looked over and saw Three Elk listening attentively, though surely he could not be understanding much of it.

Jamie, on the other hand, stumbled off and on through the

more archaic words and less concrete allusions. But his mother rejoiced when he firmly executed his performance of one of the last verses. As if it were the one thing in all the long poem that made sense to him, Jamie locked his gaze with Three Elk's and said,

> He prayeth best, who loveth best
> All things both great and small;
> For the dear God who loveth us,
> He made and loveth all.

Three grouse had been a feast, and full bellies were ample cause for celebration. But the bones were soon picked bare. The storm that had begun thin and ragged hung on more endless and deep than an ocean. Wind blew with steady vengeance, temperatures plummeted, and it was three days before Callie could manage her way down the valley to hunt grouse again.

The pattern of storms that followed over the multiplying weeks left her continually anxious about food. Her gratitude to the Lord for each addition to their diet was profuse; specific prayers of faith, like the one she had offered back on the Platte when she'd needed a horse, were her natural thought. Answers were not always immediate, but Callie credited her growing resourcefulness to the Lord.

She gathered the seeds of sage bushes and boiled them, traveled farther and farther upstream for watercress, harvested protruding bulbs from shoots of bulrushes in the beaver ponds, and toasted pinecones open for their meager nuts. In time, she learned to make a squealing sound, like that of a small animal in pain, by smacking her lips against the back of her wet hand. Then, when the first little creature came to investigate, she made quick use of the lance.

Beyond that, Callie preserved each tiny hide and the feathers from the grouse to make ear-coverings and mittens that would block the wind. Three Elk had laughed at her ignorance of squaw's work, but necessity made her listen to his instructions for tanning. These weren't chores he'd done as a warrior, yet he was endlessly amused by the discovery that she did not know how to perform them.

One day Callie came in from an unsuccessful attempt at spearing fish. As often, she was on the edge of her resilience, relentlessly worrying about what else might be nourishing, what else she could find to eat. *Nine-tenths of staying alive is food,* she reflected, considering that this need had never exclusively commanded her thoughts and energies before. *My life has vanished into a menial abyss—no circle of lady friends, no social graces, no great and inspiring thoughts beyond those I make myself—and there's nothing left of me to think that hard by the end of the day's surviving.*

She rubbed her sore feet, trying to recall the last time they'd been truly warm. A tired sort of melancholy washed over her when she realized she could not exactly recall the way it felt to slip on silk hose. She had worn them long ago, but present facts blotted out a satisfying memory.

"Mum?" Duncan called her from her reverie. "I need to show you something in one of my traps. I'm not sure what to do with it. Could you come with me? Now?"

The earnest and imperative sound of his voice warned against questions. Callie pulled her still-damp stockings and worn, wet boots back on and followed the boy out into the snow. He led her upstream, past the necessary, and paused as soon as their path had made a twist around in some rocks.

"I . . . I really don't have any snares set here," the boy began. Something in his tone made Callie bend down so her face was level with his. "There isn't anything for you to see, but I had to tell you something about Jamie. I know he'd be sore if he heard me. It's his hand, Mum—his hand!"

"What's wrong with his hand?"

"It's all splotchy and angry-looking. Big slivers are pokin' out here, all across the palm and in the muscle beneath the thumb. There's pus 'round the slivers, too."

Callie recalled suddenly, though it had meant nothing to her before, that when they left Jamie had been sitting all hunched up with his right hand hidden beneath his left arm. She patted Duncan's shoulders and stood straight again. "You're a fine boy, Duncan. I'm glad you care so much about your brother." Callie stomped her icy feet three times, and without wasting another instant, started back for camp. Duncan had to run to keep up.

"You won't tell him, will you, Mum?"

"No, Son. He'll not be cross with you."

As soon as they crawled inside, Jamie asked, "What was in th' snare?"

"Couldn't recognize it," Callie answered quickly.

"Squashed flat, eh? Told ye that rock was a might big, Dunc."

"Whittle me some kindling, won't you, Jamie?" Callie said, knowing that he couldn't perform this task with one hand.

"Could ye let Duncan do it? I'm a wee bit tired," Jamie said, yawning widely.

"You may use my knife," Callie answered, holding the complete blade, handle outward, toward him. Jamie reached out his good hand to take it, but in doing so, his injured hand became visible.

"What's wrong with your hand?"

"Nothin', Mother," the boy said quickly, withdrawing it from sight and tossing his head at Duncan. "Can't he do 't?"

"How did this happen?" Callie pressed, scooting closer and taking the tender hand in her own.

"I was curious, Mother, that's all. I was out in th' forest one day, checkin' m' traps, when I saw this strange-looking beastie chewin' th' bark off a tree. 'Twas so fat it waddled, an' all covered wi' spines like a hedgehog, but more. *What's this?* I asks m'self, thinkin' it looked a lot like th' spines o' that fancy headgear Three Elk was wearin' when first we found 'im."

Callie looked up and saw Three Elk nod, *"Heskoveto."*

Jamie went on, "An' I thought he'd like more o' them, maybe almost as much as I'd like th' fatness underneath. Th' creature was movin' slow, so I snatched a stick an' went after 't. Gave 'im a horrible punishin', but no matter how I whacked, he just kept waddlin' away. So then, I thought, 'He's not so tough lookin'. Maybe I could grab an' throttle 'im.' But the minute I touched 'im, these prickles stuck in m' hand."

"E-peva?e," Three Elk chuckled and spoke to Jamie. "It is good. You have met Thorny-one. You know his strength. To kill him you must stab here," Three Elk pointed to his nose. "Only this place will life go out."

Drawing Jamie's hand closer, Callie examined the wounds and saw that the animal's spikes were barbed at the ends. The hand was swollen, infected, unusable. "Three Elk," she pled, "What can I do?"

"For baby, this thing is coming out with many tears. For this one . . ." he spread his hands wide. "He hurts three, four suns. He not cry."

"You knew? Why didn't you tell me!"

"He is man. He choose."

"This is no man," Callie fiercely repeated what she'd asserted so many times before. "Jamie is my *boy*." Then, letting go of what she wanted and looking at sore reality, she asked softly, "Can you help him?"

"Give knife. I cut free Thorny-one's feathers." Immediately Three Elk began to heat the knife clean, just as Callie and Jamie had done that autumn night that seemed so long ago.

Seizing Susa's hand and leading her out the door, Callie commanded, "Come along, too, Duncan. We'd best be gathering firewood before dark." She did not seem in an unnatural hurry, but the two children noticed that despite the snow lying two feet deep between drifts, their mother led them farther from the shelter than was necessary, and she did not return until cold forced her to go back.

"Haahe!" Three Elk said, as Callie peeked through the door of the shelter. He was holding the knife in his teeth and he had Jamie's hand palm-up in his. The boy sat on his other hand, a thick stick about three inches long clenched between his teeth, his face pale beneath the freckles, and perspiration dampening the edges of his red hair. Callie looked at him only once; she did not look again.

"Lucky Woman," he spoke without glancing up, "you bring white root from beaver pond. Three, four root."

Leaving Duncan and Susa behind in the relatively warm lodge, Callie trudged downstream through the snow to the pond. She had to skirt it widely and come up from the farthest side, for she had already harvested the reedy banks quite thoroughly, but she lost no time in getting to work.

While she dug, snow began to fall. Heavy, wet flakes fell at first, increasing in number and then growing smaller as the wind drove them. Callie was so cold she hadn't strength to dig more than the few roots Three Elk wanted. That done, she stopped and built a small fire to dry her footgear, but such meager warmth did not last. By the time she returned to the shelter, all connection to her toes was lost, and she had to keep looking down to be sure her hand still gripped the cattails.

The Indian was eager for the roots. He mashed them between two stones and crushed more of the frilly, dry leaves from his small neck pouch into the concoction. Then he rubbed the balm onto Jamie's tender hand, wrapping it with a strip of cloth torn from his shabby blanket.

That night the five of them ate the very last of Three Elk's sausages. Callie had tried to ration them sparingly—dividing small portions at any given time and eating every other available morsel first. She had become familiar with watching the children seek sleep against their hungry stomachs, especially Jamie, who pushed the last of his supper on Duncan and Susa even when she saw in his eyes that he craved more. Once his breathing had slowed to a peaceful rhythm, she sat stroking her son's red hair with caressing fingertips.

"Brave," Three Elk said across the rippling coals of their small fire.

His eyes were on Jamie, but Callie wasn't sure if the word were an adjective or a noun. She didn't want to talk about it. At last she sighed, a long drawn-out sigh that became an extension of the tiredness stretching throughout her body.

"Three Elk, I'm afraid we have seriously depleted the game I can kill in this area. The snow keeps coming and coming—deeper and deeper! The boys' snares don't bring in as much as at first, and I am forced to travel farther and farther abroad for food."

"Cold have iron teeth. Bite hard. Not let go."

They sat wordlessly for some time, their silence a communication of agreement and equal concern. Callie wanted to ask him if he couldn't help more, if he couldn't at least try to shoot his bow. But she had seen Three Elk walk alone to the valley bottom and had read in his return that he could not yet draw back the string. Not only was his upper body strength slow in returning, but the savage couldn't walk even as far as she could.

"Do you know what else we can eat?" Callie asked at last. "The snow is so deep that Cyrus flounders. I can't ride him effectively, and if it keeps snowing, I won't be able to walk far enough."

She didn't think there was anything he could say and was immediately sorry for having asked the impossible. Not wanting to look up, lest she be forced to read the disgrace of powerlessness upon his face, Callie turned her back to the fire, clasped her hands, and approached the Lord in prayer. After the amen, she was crawling under her blanket before she noticed Three Elk was waiting to speak.

"I give new feet beneath your moccasins," he told her. "New feet that you may walk upon the snow."

TWENTY-SIX

"Come," Three Elk said, shaking Callie's shoulder and bringing her awake in darkness. "We hunt *heskoveto,* the thorny one."

They had not hunted together before, and she looked suddenly, curiously into the savage's face. There in his eyes, for one brief instant, Callie deciphered an alarming truth she had not suspected.

Callie thought about the day she had tried his weapons, the day Duncan told her how to make a pony drag, the day Three Elk had warned her not to overwater Cyrus. She realized how, in the beginning, her spine had stiffened every time the Indian tried to give her advice. She hated being beholden to him. She had despised owing him anything or knowing he had helped her in any way. She was kind because she chose to be magnanimous—that had been respectable—but she could not stand to need him.

Now, all at once, she realized that Three Elk's dignity had suffered as much as her own. He did not like having to rely on her, did not like having to eat her meat any more than she liked having to ask him where to find it.

Taking up the lance, Callie wrapped a blanket around her shoulders and followed the Indian into the predawn darkness outside. The snow had stopped falling, but the wind lashed itself into a fury, shrieking around every upright thing. Drifts whipped skyward, forming impassable hills where she had been walking; in other places, the frozen ground lay bare.

Though Three Elk's manner was composed, his step soon

lost its spring as he labored through heavy snow in the gray, luminous night. Soon they came to a place where all the trees were girdled, their bark missing in round bands. The Indian searched the ground and then pointed out the porcupine's hole beneath an inconspicuous jumble of rocks. "Watch close, Lucky Woman. *Heskoveto* not come yet." Three Elk gestured to the unsullied snow in front of the opening. "He come back to lodge soon. Big cold coming angry. Thorny-one eat good in darkness, hurry back before snow."

Then, to Callie's surprise he turned and walked away. Looking after his disappearing form, she realized that though he walked erect, he was as thin and gaunt as if the wind were blowing clear through him. She saw, too, that Three Elk was not a tall man but that he held himself straight and appeared larger than he was.

Callie wished he could at least sit with her. She wasn't very eager to fight this creature alone, especially when it could only be killed by a stab to the nose. But the thought of warm meat and fresh color in the children's cheeks kept her waiting and watching. She concentrated on merging into the ground and the snow, letting the shadows swallow her motionless form.

Her patience was rewarded. When darkness had at last been replaced by gray light, a round, spiny creature came snuffling along between the trees. Before it could take refuge in its burrow—and before she could entertain a second thought—Callie rushed forward, plunging the lance tip to its ugly task.

Callie expected to find Three Elk resting inside the shelter. She crawled through the door just after dawn, scattering snow and dragging her quarry on a pine bough to avoid the quills. She was eager for him and the children to see her success, but only the little ones were there.

Jamie and Duncan were cautiously curious, and Susa drew

back, afraid. "Is he quite dead, Mum? Are you sure?" she asked, but Callie ignored the question.

"Three Elk! Where is he?"

"Can't say," Jamie answered. "Both o' ye were gone when I woke."

At this, Callie's lips tightened down in a hard line, and she buried her concern in the task of melting snow for hot water to warm herself. She had no idea where the Indian could be, and the brief break in snowfall had given way to ice pellets riding hard on the wind. Even with the heat of their bodies, the fire had to be kept high, and the menace of the prowling wind grew loud and constant. She waited, anxious, until muffled sounds came from outside the door. As she opened it, snow swirled through the opening. Three Elk pushed in a bundle of willow sticks.

"But . . . but . . ." Callie stammered, "we already have plenty of wood. The boys can gather that."

"Not burn," Three Elk said, suppressing a shiver and pushing the bundle beside his pallet. Then, noticing her kill, he smiled, "Ah, Lucky Woman, it is good." Without saying another word, he rolled up in his blankets and slept.

Callie was unsure what to do with her stiffening beast—she'd hoped Three Elk would help her through the problem of cleaning it out and removing the prickly hide. But soon hunger got the best of her, and she dragged it outside to cut her way through the soft stomach.

During the short time it took to remove the entrails, Callie realized the gale raging down upon her was worse than the blizzard that had caught them out on the desert. Snow clung to her face and lashes. Her raw hands bled from quill pricks she was too cold to feel. Even down in this protected hollow, standing up was entirely impossible; she was forced to crouch with her back to the wind to work on the carcass. Callie could not see the necessary nor the midden, and she feared that if she ventured into the whiteness, she might not find her way back. Leaving the entrails, head, and skin in a heap beside the door, she hurried back in out of the wind.

They ate thick, hot juicy steaks that day, and Callie woke Three Elk to urge some nourishment on him.

"What about Cyrus?" she pressed. "Can he survive such cold? How will he eat?"

Three Elk gestured toward the pile of willows. "I cut for him, too. He stay in trees by water."

"But will he be all right?" Callie worried.

"You want go see?" Three Elk shrugged impatiently. "Good horse, that one. Cheyenne horse. This not his first winter." He stuffed a greasy piece of meat into his mouth, and Callie knew he would say no more.

Three Elk went back to sleep immediately after eating his fill, and that night the storm covered their shelter over so that it was impossible to force open the door cover. Jamie kept a tiny smoke-hole open in the roof, but snow and cold blew through it with arctic frenzy.

A second day was entirely gone before Three Elk woke and ate again. Callie had let the children feast on the fresh meat, eating well while she read to them from Angus's Book of Mormon. But once the third day passed, little was left of the fatty animal.

Wind-driven snow still beat upon their shelter, and the door was buried beneath a drift. Callie melted snow for water, insisting they drink from the hot pan. Firewood grew more and more scarce, until Callie gingerly pulled down bits of their shelter from its frame. The snow stayed where it had been packed against the sticks, white and hard.

She wanted to burn Three Elk's willow rods and had just decided to say so when he appropriated her pan. He boiled snow water, too, but used it to steam three willow sticks at a time, bending them around until the ends met and the middles formed a teardrop. He lashed two sets of willow rods that way, tying an eight-inch brace across the center so it would stay open.

On the fifth day Three Elk had the boys, with immense effort, work the door open and tunnel out until they found the entrails Callie had left outside. These he thawed, cut, and wove across the willows that had dried. When the gut ran out, he twisted bits of willow in and out for strength.

Night came again, colder than ever. No one had eaten all day and fuel was running dangerously low. In spite of her own shivering, Callie chafed the two little children's limbs to keep their blood moving. Duncan was surly and petulant, Susa whined, and Jamie sat with his back against the rock, whittling.

"I'm hungry," Susa cried at last. "And I want to go out."

"No," Callie answered, wrung out by the endurance of the wailing storm as much as the hunger and close quarters it enforced. "Read some more for me."

"I've been reading, and I'm tired of it, Mum. God didn't leave Lehi's family to be hungry. I just read how He made their meat sweet so they could eat it raw. But I'm hungry. Why doesn't God take care of me?"

"He does, child," Callie said in a voice so full of solid conviction it sounded harsh. "He does," she repeated more softly, though not less firmly. "You just can't see it right now. Be still if you won't read. Go to sleep."

"I slept in the afternoon, and I can't sleep anymore because my belly hurts!"

"Drink some water then," Callie's voice rose with frustration. "That's all I have to give you."

Three Elk, who had been lying silent beneath his blankets, sat up, retrieved the clean-picked bones from outside the door, and handed them to Callie. Having already boiled them once, she glanced down impatiently.

"Lucky Woman make bread. *Ve?hoo?e* like bread."

"What?" Callie recoiled.

"Look. See." Three Elk insisted. Taking two rocks from the fire circle, he began crushing the dry bones. He smiled, "We eat again."

Curiously, Callie began grinding the bones to meal. Reason told her there would be strength and nourishment there. Enough to support life? She did not know. But enough at least to ease the pain of empty stomachs.

"Three Elk," Jamie asked in a pleasant voice, "will ye tell us some stories again?"

Three Elk nodded. "Yes, I tell if you speak first."

Jamie leaned back and grinned.

Fine, Callie thought. *Maybe bones would taste better if the boy's thoughts were on spinning whoppers.*

Jamie told a tale of a mountain trapper so fierce that the dreaded Sioux war parties went miles out of their way in rugged terrain just to keep clear of him. Mother mountain lions terrified their cubs into obedience with the mere mention of his name, and when mink or beaver heard he was coming, they'd crawl right up onto the grass by the lakeshore and die rather than fight the inevitable.

Callie stopped grinding, incredulous. "Where in heaven's name did you learn to go on like that, James McCracken?"

But Jamie only smiled, muttered something about the river levees, and asked Three Elk if he was sure Cyrus was all right.

"Haahe! He eat *meno?ke."* The Indian motioned as if pawing snow from the ground. "Hunting keep him warm."

"How did ye get 'im in th' first place?" Jamie asked. "Tell us th' story 'bout that."

"Yes! Tell us about Cyrus!" Susa cried.

"I tell of coup I count with this horse," Three Elk said, and the children settled down to listen. Haltingly, using his hands to make meanings clear, the Indian told of a time when he had buried himself in a sandy dry streambed and waited for hours to ambush his Crow enemy, Naked Bear. This one, he explained, had stolen many ponies. He had taken the horse they called Cyrus, but in this brave deed, Three Elk got him back. The savage exhibited great pride in his escapade and was quick to add that Naked Bear's scalp soon hung from Cyrus's mane.

"Enough of that!" Callie announced, mixing water with the bonemeal to form a paste. "Duncan, you tell about Ammon. He was a great missionary to the Lamanites, and perhaps these two would appreciate his valor."

Duncan did a good job of relating the story, but as with every other Book of Mormon story she'd urged on him, Three Elk only grunted. Each time she struggled to ignore the impoliteness of his response, and each time Callie remained uncertain whether the grunt was one of approval or disbelief. Baffled once more in her effort to save the red man's soul, she served up their strange meal.

When the storm had blown itself out and passed off into the east, Three Elk and the boys dug a tunnel out of the shelter and up onto the surface. Clutching her blanket around her, Callie emerged, her eyes blinking and watering at the brilliant white that spread as far as she could see. She tried to stand, floundered where the boys hadn't packed the snow firmly, and then realized that she would have to keep her weight spread out if she didn't want to sink in.

"New feet," Three Elk said, handing her the teardrop-shaped willow forms he'd woven and two bindings he'd cut from the buffalo rawhide.

Eagerly, Callie hurried to strap them on beneath her boots. Placing her toe through a hole near the wide end, as Three Elk indicated, she passed the rawhide through the webbing and cinched the ball of her foot down tight. Then, standing awkwardly, she heaved forward two paces before tripping. Callie struggled up in the powder and lifted the tips of her "new feet" carefully above the snow with each step. After several chilling falls, she began to settle into a rhythm. Still, she was disappointed that she continued to sink in as far as her calves and was frustrated by how exhausting the effort was.

"These need to be bigger," she called to the Indian, unstrapping one and lifting her foot out of it. "I still sink in, and it's a lot of work pulling them out of the holes." Standing on one leg, she tossed the "new foot" to Three Elk. "Can you enlarge it?" Then she shifted weight to the other leg so that she could unfasten the second binding. Immediately, her plain boot sank down until the snow was above her hips. Callie screamed at the cold.

Three Elk laughed heartily, tossing the "new foot" back at her. Embarrassed but unable to resist chuckling, too, Callie put the other "new foot" back on and shuffled into the shelter to warm up.

He laughed at me, Callie noticed, reflecting back on those early days when she had wondered if Three Elk was incapable of emotion and pain. But here was humor bursting free between them, and undercurrents ran subtly through their interactions.

As soon as she was ready, Callie stuffed one of the last six bone-cakes into her apron pocket, tied the buffalo hide and ear-coverings on, and started upstream looking for food. Though she tired quickly, the rhythm of walking on her "new feet" grew easier, and she used the butt end of her lance to brace herself when she got stuck. She walked upstream but saw nothing. Crystalline snow lay unbroken among the pines and across the meadows.

Finding no tracks, Callie walked higher and higher up the watercourse. She had eaten the bone-cake early, thinking she would kill something soon. But it was not so. And now an iron band clamped down around her forehead and her heart tripped up to a high speed every so often. She paused frequently to rest, her breath puffing clouds in spite of the brilliant sunshine.

Yet she always pushed on, traveling higher, seeking game, and refusing to believe everything was holed up.

She had prayed as she walked, but at last she found a place where it was possible to kneel on some rocks and pour out her soul. Callie told the Lord she knew the pain in her head and her hammering heart were more the result of hunger than exhaustion. She expressed her determination and reasons for pushing on as well as her fears that she couldn't keep up the effort much farther. "Oh Lord," she begged, "it's manna time now. I'll face the cold. I'll walk all day just to fill my pockets with something for my children, but I can't return empty-handed. Please, please show me what to do . . ."

After her amen, Callie stayed motionless for some time. She recalled the way one of her prayers had been answered by Cyrus nearly pushing her over and walking across her in the blizzard, and the way the grouse had run out from beneath Cyrus's hooves when she'd been hunting in the valley. But nothing moved, and the low temperature soon drove her into action.

Lift, pivot, drop. Lift, pivot, drop. Her "new feet" methodically crawled up the stream-cut ravine, her eyes searching the dazzling whiteness for clues of other life. After an hour's continual plodding, she heard the baying of a pack of wolves. Their howls made the hair along the back of her neck prickle, and her hands shook with fear, but her mind reeled with knowing that if the wolf pack had driven something out, so could she.

Callie determinedly bent her steps uphill, clutching the lance and insisting there was no danger. The clumsy "new feet" made her feel vulnerable, but she promised herself she would watch the wolves from a distance. When she discovered the tracks of a deer, her heart caught with fear and excitement. Now she knew the pack's prey.

Stumbling along within the shadowy edges of the trees, Callie followed the frantic split-hoof trail of the deer, the circling prints of wolves' paws. At one place she came to a wide area where the snow was beaten down and the deer had floundered through a boggy place. They'd hit at him here, she knew, because blood stained the snow. From here on up the ravine, the victim's grim fate was written in every red step.

She was far behind the fight—perhaps it was already over. The wolves' howls had not reached her for some time, and the red trail in the snow was already turning to ice.

Callie pressed on. In another clearing, she saw where the deer had paused to make a stand. For three or four yards all around, the snow was torn, thrashed, and bloodied. Still the desperate animal had clung to life, managing to shake free and escape again. But this time its flight was different. From the tracks Callie could see that the deer's bounding strides were failing into short, irregular stumbles. The end could not be far off.

TWENTY-SEVEN

Callie did not go out into the clearing to investigate the prints closely. She hid among the trees, waiting for her panting breath to slow, studying the silence until she felt safe in inching ahead. When at last she reached the edge of the pines, she peered at the bloody spectacle through a thin stand of leafless aspen.

The snow in the clearing was stained crimson, shreds from the deer's torn hide and gnawed bones scattered wildly across it. Terrified by the sight, she strained her ears again, waiting for the sound of a whine, a howl, a bark, even a paw on snow. She scanned every shadow for yellow eyes, a flash of gray, the slightest movement. But the wolves were gone.

Callie scrambled into the clearing, her "new feet" shuffling across the streaked and blotted snow. Spreading out the largest fragment of bloody hide, she began tossing bones onto it as fast as she could pick them up. Then, wrapping the bundle tight, she hurried back into shelter of the pine forest, fleeing downhill as a thief flees for his life.

The burden on her back would have slowed her had fear not made her steps quick. *Don't let them come back, please, Father. They've had a whole deer . . . the carcass all to themselves . . . All I want is the bones. Please, don't let them come back.*

As she scurried along, her tired legs cried in agony at the burden of the "new feet" and the pack on her back. Suddenly she realized how high she had ventured into the mountains and that the ravine split below her. Frantic, she looked around, searching for her backtrail or that of the deer. She had not kept her own tracks in sight. Night was falling, cold and grey with no stars; soon the snowy open places slid into shadow between the trees. With a knot of fear clenching in her stomach, Callie realized she was lost.

Oh, where are my children? was her first frantic concern. *I've got to get to them tonight, got to feed them these rich, fresh bones.* Then, *If only Three Elk were here. He'd know where to go, what to do.* And finally, *What if the wolves come back now that it's dark? What if they chase and catch me?*

Then began a desperate flight. She ran wildly, the bone-bundle pounding against her back, her legs lifting and plowing forward until suddenly her knees gave out, and Callie plunged face first into the snow.

Slow down, something within her seemed to say as the chilling white powder hit her face. *You need a fire and warmth and food. You're colder than you know and beyond reason. You're making yourself a perfect prey for wolves.*

Callie labored to her knees, her chest heaving painfully with each breath, her head pounding against the iron band that seemed to ring her forehead. Ahead of her, in the branches of a five-foot pine, was a bird's nest. She swallowed panic.

Struggling toward it she stretched out a shaking hand and plucked the nest free. During those early days of digging cattails, she'd begun carrying bundles of sage tinder whenever she went foraging. Now she dug one of these from her apron pocket and arranged it on top of a piece of dead wood in the snow. Then, shielding the bird nest from the wind with her body, she struck her knife blade against Jamie's piece of flint until a spark fell into it. Quickly, she lifted the nest to her lips, blowing softly and giving thanks as wisps of gray began coiling upward.

Callie cooked some of the scavenged bones over her fire and sucked the marrow out. A warm feeling wrapped around her—the warmth not of complacence but of realistic confidence. She knew the wilderness well now, knew her limitations, and knew that she could not beat it down no matter how she fought. God made something powerful when He'd created this wilderness. Butting her head against it exhibited no more wisdom than a goat attacking a brick wall: she could not win.

But she could follow the law of the wild—the law by which its Creator had organized it. She could weary the wilderness with patience and ultimately overcome the chasm that held her from her goal. Patience . . . Didn't the Bible say "in patience ye shall possess your souls?"

Above Callie the cloud cover parted. She watched as one by one the blinking stars poked through. How many nights she had looked up at these very stars since she'd lost Angus! There was something comfortable in their sameness. She'd memorized them without ever meaning to do so.

She wondered if she'd ever looked at the stars in Yorkshire. She couldn't distinctly remember doing it. They hadn't been quite as important there, hadn't been her sentinels and companions every night as they were here.

During polite conversation once, long ago, she had referred to the stars as "God's poetry." The words had sounded nice, and everyone had nodded politely over their teacups, remarking on the beauty of His heavenly handiwork. But now . . . well, now it went beyond seeing the stars. Now she *knew* them.

When morning came, Callie found she could barely move. Cold had settled hard over everything during the night and, though she'd kept her fire burning, her joints seemed to have frozen stiff. Her legs and backside cried out against being used after the beating she'd given them the day before, and her ability to coordinate their efforts was in revolt.

But slowly, patiently, she managed to work up onto her feet

and start walking. She followed the closest ravine all the way down the mountain, only to discover that it was not the right watershed. She did not pass their little shelter huddled against the rock. This effort consumed the greater part of her day, and it was late afternoon when she began skirting the foot of the mountain, working her way west, peering up each canyon to see if it was her own.

Night had fallen before she discovered the familiar beaver ponds. Their reedy shores and red willows were lost in shadow, and off across the way she could see Cyrus stomping to get at the grass. Her progress was painful and slow, each step a careful mental exertion, but seeing their snow-covered lean-to filled her with warmth, and the stars above seemed to leap and dance for joy.

It was as if those cold, distant stars had blown open the windows of her mind. Callie saw through different eyes the moon's blue shadows stretch across the valley. As she drew closer it seemed as if the trees above her head were cradling the stars in their bare arms, just as she cradled her children. The golden glow of light escaping around the door covering of their lean-to called silently, urgently to her. But her mind also leaped beyond the cold menace of snow and ice to gaze in wonder at the larger scene of sweeping white beneath the protective curl of the barren ridge and sheltering pines.

Callie breathed deeply and lifted her right foot, and then her left, then her right again. Her mind saw the faces of Jamie and Duncan and Susa—not hunger-pinched, in her memory, but jolly and round. She caressed them, kissed them, showed them what she'd brought. Then she saw Three Elk, and gratitude rushed up inside her, for he had been there with them while she was gone. That was when Callie realized, as she approached the door of their shelter, that she would be glad to see Three Elk, too.

Callie slept, prepared food, and slept again. But in time the bones were gone and she was forced to replenish their food supply once more. Having grown wise to the deceptiveness of early-morning calm and down-sloping mountain ravines, she followed the wolf packs after their kills and dragged home the remains of their feasts. During times when winter's grip loosened ever so slightly, she carried back greens from the streambeds to supplement their diet, and the wolves cleaned the bones less efficiently. But with each onslaught of icy cold both hunter and hunted holed up in their warm places and waited for warmer days. Then she ground whatever bones she could scavenge, fighting to keep life and limb together for five souls.

The constant battle against starvation and its ever-present evidence in the thin faces of her children was anguishing for Callie's motherly heart. But quiet beneath these cares was the reassuring regularity with which she awakened morning after morning to find everyone still breathing. This miracle never failed to amaze her. Through endurance her faith grew, counterbalancing pain with hope.

Three Elk wandered away from camp more often than before. He had not brought back an overabundance of game yet, but Callie knew he was working to strengthen his legs by walking. Sometimes he carried his bow, and she felt certain he was practicing drawing it back, rebuilding his shoulder muscles with consistent exertion.

One night, when he had taken the tanned buffalo robe and left shortly after dark, Callie was sitting beside the fire reading the Book of Mormon to her children. Jamie, always the last one to persist in listening, had finally fallen asleep, and she lapsed into reading silently. Her heart tasted peace as she savored the Redeemer's words in Third Nephi, "Yea, blessed are the poor in spirit who come unto me, for theirs is the kingdom of heaven. And again, blessed are all they that mourn, for they shall be comforted. And blessed are the meek, for they shall inherit the earth."

She looked up at the fire, thrusting more wood into its hungry center. The flames ate eagerly, without sizzling, and Callie noticed the wood was exceptionally dry. Everything was dry. Night had fallen like an iron dome across the world, and the cold was so compelling that it sucked moisture out of the very air—out of everything! Her skin felt dry and tight, and her lips cracked. All evening her skirts had been snapping and crackling with sparks.

There was a sound outside the shelter door; icy cold slid in as Three Elk drew aside the cover. Silently he gestured for her to come.

Anxious to see if he had killed something, Callie pulled her blanket around her, grabbed her bonnet and ear-coverings, and followed. A wall of cold struck her face. Callie secured the door and turned, shaking loose a few snowflakes from the top of the drifted shelter. They spiraled and eddied downward, catching silvery moonlight like numberless faceted mirrors. Her nose froze and her lungs stung when she opened her mouth to breathe.

Three Elk had already gone ahead, walking northwest up the side of the ravine behind their shelter. Dry squeaky snowpowder echoed loudly beneath her boots as Callie ran to catch up. He stopped at the crest of the sage-covered ridge, staring off through the endless sky.

Callie caught her breath, and the air burned her lungs as she sucked it in. When she blinked, the tears froze at the corners of her eyes, but she gazed upward, unheeding. What could it be?

A pale red glow shone to the north of the high ridge that had barred the pony drag from going west. Like the reflection of some huge fire, it lit the night sky. *People!* she thought, lunging a few steps forward in the snow. *Bonfires!* Scattered images of soldiers and armies and burning villages tumbled through her mind. *The homes of Saints?* She stopped and peered at the lights. No, the Salt Lake Valley was too far away, and besides, this was too far north, she reasoned. Burning Indian villages, perhaps. Were they Cheyenne? Were they Three Elk's people?

Callie returned to his side, squinting hard at him; but the Indian's face was impassive as he watched—or was it? Clouds billowed from his nose, and the muscles tensed along his jaw. Callie sensed subtle, deep-flowing emotions beneath his stony exterior. Slowly, as she studied him, she concluded that he was not suppressing fear or anger. Instead, he was possessed by vibrant reverence.

Callie stared in open-eyed wonder at the sky again. She could see that the flames must be very, very far away. But then again, no, it couldn't be a fire. A shiver ran down her frame, a shiver not of cold but of awe. The ethereal color was changing from red to greenish blue. Something vast and faintly luminous began rippling upward across the immensity of the sky. It was furrowed like the sail of a ship but fine as gauze, changing color and shape again. The form was mostly silver, but its tint sometimes showed greens and blues and occasionally orange and yellow. The shimmering image trembled, drifted, reformed itself into long streaks like the plumed tail of a tremendous peacock suspended against frozen blackness.

Callie shivered again, and gooseflesh prickled along her arms as she suddenly remembered the night she'd seen Angus. Was this a sign? What was the ghostly image? "Dear Father," she whispered low. "What handiwork of Thine—?"

Three Elk began singing, or rather, chanting softly under his breath. His voice left an eerie echo in the still, iron-hard night. The order of its calm repetition reassured her, and the passion in his voice lent both ritual ceremony and human expression to the absolute silence that captivated the darkness. The sound was eerie but comforting, too. As Callie stood beside him, watching ice-fires play above the horizon, she realized for the first time that, like Callie herself, when Three Elk sang, he was praying. And with this realization, she felt a sudden unsettling certainty, a startling sure conviction that, like her supplications, his prayers were also heard.

The frozen jaws of winter stayed clamped upon the cloud-shrouded mountains and pitching plains. Edible substances of all kinds were sometimes virtually impossible to find, but Callie became expert in interpreting the calls of wolves and tracking their attacks. She recognized the long, wailing, full-throated cry of the chase, could tell it from the short, snapping bark and snarl that told her they'd cornered their quarry. Wolves never let their victim rest, she knew. The pack would harry and tire it, staying with it night and day until it was too weary to fight. She made a point of listening to their calls, never closing in fast enough to hear their growls nor watch their bloody work. Gratefully, she scavenged the scraps as soon as they were gone.

TWENTY-EIGHT

Callie tried to shut down the pounding of her heart so she could listen more keenly to the silence between the trees. She pressed against the outermost trunks that ringed the clearing. A breath of wind swept across the open snow ahead, tipping a shower of frost dust from the barren branches of an aspen, and for a moment the sunny air was bright with a glittering curtain of diamonds.

No, she told herself, waiting anxiously for the snow to clear. *There wasn't anything among the shadows beneath those pines.* She squinted again. Nothing.

Her mind was playing tricks on her—or rather, her fears were. Every time she stalked a doomed creature, her skin crawled, her nerves on edge. But she hadn't actually seen anything dangerous yet, and she wanted to cut through the clearing where the going was easier for her "new feet."

Callie stepped out of the forest's protection, following the split-hoof trail of the fleeing animal and those of the circling wolves. They were after one of the huge deerlike creatures from whom Three Elk took his name. She was surprised the wolves were chasing this one, for it had an unwounded, ground-eating gait and had been able to run far. She had followed the clean tracks at least three miles up the mountain on the hope that this pack of wolves could not possibly eat so much meat. Now she began to wonder when they would ever bring it down.

From experience, Callie knew that wolves often quarried their kill right away, though sometimes the chase took more time. But what unnerved her today was that she could no longer hear them baying ahead of her. Perhaps she was too far behind, or perhaps they had given up pursuit and gone off to stalk something else.

Callie moved tenuously out into the open and then rapidly planted step after step up the valley. She would never get used to the way the "new feet" made her count every stride, made even small distances devour time.

Halfway across the clear stretch she froze in mid-stride. A sound had cut to the quick of her soul. Behind her, down the valley in the trees where she'd just been, Callie heard the wail of a wolf.

Her ears prickled. Her heart fluttered painfully as the shock stung her fingertips and toes. Then another howl ascended from the pines that circled the clearing to the right. The mad thumping of her heart escalated. Her mouth went dry. These were the calls that had so often told her to leave camp to scavenge, the calls that indicated the pack had chosen a target. They were the death knell condemning a lone animal to die.

The wolves' howls told her they were cutting between her and safety, waiting downhill in the trees to the right. But the stream that led to the shelter was below and to her left. Clenching the lance in one hand, Callie hiked her skirts above her knees and ran in that direction.

Panic possessed her only for a moment. Then she fought it back, breathing deeply and concentrating on keeping her rhythm. She must not fall. She must not let the "new feet" trip her now. In all the wolf trails Callie had followed, only once had she known a victim to rise after it was down. *I must not fall,* she told herself with each hard-won step. *Must not fall . . . must not fall . . . must not fall . . .*

Callie reached the stream with perspiration already beading her brow. From here the drifted meadow stretched far downstream, and she hoped to make good time in the open. But she could see the wolves now. They were cutting in and out like shadows among the dark trunks of the pines. First she glimpsed them on her left, then the right, and she knew there were more ahead and behind.

At the actual sight of them, she had to fight panic again. Callie wished she could sing, but the struggle to keep her breaths deep and her strides swift above the snow absorbed total concentration. Her thoughts, keeping rhythm with her feet, were not unlike a song, and their impetus quickly turned from *must not fall . . . must not fall* to a prayer of *keep me up . . . please . . . keep me up . . .*

She had run a long distance with the wolves loping and baying all around her when Callie realized she needed to moisten her throat. Her side ached and the pounding of her heart was continually answered by the rasp of breath heaving in and out. Her lungs burned with explosive pumping. Quick, deep gasps had made her throat so dry she could not swallow. She was still at least two miles from the shelter, and she knew she must moisten her throat now.

Pausing, Callie used the hand with the lance to scoop snow into her mouth. She wiped it across her face, feeling the vigor of its coldness. But even in the instant it took her to do so, one of the ruthless creatures darted toward her, baying as if she were cornered.

"I'm not down yet!" Callie screamed at him, dropping her skirts and throwing snow. Though the wolf whined and drew back, she was not fooled. He wasn't intimidated, only waiting.

Before others could rush in, she resumed her retreat. But the freshness of her energy soon dissipated. She had to keep moving! She could not afford to fall! Callie tried to establish a rhythm and maintain it—not the headlong flight of panic but a solid steady stride. Yet in spite of her concentration the wolf pack was undeniably wearying her. Her initial burst of terror had burned a great deal of energy. She felt hollow and shaky at the center, except where the ache in her side had grown leaden. The leg below it was not responding as quickly as the other. Callie focused her attention on lifting that foot clear with every step. She passed through fingers of forest, fighting low branches and rocks within the snow, always seeking open meadows in which to run.

In one treeless stretch, she could see that the stream ran frozen beneath the snow in a boggy bowl. She knew the danger of hugging too closely to the stream and scanned the whiteness for signs of water-pockets below. But the trees closed in and forced her nearer the watercourse than she ought to go. She debated—watching the howling streaks of gray that darted around her, hearing misfortune in their full-throated cries. She was too tired to contend with the trees and still keep up her speed. Callie chose to stay in the open, hurrying directly along the edge of the creek bed.

She'd almost made it to the open meadow again when suddenly the snow gave way beneath her and one leg sank to the thigh. Icy water stung her toes through her boot. Frantic, panting wildly, Callie contended with the hard snow. Her "new foot" would not release. She could not get it back out, so she jerked until her boot came free of the binding and pulled her leg up without it. Her muscles bunched beneath her as she tried to stand, cramping from cold and relentless strain. But she commanded her legs to be stiff and used the lance to pull herself to her feet. She *had* to get upright!

This was the chance the wolves had been waiting for. Five of them emerged from the trees, circling closer and closer. Standing on her remaining "new foot" Callie brandished the lance and shouted ferociously at her attackers.

They worried at her, harrying from every side, snarling and snapping. Their ears lay back against their scruffy necks, and their teeth clashed together with a sound that promised fangs on flesh. One jumped from behind and Callie turned, swinging the lance low. His bite fell short, but the wolf's teeth locked into her skirt. Callie struggled to keep her balance, hitting at him with the lance. He dodged, his nose wrinkled in a snarl; hackles bristled along his neck. The wolf twisted, pulling at her skirt, and she wobbled on the lone "new foot," until she fell back into the icy hole the other foot had made.

Callie's skirt tore free of his jaws as she slipped, and the cold beneath the snow wrenched all air from her tired lungs. Gasping, she clawed at the snow. But the wolves were circling too closely for her to crawl out.

Again, the one behind her rushed in. The butt of the lance was toward him, and she swung in close quarters. Slashing out with all her strength, Callie felt the handle hit. She heard him yelp. But there wasn't time to turn and see, for another wolf was lunging directly at her face. She thrust the lance-point out, and he stopped just short of impaling himself. He danced backward, baring his teeth and growling low.

They could play this game a long time, she knew. There were five of them, and she was tiring so fast that it was almost impossible to think about what she should do.

The wolves growled and barked, their eyes gleaming yellow malice, the silence between their attacks threatening. They took turns drawing in close upon her from different angles. As one blackish fiend with chewed-off ears came at her, Callie had a sudden, fierce desire to throw the lance. They were so close. At least she could kill one before they got her. At least she could fight.

Yet even as she refused to give up, exhaustion was settling over her in a heavy mantle. Inwardly, she knew she should hang on to the lance. So the battle raged, with the pack flanking her, cowering back when she swung her lance like a club. Callie could see nothing beyond the yellow teeth and fangs, could hear nothing beyond the snarling sounds of the attack.

A smaller gray wolf rushed her again, closer this time, and despite her slowing reflexes she aimed the lance toward him at the very last possible instant. His bark cut short, he hung impaled, legs still working in death.

Callie fought to tear the lance free. Now was when they

would all rush in on her, she knew. And it seemed she struggled for an eternity, trying to pull her weapon from the spasmodic carcass. She wondered why they were not seizing upon her as she jerked again and again to free the lance. Then, forsaking it, she pulled her knife and faced the next attack.

Callie's blade felt small in her hand. Strength spent, her whole frame quivered as the black wolf danced around in a tormenting, growling pattern of approach and feint. She tried to slash out with the knife, spending priceless strength in an effort to stab him first. She crouched into the water-bottomed hole, gaining protection up to her armpits. But she was trapped, and Callie had nothing with which to stop the force of his ultimate advance nor did she have the ability to meet and stab him first. He would eventually set on her, she knew. And that would be the end. Even if she stabbed him, it would be too late. His fangs would already have closed around her neck.

With the strange, slow clarity that comes in terrible, deathly moments, Callie cast her eyes around. She had expected the entire pack to charge in at once, and she looked for the other snarling mouths, the other yellow teeth.

But the black wolf alone had locked his attention on her. The others were watching a dark form that floundered on the edge of the woods. For one crazed instant, Callie thought it was the elk the wolves had been tracking before they'd turned on her. But something was on its back. Her exhausted mind reeled as she recognized Three Elk gripping the pony with his legs, drawing his bow and shooting into the pack, scattering them from around her. The other wolves began moving in on him, clustering near the snow-hampered horse.

He came! Callie thought, feeling mingled joy and surprise in spite of exhaustion that dulled thought and movement. *He came to save me!* Then as an afterthought, she looked into the wolf's blood-hungry eyes with a sense of distant regret that Three Elk had come too late.

The black wolf rushed in, jaws spread open. His throat was

suddenly silent, his glaring teeth set to clamp shut like a trap. Callie threw up her arm to shield her face; the tearing vise of the wolf's jaw slammed shut on it. Pain bit where his teeth penetrated her buffalo-hide cloak. Breathless, dizzy, for an instant Callie could do nothing. She felt the warm, wet dribble of blood reach her hand, felt the wolf's hot, rancid breath upon her face. He was trying to eat through the defense of her arm so he could reach her soft, vital spots!

Rage welled up within Callie at the vicious brutality chewing on her. His jaws ground down as the wilderness had gnawed from the day they'd left St. Joseph. Gnawing and gouging and grinding . . .

But Callie's rage was not at the wolf—it was at the elemental wilderness of which he was a part. And she fought with all the fierce, bitter hatred she'd ever had for the mercilessness of this land. Jerking her arm back and forth, she battled to wrest it free. Plunging out wildly with the knife, she strove to stab over her shoulder at the wolf, but his hind parts danced away. Callie slashed and struck until she could not lift the knife once more.

Still the wolf hung on.

For an instant, Callie slumped back, panting against pain as the wolf's teeth worked entirely through the buffalo-hide covering her arm.

So this is death, she thought. And for the first time that portal loomed before her, majestic and meaningful but without strings attached—without weeping and feeling cheated, without curses of vengeance. It was simply death. Nothing more.

Her thoughts soared upward above physical distress, and she cried to the Lord, not in anguish or terror or frustration as she had so many times before, but from the perspective of sweet release. *If it is to be,* her heart said, *if it is Thy will, I know Thou wilt care for my children.*

Pain screamed shrilly, and Callie looked again at the wolf. She couldn't stab him any more effectively than she could subdue this wilderness. But all at once she saw clearly how she could use his tenacity, the very power and force of the wilderness, to defeat him. Agonizingly, she let the resistance shift and began drawing the fang-riddled arm toward her face. The snarling wolf's ears lay back, his yellow eyes bore into hers as some instinctive warning sounded deep within him. His paws shifted against the snow, and his growl sank to a rumbling even deeper in his throat, forcing its way through clenched teeth. It was not in him to let go, but he sensed that the arm now drawing him forward matched him will to will. Breath surged into breath, eyes locked, as the two of them balanced on the counterpoint of thrust versus thrust. Suddenly, Callie's upper body pivoted, her free arm rose, and she drove her blade into his neck.

Then all strength was gone; her knees buckled, and the dead wolf slid into the hole on top of her.

Callie didn't know how long it was before Three Elk came and heaved the carcass off. Comprehension was hazy, but she knew they came out of the hole as one, the wolf's jaws sunk through the buffalo hide and her flesh. And she knew Three Elk pried the viselike fangs apart and pressed at her arm to stop the bleeding. Callie remembered all this as if it had been a dream, as if it had been done to save someone else.

She knew he gutted two wolves and tied them onto Cyrus because she later remembered the sound of the horse's hooves as he nervously sidled away from that burden in the crusty snow. She remembered Three Elk whispering to the pony, calming him before he tied the dead animals on.

And then she remembered nothing more than being taken up in the arms of her friend, lifted onto the pony's back, and carried home.

TWENTY-NINE

The lance! Callie hadn't picked it up. Her fist clamped shut on nothing, and her muscles jerked painfully awake. A searing pang shot through one shoulder and arm and then eased slightly as she made a concerted effort to relax it. Callie thought she'd cried out but must have made no noise, because she heard voices nearby that neither hesitated nor responded.

"Thank ye for th' lovely hymn, lass," a familiar one said, so comfortable and easy she thought it was Angus. How nice. He was conducting a devotional of the kind she had relentlessly held morning and evening since they'd started for Zion. That was good. She was much too tired to handle it today.

"Now we will recite scripture from th' book o' St. John," the voice said with calm and pleasant authority. But it wasn't Angus speaking. Though the voice promised coming maturity, it hadn't deepened yet. That was Jamie, Callie suddenly realized. James was taking leadership because she could no longer shoulder it herself.

The sound was sweet on her ears as honey in the wilderness. Until now, she hadn't wanted to admit that the boy had grown, but he had. And, most important, he'd grown right.

"Peace I leave with you, my peace I give unto you," three voices chorused brightly. "Not as the world giveth give I unto you. Let not your heart be troubled, neither let it be afraid."

Callie lay still beneath the buffalo robe, watching them through the fireglow, making no effort to lift her hand and wipe away two tears that edged freely across her cheeks.

"Mum!" Susa cried.

"You're awake!" Duncan echoed.

Callie smiled weakly. She couldn't move; it burned her arm to try.

"Take a drink o' this," Jamie said, offering warm water. "Be y' in great pain?"

"No, Son." Callie's voice sounded croaky and weak. "I'm fine. Better than ever, I suspect."

"Haahe!" Three Elk said, offering a smile as he came through the door.

Callie lifted her good arm to blot the tears before he could see.

"She moves? It is good." He put something down by the fire and came toward where Callie lay. "Back," he said, pulling on the children. "I check bleed-place." With firm, gentle fingers, he turned aside the cover and examined the fang-riddled arm. His movements were efficient, in perfect keeping with his usual controlled demeanor. But Three Elk's touch transcended strength and stability to convey gentle caring. He had known physical pain, though he had not shown it. And Callie recognized compassion in his hands.

"You make big fight, Lucky Woman." Three Elk rocked back on his haunches when he was finished with his examination. "Black wolf want eat you ver' bad." The caring of his touch was not as obvious in his voice, but Callie identified regard behind words where once she would never have seen it.

Callie mustered a grin. "But instead we're eating him, right?"

"We eat."

"And the lance? Where is the lance?"

Three Elk pointed toward a thin shape beside the door.

"Ah," Callie sighed. "And the knife?"

"You are a warrior, Lucky Woman? To be asking first of weapons?"

Callie swallowed and closed her eyes momentarily. She wanted to express her great gratitude in some commensurate way. But words felt awkward, as if the rescue, once it was over, had been distanced by time and place. When she opened her eyes again, he was still watching her. "Thank you," she whispered, feeling remorse that the term was such an understatement.

Three Elk nodded. He started to move away, but Callie caught after him with her eyes. "H-h-how? How did you know to come?"

"I listen to wolf calling his brothers. When you go, he is running up mountain. His hunt is hard. He comes tired. He is not calling for a time. Then I hear again his call, not so far 'way. I know he hunts my friend."

Three Elk was gone most of the time during Callie's recovery. He took Cyrus and traveled down into the lowlands, returning at intervals with deer and prairie goats he had shot. Callie praised his kills with the appreciation of a fellow hunter, and she thanked the Lord daily for the returning strength in his shoulder that allowed him to pull the bow and bear the load. Hunger abated, and the children's faces grew less pallid.

Callie lent her "new feet" to Jamie so that he could more easily inspect his deadfall traps. She quizzed Duncan in math and science. Using the hides of the wolves, Callie fashioned a warm hooded cape for Susa, and from a scrap she taught her how to make another for Mrs. McGillicutty.

Warm weather finally began nudging away winter's grip; soon the snow melted in great steaming muddy patches. Callie was up on her feet by then, swinging her arm to increase movement and strength. Every time Three Elk came into camp, she prodded and pushed him to agree that it was time. But the man would not be hurried.

First he told her it was only *He?koneneheso-ese?he,* Little Hard-faced Moon, and she saw that he was right, for periods of rigid cold and heavy snows followed. But with time each of these melted more quickly. Callie walked often toward the beaver ponds. She watched the runoff as the stream ran high and white-crested against the rocks. Small snowflowers eventually peeked yellow heads from the dead undergrowth of the year before.

Again she questioned Three Elk, urging him to tell how travel was out on the prairie. And one day while gathering greens down by the beaver pond, she saw him riding into camp. Running out to meet him, she took up the dead fox he'd shot and inspected it.

"Time to go west yet?" she asked, after expressing genuine praise for his kill.

"This *Ponoma?a-hasene-ese?he.*" She waited, knowing he would translate, and after a moment he said, "Dry-up Moon."

Callie drew a deep breath. She'd been waiting months for this moment, yet instead of exulting, her thoughts rioted with questions. "What will you do?" she ventured, as he turned the pony loose to graze.

They stood on a windy hillside, watching Cyrus hurry off to crop the barely-showing tips of green along the windswept ridges. He had dropped so much weight that his bones were prominent, even through his shaggy coat, but he was wiry and still strong. She noticed that the scalps were no longer knotted in his mane, and she wondered vaguely when Three Elk had removed them. But resolving more urgent concerns kept her attention. And when Three Elk did not answer her question, Callie put it to him a different way. "Will you leave soon to find your people?"

"It is time," Three Elk answered.

"Where will you go? Are they east of us?"

"I do not know," he said, his voice deep and slow with sorrow. "When you find me, I am shot by bluecoat soldiers of Sumner. He have ver' black face for Cheyenne. Burn village, burn all meat stores for winter. Cheyenne have no place.

Buffalo coming hard to find. How my people live in cold time I not know."

"I'm sorry," Callie answered. Silently she prayed he would find his own family alive, that God would bless him for having preserved hers.

Three Elk's eyes grew as cold and hard as they had been when she first found him. He gazed out across the open country with tragic stoicism. "Buffalo soon gone. Hunger make women of warriors. Mebbe now few sing brave heart songs."

They stood in almost-warm sunshine, the winds whistling around them and out across the barren ridges to the east. At last Three Elk sighed, "I help you see Fort Bridger." Callie's heart leaped with relief and gratitude, but before she could say more he added, "Tomorrow I go. Get deer. Then you make meat to travel."

"Ready," Callie told Three Elk. "Everything's in order."

He turned toward the boys. "Where sticks?"

Proudly, James and Duncan produced four walking sticks they had cut, having carved a handgrip and initials into the bark of each. Callie did not need one. She would carry the lance.

"E-peva?e," he announced. "We go."

Callie looked back up the narrow valley at the hut they had wintered in. Their six-month shelter hunched against the rock, looking suddenly small and empty without a gray column rising from the smoke-hole. Around it circled the ridge, running sheer into the valley. And above it the pine-dotted slopes reached into the mountains, their leafless spring aspen looking for all the world like fuzzy gray wool caught in the spikes of a green carding comb.

Then Callie turned her face west again, toward Zion. She had no fears of setting out onto the desert if Three Elk felt it was safe. Recalling the fury of last autumn's storm, she noted there was no protection except an occasional scruffy beard of leafless aspen covering the lee sides of the barren sagehills. Wind reached everything, first tugging and tearing with cold fingers and then pounding in breathtaking gusts.

Late the first afternoon, they crossed the towering ridge that had previously forced her to leave Three Elk behind. And from its crest she viewed vastness reaching beyond description, an immensity of weaving gullies and ridges. Seeing the desert now, with a winter of hunting experience behind her, Callie realized how hopelessly lost she must have become if she had persisted on alone after the October blizzard. She could never have held a true course across it nor found the fort in all this distance. Her greatest problem would have been an absence of definition. For, although the land wrinkled in a series of sharp undulations, they tangled every which way, each ridge looking the same as all the others.

Several times she pulled the children aside and pointed out the dismal futility their earlier efforts would have afforded. Carefully, she reminded them that the Lord provides. In every prayer she thanked heaven for their guide and for another benefit of crossing in spring: the way snow runoff created moisture for all of them to drink where last fall the ground had been scorched dry.

In her private prayers Callie thanked the Lord for the way circumstances had molded her and Three Elk until they could work easily together. Something told Callie that before their shared ordeal he would never have let the children ride his buffalo-horse while he walked. She supposed he would never have let a woman carry his lance, either. But here they were, walking together, one or another of them riding with Susa, and every day Zion grew nearer.

They traveled steadily over the mucky hills, making good time but crawling no faster than ants across immensity. Huge drainages twisted around them, some a mile wide and a thousand feet deep, others wearying them with steep rises and falls in rapid succession. Deceptive bowls of snow were scooped out of the protected sides of towering drifts, their tops leaning over like the crests of icicle-hung waves. Yet the only thing that challenged them more than their own stark sense of smallness was the constant wind.

Squalls tore down upon the little party as they crept across the unprotecting land. Then Three Elk lashed the walking sticks and lance together, throwing the assorted pelts and hides they'd gathered during the winter over this makeshift frame. Here they huddled—often enduring a collapse of the tent, always fighting to keep it together—until the storms swept away.

They journeyed down deep, wide valleys, where Callie noticed the first green whorls of spring were creeping up at the center of last year's spiraling dead leaves. Arid mountains rose before them, each one looking like the last, each one having to be skirted. Three Elk often left Callie behind with the children to rest while he rode ahead and scouted the terrain, choosing canyons that would open onto others leading as directly west as possible.

Callie did not know what Indian tribes controlled this desert territory, and she never saw any of them. She only knew they were not Cheyenne. Three Elk had never been to Fort Bridger before, had never even seen the place. But he said he had heard descriptions of it, and to her grateful wonder, he knew the way and what must be done to get there.

At last, after two weeks' progress, they stood looking down where all the ridges and ravines emptied out onto one great plain. The view was bigger than Callie's eyes could take in; distances purpled her vision. Legions of gray-bottomed puffball clouds advanced beneath a high, thin blue sky. Between them, the rays of the sun slanted brilliantly, washing the land with gold. Buttes rose up across the desert floor, row after row hazed by distance, splotched with snow. And over all the ground lay a transparent green veil, almost invisible against the gray-brown sweep.

By the time Callie's band dropped down onto the flats, the snow was mostly melted. To her surprise, the patches she had seen, cupping like drifted bowls, were actually white alkali pools. Here the sagebrush was lower and more sparse, making the going twice as fast. Callie could not deny her pleasure at being able to walk more quickly and freely, but it seemed they had been exposed in the open for a very long time. She longed for the cover of trees.

Spring herds of prairie goats watched the travelers' approach, their black horns, eyes, and cheek patches showing up plainly against the tan and white coloring of their hides and the land. They were preoccupied with the business of fattening after the long winter but not so engrossed as to take much risk. One moment they stared motionlessly; the next instant their powerful legs bunched beneath them, kicking up billowy dust trails between the muddy sheets of runoff water.

Callie envied their speed and power to outrun danger, especially one evening as Three Elk led them over a steep ridge and into the mouth of a river bottom. Ahead, dominating buttes glared down from shadowy heights, waiting to pen them in.

"I go," Three Elk said.

Callie had just finished combing out her hair and was, according to her routine, about to begin evening scripture study. The book rested half-open in her hands as she gaped wide-eyed at her friend. "You . . . You're leaving us?" Callie swallowed hard and struggled to regain composure. "But . . . I . . . I don't know where Fort Bridger is from here."

"Not go far 'way," Three Elk clarified. "Take pony. Go up." He ran his hand around the circling buttresses that ringed the indigo sky. "The place *Sisk-a-dee-agie* is one day walking. You follow river, you come there."

"Sisk-a-dee-agie," she echoed the phrase.

"Shoshone say *Sisk-a-dee-agie.* Your people say . . . hmmm . . . say Green River."

"Green River!" Callie had heard the name, and her heart clamored a wild tattoo. "Green River? Where the Saints have ferries to carry emigrants across?"

Three Elk grunted. "Your people, yes. Later they come. Too early now for wagon. Others here first. Trappers come ronnyvoo. Shoshone, Gros-Ventre, Ute here too. Enemies of Cheyenne."

"I see," Callie breathed, and the shadows around the buttes suddenly hung with menace. "But why does that mean we should separate? Isn't there more strength in our numbers?"

"Who you meet, Lucky Woman? Bluecoat soldier mebbe? He like you—not me. He kind to you, kill Cheyenne." The man's hard tone left no room for consideration, and suddenly Callie recalled the vermilion war paint and the scalps that had hung from his horse when she'd found him. "Shoshone?" Three Elk went on, "Mebbe they kind to alone woman. Help you. Get tobac, blankets from Bridger."

"But what if they aren't kind?" Callie blurted crossly, peering into the canyon's crowding darkness. "Or what if I meet some of those others, those . . . those Utes or Gros whatever-you-called-them? Then what?"

Three Elk smiled, amused by her fiery consternation. "I ride above. I watch. I see trouble before you. Trouble not see me until—*Ai-e-e-e-e!*" He brought one hand down hard upon the other, with an abrupt chopping motion.

Startled, Callie drew away.

"It is good," Three Elk settled back in satisfaction.

"No," Callie snapped. "It is *not* good." Then after a pause she urged enthusiastically, "We'll come up on top with you! I don't like this narrow place anyway. Even the dirt is strange: orange, yellow, green. Nowhere is it a proper brown, nor is the water blue."

"Green River not blue," Three Elk chuckled, and Callie had

to admit her protestations sounded silly. But her fears were real.

"You're taking Cyrus, then?" she asked at last. "The children and I will walk alone down here?"

"Easy place to walk," Three Elk nodded, still seeing humor in Callie's concern.

"But the river?" Callie asked, shuddering as she recalled her ordeal at the Platte. "You say the ferries aren't running yet, so how are we to cross?"

"I come."

Callie looked into her companion's face, the liquid-brown eyes, the prominent nose and set chin. All joking was suddenly put aside as she realized this was a promise. He had said he would come, and she could count on it.

THIRTY

"I'm not a geologist!" Callie protested in frustration. "I don't know what makes this rock glitter any more than I knew what made that last one red." Then, seeing Duncan's head droop, she reached out and tilted his chin up. "I wish I knew, Son, but I don't. See here, maybe you'll grow up and know a lot about stones. Perhaps you'll be an architect and use them when you design great cathedrals and universities . . . or . . . or better yet, a temple!" She winked and was rewarded when the boy brightened. "Take a look at this white chalky one here." Callie picked up a small sample. "There are dozens of little shells in it."

"Thanks!" Duncan said, shoving the white crumbly rock into the bag with the rest of his collection. "Guess what Mum gave me, Jamie!"

Callie watched the two boys as Duncan pulled out one dirty rock after another. He spit on a piece of gravel and rubbed his shirttail against it until it took on a green, almost glassy shine. At one time, Callie would have scolded him for mussing his shirt, but now she watched his transformation of the stone. The shirt didn't matter. She'd long since stopped craving to boil their clothes clean. As soon as she could get her hands on fresh outfits, she would burn every filthy stitch they wore.

"Don't stray so far," she called to where Duncan and Jamie had begun prying flat pieces of shale from a dirtbank. Perfectly preserved fish fossils as long as their fingers had kept them running ahead to dig in the grayish green veins of rock all morning. But she felt uneasy, and her heart jumped every time she heard them skipping the less interesting pieces out across the water.

"Six jumps!" she heard Jamie whistle low under his breath. "'Twas a good 'un, Dunc!"

"Hurry along, boys," she called. They could keep up, Callie had no doubts, but she was worried about whom they might meet if they lagged too far behind. And she was apprehensive about crossing the river. If only she could cheer herself up as convincingly as she'd cheered Duncan.

"Glory to God on high . . ." Callie began singing softly, matching the pace to her steps. And Susa, who was holding her hand, joined in, "Praise ye his name . . . [not so loud, dear,] . . . Tell what his arm has done, What spoils from death he won. Sing his great name alone: Worthy the Lamb!"

A gnawing sense of apprehension was growing inside Callie. During the morning Three Elk had intentionally shown himself to her from high on the tops of the buttes. His stationary silhouette had reassured her; but now the sun was nearing the horizon, its glow splashing red against the rusty bluffs, coloring the dirty river crimson-gold. She had not seen him since they'd passed a towering, castlelike butte, and she wondered how he would get around it. If only he'd arrive and help her cross before dark! She'd rest better tonight with the river behind her.

Coming around a bend and directly into the sun's splash Callie saw the river twist right, pressing hard against the base of a butte whose loose rock strata formed a vertical cliff. Would they have to cross now without Three Elk and the horse? She called Duncan and Susa to her, Jamie came on his own, and together they scanned the stony ramparts for any sign of Three Elk and Cyrus.

"We'll 'ave t' get wet, Mother." Jamie squinted into the setting sun. "But there's a long sandy island this side o' th' river. 'Twould get us 'round th' hole." He pointed at the base of the cliff where Callie could see sheer rock extending down into a deep pool. "We can walk along the island, if we cross the river to 't an' then cross back onto th' same bank again at th' other end."

Callie gave up searching the northern skyline and peered where Jamie was pointing. Yes, it would be possible. The water might not be more than knee-deep. *If only this sun weren't so bright!* she thought. The glare made it hard to see properly. "Isn't there something moving over there?" Callie whispered, her eyes focusing at the same time on three horsemen splashing into the water at the far end of the island.

"Get down!" she hissed through her teeth. "Down!"

Looking again, Callie could see that the riders were Indians with feathers in their hair and weapons in their hands. *Out looking for spring mischief,* she supposed as she watched them approach at a leisurely walk. They were young, Callie realized as they came toward her, younger than Three Elk. They laughed together as they clattered up out of the golden water onto the grassy island.

She could not run. They would see her escape around the bend and ultimately ride her and the children down. There was nowhere to hide. Or was there? Callie had hunted by lying perfectly still beneath a buffalo hide. Experience taught her that in many cases, what does not move is not seen.

Her eye caught on a dead, weather-silvered tree crouching about four feet tall in the sage along the bank. Scooting the children beneath this Callie cautioned, "Take your packs off and lie still." Sliding out of her own pack she whispered, "Do not move for any reason. Pray with all your minds and hearts, but be as still as rabbits in the brush. Don't look directly at them or they'll feel your eyes." Pulling the broken knife from her apron strings, she handed it to James. "Take this in case we're seen."

He looked at her surprised, delighted, serious. "Aye."

Callie listened to the sound of the approaching Indians, gripping her lance with a white-knuckled fist. Her eyes searched the tops of the buttes again as she anxiously prayed for sight of Three Elk, but there was none. The riders came on.

"I gotta cough," Susa whimpered. "Duncan kicked dirt in my mouth."

"No," Callie whispered. "Spit it out. Quick. Then not another sound."

Urgently, she searched the wind-hewn pinnacles and flat-topped bluffs that towered above her. The canyons cutting back into them were sheer drop-offs, steeper than when they'd started out this morning and cutting farther back from the river. That must have been what was keeping Three Elk away.

The approaching savages were halfway across the island when Three Elk disclosed his position to Callie. He was above her on the shadowed side of the cliff on foot. There was only an instant when she saw him, and then he disappeared into the steep drop of a gully. Following the land with her eyes, Callie saw that the gully curled around and emptied onto the river between her and the bend. Three Elk would follow it, she knew, and come out just behind her.

As she watched the riders draw nearer, Callie realized that when they came up out of the water the hooves of their horses would pass within a few feet of her and the children. The sun slipped below the horizon, its glare no longer in her favor, and at the same instant a small black bird with red wing-bands lit on the dead tree above her. "Vaaak!" its reedy voice blared. "Vaak! Vaaaaaak!"

The raucous sound must have attracted the horsemen's gaze, because one of the riders grunted something to his companions. He pointed casually toward Callie with the tip of his lance. The others answered in low jovial tones, apparently pleased at the prospect of creating a little trouble. They kept riding, approaching her and the children without hurry, obviously anticipating easy prey.

Realizing they'd been seen, Callie frantically considered rushing out into the river or trying to climb the face of the cliff.

But reason was stronger than fear. She didn't want to fight them—savage or not, she didn't want to hurt anyone. Yet if they left her no choice, she was capable of opposing them. *They don't know I can fight,* Callie told herself with desperate conviction. *Don't know I can use a lance. They won't be expecting that!*

Suddenly, the nearest of the three kicked his horse, sprinting forward into the water.

"Run!" Callie screamed at the children. "Different directions! Fast!"

The children burst from their cover, horror propelling their legs. Duncan bolted along the river, toward the bend. Jamie ran to the mouth of the gully where Callie hoped Three Elk would emerge. Susa followed him, frantic. But her clothes tangled in the sage, and she tripped. On her knees, she tore at her pantaloons, wailing as the oncoming rider swept down on their mother with a terrifying yell of attack.

Callie recoiled momentarily, but she had been in this position before. With the wolf, fatigue had made her slow, had dulled her reflexes so that the lance came up at the last moment. The wolf hadn't been able to stop in time. Now Callie saw she could do it again. Bracing the butt of her lance against a sage stump, she waited . . . waited . . . waited until she thought the horse's hooves would dash her to pieces.

The rider bent very low off the side of his mount to strike. *Now!* Callie pulled up on the lance with both hands, angling it into the air just as the savage swept by. The shaft was ripped from her hands as its tip caught where his neck and chest met. His body was torn backward and he fell, his last breath escaping as he hit the stony ground.

Callie got to her feet before the other two horsemen rode down upon them. She ran and threw herself over Susa, protecting the child's body with her own.

Ssssss-thung! Coming out of the water in a showery spray, the leading rider threw up his hands and lurched backward off his horse. Callie glimpsed a feathered shaft sticking from his chest. Then he rolled, his body floating slowly down the river.

Turning, Callie saw Three Elk behind her, running from the dry gully. His bow was in his hand, but he hadn't had time to nock another arrow. The last attacker swerved past her, rushing down on Three Elk.

"No!" James shrieked, springing up from behind a rock. "No!"

Callie's heart plummeted and her breath caught.

The young savage rode past Three Elk, but instead of dealing a death blow, he reached out to touch the older man with his club. Then he jerked his horse around and readied himself for a second pass. Three Elk lunged forward, knife in hand, slicing at the attacker's bare leg. The horseman wheeled. Fury blackened his face. He shouted something and then rushed forward again, lifting his stone-headed club to deal a crushing blow. Three Elk made to jump aside as the horse thundered by, but at the last instant, his adversary leaped off on top of him. Dust rose as they rolled and writhed.

Callie jumped up and jerked her lance free of the dead Indian's throat. But when she looked again, James had already run forward. Three Elk kicked beneath his attacker, but the younger warrior pinned his wrists against the ground. Callie's lungs screamed for air as she watched transfixed, breathless. Standing over them, James lifted the broken blade high, clenched in his fist. As he plunged it downward, the savage threw up his own knife. He was far more experienced, holding the knife horizontally, slashing at Jamie with the speed of a snake. The freckle-faced boy was thrown back. Red soaked his front. But in that instant, Three Elk twisted aside and drove his blade home.

Callie ran to her son. Dropping the lance, she tore open his shirt.

"Fast, eh?" Jamie grinned at her. Panting, he brushed her aside and scrambled to his feet. "That bloke was lightnin'-fast!"

Callie scowled.

But Jamie was not the least bit daunted. Taking her hand in his, he smiled even more brightly. "I've landed on m' feet, Mum. 'Tis only a cut. 'Twill come out all right, you'll see." All at once his face blanched, his knees buckled, and he sat down hard. Trying to hide astonishment Jamie chuckled. "I sure could use a bit o' drink, though."

"Susa," Callie called. "Can you get free?" The little girl's tear-streaked face looked up from where she still knelt, crying. "It's safe, now."

"Don' fuss lass," Jamie agreed. "'Tis over."

Susa's breath came in hiccoughing gulps, but she stood.

"Bring the packs over here, please. And get your brother a drink from the waterskin in mine," Callie called, knowing work would help Susa leave the crisis behind.

Then, shaking so hard she could barely stand, Callie cast her eyes around to see where Duncan was. He was down at the water's edge, trying to catch and calm the horses. When he saw her looking, he whooped and grinned.

"First-rate, eh, Mum?"

Not trusting her voice, Callie waved a trembling hand.

Three Elk was already going over the dead bodies, removing their weapons and other useful items.

Duncan had retrieved two of the ponies when Three Elk went to fetch Cyrus. Choking down her sickened stomach and breathing deeply to steady herself, Callie used the lance to roll the bodies into the river. Then she sat beside James on the riverbank, feeling dusk settle protectively down around them. And before long Duncan had all three horses tethered to the dead tree on the water's edge. Then he came quietly to sit beside his mother. The black bird had returned to perch on a reed near the water's edge. It ruffled its red-banded wings and squawked, its grating voice scratching the night. Susa cradled her head in her mother's lap and lay still, watching the muddy water slide noiselessly by.

"I'm hungry, Mum," she said at last.

"Of course you are, Chickadee." Callie stroked her hair. "Of course you are."

Unhurried hoofbeats approached in the gathering darkness. "Come," Three Elk said as he leaned over to pull Susa up in front of him. He pointed to the dead men's ponies, indicating the others should mount.

Then Three Elk led them upstream, across the island the way the horsemen had come. "I see Gros-Ventre from high." He told her, waving a hand at the butte. "Have big trouble coming down."

"I should say so!" Callie declared, feeling all at once light-hearted now that the bloody scene was behind them and the pall of fear had passed over. "You had big troubles! I was beginning to wonder where you were. You got here just in time, you know."

Three Elk nodded, "Just in time, Lucky Woman."

THIRTY-ONE

Three Elk led them to a cave that hunkered under the palisading cliffs upriver. As they passed through the gap he'd found between the rocks, Callie discovered that the inconspicuous crevice was more than a split in the stone wall. In fact, the cave was surprisingly roomy, and they led the horses in as a precaution should other Gros-Ventre come along. They made no fire until it was fully dark, and by then Callie was grateful for the warmth as the urgency of the confrontation had subsided and the spring night was chilly.

Callie insisted on dressing Jamie's wound, and after she washed it she asked Three Elk if he had any more of the frilly leaves in his neck pouch. He gave her the last pieces, along with a handful of crystalline rock he'd pried loose from the cliff. She turned the white rock over twice, smelled it, and then looked at him with raised eyebrows and an expression that clearly asked, "What's this?"

Amused, Three Elk chuckled and took it back. He crushed the white crystals between two stones and dissolved this powder in hot water. The liquid had a somewhat soapy consistency, and dipping one finger in, Callie was even more astonished to find that it tasted salty.

"Wash. Make clean," Three Elk instructed.

Callie smiled her thanks to him and then set about using the mixture to wash Jamie's wound before applying the dried weed in a poultice. Tearing off the bottom of her apron, Callie bound her son's chest. The cut was long but shallow. And when Three Elk praised his fighting, Jamie seemed to derive more pleasure than pain from the wound.

Despite this she kept a close eye on him throughout the evening's devotional, and only as he settled gingerly into sleep did her worries abate. Duncan and Susa, after vigorously recounting their version of the fight to each other, fell asleep mumbling of the light biscuits they intended to eat "t' the heart's content" in Zion.

Callie sat by the fire, the scriptures still open on her lap but beyond her concentration. Like the shadows their small fire threw dancing against the walls of the cave, the events of that afternoon danced across her soul. She recalled the force as the lance entered the Gros-Ventre, the thud of his body hitting the sand, and the surprise that licked his face before expression ceased. What had Angus felt when . . . ?

No, she still could not think of it. The fire hissed and settled. Jamie moaned slightly in his sleep. She slanted Angus's Book of Mormon toward the fire, turned the pages and read. "And thus he cleared the ground, or rather the bank, which was on the west of the River Sidon, throwing the bodies of the Lamanites who had been slain . . ." She cringed as she realized how little she thought of killing another human being. Had the wilderness claimed her completely?

Rising to her knees by the fire, Callie began a fervent and far-reaching prayer. For herself, she asked forgiveness for taking a human life, even though it was clearly self-defense; she prayed for her children, who had through all their journey been protected from witnessing such violent scenes. After all they had passed through, how would they fit into Zion? She prayed for the Gros-Ventre and for those who waited for them in vain. She prayed with all her heart for Sweet Berries and Little Dog to have been preserved through the winter awaiting Three Elk's return. Finally she prayed for herself once more. Having worn out her prayer, she closed, and lifting her eyes met Three Elk's compassionate gaze across the ebbing coals.

"Sing, Lucky Woman," he ordered gently. "You sing."

Callie searched her soul and memory for a long moment and began to sing,

> The soul that on Jesus hath leaned for repose
> I will not, I cannot, desert to his foes;
> That soul, though all hell should endeavor to shake,
> I'll never, no never, no never forsake!

They crossed the river the next morning, swimming their horses. Susa rode in front of Three Elk as on the night before, and Callie was amazed at how quickly they traveled with everyone mounted. She thought it was possible they'd covered a good twenty miles before Three Elk brought them to the bank of a small river where they would camp for the night.

Now eager with anticipation, Callie woke early again, checked the horses' packs, and watered them well. She hoped the day would be warm, but there were increasing numbers of gray-bellied clouds scudding up from the horizon on a steady wind. She didn't want rain, but she was grateful for the clouds' shade as soon as they'd crossed the river again.

The rocky cliffs above Green River had been barren and dry, but now they crossed a place where even cactus and sage refused to grow. The desert was almost entirely void of plants. Here and there, piles of gray dirt heaped up like lumps of potter's clay. Dry fingerlike ditches and gullies had been washed out of the gravel-sprinkled soil, and white patches of alkali dotted the wrinkled view.

Midmorning the clouds massed together into a squall that broke with sudden fury. Wind whipped the rain in heavy sheets, so that in only a few minutes, water roared down the gulches, and slimy clay stuck three inches thick to the bottoms of the horses' hooves. Callie dismounted to lead her pony and Duncan's, but her skirts were soon heavy with the clinging muck. Progress was halting now, as she struggled against her wet clothing for each step, fearing the encumbered beasts would slide on top of her.

"Three Elk!" Her cry sounded weak against the gray veil of rain. She could see nothing. "Three Elk!"

Suddenly sweeping north, the wind changed, and she glimpsed her friend, also off his horse, pulling the buffalo robe and other skins from his pack. Jamie was there, too, framing the walking sticks to shape the hide tent.

Moving toward them she offered the lance. "I didn't know you'd brought the walking sticks along, James."

"Aye," he grinned as he lashed their tops together, mud spattering and clinging to everything. Water streamed down his cheeks from his rain-soaked hair. "Tied 'em t' m' horse for just such a pleasant occasion."

Three Elk pointed at James and Duncan as soon as they were huddled inside the makeshift shelter. "You paint face?" He squinted his eyes and nodded as if in approval. "Pretty good. Make enemy ver' 'fraid!"

Clods of mud hung in both boys' hair, and great slimy patches glistened on their skin and clothes. The sound of Susa's laughter coupled with the relief of escaping the storm rushed over them all, and they were suddenly amused by how ridiculous they looked.

The rain let up as quickly as it had begun, but travel was impossible. Three Elk and Jamie dug holes to catch the last of the runoff and then used it to water the horses. Wind continued to blow steadily, so that by day's end the ground had a thin dry crust forming across its slippery surface.

"Next sun, mebbe early, we come to fort," Three Elk spoke encouragingly, and Callie suddenly realized he had expected to arrive by nightfall.

The news brought a smile to Callie's face, but she performed her evening chores as if in a dream. Using some of the precious though silty runoff water, she boiled dry meat in the battered pot. Then she held devotional, tucked the children into their muddy blankets, and made a charcoal scratch in the back of her Book of Mormon for the last time. She'd waited so long for the coming day that it hardly seemed real. Mud spread all around her, and she was so caked with it she simply could not visualize civilization.

Yet she knew that if Three Elk told her tomorrow would bring them there, it was true. Gazing up at the clean, blinking stars, Callie wondered if she ought to feel something different, something final.

Three Elk also seemed pensive. She watched him, noticing that the unreadable mask had gradually begun slipping back over his face. He reclined on a scrap of rawhide, drawn into himself, staring up at the night.

"You'll be excited to see Sweet Berries and your boy again, won't you?" Callie asked amiably, though the words sounded surprisingly strange.

Three Elk grunted; he hadn't heard her.

"Your wife and son . . . your brother, Crazy Lodge—you'll be glad to see them again, won't you?"

He made another sound, something nearer an affirmation this time, but his thoughts were remote. Callie had been with Three Elk for seven months, yet she knew little about his family. They had been homeless, that much was clear. Homeless like she was and hungry like she was, too, without provisions or tepees during all the long, hard cold. And they had been without their father.

Compassion swelled her chest, dissolving the distance between her and the woman she had never met. Callie couldn't picture Sweet Berries's face, but she understood some of her trials. She wished she could do something for her. She wished she could do something for Three Elk. Of course she had urged on him the lion's share of the dead Gros-Ventre's provisions and equipment—anything he chose. But that wasn't enough.

Now, more than ever, Callie wished she'd been able to instill in Three Elk a vision of his own possibilities and the history of his people. She had coaxed, cajoled, reasoned, and prayed, but in matters of adopting her culture, Three Elk had been as responsive as stone. If only she'd managed to interest him in reading. Then she might have succeeded in teaching him the gospel. He could have shared it with his people, and it would have been the greatest gift, the most priceless possession she could ever have offered.

Orange coals fell, collapsing inward on themselves as Callie fingered the tattered cover of Angus's Book of Mormon. She had failed her friend. Yet she didn't want to give in. Somehow, someway, she must leave Three Elk with a singular gift, something of her that would be meaningful to him.

Spreading the pages open carefully to avoid soiling them, she began to read, " . . . And because they are free from the fall they have become free forever . . . to act for themselves and not to be acted upon . . ." Callie squinted in the fireglow and read the words again. ". . . not to be acted upon save it be by the punishment of the law at the great and last day according to the commandments which God hath given." Callie closed the book and her eyes, feeling the embers' warmth upon her face. " . . . not to be acted upon . . ."

That was it! From the start she had wanted to seize Three Elk and make him become like her, compel him to live by the rules of her society and seize the convictions of her heart. Privately embarrassed, Callie reviewed all her attempts to force her testimony on him. Three Elk was not putty. He could not be made to believe at her convenience, for her purposes, or on her timetable.

No wonder he had said, "White man's words are empty," that golden autumn morning so long ago. Her words had been void of regard for him or his culture.

I'll do more than say it now, Callie vowed as an idea took shape in her mind. She would speak with actions. Oh, she had tried to model integrity all along, but this time he would know her heart by her deed. This time Three Elk would understand.

Dawn came without a cloud in the sky. The going was messy, and the horses skidded every few steps, but before long the gullies led them to a swift stream, and beyond it spread a grassy green valley. Following Three Elk's example, they dismounted and walked into the water fully dressed, letting it wash away the clinging mud. Jamie and Duncan caught some fish, so they breakfasted while drying out. The sun was not even halfway into the sky before they remounted and started forward again.

Brilliant morning shimmered across the grassy prairie, and Callie's heart bounded. The clean water and trout had refreshed her; the lush valley opened before them invitingly. Exhilaration surged within her; gratitude glittered around every thought. She felt young, younger than the thirty-two years she had spent in this life, young as a child now that the intolerable burden of the journey was soon to be eased. And yet she felt tremendously old as well. She was old and wise as the wilderness that rolled toward the horizons, on and on and on, farther than her eye could see in every direction.

The mare swayed rhythmically beneath her, carrying her closer and closer to Zion. Spring sunshine warmed her back, and the air smelled fresh and sweet.

"I'll be feastin' on hunks an' slabs o' leavened bread this big!" Jamie boasted, spreading his hands as wide as his bandaged chest would allow.

Duncan laughed, spreading his wider.

"An' you, Little Button?" Jamie teased his sister. "Will ye be callin' for creamy milk or sweets first?"

"Both!" Susa giggled indulgently.

A meadowlark in a yellow vest and black cravat perched on a clutter of stones and whistled up a scale. Callie slowed her horse's pace to watch him. She tipped her head in greeting, prodded the mare forward, and gave way to unbridled delight as she joined him in song:

> The Lord my pasture will prepare,
> And feed me with a shepherd's care.
> His presence will my wants supply,
> And guard me with a wa-a-atchful eye.

Her voice was firm, clear, surer than it had ever been. Her confidence was rooted not in faith alone but in the knowledge of hopes tested and won.

> My noonday walks he wi-i-i-ll attend,
> And a-a-all my weary mi-i-idnight hours de-e-efend.

Three Elk turned, "Soon fort."

A knot tightened in Callie's throat. She'd imagined this moment so many times. In her estimation, getting the children to Fort Bridger amounted to nothing short of an incomprehensible miracle. She'd pictured them crawling in and felt overwhelming gratitude at the thought of them simply arriving. Never in her wildest dreams had she envisioned them riding in on horses with food panniers. True, their clothes were ragged, and the children's things were outgrown. The food was pemmican she had once turned up her nose at, and all of them were lean. Yet, here they came, not creeping and whining, but arriving with the Lord's blessing, sheltered by His hand. Her greatest needs had been met by Him: they were alive and whole!

Topping a grassy rise, Callie saw Fort Bridger. She could just make out what she thought was a wooden palisade and a rock wall. Low buildings, a few of them possibly even whitewashed, clustered a long way off.

A shout carried across the quiet morning, some loud profane curse from a soldier that once would have offended her. Now her heart leapt—it was English! In the distance a blue wagon with red-spoked wheels passed between two buildings, and she heard the sharp, ringing crack of an axe. But Callie had learned to gauge prairie distances, and she was not fooled by the astonishing clarity with which sounds carried across the fresh, clean air.

Three Elk stopped, dismounted, and lifted Susa down. As Callie and the boys followed suit, she heard far-off yelling.

"Hey, what's that?"

"John! Look! Run and get Judge Carter!—No, get his wife instead. It's a woman!"

"A what?"

"You heard me. A woman . . . some white woman with an Indian buck. Why I . . ."

Callie recoiled at the words. Whenever she'd visualized her arrival, she'd imagined being caught up by her own people and cheered. She'd anticipated a roar of hurrahs when they heard her story. But now she turned her back on them all and faced her friend.

"Say good-bye Susa, Duncan, Ja—" she started his name but couldn't finish. Her son looked as if he might gallop off behind Three Elk any instant.

The man knelt low, gently brushing stray locks of Susa's golden hair back from her cheeks, gazing fondly into her face. He remained that way for some time, and Callie felt that he was visually devouring the girl's features, impressing them upon his mind. Then, as the moment lingered, she realized he was communicating too, speaking fondness and caring through his touch, bestowing a wordless blessing of farewell with his eyes.

Rising, he pulled from his neck pouch a small stone, no bigger than his thumbnail but blue as a robin's egg, and pressed it into Duncan's hand. "This one," he said, "is balance." Three Elk spread his hands wide as if patting down the landscape, and then he repeated the gesture as if patting down his heart. "It is stone," he pointed toward the treasure, "but it is more." Again he swung his hands wide with a gesture that took in the horizons.

Turning last to Jamie he paused.

"I . . . I wish . . . ," the redheaded youth agonized. "I wish I could go wi' ye."

Three Elk shook his head. "*Ma?heo?o* gave you the hard road so you would grow a brave heart." He placed his hands on the boy's shoulders, speaking again with gaze and touch. "It is not for you or me to change our birth, only to live and die well. Sing the brave heart song."

James returned the man's words with the potent silence of respectful adoration. Three Elk's head was turned and one braid had fallen forward so Callie could not see his face clearly, but she saw him shake her son's shoulders and repeat the command. "Sing."

James swallowed hard, confused. Three Elk began intoning the chant that had once so unnerved Callie, "*Hunh-ha, Hunh-ha* . . ." and then James's voice, thick with emotion, joined in countermelody, "How firm a foundation, ye Saints of the Lord, is laid for your faith in His excellent word . . ."

Tears crowded her eyes, but Callie blinked them back. Turning away, she dug into her pack, using the effort to mask her sentiment until the peculiar duet had finished. Though Susa and Duncan were sniffling behind her, she shut out all awareness of their tender feelings lest it leave her unable to speak.

"Three Elk, I have something I want to give you." Her mind went on, telling him it was something very dear to her, something she hoped he would come to understand, but her voice cracked and the only other words that came were, "It belonged to my late husband."

The beaten Book of Mormon sat on her open hands, poised midair between them for an interminable moment. Then Three Elk pulled his shirt off, reverently wrapped the sacred volume in it, and held it to his chest.

"Medicine," he said solemnly. His eyes told Callie he valued the magnitude of her gift. He had seen her spend countless hours studying its pages, had seen her mark the charcoal lines night after night inside its cover, had seen the comfort it brought her in moments of despair. Placing the bundle carefully in his beaded leather bag, he turned to her again in a way that bespoke valued friendship.

Three Elk gestured for her to give him the lance.

"The lance?" Callie blurted, confused. He had Cyrus, his shield, his bow, and most of the provisions. She'd long ago given back the knife and its sheath, and now her precious scriptures. Must he take the lance as well? Her fingers curled around the leather grip that had come to fit so familiarly in her palm. This rod had kept her children from starvation and more than once it had saved her life. Did he know what it meant to her? Reluctantly she held it toward him.

Three Elk took the lance with slow significance. Deliberately, he gazed at it. Then, lifting the weapon high in the air, he shattered its shaft across his knee in one violent, angry blow.

Before Callie had a chance to register fully what he'd done, Three Elk thrust the broken halves skyward in both fists.

Her vision riveted on Three Elk's figure, arched backward against the sky. His entire frame was poised, all the energy of body and spirit summoned to the surface but leashed beneath tight control. Three Elk's eyes strained beyond the broken lance, deep into endless blue. His feet were spread, his tensed muscles motionless, launching the very vitality of his being upward through his gaze.

Hot tears stung Callie's eyes as she looked at the ruined weapon, sun glancing off its stone tip, wind gently tossing the feathers secured there.

The ferocity of Three Elk's actions startled her, and she struggled to understand. Why had he broken her lance? What could he intend with this display? She felt he was bestowing ceremony on their moment of parting, honoring it with the depth of something spiritual.

Three Elk turned abruptly and shoved the splintered pieces of the lance toward her.

Callie only stared.

He shook them once in a rough gesture for her to take what was left. *Take it!* his stance insisted. *Take these pieces and know their meaning.*

In spite of herself, Callie's hands rose hesitantly to receive the broken halves he thrust toward her. As her fingers touched the shattered shaft she could feel his entire form trembling.

Then Three Elk clamped his hands over hers, tightening her fingers around the splintered wood. She did not feel it in her grasp but, looking down, saw her own knuckle-white grip on the pieces.

This lance had pierced and slain, had made fatherless girls as fair-haired as Susa and left boys as full of joy and promise as Jamie and Duncan unprotected against the terrible face of nature. Every vestige of hate, abhorrence, and loathing, every hope of exacting retribution that she had ever harbored toward the brutal savages who had stolen her dear Angus now stood ready to be unleashed. She did not need to summon fury—she had earned it through deprivation and loneliness and suffering. Her children deserved it.

She glared down at the broken weapon in their two hands, his surrounding hers. Waiting.

This lance had sustained her and the children, protected them. . . . Though it had taken life, it had returned life as well. She could not deny that the crucible of the wilderness had forged a newer, greater faith within her.

Callie dared not look into Three Elk's face. She recalled the war paint . . . the scalps . . . Shuddering inwardly, Callie gasped for air and struggled to bring her feelings into focus.

From the moment she'd found him, Three Elk had kept his feelings private, controlled. Now she recognized that a message of respect lay behind this ceremonial display of emotion. Respect and something else . . . respect and appreciation for the gift of life they had given each other. She felt Three Elk was ceremonially showing the bond their trails had forged and the hand of God at work in their lives.

At that moment Callie let go of what remained of anger, pain, and hatred. She had never allowed Three Elk to see her cry, but now there was no thought of propriety or pretense. Her tears fell unchecked, washing the backs of both their hands. And as she looked up into his face she discovered her own tears mirrored in his eyes.

Three Elk's touch was warm, firm—and then it was gone. Without a sound he whirled and swung up on Cyrus's back.

Callie remained motionless beside her children. Clasping the broken lance, she watched as his pony circled once. Three Elk caught her gaze and held it one last, long time. Then he rode away, without looking back. And Callie stood weeping until he was entirely lost in the tender green of the vast windswept prairie.